A Plague of Dreamers

A PLAGUE OF DREAMERS

Three Novellas

STEVE STERN

CHARLES SCRIBNER'S SONS
NEW YORK

Maxwell Macmillan Canada
Toronto
Maxwell Macmillan International
New York   Oxford   Singapore   Sydney

Copyright © 1994 by Steve Stern

Reprint permissions will be found on page 269.

Charles Scribner's Sons   Maxwell Macmillan Canada, Inc.
Macmillan Publishing Company   1200 Eglinton Avenue East
866 Third Avenue   Suite 200
New York, NY 10022   Don Mills, Ontario M3C 3N1

Macmillan Publishing Company is part of the Maxwell Communication Group of Companies.

Library of Congress Cataloging-in-Publication Data
Stern, Steve, 1947–
A plague of dreamers : three novellas / Steve Stern.
p. cm.
ISBN 0-684-19532-1
I. Title.
PS3569.T414P57   1994   93-19253
813'.54—dc20
CIP

Macmillan books are available at special discounts for bulk purchases for sales promotions, premiums, fund-raising, or educational use. For details, contact:

Special Sales Director
Macmillan Publishing Company
866 Third Avenue
New York, NY 10022

Book Design by Anne Scatto

10 9 8 7 6 5 4 3 2 1

Printed in the United States of America

For Steven

Contents

"His guiding purpose, though it was supernatural,
was not impossible."

JORGE LUIS BORGES

"The creation of an angel in our world and the
immediate relegation of this angel to another world
is, in itself, not at all a supernatural phenomenon."

RABBI ADIN STEINSALTZ

"You can hold back from the suffering of the world.
You have free permission to do so, and it is in accordance with your nature, but perhaps this very holding
back is the one suffering you could have avoided."

FRANZ KAFKA

A Plague of Dreamers

ZELIK RIFKIN AND THE TREE OF DREAMS

I. The Lost Tribe

Even by the infernal standards of the Memphis summers, this one was unnaturally hot. So intense was the swelter in the flats above the shops on North Main Street that the wallpaper bubbled and the menorah candles melted into shapes like choirs of ghosts. Great blocks of ice dissolved in their tongs to tiny cubes before the iceman in his saturated apron could carry them upstairs. Ceiling fans turned sluggishly if they turned at all, mired in the heaviness of the humid air. Housewives cooked stuffed kishkes on their windowsills and complained that their own kishkes boiled, their brains stewed in the ovens of their claustrophobic apartments.

All day the population of the Pinch—mostly Jews who liked to call themselves a lost tribe, so far were they scattered from the more kosher habitats of their brethren—kept as much as possible to the shade. Wearing ice bags in place of their yarmulkes they gathered in panting quorums to say prayers invoking rain. In the evenings they sat in folding chairs outside their shops, fanning themselves till all hours with limp newspapers from which the print had run. Later on they brought out picnic baskets and cradles, rolled-up pallets and little spirit lamps. Then they took the short walk over to Market Square Park where they bedded down alfresco for the night.

A relatively barren parcel of land where an auction block for slaves had once stood, Market Square was tucked behind a row of shops on North Main. It was bordered by an ironworks and the red brick pile of the Anshei Sphard Synagogue, and the Neighborhood House where the greenhorns were taught how to box-step and brush their teeth. As a park Market Square had only the barest of parklike attributes. There was a dried-up stone fountain and a ramshackle band pavilion, behind whose trellised skirts local lovebirds conducted trysts. There was an enormous old patriarch oak. It was under the broad boughs of the oak, as if wanting shade from the starry firmament itself, that the citizens of the Pinch made their outdoor dormitory.

II. Friends and Relations

Famous for his cowardice all along the length and breadth of North Main Street, Zelik Rifkin spied on the other boys at their adventures. Often he went out of his way just to frown in disapproval over the foolhardy risks they took. Walking home from the Market Avenue School, for instance, he sometimes made wide detours in order to pass by their haunts. He spooked about the levee, hiding behind rafts of lumber and cotton bales, or peeked around corners, looking up into a slice of sky between alley walls. Then he was likely to see them, the redoubtable Jakie Epstein and his cronies, hurtling in their daredevil competitions from roof to roof.

Taking a dim but fascinated view of their activities, Zelik kibitzed the pranks they played on unsuspecting citizens. From a safe distance he watched them singeing a cop's moustaches with a well-aimed magnifying glass, setting fire to the gazette in a reader's hands. He watched them angling with bamboo poles for the sheitel wigs of the orthodox wives, or stealing a camera from the pawnshop to take photographs of couples necking under the bandstand, threatening to blackmail them for the evidence.

Sometimes, though it tied his stomach in knots, Zelik was a witness to their shadier exploits. He saw them waltzing the ticketholders in front of the Phoenix Athletic Club for the purpose of deftly picking their pockets, or beating up on trespassing members of the Irish Mackerel Gang in Market Square. Once or twice he was there in the alley behind the Green Owl Café, when racketeers dispatched them into Negro precincts with booklets of policy stubs. He saw them receiving the bottles that Lazar the bootlegger handed them out the Green Owl's backdoor.

If ever they caught him at his spying, Jakie and the boys might invite Zelik to join in their operations, confident that the invitation alone would scare him away. "Nu, Rifkin," they shouted, "come and help us roll Charlie No Legs for muggles. Come on already, we'll get shikkered blind and jump off the Harahan Bridge."

Flushed from hiding, Zelik would tell them, "Thanks all the same." Then pulling down his golf cap to the bridge of his beaky nose, he'd coax his legs in their baggy knee pants into motion.

He'd duck out of sight, as he did today, and run straight home to his widowed mother.

"It's me, Mama," hailed Zelik upon entering the cramped apartment above Silver's Fruit & Vegetable. He always announced himself as if the remote Mrs. Rifkin, listlessly pumping the treadle of her sewing machine, might take him for somebody else. She might mistake him for one of the dead relations she set such store by, and thus be given a fright. Behind her rose a mound of unstitched jackets and pants like a hill of straw that refused to be spun into gold.

Smiling wanly, more to herself than to her son, Mrs. Rifkin kissed the air next to the cheek that Zelik offered.

"I killed a man this morning," he confided, secure in the knowledge that she never heard him. "I robbed the Planters Bank and rubbed out a teller."

"Just so you're careful," replied his mother, absently feeding fabric to the bobbing needle. "Don't climb too high, you won't sink too low. All I ask is that you be careful. Remember, your father Mr. Avigdor Rifkin, peace on his soul, was struck down in his prime."

From his vague recollection of his father, a herring-gutted garment peddler with a fruity cough, Zelik doubted that the man had ever had a prime.

Pausing a moment in her labor, Mrs. Rifkin looked up to note the date on a calendar hanging from the faded wallpaper. Produced by a company that had created a device called a rational body brace, the calendar was decorated with illustrations of women in harness. "I see that today is your Great Aunt Frieda's yahrzeit," acknowledged Zelik's mother in a tone of dreamy anticipation. "That means we'll have to go to shul after dinner." Sighing wistfully, she tucked a strand of mousy brown hair behind an ear and proceeded with her automatic toil.

For his part, Zelik had no idea who his Great Aunt Frieda was. In fact, most of the relations whose birthdays, anniversaries, and memorial yahrzeits (mostly yahrzeits) filled every available date on his mother's calendar, were entirely hearsay to him. He and his mama were the only Rifkins, living or dead, that he knew. But in an otherwise shut-in existence, her trips to the synagogue to light candles and say commemorative prayers were Mrs. Rifkin's sole excursions into the world. They were all she looked forward to, and Zelik, with nothing better to do himself, had acquired the habit of tagging along beside her.

Dumping his schoolbooks in the curtained alcove that served for his bedroom, Zelik excused himself. "Good-bye, Mama. I'm running away to join the circus and ride panthers through hoops of flame." As he started downstairs to his afternoon job in Mr. Silver's market, he could hear his mother faintly uttering her cautionary proverb behind him.

Not gifted with an especially enterprising nature, Zelik was a less than inspired greengrocer's assistant. It was a negligence abetted by the grocer himself, who worried enough for the both of them, making the market the one place where Zelik relaxed.

A troubled man with care lines stamped into his brow as with a brand, Mr. Silver was much too busy looking over his shoulder to keep tabs on a daydreaming stockboy. He was a bachelor, the skittish grocer, said to have fled his native Carpathian village in advance of a rumored pogrom. But despite the considerable distance he'd put between himself and the Old Country, Mr. Silver had yet to feel safe from approaching disaster, and often he confused the local gentiles with the hell-raising Cossacks of his youth. His particular fear was of the Ku Klux Klansmen who staged regular mounted parades up Main Street, with both themselves and their horses enshrouded in sheets and visored cowls.

But for all his apprehensions, Mr. Silver was a generous employer, generous beyond Zelik's worth and occasionally his own means.

"You sure you didn't make a mistake?" Zelik had asked upon receiving his first weekly salary; to which the grocer, sudden prey to a blinking fit in one sad eye, replied, "Maybe you are needing more?" Then he'd thrown in a peck of apricots as a bonus, and enjoined his employee to "Give your mama a health on her head from Leon Silver."

After a while Zelik could take the hint: Mr. Silver's largess was not so much for the benefit of his assistant as for his assistant's mother. It seemed that the grocer was harboring a secret affection for the seamstress, which he was too timid to express through means more direct than his philanthropy.

At the end of the token few hours he put in at the grocery, Zelik went back upstairs for his Hebrew lesson with Mr. Notowitz. To support herself and her son after the death of her husband, Mrs. Rifkin had taken in piecework from the neighborhood tailors. But even supplemented by contributions from the Anshei Sphard widows' fund, her labors brought only a pittance, and so she had been forced to take in boarders. The current was Aharon Notowitz, a teacher of Hebrew and therefore just a cut above a common shnorrer. Chronically short of the rent, the moth-eaten Mr. Notowitz had offered to compensate his landlady by giving her son "post–bar mitzvah lessons" free of charge. It was a wholly impractical arrangement that would have added to the boarder's liability, were it not for the windfall profits Zelik had come by since going to work at Silver's Fruit & Veg.

He would find the old teacher in his windowless bedroom lit by a dirty skylight, sunk as usual in a hobbled armchair surrounded by heaps of unshelved books. Formally attired in the gabardine suit he slept in, his beard discolored by ashes and crumbs, eyes like bloodshot fried eggs, Mr. Notowitz seldom got around to actually teaching. Instead he recounted his sorrows. This was fine with Zelik, who'd long since lost the knack of taking religious instruction; it was only as a concession to his mother, who now and then nourished the notion of her son's becoming a rabbi, that he'd agreed to the lessons in the first place. Moreover, a steady diet of Mrs. Rifkin's memorial days, garnished with the threat of Mr. Silver's transplanted Cossacks, had prepared Zelik to appreciate the old melammed's complaints. By the time he came to hear them, such heartsick lamentations were for Zelik an acquired taste.

Touting himself as a once-celebrated scholar, descended on his mother's side from the archwizard Isaac Luria, Mr. Notowitz had a favorite gripe: he'd lost his faith. "To this farkokte country are following us the demons," he liked to repine, removing a finger from his tufted nostrils to examine the pickings. "But God," pointing the finger aloft, "He stays behind."

III. Prince of Dreams

That summer, secure within his circle of ritual, apprehension, and regret, Zelik found himself stealing more frequent glimpses outside it. Though he remained true enough to the routine of his days, a restlessness he couldn't account for had seeped into his reluctant bones. He was spending his evenings as always in the company of his mother, going along on her commemorative errands when it was called for. And since school was out, he worked longer hours in the greengrocery; he hung around Mr. Notowitz's rubbish-appointed bedroom. But still he had considerable time on his hands. There were stretches when, lurking aimlessly, Zelik tried to remember what he'd done during previous summers. Then it seemed to him that, every inch his foggy mother's son, he had sleep-walked through the whole of his sixteen years. But if that were the case, he reasoned, to wake up now might be a shock to his system from which he would never recover.

From a furtive vantage Zelik kept watch on the exploits of Jakie Epstein and company. He watched them with his typical nervous censure but found it increasingly difficult to turn away.

Though most of the boys had legitimate jobs of their own to attend to—they hawked newspapers, plucked chickens, sold dry goods in their family's shops—they never seemed to let work get in the way of a good time. With school out they found ample opportunities to run wild. Levy's Candy Store excepted, they tended to avoid North Main Street during off-hours, staying out from under the eyes of parents stationed at the soaped windows of their retail emporiums. Instead they preferred to lurk around the margins of things. They prowled the tenement rooftops and the wagonyards crammed with farmers' tin lizzies, the back alleys with their stables fronting for underworld goings-on. They challenged the rival Goat Hills and Mackerels to baseball in Market Square, games that generally ended in free-for-alls. But mostly they loitered about the cobbles along the levee just below the Pinch.

They sponged dimes from passengers on the paddle-wheeled excursion boats in exchange for the false promise of watching their motorcars. They shot craps in the shadow of cotton bales with roustabouts who told them stories of blown boilers, wrecked packets, crimes of passion, and floods. Defying the treacherous current (to say nothing of the undertow, the parasites, poisonous snakes, and man-eating garfish with which Zelik had heard the water was rife), they held swimming races across the river to Mud Island. On the far shore they drank "gnat's piss" and swapped lies with the fishermen, who lived there in a shantytown made from old Moxie signs.

They swarmed up the arm of a huge, freight-loading gantry crane and dived off. This stunt in itself would have been sufficiently harebrained, but the Pinch Gang liked to gild the lily. From the crane's dizzy pinnacle they executed backward somersaults and cunning jackknives, sometimes (as in the case of Captain Jakie) wearing blindfolds to heighten the danger. Barely clearing the docked barges and houseboats, they shouted obscenities and clutched their testicles before hitting the water. In this way they were sure of getting the attention of the girls, who lolled against bollards and floats pretending not to notice.

When they were done showing off, Jakie and the boys would wander over to where the girls sat sunning themselves. The clown Augie Blot, wearing only wet underpants and goggles, might shake himself like a dog in their vicinity, prompting universal screams.

Hyman Myer might invite Sadie Blen to feel his muscles and, if she complied, press her to let him return the favor. A playful tussling would ensue. But sometimes their tussling wasn't so playful, and Zelik, peeping wide-eyed from behind a packing crate or a parked DeSoto, would draw in a horrified breath.

Once he saw the overgrown Lieberman twins, Ike and Izzy, yank Rose Padauer's pinafore over her head. While Ike held the upgathered material in a meaty fist, Izzy whipped off his belt and bound the package tight. "Give a look," cried Ike, the more articulate of the two. "We made a flower."

"Yeah," said Augie Blot with mock sentimentality, "a rose."

The other boys howled, asserting that the change was an improvement, while the girls stomped their feet in angry protest. But shocked as he was, Zelik had to admit that she did indeed look like a flower: a pale yellow one with a pair of kicking, pink-stockinged stems, and frilly white drawers at the blossom's base.

When especially wrought up, Zelik imagined himself, preferably masked, swooping down Douglas Fairbanks—style to rescue the girls from the Pinch Gang's wicked designs. Afterward he was ashamed for indulging such dumb fantasies, involving as they did the childish heroics with which he had no patience. Besides, the truth was that the girls were seldom in any real distress. In fact, they usually gave as good as they got, teasing the boys relentlessly. They cast doubts on the Gang's much-vaunted experience of the opposite sex, requesting positive proof of their manhood, reducing them to sheepish blushes, then pushing the advantage: "What'sa matter, can't you take it?"

One of the girls, Minnie Alabaster by name, was particularly distinguished for her unmercifulness. Her mouth was a neighborhood scandal, causing general embarrassment whenever she opened it. "Your mother seen those warts on your palm?" was her standard greeting to the boys, after which her conversation was likely to degenerate even further. Her remarks were notorious. Regarding the Lieberman brothers, who were forever digging at themselves, she might inquire with alarm, "You guys got carnivals in your pants, or what?" And when Moe Plesofsky had his head shaved due to an infestation of ringworms, she'd thoughtfully observed, "It looks like a putz, only smaller." She always had some off-color joke ("A guy takes a girl for a ride in his car, parks by the river. 'Shtup?' he asks, and she says, 'I usually don't, but you talked me into it.'") or a fanciful aside concerning the foibles of North Main Street:

"So I'm on the streetcar when I hear Mrs. Ridblatt whisper to her husband, 'Shmuel, your business is open.' And he whispers back, 'Is my salesman in or out?'"

Nobody, not even the otherwise unassailable Jakie Epstein, was spared the sting of her tongue. Wary of it, the boys tended not to cross her, seldom daring to make her the object of their gags. Also, though Zelik had seen no hard evidence, it was generally acknowledged that Minnie was Jakie's girl. This was not so much on account of her formidable tongue as her devilish prettiness—her gimlet green eyes and puff of ginger hair cropped after the fashion of Clara Bow, her lips like a twittering scarlet butterfly. The pendulum sway of her hips in the pleated skirts that she wore above her dimpled knees. For such attributes it was assumed that nobody but the Gang's intrepid captain should deserve her, though Zelik wondered if anyone had bothered to consult with Minnie herself on this point.

Naturally he was as intimidated by her bold-as-brass manner as he was by the antics of Jakie and the boys. Minnie's forwardness, scalding his ears, was as much a subject of Zelik's eavesdropping disapproval as the Pinch Gang's hazardous stunts. All in all, he concluded, the youth of North Main Street were playing with fire, and you couldn't blame Zelik Rifkin, who played it safe, if they got burned.

But when he was alone, Zelik found that he continued to think about Minnie. He imagined that her brazen exterior concealed untapped tenderness and fidelity. She had a pure and sympathetic heart that only he, with the well-kept secret of his amorous nature (a secret to himself until now), could detect. And at night, under sweat-soaked sheets, he came to realize a not entirely welcome truth: he had conceived an infatuation for Minnie Alabaster. It was a passion out of keeping with any emotion he'd ever experienced— an immoderate, reckless passion, so lofty in its aspiration that it left him, afraid as he was of heights, a prey to chronic nosebleeds; not to mention the gnawing discontent that kept Zelik lingering a little longer in the neighborhood streets.

He became less furtive in his daily espionage, sometimes dawdling in full view of the other kids. This wasn't so much a function of audacity as imprudence, the result of an overwhelm-ing desire to be nearer to Minnie. Thanks to his short stature and the meager frame that enhanced his semi-invisibility, however, Zelik was regarded as harmless if he was regarded at all. Powerless as he was to stay put, he was thus further encouraged to step out from behind the wardrobe in front of Shafetz's Discount or the wooden Indian next to Levy's Candy Store.

At the very worst Zelik's proximity to his peers earned him only the usual spurious invitations, the standard verbal abuse. Twitching his leaky nostrils, Augie Blot might begin the chant, "What's that I'm sniffkin?" to which the choral response was, "Must be a Rifkin—peeyoo!" Occasionally even Jakie himself, ordinarily above such banter, couldn't resist taking a shot at the figure of fun. "Vey is mir," he might exclaim, popping his gum with a freckled jaw, "it's Zelik the Shiv! Run for your lives!" Then the lot of them would beat it down an alley in stitches.

Sometimes the girls would enter into the ragging, and Minnie Alabaster was often foremost among them. But Zelik had become a glutton for even her most barbed remarks. Once, with her dis-tinctive flair for the dramatic, she'd clutched at a precocious bosom heaving beneath her sailor blouse.

"Come closer," she beckoned the intruder, "Zelik Rifkin, prince of my dreams."

He knew that he ought to feel mortified; she was mocking him shamelessly, but mockery and mortification were second nature to Zelik. What mattered was that she had spoken exclusively to him, and her words—once he'd stripped them of their original context— could be savored in the privacy of his alcove. They could be recalled in such a way as to evoke a sensation that swelled Zelik's shallow breast and surpassed his understanding.

IV. Acrophile

Then came the heat wave that sent the whole of North Main Street to sleep outside in the park. Formerly, during prolonged hot spells, a family might be forced to spend the night on the roof of their building; they would haul up lamps and mattresses until they'd created a kind of poor man's penthouse. But this summer's heat was of a more hellish intensity than the most long-time residents of the Pinch could recall. All day it baked the tenements so that, even in the slightly less oppressive evening air, the rooftops remained scorching to the touch. The soles of shoes might adhere to the simmering tarpaper, arresting movement, leaving you stuck and exposed till the sun rose to bleach your bones. So the families took to the park instead.

Thus far the Rifkins had remained an exception to the late evening exodus, which included even old Mr. Notowitz. Complaining that the foul breath of demons was driving him out of his room, he'd fled the apartment bookless in his filthy suit. (Though not before loosening his necktie and unfastening his collar stud as a statement of how extreme things had become.) Mr. Silver had warned Zelik and anyone else who would listen that the blistering heat was a conspiracy: "It's the Ku Kluxers that they have cooked it up for getting in one spot the Jews. Then by a single swoop they would slaughter them all." But in the end the grocer also succumbed, preferring to be murdered out of doors than suffocated inside.

Zelik supposed that his mother, whose calendar knew no climate, didn't feel the heat so much as others. She appeared no more languid and done in from her drudgery than usual. As for himself, Zelik felt it all right, and what was worse, the terrific heat seemed only to further inflame his passion for Minnie. He yearned for her with a desire that grew like a genie let out of a bottle, too large now to ever stuff back in again. It was a longing beyond his control, that despite himself gave him crazy ideas, and would have kept him awake nights regardless of the weather.

Still, Zelik didn't need his mother with her wholesale distrust of nature to list reasons to stay out of the park. Didn't he already have her litany by heart? There were worms in the grass that crept into your liver through your feet, earwigs that crawled into your brain, mosquitoes indistinguishable in their size and thirst for blood from vampire bats. At night rabid animals stalked the perimeter of the Pinch, with now and again a werewolf among them; and never mind the marauding Klansmen promised by Mr. Silver, when the kids from rival neighborhoods were unfriendly enough.

But on this especially torrid night, as he stood in a window mopping his forehead, watching the neighbors strolling en masse toward Market Square, Zelik achieved a restlessness that challenged his legion of fears. Among the strollers he spied Mr. Alabaster the tinsmith in a knotted headrag, his broad-beamed wife in a fancy leghorn hat, with their pistol of a daughter sashaying behind them, and what once had been clear and present dangers seemed suddenly no more than superstition.

"Mama," Zelik announced at the door of Mrs. Rifkin's bedroom, "I'm off to join the wild Indians and cut the scalps from my enemies."

"Just be careful, tateleh," murmured his mother from her bed. "Chase the wind you nab a devil, stay at home you don't wear out your shoes." Though her voice was much the same waking or sleeping, she nevertheless surprised her son by rolling over to complain about the heat.

In the park the holiday mood of the gathered North Main Street community confirmed Zelik in his feeling that he didn't belong. He felt as if he'd blundered uninvited into the starlit bedroom of strangers, though he was perfectly familiar with everyone there. He saw Bluesteins, Taubenblatts, Rosens, Shapiros, Padauers, Dubrovners, Blens—all of them camped out like pashas on throw-cushioned carpets and folding cots, enjoying the after-hours conviviality. They were exchanging gossip and debating local politics, banqueting on cold chicken and assorted nosherai, decanting samovars to sip glasses of tea through sugar cubes. By lamplight, the perambulators surrounding them like circled wagons, women changed the diapers of bawling infants. They played mah-jongg in upraised sleeping masks while their husbands—in bathrobes, flicking cigars—fanned themselves with their poker hands. Here a voice was heard reciting Scripture, there another naming the constellation of Berenice's Hair. A victrola with a tuba-sized speaker, blaring a Misha Elman nocturne, vied with the Original Dixieland Jazz Band through the crackling static of a wireless radio. Children ran around in pajamas chasing fireflies, though some already lay curled up on blankets fast asleep.

Even Mr. Silver, although vigilant in his tasseled nightcap, looked sufficiently comfortable where he sat under cover of a lilac bush, nibbling fruit from a paper bag. And Mr. Notowitz, wrapped in newspapers like a fish but recognizable from his gartered ankles and volcanic snores, was the picture of one who'd slept on stone benches all his life. Meanwhile, having strayed from their family bivouacs, young people were clustered among the roots at the foot of the patriarch oak. The boys rough-housed and scratched initials on the bricks that filled the hollow of the tree trunk like a walled-up door. The girls turned their backs and conspired in whispers.

As he sidled to within earshot, Zelik could hear Augie Blot proposing a contest to see which of the Lieberman twins was the dumber. "Okay, Izzy, first question: are you Izzy or Ike?" Jakie Epstein was leaning against the tree trunk with folded arms, looking as if the whole proceedings depended on the grace of his lanky, sandy-haired presence. From her giggling confab with Sadie Blen and Rose Padauer, Minnie Alabaster turned on a dare to the silent ringleader, "Hey Jakie, you still dating that shikse what's-her-name, Mary Fivefingers?" Some of the neighbors in Zelik's vicinity commented in exasperation over the mouth on that Alabaster girl.

Then Augie went into his nose-twitching routine. "What's that I'm smellik?" he called out once or twice before he'd elicited a half-hearted chorus from a couple of the boys: "Must be Zelik." "Rifkin, man of the hour," greeted Augie, showing teeth like blasted hoardings. "Jakie, wasn't you just saying how we needed Rifkin to complete our minyan?"

Jakie frowned his irritation at Augie's putting words in his mouth, especially concerning so uninteresting a subject. But then there was always the chance that, under Augie's instigation, something interesting might develop.

Zelik knew it was time to back off and dissolve into shadows, but in the moment that he hesitated (a moth drawn to Minnie's flame) the Liebermans took hold of his arms. They ushered him forward and planted him directly in front of Jakie, who took his measure with a dispassionate gaze that made him shrink. He shrank further from his acute awareness that Minnie was looking on with a sardonic grin.

Man of action though he was, Jakie condescended to speech when his office obliged. "You see, Rifkin," he began with a pop of the jaw, "we got this problem. Seems there's this . . . ," leaving the problem for Augie to define.

"This kite," supplied Augie, pointing straight up.

"There's this kite," continued Jakie, "which it is stuck in the top of the tree—ain't that right, Augie? And ain't none of us got the beytsim [Augie, acting as interpreter, clutched himself between the legs] to climb up and fetch it down."

At this Zelik began to struggle against his detainers to no effect. While Augie assured everyone what a lucky break it was that Fearless Rifkin had happened along, the Liebermans hoisted their captive onto the bottommost branch of the oak. When he tried to scramble down, they prevented him, shoving him back onto his swaying perch. Augie Blot struck a match and waved it under his shoe soles until Zelik also had to draw up his dangling feet.

"Now don't he look natural, Jakie," said Augie, stepping back to feign admiration. "A regular Tarzansky, wouldn't you say? He's hugging that branch like I think he must be in love."

"Yeah," concurred Jakie, known sometimes to wax philosophical. "Rifkin wasn't never at home on the earth."

Clinging to his knotty tree limb in a panic, Zelik pleaded, "Have a heart!" He appealed to the neighbors in the grass beyond the serpentine roots, and was told to pipe down, they were trying to sleep. Besides, since he was less than six feet from the ground, those who noticed were more inclined to see humor than danger in his situation.

"Help!" he cried to universal laughter and taunts, one of which resonated in his ears more than the rest.

"Don't worry, Zelik. If you start to fall, you can hang on to your mama's apron strings—which he also uses for tefillin, I got this on good authority."

It was Minnie Alabaster, in whose voice Zelik could take no comfort now. He saw himself, through her eyes, for the pathetic, cowering creature he was, and again in a single night his fears had met their match, overcome this time not by restlessness but shame. And shame, like restlessness, shook you into action. It made you want so badly to distance yourself from the insults hurled from below that, unable to descend, you had no choice but to start climbing.

With a painful deliberateness, his groping all the clumsier for the racing heart that tried to hasten his ascent, Zelik hauled himself aloft. At every stage he paused to catch his breath, embracing boughs hatched with crude hieroglyphics, taking note of a whole new dimension of things to be scared of. There were enormous ants and acorn weevils scurrying along the rope-veined branches like scorpions, warts like eyeballs on spatulate leaves. An unseen owl hooted nearby and Zelik froze, snuffling back tears and wiping his nose, which had begun to bleed. Then a fresh round of abuse spurred him into motion again.

Somewhere during his vertical crawl, far beyond the point where he could see the ground anymore, Zelik realized that the taunts had actually turned to encouragement. Jakie's gang were calling him Shipwreck Zelik after the famous flagpole sitter, saluting him for the way he'd risen to the occasion. That's when, rather than cheered, Zelik was struck by the magnitude of what he'd done, the impossible height he'd attained, and he held fast with all his might to the tree.

Afraid to look down, he squeezed his eyes shut but was afraid of the darkness behind his closed lids. So he opened his eyes and looked up. Just above his head was what appeared to be a cobweb shaped in a spiral like a miniature galaxy. Or could it be in fact the raveled tail of a kite caught in the topmost fork of the oak? His cowardice still screwed to the sticking point, Zelik didn't even dare to reach for it. Instead he clung tighter to the slender bough that nodded with his weight, its bark smooth and unscored by anyone who might have been there before him.

"Attaboy, Zelik!" they shouted; "Rifkin at the roof of the world!" their fickle turn-around galling him even more than their contempt. But though he'd climbed as high as he could manage on the strength of his shame, the wish to get farther from their voices gave him one last boost, and Zelik rose another foot or two into the breezy air.

His head had penetrated the cobweb, which turned out to be nothing more than a patch of fog. It cooled his brain, stilled his heart, and left him with eyes wide open, but what Zelik saw made no earthly sense. He was after all in the top of a tree, a fact miraculous enough in itself. But what he seemed to be looking at, from the level of the pavement no less, was North Main Street—the shops and the firehouse, the tenement flats, the movie theater, the cigar factory, the trolley car lines. It was the same shabby street he lived on, its alleys rank with weeds and wisteria, the cooking odors mingling with the stench of the river and the horse poop of mounted police, though here and there some telling detail suggested a difference.

For one thing there was a moon, a crescent like a silver fishtail, where previously the night had been moonless, and its light was strong as sunlight, if softer, and grainy like a fine yellow mist. The buildings looked mostly the same in their uniform need for repair, though the paint-chipped facades were relieved in some instances by an odd architectural flourish: the laceworked wrought-iron balcony, entwined in orchids, jutting from the widow Teitelbaum's window; the giant barechested caryatids, which seemed to be breathing, holding up the cornice on either side of Tailor Schloss's door. Projecting from the chimney of a tiny frame house, where a colored family lived beside Blockman's junkyard, was a tall mast complete with yardarms and a billowing, bloodred sail. While the shops were identical to those on the terrestrial street, there were certain items out of keeping with the standard merchandise: the golden ram's horn and the pair of magnificent ivory wings, for instance, among the tarnished brass watches and battered ukeleles in the window of Uncle Sam's Pawn; a manikin decked out in the naughtiest Parisian lingerie and an eye-catching coat-of-many-colors among the racks of irregulars in front of Shapiro's Ready-Made. Through the windows of the Main Street trolley, whose tracks passed not three feet from Zelik's head, he could make out an interior as opulent as a club car on the Twentieth Century Limited.

The neighbors were going about their more or less ordinary business, despite random intrusions of the extraordinary. Mr. Sacharin rolled a herring barrel backward down a ramp from a delivery truck; Mr. Krivetcher arranged his show shelf of only left shoes. Mr. Dreyfus, at a workbench in his shop window, polished a pearl the size of a swami's crystal ball. Max Taubenblatt, in the window of his haberdashery, wearing the hat and tails of a stage magician, prepared to saw his talky wife in half, while next door Lipman the asthmatic cobbler, in lion skins, collapsed the doorposts of his building with a mighty shrug. On a corner Itzhik Bashrig the luftmensch, holding his pail under a faucet, coaxed a pinging shekel from the tap with every flick of his wrist. A woman rode past on Blockman's swayback horse, her naked body concealed by her Godiva hair. The thick blonde tresses were parted in back over a prominent dowager's hump that identified her as Mrs. Blockman herself, the pious junkman's wife.

There was a moment when Zelik wondered if he could have reached heaven. But the monkeyshines of his neighbors were not altogether of the type he associated with a kosher idea of heaven. Besides, so far as he knew, none of these people were dead yet. Having made this assumption, however, Zelik figured he ought to confirm it, and immediately thrust his head back under the quiet whirlpool of fog. He looked down through the web of branches at the sleeping neighborhood spread out around the base of the tree. Then it occurred to him: what sleepers did was dream. And dreams, one might suppose, rose like heat until they found their common level. There they might settle at a height where some dauntless climber, provided he had the means of ascent, could reach them. He could enter the community of dreams and witness the high jinks to his heart's delight.

But as he looked down Zelik lost the sense of rapture he'd had only moments ago, and with it he very nearly lost his balance. Reminded that he was still, God forbid, umpteen feet above the earth (where dawn was already breaking), Zelik's fear of heights reasserted itself with a nauseating rush. Desperate, he clung to the oak for dear life.

Once the nebbish had climbed out of sight and shown no signs of coming down, the Pinch Gang began to lose interest. Augie Blot started torturing a bullfrog, pretending to read the future in its entrails, which were ultimately used to terrorize the girls. Eventually, grown bored and sleepy, they'd all wandered off to join their families. In the morning, reassembled at the foot of the oak, yawning and disheveled from a night under the stars, the remnants of last night's party remembered Zelik. Because the leaves were too thick to determine if he was still dangling somewhere above, Augie Blot was for calling the fire department, while Jakie dispatched his nimbler lieutenants to investigate.

When they saw him being lowered through the branches from which he'd been pried, they marvelled that he'd stuck it out overnight. Moe Plesofsky and some of the others proposed that Rifkin be made an honorary Gang member on the spot. Such fanatical endurance surely entitled him to waive the trials by fire, water, and theft that constituted a traditional initiation. But on closer inspection, when he'd been dropped to the ground in a limp but still quivering heap, they thought better of their benevolent impulses. All of a sudden it was clear that, regardless of what may have compelled him up the tree in the first place, it was fear that had kept Zelik aloft.

"Jellyfish Rifkin," jeered Augie, stepping over to lift one of Zelik's scrawny arms, "the winner and still champeen coward of North Main Street." Several others joined in the derision, but ramrod Jakie Epstein advised them to button their lips. "He ain't worth the wasted breath," Jakie added quickly, lest they mistake him for a defender of the underdog.

Some of the neighbors, pulling up suspender straps and massaging sore spines as they passed on the way to their homes, did a double take at the sight of the pitiful Rifkin kid. They gazed at him as if, though familiar, he was a stranger whose face they'd seen somewhere before. Among the passersby were the Alabasters, with their tousle-headed daughter in tow. Getting a load of Zelik, she gave him a flirtatious wink, then screwed up her face like she didn't know what had gotten into her.

For his part, Zelik—cap caked in bird droppings, shirt and plus fours hung with twigs—wondered if he were still in a dream.

V. Shedding Skin

Trudging home in the already hothouse sunshine, Zelik found his mother, who'd yet to miss him, dragging around the kitchen in her tatty dressing gown. She was setting the breakfast table with typical burnt offerings.

"Today's the anniversary," she announced with an enervated reverence, "of your great grandma, the Bubbe Bobke's passing, who died of what they died of in those days. So after supper you'll come with me to shul?"

"Mama," confessed Zelik, presenting the bedraggled spectacle of himself as evidence, "I spent the night in a tree."

"As long as you were careful, my yingele. If you climb a ladder, count every rung. You know, your father Mr. Rifkin . . ."

Not that Zelik needed any reminding about the perils that awaited him abroad. Hadn't last night's adventure been lesson enough, leaving him more than ever a bundle of nerves? Should someone say boo, he'd have clung to his mama's bristly ankles and pulled her gown over his head. So jangled was he this morning that he could scarcely recollect how, for a while in the crown of an oak tree, he'd been brave.

But as the day progressed and Zelik went through his perfunctory paces in Mr. Silver's market—grinding coffee, weighing cantaloupes, shucking corn to the weary rhythm of she-loves-me, she-loves-me-not—he began to recall with more clarity what he'd seen from the top of the tree. Or rather, the memory overtook his brain despite his best efforts to resist it. The exhilaration of the previous night returned, dispelling his nervousness, infecting his tepid bloodstream till his insides ran with rapids and cascades. In the end, Zelik's vision of a cockeyed North Main Street eclipsed even his hopeless mooning over Minnie, and he longed to see that ethereal place again more than he longed to see her.

Later that afternoon in Mr. Notowitz's bedroom, as his teacher belched whitefish and remembered past glories, Zelik thought he knew precisely what the old man was talking about. There was the part for instance where, wiping his face with the fringe of his flyblown beard, the teacher brooded,

"Once the Tree of Life I have climbed and plucked the sacred citron—I, Aharon Notowitz, that knew personally what are calling the wise men a holy influx. This by the heart and yea even in the pants I am knowing, when I would wear the garment of light that it was custom-tailored. . . ."

"I know just what you mean," put in Zelik from the edge of his chair.

"You?" said the teacher, his blood-rimmed yellow eyes coming to rest on his student for possibly the first time in their acquaintance. "Pishteppel, what do you know?"

The concept being brand-new to him, Zelik had to grope for the words. "It's like . . . being awake in your dreams."

"Dreams shmeams," grumbled the old man, though Zelik thought his sourness lacked its customary conviction. "Kholem iz nit gelebt, dreamed ain't lived."

Zelik looked forward eagerly to accompanying his mother to the synagogue that evening, if only for the time it would kill. Absorbed as he was in his anticipation, however, he couldn't help noticing that, despite the ever-oppressive heat, Mrs. Rifkin looked a touch livelier than usual. The indications consisted in nothing more than a slightly diminished slouch to her walk, a clean frock, a hint of rouge, a head-hugging flapper chapeau. But they were enough to make her son question whether the exuberance he could hardly suppress was somehow contagious.

Because sundown came so late during the summer months, the service on this Shabbos evening didn't begin till after nine o'clock. It was ordinarily a lengthy affair, during which, in a ritual unique to North Main Street, prominent citizens were called up to read from the Torah. Leaving their seats by the eastern wall, these men, often dressed as if for the links, would whisper in the sexton's ear before ascending the bima; then the sexton would relate in a booming voice their competitive contributions to the synagogue building fund. But tonight the service was cut short on account of the general asphyxiation. After Cantor Abrams had lifted his megaphone for a show-stopping "Adon Olom," Rabbi Fein rose puffing in his bowler to make an announcement: The ladies of Hadassah would be on hand with provisions for those who elected to stay the night in Market Square.

To Zelik's astonishment his mama, who as a rule never ventured farther from home than the shul, heaved a sigh and submitted fatalistically, "Who knows, maybe it'll do us good. Coming, kepeleh?"

In the park Mrs. Rifkin set about her mechanical housekeeping as if she were accustomed to sleeping out of doors. Choosing a spot on the edge of the crowd—somewhat duplicating the apartment's floorplan in its vicinity to Mr. Notowitz on his bench—she spread the horse blanket dispensed by the Hadassah. She kicked off her shoes, removed her costume jewelry, and took a yahrzeit candle from her purse. Zelik wondered why he should have expected that the candle would already be lit.

Nearby under the lilac Mr. Silver sat, nibbling dried fruit. Upon seeing the Rifkins he rose and shuffled over, removing his sleeping cap. Zelik waited for him to warn them of impending disaster, but instead he only offered some of his prunes. "Very good on my ulcer, they told me, and for the voiding of the bowel," he assured them, risking an experimental smile at Mrs.

Rifkin. It was as close to a declaration of affection as Zelik had ever known him to make. Something, it seemed, was in the air.

Zelik stuck close to his mother, who, after muttering prayers and laying her head beside the flickering candle, surprised him again by the ease with which she fell asleep. Once asleep, however, she was her old self again, moaning in the way that distinguished her troubled slumber. From where he sat in parched grass that still retained the heat of the day, Zelik could just make out the other kids under the tree. He strained for a glimpse of Minnie but felt no special disappointment when he couldn't see her. Instead he was content to lean back against the pillow of his wadded sack coat, listening to the A&P Gypsies drowning in a surf of static, the laughter of his neighbors growing spotty before subsiding into yawns.

The hour was late and he too ought to be dog-weary, having had not one wink of sleep the night before, but tired was the last thing that Zelik felt. Warily he got to his feet, beginning to creep about the margins of his neighbors' encampments, picking his way toward the base of the oak. He looked here and there amid the lumbermill of snoring to make certain that no one was watching, then jumped up to grab hold of an overhanging limb.

"I don't do this," Zelik reminded himself as he clambered for a foothold. "Zelik Rifkin doesn't climb trees." So who was it clutching that knot shaped like an old man's grimace, who fending off the flapping of an angry bird whose nest he'd nudged with his head? This is not to say that the dread of almost everything, by which Zelik identified himself, wasn't perfectly alive and well in his system. But tonight anxiety didn't rattle his nerves so much as strum them, tuning them to musical vibrations as he climbed into the cooler air.

In the giddy branches at the top of the tree, without hesitating, Zelik stuck his head through the spiral ceiling of fog. Again he was presented with the street of dreams. Citizens passing by on foot or in automobiles waved cordial salutations to Zelik's disembodied head. Blind Eli Rosen sounded an aooga horn as he rounded the corner in a block-long, articulated touring car; Miss Bialy of the Neighborhood House fluttered her hankie from the window of a solid glass four-in-hand. Filling his lungs with the fumes and aromas that were a tonic to him now, Zelik exchanged his grip on the oak for a hold of the pavement. He pulled himself up, scrambling from what turned out to be a manhole, its cover lying to one side like a huge plug nickel.

He stood in the middle of the street, poised to investigate, when he was struck by a mildly disturbing thought: What if, just as this morning he'd nearly forgotten last night, in wandering away from the manhole he forgot where he'd come from. To refresh himself with regard to his bearings, Zelik dropped to his knees and poked his head back into the hole. What he saw under the fog was a skinny kid in golf cap and baggy knee pants, hugging the wavering branches of a tree.

"This is me," Zelik surmised, curiously inspecting the flesh and bones out of which he seemed to have climbed. It troubled him a bit that his abandoned self should have reverted to so terror-stricken an attitude. Feeling, nonetheless, quite corporeal from his loftier vantage, fully clothed and ready for a little fun, Zelik withdrew his head from the fog as if he'd kept it under water too long. Then, with another breath, he took another look: still there. Again he raised his head, gave a shrug, then got to his feet and set off to explore.

He began with the Idle Hour Cinema, where, as a regular feature of the Amateur Night venue, the little Elster girl was winding up a tapdance in blackface and bubble eyes. Following her the manager, Mr. Forbitz, announced, "For your special delectation . . . ," drawing a curtain to reveal Tamkin the cobbler's apprentice immersed in an outsize fishbowl, a knife in his teeth, wrestling a large man-eating reptile with a thrashing tail. At the Phoenix Athletic Club they were dragging Eddie Kid Katz, the local palooka, out of the ring, after which the cadaverous Galitzianer rebbe entered in satin trunks. Coached from a corner by a party resembling the champ Benny Leonard himself, he delivered a sucker punch to the apparently glass jaw of a giant wearing biblical sandals and a ribbon-braided beard. From a dolphin's-head spigot on the marble fountain in his candy store, Mr. Levy filled a glass with sparkling liquid, levitating as he sipped it several inches above the sawdusted floor. In his butcher shop Old Man Dubrovner, tiptoeing into the meat locker, parted hanging slabs of beef to behold what looked like the Queen of Sheba, suspended in a block of ice.

Zelik took in everything with the peculiar wisdom with which he felt himself newly endowed. He understood, for instance, that, although most of these prodigies were authored by individuals, there were some involving two or more dreamers at once. This could of course be explained by the fact that the neighborhood slept together, and their dreams were therefore likely to mingle and converge. It was a condition that sometimes made it hard to determine where one person's dream left off and another's began.

Such was the case in the mikveh where the Rubenesque Mrs. Kipper, her lower anatomy that of a glittering goldfish, was performing a solitary water ballet, while Mr. Shafetz of Shafetz's Discount looked on indulgently in his fez, blowing words of love in the smoke from a nargileh pipe. It was the case with the Pinch Gang, who were everywhere, performing stunts compared to which their daylight exploits were sissy stuff. They danced without nets on crisscrossed clotheslines strung high across the alleys. At the river they commandeered the sumptuous barge of the Cotton Carnival royalty, dallying with the maids of honor after forcing their irate escorts to walk the plank.

Returning their greetings, Zelik heartily applauded their reckless abandon. He felt that, while only a spectator, he somehow as good as participated in their mischief. In fact, it occurred to him that being wide awake gave one a sort of edge over the dreamers.

You had the power, should you want to use it, to interfere with or even alter the course of their dreams.

But why would you want to do that when everyone already appeared to be having such a good time? Or rather, almost everyone—because, across the street at Silver's Fruit & Veg, the harried proprietor cringed behind his cash register with his apron over his head. A posse of mounted Ku Klux Klansmen, wearing cowls that bore the insignia of the Black Hundred and brandishing Cossack sabers, had ridden roughshod into the grocery. They were dangling a thick noose from a light fixture, threatening to stretch the grocer's Jew neck.

"We gon' do you like they done that'ere Leo Franko down Atlanta-ways."

Nor was everything hunky-dory in the apartment over the market. Mrs. Rifkin was as usual at her sewing, but back in his stifling bedroom Mr. Notowitz was beleaguered by giggling demons. Shaggy little creatures with beaks and crumpled horns, with goat shanks and barbed tails that struck sparks from whatever they touched, were tearing pages from his sacred texts and tossing them gleefully into the air. Bleating depravity, they tugged at his soup-stained beard and knotted the wisps of his hair while the old man asked the Lord why he'd been singled out for such a distinction. And when he looked again, Zelik saw how his mother, idle behind her antiquated Singer, was staring in dumbstruck confusion at the calendar on the wall. She was studying the glaringly empty square of a single vacant day wherein there was nothing at all to commemorate.

An old hand at nightmare himself, Zelik certainly knew them when he saw them, and so backed away from the situations of his mother and friends. It wasn't that he was frightened; nothing here seemed to frighten him, which was the point. All of a sudden Zelik missed his native jumpiness, the nerves that set off alarms throughout his body. Light-footed, he missed the lumpish body in which he'd never felt much at home. Maybe, he thought, it was time to go and check on himself in the tree.

Making one last scenic loop on the way, he passed by the Anshei Sphard shul, through whose portals he saw dreams that had not so much merged as collided. Inside, Minnie Alabaster was being manhandled, dragged kicking and screaming down the aisle by the Lieberman twins. In a gown of white chiffon and a veil sent flying from her tossing ginger hair, she shouted oaths that caused even Jakie's goons to turn crimson about the jug ears. On the altar stood Captain Jakie himself, looking a little chafed in his top hat and cutaway, with his best man, Augie Blot, beside him in snazzy pinstripes, a pistol trained on the frowning Rabbi Fein.

In the door of the synagogue Zelik had reached the conclusion that, given such complicated circumstances, you could hardly apportion blame, when Minnie twisted in her struggle to cry out to him, "Shmuck, you got lead for bones or what!" At that moment, having wrestled her up the stairs to the canopy, the Liebermans hoisted her wedding dress and bound it tightly over her head. They held her pinned in place but still kicking as the rabbi began dolefully to read the marriage vows.

Satisfied that all was not only big fun in this quarter, that one person's dream might be another's nightmare, Zelik turned and retreated to his manhole. He dropped back into his vacated skin, which welcomed him like a warm bath of worry and fear.

VI. In Which Zelik Has An Agenda

With the ounce of residual chutzpah still left to him, Zelik managed a slow descent on his own steam, reaching the ground just in time for sunrise. Where yesterday his muscles had smarted exquisitely, unaccustomed as they were to strenuous exercise, today he hurt in his very bones, not to mention his head and his heart. All that afternoon in Mr. Silver's market he groaned aloud with every least effort, until the grocer was moved to say, "You don't look so good already. Have a sit." No martyr to his condition, Zelik wanted to tell his employer, unusually spruce of late in a rakish straw boater, what he knew no one would believe. In fact, but for the souvenir of his general aches and pains, Zelik was no longer so sure what he believed himself.

"Maybe I overdid it in this heat," he agreed with Mr. Silver, and sat down.

Later on he swapped complaints tit-for-tat with Mr. Notowitz, griping about the unpleasant consequences of slipping in and out of one's own skin, but fell into a self-conscious silence when he had the impression that the old man was listening for a change. He was irked by his mother's unbecoming friskiness that evening, her air of expectancy. Why should she be in such an all-fired hurry to get to Market Square, where all she did, after a brief chat with Mr. Silver, was lie down and sink abruptly into fitful sleep?

As it turned out, Mrs. Rifkin wasn't the only one bent on retiring early. All around the neighbors stretched ostentatiously, excusing themselves from bridge circles and checkers, plumping pillows as if they couldn't wait to commence the business of dreaming. Not a bad idea, thought Zelik, who'd had no rest for two nights running, but he was still too keyed up and racked with pain to relax. Unable to get comfortable, he rose, feeling that despite wide-open eyes he was walking in his sleep, limping resistlessly toward the oak. He was in no shape to even consider climbing, which thank you but he'd had quite enough of in any case. Though didn't the conventional wisdom have it that more of what brought on the affliction was sometimes the best remedy. . . ?

At the top of the tree, hoisting himself with an excruciating effort into the dreamscape of North Main, Zelik was buoyant and light-headed once again. What's more, he found himself in possession of a program. Making straight for the greengrocery, where Mr. Silver's recurrent nightmare was still in progress, he leapt adroitly astride the haunch of one of the horses, unseating its hooded rider with a shove while retaining his sword. He spurred the spirited Arabian into the market, laying about with his blade and snatching up the terrified grocer, whom he folded over the horse's flying mane. The Klansmen reared and spat curses in the name of the Exalted Kleagle before beating a frustrated retreat. Leaving Mr. Silver seated now upon the charger, proudly erect as if posing for an equestrian portrait, Zelik dismounted and picked up a Klansman's fallen hood. He took a grease pencil from the checkout counter, scrawled a star of David above the peepholes, and pulled the linen cowl over his head—a wizard's hat.

He shot upstairs past his wilted mama, saying, "Don't go away!" then burst into the room where Mr. Notowitz was suffering from demons. "It is I, your hallowed ancestor Isaac Luria," he announced, "scourge of goblins and fiends." He took up a book at random from the gutted pile on the floor. "And this is the Book of Raziel that the angels gave to Adam, which he lost like a klutz when he got kicked out of the Garden. It's the book that answers the question how to look on the Almighty without you should go crazy or blind." He licked a finger, fanned the pages, gave a satisfied nod, and addressed the assembled evil spirits by name:

"Igrat, Pirpik, Qatzefoni, Asherlutz, Hormin son of Lilith,
Mahalath
  ahalath
   halath
    alath
     lath
      ath
       th
       h, enough already! Shoyn genug!"

Whining that they'd been dealt with unfairly, calling Zelik a spoilsport and worse, the demons began to vanish from their hooves and chicken feet to their spiky, cyclopean heads. To the tune of his old teacher's blubbering gratitude, Zelik made his exit and doffed the hood. He marched past his mother, who was mired in fabric, and stepped up to her calendar, writing boldly with his marker in the single vacant square (whose date was incidentally the present day): RACHEL RIFKIN'S COMING OUT. Then, gently, he raised her from the sewing machine and led her out of the cramped apartment down into the enchanted street. There Mr. Silver, saying "Hi ho, Leon Silver!" invited her to take a ride on his milk white steed.

After that Zelik might have rested. On earth he would have rested, tuckered out from the sheer exertion of having imagined such events. But here one thing led to another, the momentum building, carrying him forward as on the crest of a wave that crashed at the threshold of the Anshei Sphard shul. Entering, Zelik plucked the cantor's megaphone from its wall sconce, thinking it might come in handy. He stole into the women's gallery to better survey the scene on the altar, still in full swing, the hostage rabbi still pronouncing nuptials over a battling bride. Zelik tapped his temple until a strategy revealed itself. He untied from the railing a rope attached to the Everlasting Light, which in turn hung suspended from a rafter over the wedding canopy, directly above the head of the gun-toting Augie Blot. Then he let go, allowing the lamp, like a small red meteor, to drop through the canopy and flatten Augie's yarmulke. As Augie crumpled, Zelik broadcasted through the booming megaphone, "It's the voice of the Lord here. Now cut the hanky-panky."

Exchanging fearful glances, the knuckleheaded Liebermans unhanded their captive and bolted, tumbling over each other in their efforts to be first down the aisle and out the doors. Meanwhile Jakie Epstein, ferocious when provoked, had taken up the fallen Augie's pistol, pointing it left and right. "What's that I'm sniffkin!" he called out, proving it wasn't so easy to pull the wool over his eyes even in dreams.

Welcoming the challenge, Zelik mounted the railing, the rope that held the counterweight of the lamp still in his hands. He swung down from the gallery in a sweeping pendulum arc, neatly kicking the gun out of Jakie's grasp and catching it on the upswing in midair. Then he dropped to the altar and aimed the gun at Jakie, who raised his arms in defeat, muttering as he retired that they would see who had the final laugh. Nevertheless, Zelik thought he'd detected a trace of the ringleader's smile, as if Jakie were pleased at long last to have a worthy adversary. Tossing aside the pistol, Zelik unfastened the knot that bound Minnie's dress over her head and stepped back to watch the lace and chiffon fall like petals unfolding. As they faced each other—Minnie drinking in an adoring Zelik with quizzical jade green eyes—the rabbi read the conclusion of the ceremony and advised the groom to stomp the glass.

Lifting Minnie in his arms, thrilled to his toes by what a featherweight she proved to be, Zelik carried her down the aisle past pews now filled with neighbors shouting, "Mazel tov!" With his thoughts turned toward their honeymoon, he carried his bride out of the synagogue to a manhole in the middle of North Main Street. But when he'd stepped into the tree and settled back into his skin, he found that he was empty-handed except for the swaying branches he clung to for dear life.

The next day was agony all over again. Having never been drunk, Zelik thought this was what it must feel like to be hung over, so muddied in his brain were his memories of nocturnal derring-do. "Reckless shmeckless," he scoffed at himself Mr. Notowitz–style. Nervous and full of self-pity, he was valiant only in dreams.

Building a pyramid of apples in front of the market during the hottest part of the afternoon, Zelik pictured himself a slave in Egypt. Mr. Silver he tried to cast in the role of pharaoh, which wasn't so easy given the grocer's recent high spirits. How could you account for such a change in the timid little man? Where he should have been bemoaning evil prospects for the future, here he was making plans.

"So, Zelik, I think maybe I'm purchasing to raise them in the yard some chickens. I would make a competition by Makowsky and Dubrovner that they could use a kick in the toches. Don't you agree?" Then he inquired as to what time the Rifkins might be walking to the park tonight.

Zelik had no opinions to speak of concerning Mr. Silver's business, but for all his nagging discomfort, he wasn't unflattered that his opinion should have been sought. He even went so far as to make a pretense of weighing the matter thoughtfully.

Later, stepping into the hotbox of Mr. Notowitz's bedroom for his abortive Hebrew lesson, Zelik found the teacher poring feverishly over his texts. Stripped for once to his threadbare shirt-sleeves, he was squeezing a boil on his neck with one hand, jotting notes and drawing diagrams in the broad margins with the other. When Zelik hemmed, the old man looked up and greeted him with unprecedented warmth.

"Ah, my prize pupil, make a guess what I do. Go ahead, make already a guess." Zelik opened his mouth to say that he hadn't a clue. "I, in my capacity that I call myself the Pseudo-Abulafia, am hereby attempting the splitting of the Ineffable Name. So what you get when you do strictly by the formula from *The Kumquat Orchard* of Rabbi Velvl . . ." here he made a few more mad scribbles " . . . is you get for your trouble a fair likeness of the Cosmic Adam in his magic hat!"

"Come again," was all that Zelik could think to say.

But the old man's enthusiasm remained irrepressible. "So nu, what are you waiting?" he urged. "Give a look."

Zelik looked and saw a doodle resembling one of the multiglobed streetlamps along North Main, lit upon by a flock of crows. This he reported dutifully to Mr. Notowitz, who exhorted him to look again. "Don't tell to me you can't see him. Of course you can see him," the teacher assured his student, his optimism generating acid in Zelik's stomach. "Is possible, anything!"

Having deserted her sewing machine early that evening, Mrs. Rifkin was not to be found in the kitchen either. Zelik located her in her bedroom, primping in front of a mirror. She was mildly distressed at having nearly forgotten her Cousin (three times removed) Zygmund's yahrzeit, who had died of something someplace far away.

"But what's the fuss, eh toteleh? After all, the old fortz was cold before I got born. Now tell the truth, which do you prefer?"—holding up two kinds of earrings—"these ones or these with the thingamajigs that look like . . . " She laughed throatily, then blushed over what she thought they looked like.

Zelik was further bewildered at the attention paid him by his neighbors in Market Square. Before tonight, the most he could have expected from the citizens of North Main Street was their indifference, but now they hailed him with an amiable familiarity. They pinched his knobby shoulder and patted his back, gave him good-humored cuffs on the ear. Some paused to pass a little time in his company, asking his views on the affairs of the day: from the bull market to the films of Vilma Banky, the prospects for Prohibition repeal, the Monkey Trial, the duration of the heat wave, the fashionable positive thinking method of Dr. Emil Coué. When Zelik protested that he wasn't really up on current events, they pooh-poohed his modesty. And Minnie Alabaster blew him a kiss.

Her parents had stopped by the Rifkin bivouac to get Zelik's thoughts on a touring company currently playing the Orpheum Theater. This was when their daughter, posed beside them with one arm akimbo, touched her fingers to her full, pursed lips and blew in Zelik's direction. Stupefied, he slapped his cheek, having actually felt the sting of her kiss, though it may have been only a coincidental mosquito bite.

What was happening, Zelik wondered, that everyone should be giving him such a red carpet treatment, after years of either ignoring him or making fun? Why this sudden about-face? They were a fickle bunch, his neighbors—that was all he could figure, and Minnie he deemed the most fickle of the lot. Another thing Zelik couldn't understand was how he could feel so crippled with exhaustion and still not be ready to sleep. He blamed the capriciousness of North Main Street for playing on his nerves. This was not to say he would have wanted them to fall back on their former disposition; it was just that this being regarded as a person, for whatever reasons, was new to him. It would take a little getting used to. In the meantime the wisest course might be to stick to the shadows, keeping a safe distance from unpredictable neighbors, going where—once the park was quiet and he could rouse his aching bones—Zelik felt himself to be in control.

VII. *Mensch*

Though the summer never relented, the population of the Pinch seemed less oppressed by it than before. Something of the festive mood they displayed in the park at night was now extended to their daylight behavior. Rather than languish in helpless misery, they invented ways to beat the heat. They became less rigorous in observing their shop hours, taking siestas and making frequent trips to the public baths. Mrs. Bluestein designed a tunic made from twin enema bags filled with ice, which she threatened to have patented when it was copied by the Tailor Schloss. Another trend was set by Mr. Shapiro, who strung a hammock between his shop awning and show rack, then hired neighborhood children to fan him with broad-brimmed fedoras. Everyone wore looser, skimpier garments, even pajamas and dressing gowns by day, lending North Main Street the aspect of a Baghdad seraglio. And one and all went out of their way to pay their respects to Zelik Rifkin.

With never a mention of any event that might have led to their change of heart, the shopkeepers sought him out. They asked his advice about embarrassingly personal matters, about the finer points of religious law as if he'd been a rabbi; they showed him a deference they might have accorded a local hero. Nor did they flinch at the improvised answers that Zelik had begun to find the temerity to hand them. Their wives dropped by to worry over him, agreeing with clucking tongues that the boy was too thin, plying him with pastries and noodle puddings that he should keep up his strength—though they never said what for. Sometimes they teased him that what he needed was a nice girl.

Grown accustomed to their attentions, Zelik had stopped wasting time in wondering whether he deserved them. What went on during business hours was of little concern to him, his days being only anxious preludes to his nocturnal escapades. After all, in the small hours, between foiling various nightmares, outmaneu-vering Jakie Epstein along the way, he was with Minnie. A doting spouse, she'd set up housekeeping on a tiny painted ark drawn by swans in the Gayoso Bayou, and had begun to hint mysteriously that they might one day need an extra room. Reluctantly leaving her ardent embraces, Zelik set off on his self-appointed rounds of interfering in dreams. When there were no horrors to vanquish, he contented himself with making matches, such as the one between the bookish spinster Miss Weintraub and the handsome young novelist F. Scott Fitzgerald, his first marriage annulled after his wife discovered his Jewish descent. All were in attendance at the reception atop the fleabag Cochran Hotel, where a lavish roof gar-den had miraculously appeared. There was a cake the size of a Carnival float, Kid Ory's Creole Band playing Old World klezmer standards, and Zelik himself in the role of wedding jester, using risqué material gleaned from his pretty bride in another life.

So, if the neighbors wanted to treat him like a celebrity, it was their affair. Zelik saw no reason why he ought to discourage them. Moreover, since his body had adjusted to its nightly dislocations and he was no longer bent double with pain, he was better pre-pared to receive their solicitous gestures with a certain grace.

Around the market these days Mr. Silver, his perspiration glistening hair oil, hummed freilach airs as he weighed the produce, striking cash register keys to end a refrain. He spoke now in a jovial singsong to his customers, attempting jokes that he generally mangled, tossing the bonus of an extra string bean into their sacks. With his popular employee he liked to intimate how he had in mind a certain someone for a partnership, just as soon as that someone finished school.

"Incidentally," he would always inquire after his exchanges with Zelik, brushing off the freshly starched apron that Mrs. Rifkin had monogrammed, "what time do you and your mama walk tonight in Market Square?"

A little earlier every evening Mr. Silver and Mrs. Rifkin— he in his spats with a hamper of laxative fruit, she all done up in her veiled cloche and high-vamped shoes—strolled to the park, shmoozing animatedly on the way. Zelik would trail behind them as discreetly as possible given the attention he drew wherever he went. Sometimes Mr. Notowitz also joined their party, his informally open collar allowing the free sway of his wattled throat. Taking his student's arm, he might assure him he had the makings of an authentic tsadik, and once paid Zelik the highest compliment: "I am seeing in you the young Aharon Notowitz." If the student reminded his teacher that he'd never before shown any special aptitude for learning, the old man insisted that such modesty was itself a sign of wisdom. Then Zelik would have to gloat a bit despite himself, grinning complacently at the back of his mother's head. For the newly bobbed curls that peeked from under her hat, her coquettishness bespeaking a second girlhood, he felt in part responsible, though he couldn't say exactly how.

In another development Jakie Epstein had begun to send around delegations inviting Zelik to attend various functions of the Gang. While making change or uncrating bananas (careless lately of tarantulas lurking among them), Zelik might feel a tug at his sleeve, then look up to find Augie Blot in his aviator goggles.

"Jakie wants to know if you'd like to be a umpire," he might say, spitting tobacco juice through a gap in his teeth to show it was all the same to him; or, "Jakie wants to know if you'd like to watch us beat the kreplach out of the Mackerel Gang."

At first Zelik tested the water gingerly, thinking he smelled something fishy. Since when had they ever requested his company except to make him the butt of a joke? But now, putting his suspicions to rest, they seemed genuinely pleased to see him, asking his advice about everything from placing numbers bets to the speculated girth of Mrs. Kipper's bosom. Encouraged, Zelik began hanging around with the boys more often. He was tickled to have been accepted without having to spend the night on Beale Street or set fire to a schoolmistress or desecrate the Torah scrolls. But what was most appealing about his chumminess with the Pinch Gang was the opportunities it afforded Zelik to be close to Minnie.

Meanwhile she was making unashamedly aggressive overtures toward him. She'd begun by targeting him as the particular audience for her dubious humor ("So, Zelik, Doc Seligman walks into the deli and asks Mrs. Rosen if she's got hemorrhoids. 'Sorry, darling,' she says, 'only what's on the menu.'"), then graduated to a more personal approach. "They say you been hiding your light under a bushel basket at Silver's," she might tease him, pouting provocatively. "Mind if I take a peek under your bushel?" Eventually even less circumspect, she would steal up behind him to whisper pet endearments: "Zisss-keit, Sweet Patootie, my naughty Uncle Zelik, when are you coming to baby-sit your ickle Minnie?"

Always in his presence she managed to be fiddling with a stocking or dropping a scented handkerchief. Inhaling a lipstick-stained cigarette, she blew smoke rings that settled like halos over Zelik's head. And if the other boys, Jakie included, ever thought it unfair that the nebbish should command so much of Minnie's attention, they never let on.

Amazingly, Zelik wasn't afraid of her anymore. After a while he could weather her flirtations without his heart beginning to hum like a beehive whose vibrations he could feel in his pants. Cozy under his mantle of local maven, he forgot all those weeks of desperate yearning, and received her advances with a courtliness due the tender bride he knew her to be in her dreams.

He even found the nerve to return her flattery, if not quite in kind. "Minnie, you're a doll," he'd attempted on a note of confidence that fizzled when the words wouldn't come. "You're a . . . doll." But when the object of his tribute, instead of mocking him, winked as though the sally had struck home, Zelik was heartened. He could do no wrong. Moved to bolder experimentation, he cribbed lines from "The Song of Songs," domesticating them to the immediate surroundings.

"Thine eyes are as sunbeams in wine bottles," he extolled, reading from an unscrolled scrap of paper with halting formality, "thy hair like when you lift the lid on a stove, thy teeth like freshly scrubbed stones in the potter's field. Thy neck is the obelisk in Confederate Park, thine tsitskehs a pair of puppies. The smell of thy garments is the smell of Ridblatt's Bakery. Behold, my neshomeleh, leaping on the cobbles, skipping on the shells of snapping turtles . . ."

Minnie rewarded him by squirming kittenishly, the words seeming to have touched her in intimate places. "Stop!" she pleaded, pulling her beret over her ears, after which she purred, "Sweetie, I'm yours!" Guilty of having kindled blushes in so many others, Minnie turned crimson herself, then grew sober: it was a grave responsibility to be thus adored. She dropped her forward manner and her trademark salty language, swapping them for an uncharacteristic hauteur. Having absorbed by association some of the fawning respect universally heaped on her "fella" (as Zelik was lately acknowledged to be), Minnie Alabaster began to put on airs.

•   •   •

It seemed to Zelik that he now had just about everything one could want in this world, and assumed it had all come about by the grace of his activities in another. But since his neighbors had never once referred to having seen him in their dreams, you might have argued otherwise. You could believe, for example, that they'd simply come around to appreciating virtues in the kid that he himself had not recognized before.

At first their homage had served only to violate his privacy; it distracted him from the driven anticipation of his nightly ascent up the oak. Nothing on earth was as beguiling or even, paradoxically, as real as what waited for him in the top of the tree. Then the quality of life in the Pinch had changed: the neighbors ceased to utter discouraging words except about the weather. And, wonder of wonders, Minnie had given him her affection. Suddenly the daylight North Main Street was making a bid to compete with its nocturnal counterpart. In fact, they were neck and neck, and Zelik, drawn irresistibly to each, was never so content as to spend his days in one and his nights in the other.

Honored in the greengrocery, he still went through his stockboy's motions, though he was often interrupted by neighbors dropping by to bend his ear. Mr. Silver, if he worried about anything beyond the knot in his new cravat, worried that his assistant might become fatigued. With a paternal interest in Zelik's welfare, not to say a newfound sympathy for matters of the heart, he would advise his employee to take off early and go visit his girl.

A creature of habit, Zelik never failed to look in on Mr. Notowitz, whom he frequently found in the throes of mystical transport, naked but for his holey underwear. "Here by the gate of paradise is Notowitz!" the old man might proclaim, the sparse hair horizontal at his temples. "Behold that it is as an elevator up the trunk of the Tree of Life—I'm talking my room. You are maybe wanting to ride?" Zelik, who never rode when he could climb, would tell the teacher, "I'll take a rain check," then excuse himself and hurry off to preside over the doings of the Pinch Gang.

With Minnie on his arm he was practically holding court, a solemn and discerning presence at their assorted pranks and brawls. They even made sure he had a grandstand view of their more disreputable enterprises—the bootlegging, the petty thefts. For himself Zelik was happy to turn a blind eye to such proceedings, but sometimes, lest they offend her sensibilities, he thought it better to lead Minnie away. He took her for walks to show her off along streets where he had previously wandered in stealth all alone; and in the evenings, touching fingertips to each other's lips, the sweethearts exchanged a fond good night. The moment seemed all the more delicate against the backdrop of the noisy park, its racket increased by the conspicuous billing and cooing of Mrs. Rifkin and the grocer. Afterward, when everyone else was bedded down and sleeping, Zelik would climb the tree and meddle in their dreams.

It was an embarrassment of riches, the bounty that he now enjoyed, though it had displaced somewhat the sweet suspense of waiting each day for night to fall. Lately, while his body still longed in every fiber to make the climb, Zelik, his mind becalmed, wondered what was the hurry. Owing to his popularity, the neighbors had relocated their encampments until the Rifkins replaced the oak as centerpiece of the gathered community. This made it chancier to go creeping among them. Moreover, should anyone catch him climbing, what with their great concern for his welfare, they would insist he come down at once before hurting himself. And sometimes it occurred to Zelik that, for their sake, maybe he ought to be a bit more careful.

Also, when he thought of it, his meteoric rise to respectability rivaled anything he'd encountered in dreams. Dreams could scarcely improve on the bliss that was Zelik's daily fare. In coming to share his neighbors' estimation of himself, he felt almost as if North Main Street, in both its terrestrial and celestial manifestations, belonged to him; as if all that went on in that neighborhood above the sleeping park were contained in a dream of Zelik's own. Or was it a hallucination, since who wouldn't start to see things if they'd missed as much sleep as he?

Then came a night when the thought of his marathon wakefulness made him yawn. All around him his neighbors were already deep in slumber, and exposed as he was, Zelik figured it must be catching. Maybe a short nap would refresh him for the climb. Yawning luxuriously, he stretched out on the davenport that Shafetz's Discount had donated for his comfort. (His mother had been provided a chaise longue.) With his fingers locked behind his head, eyes closed to the shooting stars, he began to doze, falling into a dream about Minnie. In it he was dissatisfied with their hand-holding dalliance, and had begun despite her giggling protests to fumble under her clothes. He was jolted awake to a throbbing sense of something unfinished, but presently succumbed to drowsiness again.

VIII. *A Change In The Weather*

In the days following the abandonment of his nightly climb, Zelik looked forward to sleeping as much as he'd previously looked forward to scaling the oak. He slept long and deep, and in the mornings had to be roused by his mother with persistent shaking. Throughout the rest of the day he took every occasion to catnap, catching his winks where he might, convinced that his record insomnia had finally caught up with him. Meanwhile his neighbors continued to greet him affably enough, though they sometimes caught themselves in midsentence, pausing in irritation as if suddenly aware of having transgressed some personal code. Frequently stuporous, however, Zelik was the last to notice that their attitude toward him had grown chillier and more remote.

Even his closest acquaintances got into the act. There was the afternoon, for instance, when, sacked out for a snooze on a cooler at the rear of the market, Zelik was rudely awakened by the grocer.

"Stop with the loafing already," snapped Mr. Silver, his cheeks sagging from the weight of the bags under his eyes. "Troubles I got enough of without I should have a goldbrick on the job."

Hitting a snag in his mystical investigations—the critical twelfth combination of the letters of the Tetragrammaton having failed to induce the visionary state—Mr. Notowitz, who'd reverted to his moss-grown suit, blamed his difficulties on his student's untimely entrance.

"Where you been, you never heard of knocking?" he demanded, rapping his forehead with a bony fist until he'd raised a lump. "Come in, Mr. Rifkin, that he walks in the way of the Torah repairing its breaches. Better he should walk in the way of his mama repairing britches." With this he violently blew his nose in the crook of his sleeve.

Dowdy again in a washed-out housefrock, her face lackluster in the absence of shadow and rouge, Mrs. Rifkin asked her son if he'd mind correcting the tilt of her neglected calendar. And while he was at it, he should tear off the July page, since August was already half over, though where the time had gone she didn't know.

There was also discontent in the ranks of the Pinch Gang, who'd begun to express impatience with the way Zelik remained always the spectator. It started one late afternoon on the levee, when Ike, the semiarticulate twin, asked Zelik, "How come you don't never do nothing but sit and look?" Seated on a bollard with Minnie beside him, her elbow resting on his shoulder, Zelik rolled his eyes in a groggy smirk. He expected others to do the same rather than dignify such a stupid question. But Jakie himself, drying off after a dip in the river, his stringy muscles atwitch in his soaking skivvies, seconded the Lieberman's query. This left it to the irreverent Augie Blot to set them straight.

"'Cause he's a rare bird, ain't you heard? A yellow-bellied Zelik." He went on to call him names intended to dissolve any lingering illusion that the emperor was wearing clothes.

Zelik puffed himself up, speechless at Augie's show of insubordination. Truly, it was a harsher judgment than the others seemed prepared to accept, and with a pop of the jaw Jakie offered the accused a chance to allay their suspicions.

"Whyn't you dive off the crane if you ain't afraid?"

Swallowing hard, Zelik maintained his composure. "What for should I want to get all wet?"

When Augie suggested he already was, Minnie cut him short, forgetting herself in a curse that dismissed Jakie's mouthpiece for a pink-eyed, limp-petseled bed wetter. Then swelling the bodice of her sailor blouse, she was haughty again. "Go ahead, sweetie, give the monkeys a thrill." She patted her mouth in a yawn, bored at the prospect of yet another example of her boyfriend's fearlessness.

Aggravated, wanting a nap, Zelik turned to remind his companion that he didn't have to prove himself, when he saw in the set of her features that he must. Petulantly, he slid from the bollard and kicked off his shoes. He removed his cap and shirt, handing them to Minnie, who received them as if this were part of an established routine. Aware of how his pallor contrasted with the suntanned bodies of the Gang, he was also conscious of the fact that Jakie Epstein didn't have a corner on knotty biceps, Zelik's clandestine tree-climbing activities having whipped him into pretty fair shape.

He strolled up to the greasy traveling platform from which a tall crane leaned out over the river, and sprang onto the ladder. In seconds he was scrambling up the girders of the crane itself, using the large bolts encrusted with pigeon drek for toeholds, climbing with an easy agility. Then it was bracing to demonstrate before an audience what had become for Zelik an almost involuntary exercise; although, as he mounted higher, he discovered he was a little out of practice. He was slightly winded as he neared the top, not to say dizzy from the contraption's tilt and sway, and the sun, glinting off the tin roofs of houseboats and the river, stung his eyes whenever Zelik dared to look down. Here he awoke to the realization that, for all his dream heroics, he had yet to disprove the famous Rifkin chicken-heartedness by day. It was a truth that stopped him cold, left him clinging to the girders for dear life, listening to insults hurled from the cobbles and feeling his nose begin to bleed.

After that Minnie became increasingly difficult to live with, though she continued to stick by Zelik with a stubbornness that challenged anyone to so much as look askance. But where her beau had turned back before her eyes into a milquetoast, Minnie had begun to act the floozy again. She'd revived her teasing manner that called into question the virility of the other boys, sometimes suckering them into flirtations that she abruptly thwarted. Once more she was telling stories that cast their families in compromising roles: "So Nathan Shapiro meets his papa coming out of a bordel on Beale Street, and his papa says, 'Don't be angry, sonny. Would you want I should wake your mama at such an hour for a dollar?'" And always she looked over her shoulder for Zelik's reaction.

Then the first time he'd presumed to suggest that this kind of behavior wasn't becoming, Minnie turned on him. She yanked him behind the Market Square bandstand and offered him another chance to prove his mettle. "What do you say, my big strong ape-mensch," she breathlessly invited, watering Zelik's eyes with her cheap perfume, "won't you give your angel food girlie a little fun?"

"I don't know what's got into you, Minnie." Zelik tried to stand firm in his disapproval, though neither of them was fooled. Both understood that he was simply afraid to touch her, at least in her fleshly daylight incarnation.

"Okay, kiddo," sniffed Minnie, twisting her neck to admire the bare shoulder that her boat-necked blouse revealed, "if you can't show me a good time, there's others who can." Pausing to light a cigarette, she flicked the match at Zelik before traipsing off.

Brooding but undaunted, Zelik resolved to fix things the next time he saw her, if not here on earth then elsewhere. He determined to make good again in dreams what he'd botched in waking life. How had he let the situation get so out of hand in the first place? It was true of course that, during his drowsy absence, the street at the top of the oak had all but faded into unreality; but now this only increased Zelik's urgency to reconfirm what had to have been more than just the fruits of an overwrought imagination.

At dusk on the same day that Minnie had called his bluff, however, there was a distinctly literal chill in the air. There was a breeze that the neighbors were welcoming as the harbinger of an early autumn, their reward for having survived such a scorching summer.

"Thank God that tonight in our own beds we will sleep," sighed Mr. Silver, who had recently begun talking about Klan raids in the park again.

"What are you saying!" cried his young assistant, on hand to fly into a panic. "This summer ain't over by a long shot. You'll see, the temperature'll soar. Don't be taken in by a little breeze."

The grocer was perplexed that anyone should seem to want the heat to endure. "Meshuggeh," he grumbled, turning away, washing his hands of an employee who, beyond feckless, was crazy to boot.

Zelik wandered up North Main Street, listening to the shopkeepers trading expressions of relief over the change in the weather. Taking every opportunity to contradict them, he insisted they shouldn't relax: "Don't you know we're in for more of the same!" But the neighbors only shook their heads, no longer influenced by what the screwball Rifkin kid might believe.

That night Zelik went to the empty park all alone. Not only had the wind picked up, with a blustery edge that gave him gooseflesh, but a fierce storm was threatening. Huge, billowing thunderheads obscured the moon, their interiors lit like intermittent X rays. Then the sky cracked open and a gullywasher ensued.

Running home in the torrential downpour, fording gutters flash flooded to his knees, Zelik was drenched to the marrow. Even changed into his nightshirt and nestled under the covers, he couldn't stop trembling.

At first unable to sleep, he fell at length into an agitated insensibility, dreaming that the oak was struck by lightning at its crown, riven limbs tumbling to earth in sizzling flames. He woke up sopping all over again, the sheets clammy from his sweat. For an instant Zelik thought his prayers had been answered: the heat had returned with an intensity that made a furnace of the apartment. But how could this be, when the rain was still drumming away in the alley outside? It was a mystery that goaded Zelik into abandoning his bed for the cluttered living room. His mother and Mr. Notowitz, a sheet draped like a prayer shawl over his shoulders, were already at the windows, looking onto a stormy North Main Street aglow beneath a hyacinth orange sky.

The word went from building to building that the great wooden barn of the Phoenix Athletic Club had been struck by lightning. "It went up just like matchsticks," everyone said. Although the boxing arena stood a block away on Front Street, the heat from its conflagration was so furious that the windows of the Rifkin apartment were too hot to touch. Over the clanging engines from five alarms, they could hear the nickering screams of horses in a stable near the arena that had also caught fire. They could hear the sound of shattering glass as windows were bursting all over the Pinch.

IX. Jacob's Ladder

For a day or so it was hard to tell whether the overcast sky was due to dark clouds or the smoke from the smoldering arena. But soon the cooler air blew away the smoke, the sun reappeared, and the season turned.

By now Zelik's status in the community had degenerated from merely discredited to outcast. Nostalgic for his former condition of near-invisibility, he lurked in backstreets, avoiding as best he could the scornful glances of his neighbors, the taunts of Jakie's gang. From the way everyone behaved, you'd have thought he was personally responsible for whatever disappointment they'd experienced in life.

To make matters worse, Zelik's friend and employer, reeling from a recent attack of gentile phobia (he claimed it was the Klan that torched the boxing arena, infested as it was with a certain ghetto element), informed his so-called assistant that he would have to lay him off. "It ain't so hotsy-totsy, the produce business," explained Mr. Silver.

Zelik put up a token resistance. "So what happened to 'With a certain cute boychik, soon I am making a partnership?'"

"That was couple weeks ago already," said the grocer, pausing a moment to plaintively recall the past. "To tell the truth, what it is that ain't good for business is you."

Neither was it good for business, thought Zelik, that Mr. Silver shook in his bluchers every time some yokel walked in from the wagon yard. And what about his recent quarrel with Mrs. Rifkin? (It had begun trivially enough with the seamstress accusing her suitor of having falsely advertised inferior merchandise, but ended in the mutual dissolution of their romance.) Let Silver deny that had anything to do with the sudden dismissal of his faithful employee. But Zelik wasn't really inclined to argue. The job had entailed more public exposure than he had the heart to suffer, and, besides, who needed the grocer's penny-ante charity?

Meanwhile Mr. Notowitz's experiments in practical kabbalah had entirely broken down, and the old teacher had withdrawn into a sullen and demon-ridden silence. If he emerged for meals, he ate little; he complained that feasting all summer on the fruit of the Tree of Life had given him terminal gas. As for Mrs. Rifkin: with the courtship of Leon Silver blotted from her memory, she'd resumed her fanatical devotion to the calendar of events in other people's lives.

As the following months ushered in the bitter winter of Zelik Rifkin's discontent, no one else in the Pinch appeared to be doing much better. Everyone griped that business had fallen off. They blamed their lack of prosperity—which was a new line, as if they'd just waked up to the fact that they were poor—on the treachery of their Irish and Italian competitors; though the butcher Makowsky was heard to say of the butcher Dubrovner, who promptly returned the compliment, that he was not above certain underhanded practices of his own. Most agreed with Mr. Silver that the mayor of Memphis, a self-styled potentate nicknamed the Red Snapper, was perfectly capable of reinstituting the blood libel. A pogrom might be imminent.

But of all the available scapegoats on which the neighborhood pinned their woes, Zelik remained a sentimental favorite, the Pinch's own resident Jonah. The latest complaint to become popular along North Main Street was chronic insomnia, which had infected enough to be declared an epidemic. Despite unusually cold weather otherwise suited for a deep winter's hibernation, the neighbors grew ever more irritable from loss of sleep. For this they were also disposed to blame the Rifkin kid, though direct expressions of annoyance had to be reserved for the rare occasions when he was sighted. Thus, having once been revered for no apparent reason, Zelik was now just as unreasonably despised.

The worst was of course that Minnie wanted nothing to do with him. In the face of her active disdain, however, Zelik's pining for his ginger-haired precious had if anything intensified. But this was not the wistfully chivalrous brand of longing that had satisfied him in the days when he was secure in her adoration. Now Zelik wanted to encircle her slender waist and squeeze for all he was worth. He wanted to nibble her succulent earlobe, bury his nose in the warmth of her boobies, bite the delectable flesh above her rolled stocking while murmuring forbidden words. He cursed and berated himself for the opportunities he'd let slip by, for neglecting to act on the nerve that he'd deceived himself into thinking he had.

Leaning out of doorways in his earflaps and ulster, parting racks of pants gone stiff from the chilly air, Zelik spied on Minnie. He watched her gossiping as she left Levy's Candy Store with Rose Padauer and Sadie Blen, heard her twitting the boys with her racy remarks, the choicest of which she'd begun to save for Jakie Epstein. Holding his breath so its steam wouldn't give him away, he saw Minnie urge Jakie to drop back from the others, tugging him into an alley where they could bundle and pet.

The unending cold snap did nothing to take the edge off his terrible wanting, and eventually a day arrived when desire got the better of fear. Having waited for the lovebirds to part company in a gravel drive behind the cigar factory, Zelik pitched forward through a sprinkling of snowflakes to block Minnie's path.

"M-n-n-n." His chattering teeth prevented him from getting beyond a blue-lipped approximation of her name.

Hugging herself in her mackinaw against the raw January wind, Minnie wondered aloud, "What did I ever see in you? Gevalt!" She slapped her brow with a mittened palm. "I must of had a hole in my head."

In the instant before she started away, Zelik saw in her emerald eyes that she scarcely even considered him worth pitying. Frantically hoping that a second look might erase the first, he lunged for her arm and spun her around.

"Nobody!" she hissed. "You got wet lokshen noodles where your backbone ought to be."

He was sobbing when he embraced her, the sobs mounting to a caterwaul as they tussled, as he tried to thrust his fingers between the buttons of her coat. It was a clumsy assault, too blind and confused to be effective, and Minnie handily repulsed him with a knee to his groin. He slumped against a bill-plastered wall and slid to the gravel, Minnie already showing him her heels, though she turned back briefly to deliver a kick for good measure to his shin. While the hot tears cooled to an icy glaze on his cheeks, Zelik surrendered to the contemplation of his basest act of cowardice so far.

Warmer weather brought little relief, though with a heady bouquet of growing things in the air, the open hostility of his neighbors toward Zelik seemed to have subsided. His disgrace, lacking any sound basis in circumstance, was apparently forgotten along with the dreadful winter, and the street resumed its original indifference with regard to the Rifkin kid. Not that it mattered. By now Zelik had more than enough disgust for himself to compensate for what his neighbors no longer took the trouble to feel.

He had for some time discontinued his spying operations, leaving home only to attend the Market Avenue School, in whose dusty corridors and classrooms he'd perfected his nonentity. Otherwise, except on those evenings when he accompanied her to the synagogue for prayers and yitzkor services, Zelik remained his mother's shut-in companion. He left his days to be defined, like hers, by the calendar of banner events—a new calendar published by a company that made wrought-iron anvils. Avoiding their cranky boarder, Zelik occupied himself with daydreams in which nobody ever turned out a hero, though sometimes, if only to break the monotony, he might be moved to inquire about the relatives they mourned. Maybe one of them had an interesting life. But in the end he dropped the questions, having confirmed that his toilworn mother hardly knew any more about them than he.

School let out and spring turned imperceptibly to summer, a mild summer like an apology for the previous year's inferno. But the balmy days were too good to last, and somewhere around mid-July the heat was once again cranked up full force. The shopkeepers lolled in their sweaty undershirts, their faces hidden beneath wet rags. On their heads they wore newspapers folded into admiral's hats, smeared headlines declaring no end in sight for the dog days. The k'nackers claimed they were dredging boiled mussels from the river, that Kaplan the realtor had cornered the market in shade, while the pious tended to view the heat wave as a finsternish, another plague visited for their sins on North Main Street by an angry God. Eentsy Lazarov had been spotted in the arms of her shaigetz in the balcony of the Orpheum Theater, Morris Hanover seen departing a hog-nosed café on Beale Street eating treyf. Though if it occurred to anyone to blame the unbearable weather on Zelik Rifkin, they were never heard to say.

Like every other apartment in the Pinch, the one above Silver's Fruit & Veg was practically beyond habitation. Its occupants were unable to draw a breath without feeling as if someone else had drawn it before them; there seemed not enough of that torpid air to go around. This, Zelik told himself, was what he deserved, though the heaviness of this particular afternoon left him wondering if there might be a limit even for him. Raising himself from his prostration atop a pile of clothes in need of mending, he panted hopefully, "Did anybody die today?"

With barely the strength to pump the treadle on her hobbling machine, Mrs. Rifkin glanced at the calendar. "Your Great Uncle Gershon," she sighed.

Of Uncle Gershon Zelik knew only that he'd perished of death long ago in some unpronounceable village in Europe, and that his memorial meant he and his mother, please God, would leave the apartment tonight. It never entered his head anymore that he might go out alone.

Because it was Shabbos, the whole of North Main Street was in the synagogue, flapping their prayerbooks like an aviary to try and stir a breeze. There were several instances of fainting, not to be confused with swoons in the gallery during the cantor's megaphone vocals. Dehydrated babies wailed and daveners gibbered in no identifiable tongue. Finally Rabbi Fein, so farshvitst you'd have thought his bowler was an upturned bucket, hauled himself onto the pulpit to deliver his benedictory sermon. Wrapped in his wringing tallis like a bath towel, he reeled as he recited what purported to be a midrash on the subject of Jacob's Ladder.

". . . You had at the bottom of the ladder the angels, that they looked like old men in their caftans, their wings scrawny as a chicken's. But the closer they are getting, these angels, to the top of the ladder, the more antsy-pantsy and fuller of pep they become. Then it's off with the clothes, they're throwing them willy-nilly, and hallelujah! youthful figures they got now, with lovely wings that make a nice cool breeze. . . ."

The rabbi cleared his throat and recovered his composure. "The lesson from this text we are learning," he began with authority; then his eyes started to shift and he muttered hastily that the congregation were free to draw their own conclusions. He raised his voice to announce that the ladies of the synagogue auxiliary would be on hand with provisions for those who elected to stay the night in Market Square.

X. *The Ceiling of Fate*

Too depleted from the ordeal of the service to protest, Mrs. Rifkin allowed her son to lead her across the street into the park. There they joined the others milling about like survivors of a shipwreck, receiving from the ladies blankets for making pallets and collapsible cups of iced tea. On the far edge of the circle of neighbors, Zelik spread the blanket and saw that his wilting mother was settled comfortably for the night. Sitting beside her, he patted his chest through his shirt in an effort to quiet the frightened fluttering within.

Everyone was there: Mr. Silver beneath the lilac with his galluses hanging, swilling stomach bitters to chase down his prunes; Mr. Notowitz disguised as refuse on his bench. Some members of the Pinch Gang could be seen shadowboxing under the tree, a knot of girls (Zelik wondered idly if Minnie were among them) conspiring nearby. Now and then neighbors passed seeking extra hands for card games, looking to stake claims on unoccupied pieces of ground, but not one gave the Rifkin kid so much as a "How-do-ya-do." They ignored Zelik so completely he might have doubted his very existence, which, under the circumstances, he found somehow reassuring.

In the moonless sky, however, there were occasional flashes of lightning, promising rain and threatening to reduce the oak to a burning bush. Zelik could feel this particular worry beginning to spawn nameless others until he was permeated with a general dread. Over and over, as the neighbors extinguished their lanterns and allowed their victrolas to wind down, he had to remind himself that this was only heat lightning, which was nothing but the echo of a storm too far away to matter.

To his mother he whispered, in order not to wake her, "Good night, Mama, I'm off to climb a tree to the Land of Nod," then started at her mumbled words of caution. He got to his feet and made his way among his neighbors, casting rueful glances at their recumbent forms, as if they'd fallen in battle instead of merely fallen asleep.

He stepped onto a humpbacked root and jumped, clambering painfully aloft. Due to a long inertia his muscles were unused to climbing, never mind the state of his nerves, and Zelik groaned his torment at every stage of the ascent. Too scared to look down, he nevertheless managed to lose his footing from time to time, and had to hug the tree until his breath returned. Somewhere during the climb his groans turned to whimpers, though after a certain height Zelik's suffering began to sound in his own ears as if it belonged to someone else.

When he'd surfaced from under the fog, he filled his lungs with sparkling courage, his eyes with crazy dreams. Slipping neatly out of his body, Zelik stood astride the manhole to watch the shenanigans of North Main. The widow Teitelbaum was on her balcony, serenaded by a singing cowboy bearing a marked resemblance to Cantor Abrams in Stetson and chaps. Sacharin the herringmonger tossed promotional handbills from on board a flying fish, and Lazar the red-whiskered bootlegger, unscrewing a fire plug, deluged the gutters with an amber flood of beer. But anxious as he was to commence his rounds, Zelik restrained himself; there was a piece of business he had first to attend to.

Dropping back into the tree, he hung by his knees and surveyed the park below. From this topsy-turvy vantage Zelik felt almost as if he were at the bottom of the oak again, looking up into a dark canopy hung with dreamers. He judged that all was as it should be with them, just as it was with his own outmoded self, fearfully clutching the branches under the ceiling of fog. Reaching down, Zelik took hold of those tenacious fingers and endeavored to pry them loose. His old golf-capped, knee-pantsed, skin-and-bones double struggled to retain its balance. To make sure that it didn't, Zelik gave it a little shove. As he swung back up onto the airborne pavement, he heard the thrashing beneath him, the desolate shriek, which he muffled by sliding the iron manhole cover in place. Then nothing remained but to stroll off into the thick of things.

HYMAN THE
MAGNIFICENT

I. The Straitjacket Challenge

I was in the audience at the Idle Hour Cinema with my mother
and father for my friend Hymie Weiss's Amateur Night debut.
This was on North Main Street in the spring of 1927. Of the
several acts preceding Hymie, the first was Mr. Dreyfus the jeweler, who'd aspired to be a comedian ever since Mogulesco's touring
company had played the Workman's Circle lodge hall. The problem was that Mr. Dreyfus knew only a couple of jokes, which he
repeated at each performance, so that everyone already had them
by heart. As a consequence the earnest jeweler found himself in
the role of straight man to his own shtik of riddles and gags.

His favorite was the one that went, "What hangs on a wall, is
green, and whistles?" to which the audience would answer in a
chorus so loud that plaster fell from the ceiling, "A herring."

Says Mr. Dreyfus, flapping his baggy pants in case you hadn't
noticed: "Since when does a herring hang on the wall?"

Audience: "Who stops you from hanging it?"

Mr. Dreyfus, adjusting a rubber nose scarcely larger than his bulbous original: "Is a herring green?"

Audience: "You could paint it."

Mr. Dreyfus: "But who ever heard a herring whistle?"

Audience: "Nu, so it doesn't whistle!"

Mr. Dreyfus does a modest hornpipe to Mrs. Elster's organ, exiting to raucous applause.

Next the little Elster girl, done up in blackface like Topsy, commenced a bubble-eyed tapdance, making window-washing gestures with the flat of her hands. Her mama, the resident organist, accompanied her in a medley of Stephen Foster tunes. Wearing a false beard that covered his goiter, Ike Taubenblatt, the shoe repairman, did the "Blow wind, crack your cheeks!" speech from Shakespeare. Mrs. Padauer juggled three rolling pins and Mannie Blinkman swallowed a light bulb, only to belch it back up again. Cantor Abrams sang his three-handkerchief rendition of "The Czarist Recruit's Farewell" through a megaphone. Then it was Hymie's turn to perform what he'd talked Mr. Forbitz, the theater manager, into announcing as the evening's pièce de résistance.

He came on dressed like the Phantom of the Opera in a getup borrowed from Nussbaum's Drygoods Emporium. With a flourish he doffed the top hat and removed his silk cloak, revealing a sleeveless undershirt that showed off his stringy physique. When he handed the hat and cloak to his assistant, my sister Miriam, there was polite applause, though whether it was for Hymie or Miriam (who was an uncommonly dishy girl) was hard to say. In either case Hymie had the attention of the house.

Having placed the accessories over a chair, Miriam took up the stiff sailcloth straitjacket trimmed in leather. This while Hymie, running a hand through his upstanding auburn hair, announced gravely, "Ladies and gentlemen, for your express delectation I will attempt Houdini's famous punishment suit release." Then, as Miriam held the straitjacket in front of him, Hymie thrust his hands into the sleeves, which overlapped the ends of his outstretched arms. He gave her the nod and Miriam turned to the tittering crowd.

"Hymagnimummm . . . ," she mumbled to her sandal-shod toes, nervously flouncing the handkerchief points of her skirt. But when some of the onlookers demanded she speak up, she repeated almost defiantly, "Hyman [pronounced High Man] the Magnificent requests volunteers from the audience."

Practically all the young men in the theater, eager to assist Hymie's assistant, rose and stampeded the stage. Miriam glanced sheepishly at Hymie, who maintained his rigid pose but rolled his eyes, as the small stage was overrun by the sons of North Main Street. Conspicuous among them was Bernie Saperstein, the most aggressive of my sister's suitors, looking spruce in his canary blazer and waxed mustache. Shouldering his way to the forefront of the would-be volunteers, he left Miriam no recourse but to choose him to help fasten Hymie's restraints. She also chose, probably to compensate for Bernie's vigor, the consumptive Milton Pinkas.

Exercising somewhat more zeal than was called for, Bernie went to work on the buckles and straps, slapping down Milton's hands whenever he tried to pitch in. With his torso constricted until he'd turned the blue of moldy cheese, Hymie spoke in a voice trapped somewhere in his diaphragm. "The committee will confirm," he managed hoarsely, "that the punishment suit is secure." Bernie tugged at the jacket and smugly grinned his assent. "And now," croaked Hymie, "as I say the mystical word 'Anthropropolygos!' [which I mouthed along with him], Miss Rosen, if you please—"

Miriam rolled out a gauze hospital modesty curtain from stage left and folded its panels around Hymie. Then she said what she'd been coached to say, the phrase uttered by Bess Houdini before shutting up her husband in his various cabinets: "Je tire le rideau comme ça!" "It means 'I draw the curtain thus!'" I told my mama next to me, who grunted that I shouldn't be such a wisenheim. Stepping to one side, Miriam made an artistic gesture and smiled unconvincingly, embarrassed as always by her own drop-dead beauty.

Mrs. Elster played an appropriately suspenseful signature on her organ, while I pictured Hymie behind the curtain, drinking in the moment he'd waited for. Mentally I prompted him, reciting under my breath the pertinent passage from *Magical Rope Ties and Escapes*: "The first step necessary in freeing oneself from the jacket is to place an elbow on some solid foundation and by sheer strength . . ."

The ordinarily boisterous Amateur Night audience were subdued as they listened to the sounds of the struggle behind the curtain. They remained almost reverent, even as the curtain toppled over on its clattering frame, revealing Hymie wrestling furiously with himself. He thrashed around like a cat in a bag, flinging his hampered body here and there, assuming contortions certain to cause him an injury. Against the painted asbestos backdrop Miriam had begun to chew her braid, her pale cheeks gone intensely crimson. The jaws of the volunteers hung collectively open. Then Bernie Saperstein, always the joker, called out, "Somebody get the rabbi, there's a demon in Hymie Weiss!" and the whole theater split their sides. This was Mrs. Elster's cue to strike up a rollicking tune.

The general hilarity seemed only to encourage Hymie's violent behavior. Puffed with concern, Mr. Forbitz marched out of the wings, shooing everyone from the boards. "All right, Weiss," he blustered, dewlaps swaying, "that's enough already, shoyn genug!" "Stop it, Hymie!" cried Miriam, stomping her foot, but her agitation on his behalf if anything only fueled his abandon.

At length Mr. Forbitz returned to the wings and lowered the movie screen with a dust-raising thud, thus separating the spectators from Hymie's ordeal. He stepped back out again to signal the projectionist, upon which the lights went out, a beam shot over our heads, and the picture began. It was a John Barrymore melodrama entitled *The Beloved Rogue* ("Even torture could not quell the spirit of the vagabond poet," the posters read), for whose credits Mrs. Elster modulated her rollicking organ. The rooftops of medieval Paris, brooded over by Notre Dame, appeared to be caught in a blizzard of blackbirds, so poor was the quality of the film. What's more, as the dauntless vagabond swaggered into the frame, the screen, patched and seamed as an old topsail, began to flutter from the goings-on behind it. The crooked streets rippled as if in an earthquake and the audience howled over the distortions. Then, in the side of a house from whose window a bosomy lady was waving, a fissure opened and Hymie hurtled through. Still in the throes of his desperate struggle, he lurched headlong into the orchestra pit, breaking an arm.

II. *The Passing of the Torch*

He was an orphan, Hymie Weiss, raised by his Aunt Frieda and Uncle Shaky Nussbaum above their drygoods store on North Main. All he knew about his real parents was that his father was a tinker who'd perished in a cholera epidemic in the Old Country; his mother, fleeing shortly thereafter, had died giving birth to the infant Hymie in the steerage section of a steamship en route to the Golden Land. Aunt Frieda and Uncle Shaky, his mother's brother, had traveled to Ellis Island and brought the baby back home to their emporium in Memphis. That was the story, though Hymie had always reserved the right to be skeptical.

Taking down the snuff-brown photograph of a bearded man in a dented bowler holding a book, the woman beside him in a kerchief with fearful eyes and cheeks that looked stung by bees, he would impersonate his straight-faced Aunt Frieda: "They was good haimesheh people." Then reverting to his own wistful voice, he'd say, "I ask you, Stuart—" (He always called me Stuart, for which I was grateful, because everyone else called me Stuie, my mama frequently shouting it so that it sounded like when the yokels called their hogs. I was a fat boy and sensitive to the pronunciation of my name.) "I ask you, Stuart, do these people look like the parents of a hero?" That's the way he talked, which somehow never sounded boastful or immodest, so deep was Hymie's conviction that he was marked for greatness.

Of course he was all talk at first, but that was before he took up with my sister, or rather Miriam took up with him. She cultivated Hymie's friendship on account of his being too absorbed in dreams of glory to take much serious notice of her, or so she must have thought.

You see, most of the guys in our neighborhood, which was called the Pinch, were starry-eyed over Miriam. They lined up at my parents' delicatessen, where she waited tables, just to watch her toss her midnight braid over a shoulder. Or lift her sea green eyes to dart a look from under drowsy lids, or draw back the taut bow of her smile, making wrinkles like parentheses in her otherwise satin-smooth cheeks. Never mind the way her languid bones gave the impression that they ebbed and flowed under a summer chemise. Even the gentiles came in to suffer my mama's Hungarian meatballs, word of my sister's comeliness having reached as far as Front Street and the Cotton Exchange.

The guys outdid each other in their efforts to try and get her attention, taking great pains in their personal appearance like Bernie Saperstein, or showing off like Herman Blen, who rode into the deli on horseback. There was Mickey Graber who recited odes under Miriam's window, the Lieberman twins who made themselves into human stairsteps when she got off the trolley, Max Bluestein who had her name tattooed on some part of his body that he promised to show her once they were wed. There was Sy Plesofsky who threatened flatly to cut his own throat if she didn't attend a Menorah Institute dance with him. In fact, my sister, or at least the distraction she caused, was often blamed for a rash of local injuries, self-inflicted or otherwise—to which was added the insult of her refusal to choose from among her many suitors.

What with the guys competing and the girls all taking pot-shots behind her back, no wonder Miriam preferred the company of the preoccupied Hymie Weiss. Though in the end he began to fall for her like everyone else. Not that he let on; she would have dropped him like a hot potato if he'd let on, but by now I was used to spotting the symptoms. The first I saw was the time in Levy's Candy Store, when he asked her, a little sarcastically I thought, what he'd done to deserve the distinction of being Miriam Rosen's pet.

"Why me?"

My sister lowered her lashes, so long they sometimes seemed to beat like wings, and whispered, "Because you don't make me sorry I'm beautiful." Then she perked up. "Tahkeh, you're so hare-brained you don't even know I'm alive."

"I know you're alive," Hymie had muttered into his root beer, which was when I knew for certain he was hooked. It was shortly after that he started trying to act out his fantasies.

Nobody regarded Hymie, harmless daydreamer that he was, as a serious rival for my sister's affections, but that didn't stop their disliking him just the same. They disliked him for always being in the way. For Hymie's sake I resented their attitude, since I consid-ered him my friend as well, which is not to say I paid any more attention to his big ideas than anyone else. It's just that being pudgy and something of a bookworm, I had to take my pals where I could find them. Naturally all the older guys went to some lengths to be nice to me, but that was only to win my sister's favor. Hymie was different though, being as hard up for pals as myself, and despite the fact that I was just a kid we became kind of close.

I was the one, after Miriam, to whom he confided his theories, the most notable being that Americans of Hebrew extraction could do anything they put their minds to. As evidence he produced newspaper clippings describing the progress of the singer Al Jolson or the fighter Benny Leonard. His roll of the illustrious was dizzying for its variety: Ziegfeld the impresario, Rothstein the gangster, Baruch the adviser of presidents, Berlin the composer of popular songs—all of whom had delivered themselves from humble origins to become figures in the public eye. As an orphan, Hymie reasoned, his own ties to family were less rigid than those of his fellows on North Main Street, committed as so many were to repeating their father's trades. He was freer than most to pursue a singular destiny, which, as in the cases of those he admired, would carry him far beyond the boundaries of the Pinch.

Exactly what that destiny was depended on what day of the week you happened to run into him. In the beginning it was all idle talk like I said, which amused my sister no end; she became less amused when more and more he was moved to action. It started when he began carrying around sheet music he couldn't read, singing "Carolina Moon" in an anguished soprano he pestered Cantor Abrams to help him refine. He hounded the neighborhood palooka, Eddie "Kid" Katz, into giving him boxing lessons, which began and ended with Eddie's famous sucker punch during their first and last workout at the Phoenix Athletic Club. For a while he used a lot of mobster lingo, like "yegg" and "gunsel" and "swag," trying it out on the bootleggers at the Green Owl Café until they threatened to relocate.

His aunt and uncle had thus far patiently endured their nephew's vacillating interests, Aunt Frieda attempting to put the best face on things. "Good on him," she'd say, her remarks duly communicated by Hymie, tugging at an imaginary corset, "he should be a credit to the Jewish race." Then he'd do Uncle Shaky, scratching his chin: "Credit we don't take on North Main Street. Cash'n-carry's the name of the game." (Once I asked him why, with his gift for mimickry, he didn't want to be an actor—like for instance Paul Muni, né Weisenfreund—but Hymie'd scoffed at the very idea of pretending to be someone else when what you

wanted was to be completely your own man.) They'd never interfered with his notions, the Nussbaums, so long as Hymie
remained a mostly reliable if uninspired clerk in their drygoods
store. But Houdini's three-part traveling show arrived to change
all that.

He'd taken me with him to the matinee at the Orpheum where
we sat in the second balcony, but even from there you were captivated by the magician's presence: his chiseled features framed by
the graying temples of his unruly hair; his fierce, penetrating eyes.
He did his "Noah's Ark" illusion, materializing pairs of animals
from a fountain, and "Paligensia," chopping a man into pieces and
making him whole again. He presented the celebrated
"Metamorphosis," in which he magically changed places with his
pixyish wife. He recreated the effects of phony psychics, the ectoplasm and floating trumpets, challenging anyone to produce a
phenomenon he couldn't duplicate, and for his grand finale he
escaped the Chinese Water Torture Cell. If I was no more spellbound than everybody else, Hymie was shaken with awe to his
bones.

"Stuart," he gasped, clutching my arm, "we're a witness to
miracles!"

He went back alone to every performance during the remaining two days of the tour, both matinees and evening shows. After
that he began combing newspapers and periodicals for more
information about the magician. He took out a subscription to
The New York World, which contained weekly supplements by
Houdini, and Houdini's own personal organ, *The Conjurer's
Monthly.* He managed to obtain copies of all the scholar-magician's
published works, from the pamphlets to the full-blown exposés,
and even bought the comics and dime novels depicting apocryphal
tales of Houdini's great escapes.

Every Saturday morning for fifteen consecutive weeks he took
off work to see the serial installments of Houdini's cliff-hanger,
"The Master Mystery." He saw all the features too, including his

favorite, "The Man from Beyond," in which Houdini, as Howard Hillary, is chopped from the ice still alive after having been frozen for a hundred years. With nothing better to do I tagged along, but even at age twelve I knew enough to groan over the magician's wooden acting, especially his obvious embarrassment during the romantic scenes. Still, I wasn't so unimpressionable that I didn't catch something of Hymie's bug.

"Stuart," he would have me to know, "for centuries the Jews did nothing but read books and get clobbered by Cossacks, but this one—" More than just a showman, this Houdini, born Ehrich Weiss, was a millionaire and a movie star, a friend of presidents and a pilot of flying machines. He threaded needles in his mouth, produced lit candles and miles of silks from his pockets, unmasked mediums, walked through walls, made elephants disappear with a clap of his hands. But most of all he escaped: from every variety of fetter and shackle, from caskets, racks, and iron maidens, police vans and sausage skins and kegs of beer, from the bowels of prisons and the bellies of monsters, from vaults lashed with chains and dropped into the sea.

So immersed was Hymie in the exploits of "the elusive self-liberator" that there were times he forgot where Hymie Weiss left off and Harry Houdini began. Taking his orphan's prerogative, he'd begun to revise his own past, setting great store by the fact that he and Houdini shared the same surname. Then there was the little-known biographical tidbit that the magician's first partner was a fellow called Jack Hyman. From this Hymie concluded that, if Houdini had had a son (through some scandal that all concerned parties were obliged to hush up), he might have named him Hyman Weiss. Although known to broadcast his theories to any available ear, Hymie asked that I keep this one to myself.

Then suddenly Houdini was dead. He'd died on Halloween at the age of fifty-two of the poison released in his system from a ruptured appendix.

"It's like I lost a piece of myself," Hymie brooded to my sister, who agreed with all due respect that he did indeed seem to be missing a piece or two.

Distracted at the best of times, he stumbled through his paces at the Emporium, mistaking fish scalers for bath yokes and making incorrect change. He told me out of Miriam's earshot that, beyond his grief over the premature loss of his hero, there was something else. There was the feeling he had that, while a chapter had ended, another was about to begin. When I asked what he was talking about, he confessed he didn't know.

The papers said that Houdini was going to try to communicate from the other side; this they announced as if advertising another of his death-defying feats. His wife, Bess, was to receive a coded message, and likewise his friend, the writer Conan Doyle, who was convinced despite the magician's protests that Houdini was a physical medium. Maybe the message was what Hymie was waiting for. But if word was forthcoming from that quarter, it had yet to reach the muggy backwater of Memphis, never mind the Pinch.

Not that Hymie believed for a moment in such mumbo-jumbo. In fact, he was surprised that Houdini, himself the scourge of every four-flusher and fake, had succumbed to superstition in his final hours. No, decided Hymie, the maestro had at last been confined to a place even he couldn't come back from. Now it was the task of some worthy someone to take up the fallen magician's torch and carry on his legacy.

"So why not me?"

At first I thought he was kidding; I think he also thought he was kidding—this skinny, earnest-eyed son of an alleged tinker with his woodpecker's crest of unkempt hair. In those days Hymie talked a lot about his heart: when Houdini died, his heart felt like it had fallen through a trapdoor in a stage. Now his heart released endless silk streamers and doves. "Don't you get it, Stuart? By dying Houdini called my bluff." You could run from a thing like this, he assured me; like Jonah you could hide in the belly of a whale, or be buried alive behind a drygoods counter. But in the end you would be forced to break out of your situation, if only to prove it was possible. And emerging, what choice would you have but to take up the master's mantle and step on to the stage of the world.

It wasn't my job to worry about him, as my sister usually took care of that department. But since he was keeping his most fantastic notion a secret even from Miriam, at least until he was ready to announce himself, it was left to me to tell him he was nuts. Not that he listened. For Hymie the only question was how to proceed.

Steeped as he'd become in the lore, able to recite his hero's whole repertoire chapter and verse, he'd yet to attempt a single trick, not the most basic illusion. But then it wasn't the parlor magic—the sleight of hand, the spirit knots and vanishing wands—to which Hymie was attracted. Houdini the illusionist, he stated frankly, was not all that easy to distinguish from other magicians. Rather, it was to the escapes that Hymie was drawn. In them you found the vintage Houdini and in them he believed his own destiny lay.

Setting a date for his debut on an Amateur Night in spring, he began to make preparations toward that end. He reapplied himself with assiduous devotion to the master's texts, paying special attention to *Handcuff Secrets* and *Magical Rope Ties and Escapes.* Gripped by a singleness of purpose, Hymie turned to the matter of his puny frame. He clipped a mail-order form out of *Weird Tales* magazine and sent off for the Eugene Sandow Physical Culture System. This consisted of a pair of dumbbells and some literature outlining exercises and their guaranteed results. Occasionally moved to actually swing the dumbbells in the backroom at Nussbaum's Emporium, Hymie pored over the illustrated pamphlet, savoring phrases like "melon deltoids," "cannonball biceps," and "washboard abdominals." After such sessions he posed in front of the mirror, stripped to the waist, convinced that his weedy torso was toughened, the muscles more dramatically defined.

"It's a strength that you can see it even in my face," he declared.

As the night approached Hymie attended to more immediate details. Having elected to open in high style with the show-stopping punishment suit release, he arranged with Mr. Crouch the watchmaker, whose wife sometimes had to be restrained, to borrow his straitjacket. The watchmaker, however, was reluctant to lend the jacket for more than an evening, and then only provided his wife was tranquil, which posed a problem: it would be impossible to rehearse the escape. Still, with his firm grasp of the science of escapology and his general readiness, Hymie was nonetheless confidant. Hadn't he practiced the stunt a hundred times in his head? Besides, he pointed out, you couldn't really claim to have succeeded in any feat unless an audience was on hand to acknowledge it.

It occurred to him he could use an assistant, preferably someone decorative (which disqualified me), someone who could do for Hymie what Bess Houdini had done so faithfully for Harry over the years. This was where Miriam came in.

"Challenge? What challenge? Who challenged you?" she'd demanded over her vanilla phosphate at the fountain in Levy's Candy Store. Hymie, in training, was drinking seltzer, and I, seated next to him, was eating ice cream that dribbled down the cone onto my arm.

"I challenged me," asserted Hymie, who, disappointed she hadn't gotten it the first time, began to detail his program again: that having discounted the efforts of the magician's brother to carry on the tradition, never mind the attempts of a legion of cheap impersonators, he, Hymie Weiss, had appointed himself successor to the great Houdini.

"Hymie." Miriam softened her tone, unknitting her brow so that you kind of missed the imperfection. Like everyone else I was a helpless observer of the seasons of my sister's face. "Don't you think this is a little farfetched even for you?"

For a brief moment he did appear to reconsider. "Maybe you're right," he conceded, gnawing the inside of a freckled cheek. "You know, Houdini himself was afraid of going mad. He wondered how, when he lost his mind, they would ever find a cell that could hold him." Hymie was full of obvious admiration.

Miriam clucked her tongue, shook her head. "You're impossible," she sighed, placing the back of her hand to his forehead as if to check for a fever. There was a beat during which Hymie might have enjoyed the coolness of her hand before pushing it away.

"*You're* impossible," he countered, which seemed to surprise my sister, but I thought I knew what he meant. He meant it was impossible that the likes of her should care for the likes of him, though what he said was, "Sometimes I think you don't take me serious."

"Take you serious?" gasped Miriam. "I don't even take serious you should ask why I don't take you serious! Whoever takes Hymie Weiss serious, that person is meshuggah as Hymie Weiss." While you could see she'd hurt his feelings, she still wouldn't leave it alone. "Is that what this is all about? You want to impress me by becoming Houdini? Give me a break, will ya. You're as bad as Sy Plesofsky."

It was the worst thing she could have said. Hymie expanded his chest to show off what Eugene Sandow referred to as "Marine-tough pectorals," mostly imaginary in his case. "Not everything that goes on around here is for the amusement of the famous shainkeit Miriam Rosen," he assured her. "Some of us got ambitions of our own."

Miriam tried her best to stay nettled. He shouldn't have mentioned her beauty, which she regarded as a nuisance, the source of the hostility she suffered from all the guys she would never belong to. This was hitting below the belt. But you could see that she saw the justice, and even as she turned back to her phosphate she'd cocked a brow, as if it wasn't lost on her that for once Hymie had noticed.

"I mean it, Miriam," he persisted, "this is real. Next Thursday night North Main Street will witness the debut of the new Houdini, reborn in the person of Hyman the Magnificent."

Sucking on her straw, Miriam choked slightly, then swiveled toward Hymie with an expression of tolerance under pressure.

"I thought of 'The Hebrew Mahatma,'" he went on, idly flicking a fly from his sleeve, "but decided that 'Magnificent' says it all. Kind of no-nonsense, don't you think?"

She swept her heavy braid over the shoulder of her apple green pinafore, the better to search his face. It was the gesture that stopped them cold in the delicatessen and you could tell it was having its effect on Hymie. Craning, I saw how his eyes dodged here and there but kept returning to an uncovered blue vein in her neck, blinking with every pulse. Whether consciously or not, he'd reached for a soda spigot, holding on as if to steady his resolve.

"Hymie," Miriam said finally, "you want to do amazing feats? Try growing up, why don't you. Join the living." She swiveled her stool back toward the fountain, propping her elbows on the marble counter, her chin in her hands. "Find a girl, get married, have little Hymies, raise them up to be . . . magicians for all I care."

As this last was said dreamily, like sentiments having more to do with herself than with him, Hymie relaxed: the danger was past. Off the hook, he brazenly took up again the matter at hand. "And Miriam," wiping the sweat from his upper lip, "I'll need an assistant."

"Oh no." She shook her head fervently. "You want to make a horse's caboose of yourself in front of the whole neighborhood, that's your business. Leave me out of it. Ask your shadow there with the pisk full of tutti-frutti."

For a second I was scared he might actually take her advice. But when he only winked at me over his shoulder, I felt a little let down, though I wanted no more part than my sister of what I saw coming.

"You still don't understand, do you Miriam?" said Hymie, like it was him doing her the favor. "I'm—"

"You're cracked is what you are!" snapped Miriam, with perhaps more irritation than she'd intended. "You don't need an assistant, you need a keeper."

Above it all now, Hymie raised his eyes to the bossed tin ceiling, a move borrowed from his Aunt Frieda, who frequently called on God to give her strength. "Okay, I tried. Nobody can say I didn't try, even though I knew she'd only be in the way."

"Hymie."

"Even though she'd just hog the spotlight, being such a notorious glamor puss and all."

"Hymie." She'd given his cheek the gentlest slap to turn his head, forcing him to look her full in the face. I saw his nostrils flare from the chopped liver and pickle brine scent of her fingers, which on Miriam smelled somehow exotic. Satisfied that she'd brought him back to earth, my sister asked Hymie, "What is it you want me to do?"

III. The Procrustean Bed Mystery

When I saw him just after the Amateur Night fiasco, I could have sworn he'd learned his lesson. He was relieved to have gotten Houdini out of his system, and I expected that in a couple of days he would be riding another hobbyhorse. But by the time my sister had calmed down enough to go around to Nussbaum's, he'd relapsed. Sporting the plaster over his swollen eye at a jaunty angle, he grinned piratically with a pair of shears in his teeth. He was waiting on Mrs. Altfeder, the seamstress, unrolling a bolt of cloth with his good hand, stabilizing it with the elbow of his right arm in its sling.

Reading disapproval in Miriam's rueful countenance, Hymie took the shears from his mouth and cautioned, "Don't say it. I heard it already from my aunt and uncle." With a glance over his shoulder to make sure they weren't watching, he went into his Frieda and Shaky routine. "'It don't look good for the Jews.'" This was Aunt Frieda, whom he had down even to her spitting against the evil eye. "So I tell them it looked good enough when Houdini did it, and my uncle says, 'Houdini don't fall off the stage, which it makes the whole theayter to pish in the pents. . . .'" He aped Uncle Shaky's wheezing laughter.

Mrs. Altfeder, waiting beside him for her yard of chenille, tapped her foot and hemmed impatiently. Right-handed, Hymie began trimming the cloth at a reckless zigzag with his left, declaring as he worked that next time he'd be better prepared. Almost to himself he mused, "If I can wow them so much by bungling, just think what they'll do when I succeed." He presented the ragged-edged fabric to Mrs. Altfeder, who huffed and turned smartly away.

"Did I hear you correct?" said Miriam, cupping an ear. "What next time? Am I wrong or wasn't that you they had to scrape out of the orchestra pit and carry the pieces to Doctor Seligman?"

Hymie admitted he still had some kinks to work out. "But by the time the doc takes my cast off, I'll be ready. I got a brand-new act in mind, what I call the Procrustean Bed Mystery."

"Come again?"

"It's my version of Houdini's Spanish Maiden Escape, only I plan to use a Murphy bed. There'll be these iron spikes in the mattress, see, and I'm standing inside the closet. . . ."

"Hymie, this is too much."

". . . then the committee folds up the bed. . . ."

"Hymie!"

Eyes that weren't already on Miriam turned toward her now, customers setting down dress suspenders and ribbed union suits to listen. Since there were no other sounds in the store but the creak of the ceiling fans and the zing of a receipt sent along an overhead wire, my sister stepped closer to Hymie and lowered her voice.

"What happened to my friend who knows the difference between real and make-believe?" she asked.

He tried to explain that the new act wasn't dangerous; in fact, it involved so little risk he was almost ashamed. But Miriam wasn't having any of it.

"It's not the act that scares me so much as you. All of a sudden I don't know you anymore."

"That's because," began Hymie in a phony theatrical tone of voice that assumed a certain dignity as he spoke, "Hymie Weiss fell off the stage, but it's Hyman the Magnificent that gets back on." He took his arm from the sling to reveal his stage name splashed in scarlet tempura across his cast. If I hadn't known him better, I'd have thought he was trying to get her goat.

Miriam stared hard at Hymie as if she were making an effort to believe him. Then she blinked, after which her features lapsed into pity, the pity dissolving to exasperation in another bat of the eye. Hymie followed the changes like someone observing a total eclipse.

"You should just hear yourself," she scolded, and her pleated skirt whirled, her flying black braid brushed his cheek as she turned on her heel. Watching her leave, Hymie touched the cheek gingerly.

"Women," shaking his head, "who can figure 'em, eh Stuart?" Now he was philosophical, the faker, shoving a ruler down his cast to scratch, still refusing to admit the pain of his bruises, the torn muscles and broken bone.

"Come off it, Hymie," I told him, encouraged enough by my sister's example to take a potshot of my own. "Who do you think you're fooling?"

He looked over with an expression so injured it could have fooled me.

Several weeks later a Murphy bed, unfolded from its upright mahogany cabinet, its mattress bristling with spikes, stood before the box office of the Idle Hour Cinema. Tacked inside the cabinet was a homemade handbill announcing in eye-catching colors:

!!!

Tonite

HYMAN THE MAGNIFICENT

will attempt to escape

The Tortures

of the

PROCRUSTEAN BED

!!!

Purchased from Shafetz's Discount, the bed had cost Hymie the better part of three weeks' wages. Then there was the expense of hiring Lieberman Movers & Haulers to shlep it over from the Emporium. Add to that the railroad spikes from Blockman's Salvage, the bolts, brackets, and tools from Hekkie's Hardware in Commerce Street, and you had quite a sizeable investment. But Hymie never doubted that this laying out of capital would have instant dividends. Who knew but some scout from the Pantage's Circuit would be in the audience, prepared to offer him top billing to take his act on the road.

"Then it'll be good-bye North Main Street, Stuart my man, and hello Atlantic City, Rio-by-the-Sea-o, Zanzibar. . . ."

In displaying the bed prior to his performance, Hymie had taken a cue from the master, who'd been, among other things, a wizard at self-promotion. So certain was my friend of packing the house that he felt justified in approaching Mr. Forbitz about a percentage of the take.

"Gruber yung!" This was Hymie's impression of the manager's reply. "Where you been, you don't know what it means the word 'amateur'?"

Hymie was the first to concede that it was early in his career to think in terms of a turning point. But with the Procrustean Bed—the name implied stretching and compressing rather than being impaled, but he couldn't resist the mythical ring—he felt he was expanding his repertoire. He was introducing an entertainment involving illusion and split-second timing, instead of mere physical dexterity. A measure of showmanship was called for that the straitjacket release, for all its drama, had lacked. Besides, his right arm was still weak after its removal from the cast, its color unwholesomely sallow, the bone somewhat crooked from not having properly set. So it made sense that his follow-up act should rely not so much on athletic prowess as technical expertise.

You couldn't have accused Hymie of being handy. In fact, he'd always congratulated himself on his *un*handiness, this for the doubt it cast on his descent from his supposed father, the tinker. (Albeit the Nussbaums had informed him that the tinker wasn't so handy himself, scholarship having taken precedence over his trade.) But in outfitting the dummy wardrobe of the Murphy bed to create his mystery, Hymie'd begun to take some pride. Rather than the ill-fated character in the snuff brown photograph, he'd decided it was his spiritual father who guided his hand. It was Houdini himself, in his alternate capacities as carpenter, mechanic, and locksmith, whose skill Hymie had inherited, and as he worked he was inspired to a less woolgathering, more hands-on attitude toward escapalogy.

When I got over the feeling that he was building his own coffin, I began to take an interest in Hymie's handiwork. What he'd done was to rig a sliding panel in the back of the wardrobe. Attached to a post itself attached to no other board in the cabinet, the panel was fitted with abbreviated screws that looked to be securely fastened. So neat was its construction that the mechanism could stand the closest examination without being detected. Further, Hymie'd chalked an outline of himself on the mattress ticking, then perforated the down stuffing with railroad spikes sharpened to glistening points with a file. He lay down in a flurry of feathers, satisfied that when the bed was folded up, the strategically placed spikes would never so much as graze him.

Despite myself I'd begun to grow convinced. I couldn't stay away from the backroom at Nussbaum's where he worked on his free-standing wardrobe, and when he asked me to help with a run-through, I spat on both hands. But soft in the spine, I couldn't lift the iron-clad bedframe alone. No one else other than Miriam was in Hymie's confidence, but after all it had taken to talk her into playing his assistant again, he didn't want to press his luck. Instead, taking up his position in the cabinet, Hymie simply described what would happen, which he claimed was all the rehearsal he needed.

"I stand inside the dummy wardrobe like this, right? Then the committee raises the bed. They close the cabinet doors and lock them with padlocks, and Miriam draws screens around the whole contraption. She says, 'Behold, a miracle!'" At that the screens would be removed, the doors unlocked and opened, the bed unfolded to reveal an empty space where the magician had been. While the audience gasped (Hymie made sounds of universal astonishment), he, having slipped out the back of the wardrobe and into the wings, would shout from the rear of the theater, "Here am I!"

As Hymie'd predicted, the Idle Hour was filled to capacity. Rather than excited, however, the North Main Street families who typically comprised the Thursday night crowd looked nervous to me. For excited you had our Irish and Italian neighbors, not normally in attendance though tonight they were out in force. Stomping and clapping, they demanded that Hyman the Magnificent appear without further ado. It seemed that Hymie's previous debacle had indeed stirred the local interest, if not the kind ("Your friend Weiss is a scandal," grumbled my mama beside me) the Jews were comfortable with.

In keeping with tradition Mr. Dreyfus the jeweler was scheduled to open the show. He was to be followed by Eddie "Kid" Katz's punching bag exhibition, after which Miss Bialy from the Neighborhood House would perform her eurythmic dance. The program also promised another dramatic recitation from Ike Taubenblatt and his pantomime beard. But due to the ruckus Mr. Forbitz was forced to delay the other acts in favor of starting with the headliner, which Hymie considered himself to be. Though he was backstage, I would've bet I knew what he was thinking: he was thinking how the other performers had been similarly preempted during Houdini's engagement at the London Palladium.

True to her word, Miriam came out alongside him, in a dress of airy chiffon sashes that floated around her like smoke. Her hair was loose and luxuriant, her tortoiseshell combs like trellises overwhelmed by inky tendrils. She looked so farputzt, my sister, you might have wondered if she was a little stagestruck herself, since she generally tended to play down her own luster. But I figured it was her way of showing good faith.

Behind them on stage Hymie's nightmare furniture had already been erected, its jagged mattress lowered like a cruel underjaw. Again a committee was invited from the audience, and again Bernie Saperstein, dapper in his Oxford bags, was foremost among the gang of volunteers. Having removed an orange toweling bathrobe, Hymie stood in a one-piece bathing costume that highlighted his ribs and knobby knees. (This was in lieu of the formal accessories the Nussbaums, boycotting the performance, had refused him the loan of.) He made a brief but impassioned speech describing the danger in whose face he spat. Then with a studied swagger that won him cheers from the Zanones and Keoughs—while the Shapiros, Pinskys, and Plotts groaned audible oys— Hymie took up his stance in the hollow wardrobe of the Murphy bed.

Miriam stepped forward to announce above Mrs. Elster's ominous organ roll that "Hyman the Magnificent will now be confined—" But whether owing to her self-consciousness, her anxiety for Hymie, or the constant winking that Bernie subjected her to, my sister got tongue-tied over the word *Procrustean.* She had such trouble that Bernie and his minions, rather than wait until she could spit it out, took the liberty of jumping the gun.

They lifted the bedframe at its foot, slamming it shut with such zest that the whole wardrobe fell over backward. It hit the stage with a loud report that hushed the house. The hush endured until the dust began to settle, the cabinet to rattle, muffled sounds of distress emanating from within. Then, as energetically as they'd knocked it over, the volunteers righted the Murphy bed. They opened the wardrobe doors and pulled down the mattress, revealing a stupefied Hymie squirming from the spike that had entered his thigh. As he was lifted limp and bleeding from the cabinet, that part of the audience who'd already broken their silence let loose a thunder of hilarious applause.

IV. The Inverted Rope Tie Release

"Okay, I flinched, so sue me," was his unrepentant excuse when I finally went around with Miriam to see him. This time I'd stayed away too, my disappointment in Hymie having outlasted even my sister's aggravation. In fact, she'd already been around once on her own, but Hymie's wound from the rusty spike had turned septic, leaving him too feverish for visitors. The Nussbaums had even hinted at a little delirium, though I wondered how they could tell. Anyway, he was better now, and Miriam's concern had nudged my own.

It was the first time, to my knowledge, that she'd ever been in his bedroom above the Emporium, and I could tell she wasn't prepared for what she saw. It wasn't bad enough he was skin and bones, his general color as yellow as his withered arm, his pajamas cut off at the thigh to accomodate the swollen leg propped on cushions in his sagging bed. But the bed has to be littered with books and pamphlets, their covers bearing the image of a man in chains, with handcuffs and padlocks culled from the eclectic merchandise at Uncle Sam's Pawn—further evidence of Hymie's fanatical condition.

Then he said the thing about flinching, to which Miriam could only sigh, "You really are cracked, aren't you, kiddo?"

For a moment Hymie appeared to have lost his focus. The way he stared at my sister, you'd have thought one of the dandelion puffs floating through his open window had burst into a radiant girl. When the moment passed—God forbid she should catch him openly admiring her—Hymie hauled himself, wincing, to a seated position and started to talk.

"So Doc Seligman tells me: 'Weiss,' he says, 'just make sure that foot you favor, it ain't already in the grave.' 'Better one foot in the grave,' says I, 'than two behind the counter at Nussbaum's Emporium.'" Then he did his Aunt Frieda complaining that the Jews don't have tsores enough but this one asks to suffer on purpose, and Uncle Shaky saying it was a crying shame. "'It's a kiddush ha-shame, I'm calling it. You know kiddush ha-shame, Nephew? That's a suicide.'" He mimicked his uncle wheezing laughter until he choked.

It was quite a performance, even by Hymie's standards, and I wondered whether it was the fever speaking or his nervousness at having my sister in his room. At any rate, he rattled on, contemplating aloud what he would do when he was back on his feet. He might attempt some of the challenges Houdini had never gotten around to, such as the escape from a casket plummeting over Niagara Falls. Or a straitjacket release while dropping from the

top of the Woolworth Building by parachute. Hymie supposed
the roof of the local Cotton Exchange would afford him the
needed height, though he balked at the planning involved. With
the Procrustean Bed he'd learned a valuable lesson; he'd gotten
more or less what he deserved. He should leave all that stagy
deception to the dime museum conjurers and stick to more fun-
damental displays of derring-do.

At this point Miriam tried to get a word in, but Hymie was
still gibbering to beat the band. He was suggesting that, when he
took his act on the road, she might like to come too.

"Hymie—"

"We could do 'Metamorphosis' for spice," he said, which was
how I knew he wasn't in his right mind, because it came out
almost like a proposal. "You know, the one where the magician
and his assistant trade places . . ."

"Hymie," repeated Miriam, this time with a firmness that
would tolerate no interruption, "I may not always be content, but
I'm not so screwy that I would want to trade places with you.
This is it, Hymie, no more assistant. I'm handing in my resignation. I won't watch you hurt yourself anymore."

When she was gone, he slumped back in his bed as if her
departure had pulled the plug. Suddenly the soft breeze from his
window, scented with honeysuckle and fresh challah, was overpow-
ered by the stink of his suppurating thigh. He looked so spent
that I was startled when he sat up again, a corpse sitting up at his
own wake.

"Easy come, easy go, eh Stuart?" said Hymie, though you
wouldn't have known if he was asking or telling.

I shoved him back gently into the pillows and he let go a sigh.
"You know, sometimes I think every guy on North Main Street is
under your sister's spell." Which wasn't exactly news, but then he
went on to develop a theory: they were hypnotized by the swish of
her skirt, the tic-toc of her braid. If it wasn't for their fascination
with Miriam, maybe his whole generation could get the hell out

of the Pinch. They could leave the miserable grind of shop hours, let the shops crumble to dust, and go off chasing wild destinies. "But for that you need the spirit of a Hyman the Magnificent," he sympathized.

I sat with him a little longer while he enumerated the stunts that would make him the toast of a waiting world. There was this dumbwaiter escape he'd been toying with; he'd always had a soft spot for dumbwaiters, and grandfather clocks, to whose pendulums you might fasten an axe blade. But these ideas he discarded as too gimmicky, and besides he was no closet artist. What he wanted was an outdoor event, something to capture the imagination of the clamoring crowd; not to mention the agents outbidding one another to book him at the Roxy in Peoria, the Circus Busch in Dusseldorf.

Then he hit on just the thing, a presentation brought to mind by a pet name Miriam was fond of calling him—Hymie (which rhymed with Tie me) Upside-Down.

During the following weeks I kept my distance. School was out and I was expected to help around the delicatessen; afternoons I was studying for bar mitzvah with Rabbi Fein. Moreover, I'd come to share my sister's frustration with Hymie, or so I told myself. But who was I kidding? The guy was frankly beginning to scare me. Where before he'd been a likeable eccentric, good for a laugh, now he appeared seriously farmisht; he made everyone uncomfortable. Now, when he limped along North Main Street, the shopkeepers, even as they spread rumors about him, looked the other way. They pretended he was invisible, as if he'd vanished successfully from his dummy wardrobe and stayed disappeared.

This isn't to say I didn't know what he was up to. Mutterings had reached Rosen's Deli, a regular clearing house for gossip, almost the instant he'd tacked his sign to the oak tree in Market Square. Even Miriam must have known, though she hadn't mentioned his name since the day she'd traipsed out of his room.

Of course she also had her hands full lately. Without Hymie around to cramp everyone's style, Miriam was fair game for the lovelorn sons of the Pinch. The Lieberman twins showed off wrestling holds in front of the deli and Mickey Graber recited sonnets outside her window on stilts. As usual Bernie Saperstein was relentless in his overtures. With his father's market just across the street, he was practically camped out in Rosen's, airing his prospects, sporting his China silk neckwear under a soiled apron bib. What's more, it began to look like he was making progress. The truth was, he wasn't a bad-looking fellow, Bernie, with his center-parted hair slick as sealskin. He was a smooth talker, a comer as was bruited along North Main Street, his fishy odor effectively suppressed with bay rum.

"I'm a born family man," I'd heard him boast more than once to my sister, whose resistance seemed to be weakening. Sometimes, during a break, she might sit down at his table and look almost interested, while Bernie basked in the jealous admiration of his peers.

In the end, however, my curiosity got the better of me, and I waited round the corner from Nussbaum's on the Saturday afternoon of the event. I'd meant to keep out of sight but I must not have hidden too well, because Hymie, hobbling along in his bathrobe with a coil of rope over his shoulder, spotted me right away. Greeting me like he saw nothing strange in my hunkering in doorways, he went straight into impressions of his aunt and uncle's latest reproofs.

Aunt Frieda: "Shame on you that you ain't got sense to be shamed for yourself."

Uncle Shaky: "If you see Hymie Weiss, tell him our door is always open. As for Shnooko the Magnificent, on him we are changing the locks every day. Which it is too good for him, eh Frieda?—fresh lox every day." He did the wheeze that was typically terminated by Frieda's slapping Shaky's back till he brought up phlegm.

Hymie talked all the way to Market Square, a dirt patch of a park tucked behind the shops on North Main. It was packed with a rabble of curiosity-seekers, many more than could have been contained at the Idle Hour—where Mr. Forbitz, even as they'd carried the injured Hymie from the theater, had forbidden him to appear on his stage again. There were dusty farmers' families fresh from the wagon yard, toting the trussed and squawking poultry they'd come to town to trade. You had the clerks from Main Street proper on their lunch hour, the Irish toughs from Goat Hill, and even a scattering of Negroes on the periphery of the crowd. These last hung about despite the park's taboo associations, Market Square having once been the site of a slave auction. They'd come, according to Hymie, who was feeling his oats, to watch a man break free in a place where their people had been so unmercifully bound.

"I'm a universal symbol of liberation already," he maintained.

Still, you couldn't help noticing that, for all its numbers, the gathering didn't include many Jews. This you might have credited to the fact that it was Shabbos, though nothing else in the Pinch stopped for Shabbos; nor was it lost on Hymie, the scarcity of our neighbors. "Funny how your own kind will turn their back," he complained, searching the faces of rowdy strangers who slapped his shoulders and cleared a path, "just when you start to belong to the world." He appeared to me to be looking for someone in particular.

In any case, Bernie Saperstein was there at the foot of the towering oak, along with some others—Kipper Shapiro, Herman Blen. (It wouldn't have done for the sartorial Bernie to miss an opportunity to help Hymie Weiss risk life and limb.) Beyond the crude advertisement Hymie had nailed to the tree trunk, he'd also managed to put an apparatus in place: a block and tackle attached to a heavy rope, the rope in turn looped through a pulley hung from a lofty branch. Given his bad arm and still-festering leg, this seemed enough of a feat in itself.

Hymie took off his robe and handed it to me, which I hadn't expected. My initial twinge of pride passed with the onset of cold feet, and allowing the tatty toweling to slip from my fingers, I melted back into the crowd. I don't think Hymie noticed. Stripped to his bathing costume, a stained tourniquet around his thigh, he'd shrugged the rope from his shoulder and commenced his speech.

"I use only the finest-quality braided lariat, certified by the honorable Hekkie Schatz of Hekkie's Hardware on Commerce Street. . . ."

Before he could finish, though, Bernie had come forward, boasting his credentials and presenting himself as the only candidate for the job. "Ain't I wrapped enough cold fish in my papa's market?" But despite his braggadocio, he was rudely shoved aside by a pair of yokels in bib overalls, one of whom proclaimed himself "champeen hog-tier of She'by County."

"You oughtn't to talk like that, Eugene," cautioned the other, pushing Hymie into the dirt and stooping to wind the rope several swift revolutions around his ankles. "This here's kosher meat."

"Kindly takes the fun out of lynchin' when they ask to be strung up," said Eugene, taking charge of binding Hymie's chest and arms.

There was a good deal of laughter and catcalls as the two men hooked Hymie's feet to the block and tackle, then tugged at the thick hawser cable to haul him aloft. Looking on, I hoped that Hymie'd had the presence of mind to recall Houdini's advice, swelling his muscles (what muscles?) during the binding, contracting them after to gain the necessary slack. By various hunchings and flexings (I remembered from when I'd quizzed him) you could "misguide" the tier, or failing that you could fall back on "main strength." But I feared that what main strength Hymie had had been squeezed out of him by the snugness of his restraints. They'd done him up so thoroughly that he was bug-eyed even before they'd turned him toches over elbows, which left him further flushed from the blood that filled his head.

Spun by balmy breezes several stories above the earth like a dreidl at the end of a string, dappled in sunlight through a canopy of leaves, Hymie had begun his struggle. He bucked valiantly against the ropes and, with a mighty effort, managed to get one shoulder free, but in doing so let loose a shrill cry of pain. This suggested that the shoulder, unnaturally contorted, was dislocated. I told myself not to worry, that Houdini could dislocate his own limbs at will: it was the prelude to all his escapes. But Hymie's lunatic wriggling and jerking was putting an extra strain on the branch that held him, which nodded lower and lower as if succumbing to melancholy. The spectators, who'd gone silent a spell after hearing him cry out, were rambunctious again. Somebody started up a mock cradle song: "Rockabye Hymie in the treetop . . . ," and was joined by others in an off-key choir. Then came a sound like a whistling teakettle, a stuttering hinge, and the swaying bough splintered and broke.

V. The Milk Can Test

Although I didn't see him again until some time after he was out of the hospital, I kept track of him through the grapevine— though, to tell the truth, gossip about Hymie was growing scarcer, and many of those who turned away from him in the street now avoided his name like a dirty word. Anyhow, I knew he hadn't broken his neck. This much I'd determined in the park, as the yokels carried him off in the makeshift litter of an old horse blanket. All his bouncing from branch to branch had slowed his descent, diminishing the impact of his collision with the ground. Beyond his separated shoulder and the contusions from head to toe, the lingering shock that had knocked his internal compass awry (leaving him with the tendency, according to various sight-

ings, of pausing at streetcorners in bewilderment), notwithstanding the original handicaps of his crippled arm and leg, Hymie was
reasonably intact.

Turned out of the Emporium by his aunt and uncle, who'd
stuck to their guns, he'd taken refuge at Blockman's Salvage,
where the pious Mr. Blockman treated every shnorrer as if he
might be Elijah. The ones currently in residence were the sodden
Itzik Bashrig and Yudl the Mute. For helping them collect and
sort junk, Hymie was given a nominal wage and allowed to sleep
in the warehouse loft. I didn't think I wanted to see him in such
circumstances, but Miriam, cornering me in the deli kitchen,
where I was stealing a nibble of brisket between meals, pressed me
to think again.

"Chazzer," she accused, snaring my hand on its way to the
mustard, "when was the last time you spoke to your friend Hymie
Weiss?"

I might have asked the same of her. Naturally I was aware that
she'd been biting her tongue over the subject, dawdling at tables
where his antics were under discussion. Even so, she was keeping
company more than ever with Bernie Saperstein, who was after all
more effective than Hymie (whom no one had confused with
competition) at shooing her other suitors away. She went dancing
at the Dreamland Gardens with Bernie, and for moonlight cruises
on board the *Island Queen,* where you can bet he showed her off
like a custom watch fob. So who was the guiltier party here? But
my sister's beauty carried a certain authority in our family, which
was not an otherwise attractive family, and when she suggested it
was time I paid Hymie a visit, my conscience stayed pricked.

As I turned the corner into Auction Street, I saw the junk
wagon rattling over cobbles through the salvage yard gate. It was
drawn by Mr. Blockman's moon-blind mare, Queen Esther,
remarkable for a back so swayed that her belly dragged the
ground. On the wagon box were Itzik Bashrig, tilting bootleg
shnapps into his bristling, prognathous jaw, and his scarecrow

sidekick Yudl, called the Mute on account of the endless stream of nonsense he spewed. The bed of the wagon was piled high with rags and gutted mattresses, cast-iron stove plates, mangled trombones, and busted sewing machines, and perched atop the heap was a character at least as bedraggled as the others. It wasn't until the wagon had vanished through the gate that I realized the third junkman was Hymie.

He didn't hail me with his usual exuberance, nor did he scold me for staying away. Instead, as we sat in the warehouse—I in a prickly nest of copper tubing and Hymie on some baled magazines—he seemed thoughtful, possibly even contrite. Half-heartedly he did his rendition of Doc Seligman's ultimatum: "Keep up this shtus, Mr. Magnificent, and you can find yourself another sawbones. A specialist in whatchacallit, escapology. Somebody who, when you put on a straitjacket, don't help you take it off. You're a menace to yourself when you're free." Then he asked me by the way how was my sister.

Troubled by his wasted features, his involuntary spasms from shooting pains, I answered his question with another. "Hymie," I asked, because I honestly couldn't remember, that is if I'd ever known, "why are you doing this?"

Rather than reply, he fell into sullen musing. "In my memoirs this is the chapter called 'It's Always Darkest Before the Dawn.'" He went so far as to propose the chapter's opening sentence: "Shloss the tailor had his cot and Ridblatt the baker his hide-a-bed, but Hyman the Magnificent, orphan of the world, had no place to lay his head . . . almost." Rolling his eyes toward the loft where Itzik and Yudl (babbling obscenely) were brewing some malodorous tsimmes on a lamp stove.

I suggested that, having had sufficient time to cool off, the Nussbaums might take him back again. But this only served to remind Hymie of a favor he needed to ask: would I mind going round to the Emporium to fetch some of his things? I figured clothes, since grubby shmattes were what he was wearing, but all he wanted was his Houdini stuff. Of course he could pick any lock he fancied at will, but breaking and entering violated his ethical code.

The Nussbaums, who always seemed to me to be somehow impersonating themselves, were nevertheless obliging. Along with the books and paraphernalia, they threw in—each cautioning me not to tell the other—some clothes and assorted perishables. Hymie's spirits picked up instantly. Expansive again, he pointed out how the maestro had also taken his knocks early in his career. He'd traveled with medicine shows and two-bit circuses, surviving all manner of situations, including one from which he'd carried the souvenir of a bullet wound.

I think Hymie'd begun to confuse his own junk wagon rambles with Houdini's travels, taking him as they did beyond the raised brows and cold shoulders of the Pinch. If you rose early, you could see him reclining in the bed of the wagon, basking in the humid sunshine that had given him back some of his color. Itzik would be flicking the reins and taking a furtive nip while Yudl sang indecent ditties, dangling his short-arm scales like a dancing doll. Thus did Queen Esther begin her slow clopping progress out of the city, down into the Delta where they made the rounds of plantations and slept in the barns.

All this I reported dutifully to my sister, who goaded me for information, then pretended not to care. "To think I was ever mixed up with such a nut case," she repined; and now he was out of the picture, you did have to wonder where he'd fit in. Sometimes Miriam wanted to know if Hymie ever asked about her, blushing peevishly when I told her, "Only to ask if you ever ask about him." Still, she was relieved when I assured her that he'd yet to make any reference to future stunts. But that was before he showed me his milk can.

He'd found it in one of the bins in the scrapyard, a large galvanized iron railroad milk can, only slightly the worse for wear. Dragging it to a remote corner of the warehouse, he kept it under a greasy canvas tarpaulin, which he'd removed for me as if unveiling a masterpiece. Late at night, beneath the loft that trembled from Itzik's crapulous snoring and Yudl's lewdly talking in his sleep, Hymie worked on the can by lamplight, a wizard's apprentice. From previous stunts he'd learned what comes of relying too exclusively on gimmicks or physical bravura alone. With the Milk Can Test he would strike a new balance, the perfect marriage of showmanship and chutzpah. While involving a measure of illusion, the new stunt also exacted a risk worthy of his unflinching nerve.

"After all, you can argue the success of my escapes, but nobody can say my nerve ever failed."

Once I sneaked out of the apartment while my family were sleeping to watch him work, and again I asked him why. When he opened his mouth, I told him, "If you say *destiny,* I'll scream!" He closed his mouth, looking slightly offended, but made a show of considering. Was it the crowds? I suggested, since despite being a local embarrassment, he'd achieved a certain freakish notoriety beyond the Pinch. He allowed that his public appeal was indeed a stimulus, plus the fact that he'd been born to escape—but there was something else, which seemed only now to have dawned on him. Something personal. I asked what he meant and he told me it was just that he loved it. Loved what? "You know." But I didn't, though he repeated, turning to admire the milk can with a fondness he'd formerly reserved for my sister, "God help me, I love it."

With tools less suited to creation than destruction—the crowbars and hacksaws lying around the warehouse, cutting pliers that had taken the digits of more than one hired hand—Hymie patiently fashioned his theatrical property. Subject as he was to dizzy spells, the precision called for often made his head swim. He lost sleep, though who could sleep in that stinking loft with his noisy companions? And he ached all over, especially in his shoulder, which, taken too soon from its sling, was giving him fits. But his industry overcame all obstacles.

He explained to me how it would work: having enlarged the neck of the can, he'd fastened on heavy staples and hasps. During the performance these hasps would be padlocked, making the (incidentally water-filled) container look escapeproof. However, the neck of the can—"Here's the ingenious part"—was attached to a collar adapted in turn to the tapering portion of the cylinder. The collar was studded with false rivets that fit too tight to be detected but could be easily punched out from inside. Then collar, neck, and all could be lifted off, and the artist release himself from the flooded compartment. Once out, he'd replace the whole business, including sham rivets, so no one would be the wiser when the curtain opened.

So proud was Hymie of his construction that, on completing it, you'd have thought the feat was as good as accomplished. But even he admitted that, though he'd lacked the wherewithal to practice his other stunts, this one begged a rehearsal. Already he'd gone beyond his usual blind faith to try and improve his lung capacity. No one knew exactly how long Houdini had been able to hold his breath; some said four to five minutes, others to the point where the brain, depleted of oxygen, would cease to function in an ordinary man. Though Hymie was confident he could increase the thirty seconds he'd thus far attained, he still felt a trial run wouldn't hurt.

Because there was an amount of water to be carried and a cumbersome lid to be fastened in place, Itzik and Yudl were the obvious choice to assist. But unwilling to trust them with the secret of the milk can, Hymie turned instead to me.

"Not on your life!" I told him, cursing myself for the instant I'd hesitated. Then I beat it out of the junkyard, vowing never to return.

I wondered that Mr. Blockman would let him use the yard, never mind charge admission, but then the old man was so distracted, always reading scriptures tucked in his account book, that he seldom knew what went on under his nose. Besides, the performance took place on a Saturday, when the scrap dealer would have been in shul. Hymie had called it a matinee, advertising it on a hand-painted banner hung from the rear of the junk wagon:

ESCAPE
from the
Inundated Chamber
of the
!MILK CAN!

The Jews read the banner as if some evil mandate were being issued against them, shutting doors and pulling blinds when the wagon passed. But the goyim had turned out in droves.

I knew because Bernie Saperstein, chortling into a cufflinked sleeve, had brought the story to my sister, who'd clapped hands over her ears and fled the room. Unabashed, Bernie continued telling me. Notably absent himself, he'd had it from Patsy Quinn the ice man, who said they'd come from all quarters— not just the Goat Hill roughnecks and Mud Island fishermen, but Union Avenue swells in white linen, passing hip flasks to the personality girls on their arms. Everyone pitching their dimes without protest into the sacks that the pie-eyed Itzik and the toothless, yammering Yudl held at either side of the gate.

Of course it had been a total catastrophe. A self-appointed committee had stormed the loading dock in the middle of Hymie's speech, lifting him by the armpits with his legs cycling the air and stuffing him into the milk can. They'd formed a bucket brigade, making jokes about baptism as they repeatedly drubbed him, then screwed on the lid and snapped the padlocks. The only time the obstreperous mob had piped down was when Itzik and Yudl dragged out a circular shower stall and drew the curtain around the container. (At which point you could hear a victrola playing its skipping rendition of "Asleep in the Deep":

"Sailor beheeware, beheeware, beheeware . . .") Then they opened
the curtain, revealing the can but no Hymie, and the same tools
employed in constructing the ruse were used to pry off the lid.
When they'd poured the water-logged escape artist onto the dock,
the cheers went up, Hymie's first professional engagement sounding from a distance like a ringing triumph.

VI. The Packing Case Plunge

"Some wise guy sat on his chest and started working his arms like
oars," said Bernie, convulsing, "singing 'Paddlin' Madeline
Home.'" There had eventually come a trickle from Hymie's blue
lips, followed soon after by the opening of the sluices full force.

I trotted straight to Blockman's to see the damage for myself.
He'd developed an infection from water retained in his inner ear
and was burning up on his mildewed mattress, drifting in and out
of a fugue state. (Doc Seligman had prescribed antiseptics but
refused to pay a second house call.) Between odd moments of
coherence, Hymie's babbling out-Yudl'd Yudl, who silently
endeavored to spoon-feed him a reeking broth. He confused the
junk collectors and myself, interchangeably, with key figures from
Houdini's life—his brother Dash, his man Friday Franz Kukol,
and Sir Arthur Conan Doyle. Sometimes he called for Mama
Weiss, which could have meant either the magician's mother or
his own, and once he shouted, "I will escape the clutches of a mermaid with tentacles of midnight hair!"

Then he came to his senses and gave what for him was a plausible excuse—"They should've filled the can before they put me
in it . . . " Etcetera. With detachment he reviewed his condition:
the now permanent hardness of hearing in his left ear had upset
his sense of balance, which was frankly not so good in the first
place, especially since he'd begun to drag his right leg. He con-
soled himself that his injuries were more or less evenly distrib-

uted, small comfort when his shoulder remained constantly inflamed; and his opposite arm had such poor circulation that, despite the August heat, his fingers were often numb. In addition, his more frequent dizzy spells left him with a sensation of swallows loose in his head.

On the other hand, he was rich. Even after paying their share of the gate to the junkmen, who'd been seen spending like sailors on North Main Street—Itzik had turned the lining of his rain slicker into a portable liquor cabinet, Yudl bought a sombrero for himself, a sunbonnet for Queen Esther—Hymie had close to fifty bucks. It was enough of a nest egg to launch himself with, kick the dust of the Pinch from his heels for good and all. Though why should he spend his own savings to mount a traveling show when the shows ought to be paying hard cash to hire him? Now he had only to sit tight and wait for the booking agents to come around.

"But let's face it," Hymie conceded, "vaudeville is dying." So what did I think, he should wait for the movie offers?

He decided he needed a more dignified door than Blockman's for the world to beat a path to. There was the Hotel Peabody, for instance, its lobby full of cotton barons and potentates fraternizing around a chuckling fountain. But it would also be crawling with autograph hounds and manufacturers eager to share his spotlight. They would pester him as they had Houdini, challenging him to escape this sealed envelope or that glass box for their product's greater glory. Better they should have to seek him out in more modest accommodations, like say the fleabag Cochran Hotel on North Main Street, where nobody seemed to know him anymore.

"Which it's because Hymie Weiss is banged up beyond recognition. Don't you see, Stuart, Hymie Weiss is the perfect disguise."

In his ovenlike hotel room—pipes coughing, mice scurrying

behind sweating walls—he gathered perspective. He took the leisure to reflect on how far he'd come from his days as the orphan clerk of Nussbaum's Emporium, when he was the lapdog of a small-time femme fatale.

Like everyone else in the neighborhood, my sister had become silent on the subject of Hymie. She didn't ask anymore, though I told her all the same how awful he looked, the skin over his cheeks stretched taut as old rubber, the circles round his eyes like a purple mask.

"So what am I supposed to do about it!" Miriam turned on me, her braid a cracked whip. "Aren't I the princess shaineh maidl of Rosen's Delicatessen, the dream of every boy? Miriam Rosen, who could have heroes if she wanted but doesn't want, who is incidentally thinking over Bernie Saperstein's proposal—she should run to this broken-down shmo and soothe what hurts? She should say to him, 'Hymeleh, be a person already, join the rest of us stiffs and live a little longer'?"

I hadn't really thought she was listening. When she flashed like that, my sister, you wanted to take cover; you looked out windows to make sure the heavens hadn't followed her lead.

I figured she'd seen him taking his clunking constitutionals, the new duds from Nussbaum's bellying around his wizened frame. I guessed he'd seen her too, because he'd developed this theory that Miriam's looks had certain healing properties, which to Hymie's way of thinking was no virtue. "Stuart, my bucko," he confided, his face atwitch from various irritations, "pain is the spur."

What could you say to that?

At the end of a couple of weeks he was down to peanuts. I wasn't sure where the money had gone, since he had no real expenses other than his hotel bill and the fetters he continued collecting from Uncle Sam's pawn. He hardly ate, though his room was a storehouse of groceries that the Nussbaum's (unbeknownst to each other) were forever insisting I carry round to

Cochran's. Beyond the occasional stroll he'd been content to lie in bed, reading dubious accounts of the dead magician and fiddling with locks.

Then Hymie let me in on his big surprise. It seemed that he'd had some handbills printed up at Shendelman's, complete with a lithographed illustration of a wooden crate in flames. The crate was cut away to reveal the crude self-portrait of a shackled Hyman the Magnificent, beneath which was the caption:

SEE
the daredevil and impetuous
!!!PACKING CASE PLUNGE!!!

On inspecting the handbills, I couldn't help it, I started to sob, which Hymie mistook for tears of joy. "I knew you'd get a kick out of them," he exclaimed, rubbing his hands gleefully. He went on to allow that the practical artist, one accustomed to playing it safe, would've returned to the salvage yard where his fortune was assured. But Hymie preferred to up the ante. Besides, rather than invite his audience back to the Pinch, where the prophet was without honor and so on, he'd decided it was time to take the show to his audience. He would offer an escape so spectacular that, ever after, he could ask his own price from the crowned heads of who knows where.

I wanted to clobber him for all the good it would do. "Shmuck," I yelled through my sniffling, "where are your marbles!"

As always he guaranteed that the danger was minimal: a skeleton key tucked in a seam of his bathing suit would unlock his chains, and the packing case would be fitted with a special gag panel, undetectable, etc., that could be slid aside for a hasty exit. The flames were a pure theatrical touch and would be extinguished once the box began to sink; as for working under water, the Milk Can Test would stand him in good stead. For his most ambitious event Hymie was taking his most elaborate precautions, doing everything short of actually rehearsing the stunt.

When I told him it wouldn't wash, he gave me his look of wounded indignation, like contusions and broken bones might not hurt him but words could still cut deep.

"I thought you understood, Stuart. I'm an escape artist, it's what I do."

But he didn't have to do it, nobody could tell me he had to. Saying as much, I charged out of that cheesy hotel room Miriam-style, though we both knew I'd be back again.

He'd determined on an evening performance, since darkness would heighten the dramatic effect. It was only September but for days there had been a slight autumn nip in the air, and leaves fell as the lantern-hung wagon, drawn by Queen Esther, rattled along North Main at dusk. Itzik and Yudl were on the box, Hymie standing shakily in the wagon bed, supporting himself against a large wooden packing case. A new silk dressing gown was draped over his shoulders, flapping in the breeze, the monogram *H the M* (ruggedly handstitched in gold lamé) blazoned across his back. At his feet lay an assortment of handcuffs, padlocks, legirons, and chains; there was also a jug of kerosene and a sack brimming over with bottle rockets and Roman candles.

The turnout on the street was inconsiderable: a few kids tried to follow but were quickly recalled by their parents. Some old men left their liars' bench in front of the barbershop and stumbled funereally behind for a block or two, then turned off toward the Market Street synagogue for havdollah services. Watching from the deli window, I saw the wagon cross Poplar Avenue, departing the neighborhood, the handbills that Yudl tossed from his sombrero scattering among the dead leaves.

The article in the morning paper, headlined PINCH MAN TAKES DIVE, was whimsical in tone, uncertain whether to identify Hyman Weese, 20, of North Main Street as culprit or victim. It made much of his having stopped traffic on the Harahan

Bridge, said that the density of the crowd had kept officers at the scene from reaching Weese in time to prevent his plunge. The packing case had shattered to splinters on hitting the river, the aforementioned—fished from the water by the crew of the *Island Queen*—escaping with broken ribs and superficial burns. But the photograph told it all.

In it Hymie was posed in the wagon, looking beyond the crush of spectators to drink in the grandeur of the moment. Although the picture was a grainy black-and-white, I knew what he must have seen—the last salmon smudge of sunset over the Arkansas delta, the spilled mercury of downtown lights in the river, the *Island Queen* excursion boat backpaddling under the bridge. I imagined that, after the kerfuffle over whether he was doing the stunt or the stunt being done to him, after he'd been trussed and dumped into the crate, the crate manhandled onto the railing and set aflame, scarlet pompoms had shot off in all directions. Roman candles sprayed the evening sky with peacocks' tails and Hymie's packing case doubled for a meteor.

A cartoon adjacent the article served as postscript: a character wrapped in bandages like a mummy, his head crowned with stars and bedsprings, the caption reading, "For my next trick . . . "

Miriam, who'd been peering over my shoulder, snatched the paper from my hands and set off straightaway out the door. I chased after her as she boarded a streetcar to the hospital, where we found him on an ammonia-ripe charity ward looking not unlike the cartoon. His chest was girded in adhesive tape, his exposed flesh lobsterish with blisters, and the combination of singed eyelashes and hair like molting feathers gave him an almost extraterrestrial aspect. In what I took to be a morphine stupor, he smiled goofily at my sister, the smile of a showman anticipating applause.

"You're a sight for sore eyes," he said.

"What have you got that isn't sore?" Miriam wondered aloud, maybe thinking of a possible answer because she blushed. Hymie shuddered as if her blush were more warmth than his sensitive skin could stand. He turned his good ear in her direction and replied, "Beg your pardon?"

"I said you're a mess."

Like this was news, Hymie actually tried to take stock of his injuries, but the effort of sitting up proved more than he could manage. When Miriam, settling herself at the edge of his bed, leaned over to plump his pillows, he inhaled her spicy proximity and closed his eyes. To himself he intoned, "I'm Hymum Manimmm, syml a mankind fusal live in chain . . ,"

"And y-t-t-t-t-teh." Miriam cut him off.

He opened his eyes one at a time, their pupils dilating as if to accomodate the full reality of my sister. Maybe he'd thought he was dreaming before.

"Hymie," she said in her reasonable voice, "they're all laughing at you, y'know. Look at this." She took the ragged clipping from her purse, unfolded it, and stuck it in Hymie's gauze mittens for him to read. As he perused, he began to look pleased with himself, his chest swelling visibly, stretching his fractured ribs until he winced. Seeing he was still unremorseful, Miriam seized back the paper and wadded it up to throw at his spiky head.

"North Main Street can't watch, only the goyim like to see you murder yourself! What's the matter with you, you don't know from the truth anymore?"

Hymie protested, if feebly, "Did they want to see Houdini die? When he escaped, the men and women, they hugged each other and weeped."

"Escape!" Miriam was incredulous. "Who escapes? You never noticed every stunt you pull ends in disaster? You think you're a cat, you got nine lives? Well I'll tell you something, sweetie, you got only one, and it you mostly used up. You're pushing your luck, Hymie. For God's sake, take a look at yourself."

"I tried that already," said Hymie, starting to sulk.

Now he was at a disadvantage, I hoped my sister might press

her attack, but having worked herself up to such a pitch, Miriam let it go in a sigh. "Hymie," she said, her tone a mix of sorrow and resignation, "I got something to tell you. Me and Bernie, we decided to tie the knot." Then, perhaps realizing the expression might have other connotations for Hymie, she added, "We're getting married. Rabbi Fein is going to do the honors right after Sukkos."

Though he shrugged once to show it was all the same to him, Hymie's color changed from rust to olive drab. He looked the way I imagined Houdini must have looked on that fateful night backstage, when the magician was poked in the gut before he could brace himself against a punch that set loose the poison in his bloodstream.

"Mazel tov," Hymie eventually muttered.

Miriam bit her lip in contemplation, rolled her eyes this way and that, taking in the length and breadth of the whitewashed ward. All up and down the row of beds, patients in traction with tubes up their rectums, some looking already dead, endeavored to raise themselves to get a load of my sister. Wearing a thin sundress cinched at the waist with a primrose ribbon, she was in curious contrast to the wire mesh windows and cracked enamel bedpans. Then she stood up, having apparently come to a decision. She stepped over to where a couple of modesty screens were folded against a wall, and proceeded to wheel them around Hymie's bed. When she was done, the two of them were hidden from view.

"Je tire le rideau comme ça," I said to myself.

The other patients, some perhaps with a final effort, were straining toward the curtains, one of which I parted from its frame to peek inside. She was bending over him, both their faces concealed by the further curtain of her midnight hair, but still I could hear her whispering: "Escape this." There was a rude sound like a stopper being pried from a bottle. For a moment Hymie's limbs were slightly elevated from the bed as if in an authentic struggle, then he relaxed. If he was able to think, he was probably remembering how Bess Houdini would sometimes pass Harry a skeleton key in a kiss, this in preparation for his naked prison breaks.

VII. *Buried Alive*

Released from the hospital, Hymie went where he must have felt that in his state he belonged, back to Blockman's. It was his own decision, since his aunt and uncle had come to his bedside to beg him to return to the Emporium. Forgoing the satire, he told me their mistake: they'd promised him everything would be the same as before.

He looked more a part of the junkscape than ever, more dilapidated than either of the resident ragpickers. Leaning on a stick to walk now, he was no longer certain which of his injuries had left him lame. Oddly, however, his spirits were good, almost you might say blissful. The painkillers had surely worn off, and while he sometimes resorted to medicinal snorts of Itzik's rotgut, I didn't think this accounted entirely for his mood. His smile was serene and he spoke in pensive platitudes, such as "Faint heart ne'er won fair lady" and "Only the brave deserve the fair"—as if, having reached these conclusions, he was at peace. In the end I supposed he was just exhausted, because after a week or so he snapped out of it, announcing somewhat grimly that his priorities were straight again.

He had a theory that the failure of his escapes, notwithstanding the fame they'd earned him among the gentiles, was Miriam's fault. A headache for the whole neighborhood, she'd been his special burden to bear. "It puts me in mind, Stuart," he said in the tone I had come to resent, "of Houdini's obsession with flying. You'll remember how it kept him awake for the couple of hours he slept each night. It left him muddled and spoiled his timing." The point being that Miriam was Hymie's obsession with flying.

"So what, you might ask [though I'd had no intention of asking], was the maestro's solution? He took apart the Voisin biplane, which by the way he was the first aviator to fly over Australia in. He packed it up and never flew again. Then he devoted himself with a vengeance to greater and more dangerous stunts."

Meanwhile my bar mitzvah had come and gone; I'd become a man and hardly anyone noticed, the affair having been overshadowed by preparations for my sister's wedding. Invitations had to be sent out, a bridal gown fitted, arrangements made to secure the hall at the Workmen's Circle for a reception. All day my parents made noises, which were boasts thinly disguised as complaints, about the lavish extent of catering involved. The whole street was caught up in the anticipation, since despite disappointment and envy in certain quarters, the marriage of Miriam Rosen would be a load off of everyone's mind. To tell the truth, I was a little exhilarated by it all myself. I barely flinched when Bernie Saperstein, strutting around the deli like a pouter pigeon, rubbed my head and called me "brother-in-law."

For her part, my sister couldn't manage to keep her mind on her work, which everyone said was natural in a prospective bride. Still, instead of the fussing and fluttering you would have expected, Miriam seemed merely distraught. She kept gazing out windows, ignoring customers calling for their kneydlach and buffalo fish. Some remarked that the direction she looked in was forward to the date of her nuptials, though I wondered if she might be waiting for something else. In the evenings, when the deli was closed, she begged off Bernie's solicitations with the excuse of fatigue—"too much excitement, y'know." Then she went up to sit on the roof of our building. When I followed, she forgot to accuse me of snooping, but instead said aloud what I wasn't sure I was supposed to hear.

"He used to be my lost cause," she brooded, seated on the

parapet, a silhouette but for the corona the streetlamps made of her hair. "Now he's everybody else's."

If there'd been any question as to whom she was talking about, she spelled it out soon enough. Again and again she asked how it was possible that a legendary beauty like herself, with such an angel head on her shoulders, could stoop to care for a zhlub like Hymie Weiss. Anyway, it was too late for him. It had always been too late for him, and if it hadn't been strictly speaking too late for him before he'd become such a mutilated fragment ("Oy, such a fragment!"), then it was certainly too late now. Because once the machinery of a Jewish wedding was in motion, no power on earth could turn it around.

I wasn't exactly neglecting Hymie. Since the only thing that scared me more than watching him was letting him out of my sight, I kept an eye on him. But with so much going on it was easy to forget about Hymie for days at a time. It was convenient to think he was finally too crippled to perpetrate any more funny business; though on my next trip to the junkyard I found I had another think coming. He was considering a new escape. Not just any escape, mind, but the one that had nearly been the maestro's own undoing—namely, being buried alive. The miscalculation that had resulted in Houdini's almost suffocating made it a kind of ultimate stunt, and Hymie was determined to pull it off without a hitch. It would be his crowning achievement, and afterward . . .

"But who cares about after, eh Stuart?" The escape was the thing, its faultless execution all that concerned him. Rising with a groan to support himself on his stick, he resolutely declared, "This one I'm going to rehearse."

To buy a little time I reminded him that, according to one of his own pet theories, you couldn't call a stunt accomplished without an audience on hand to applaud—to say nothing of saving you from your own botched devices. Hymie thought this over and said he was wrong; he'd been wrong all along. A stunt ought first to be perfected in solitude. Driven to the usual frustration, I could only state the obvious, that he was in no shape to perform anything more strenuous than tying his shoes. Cupping his good ear to hear me out, he agreed to a compromise.

"All right, Stuart, you be the audience."

He said it might be appropriate to do a dry run on the anniversary of Houdini's death, which was coincidentally Halloween. This was tomorrow.

He'd decided to try it out under cover of darkness, thus reducing the chance of being disturbed. For what it was worth, I pointed out a flaw in his logic, since Halloween was one of the more populated nights of the year. The neighborhood was swarming with pint-sized ghosts and witches, which the local Hasidim (who kept indoors) complained were indistinguishable from actual dybbuks on the prowl. I myself had left the apartment on the excuse of trick-or-treating, stretching the seams of the skeleton outfit my mama had made me two seasons ago. "Who ever heard of a zaftig skeleton?" she'd remarked at the time, and I'd put on a few pounds since then. But if I was keeping company with Hymie Weiss, I would just as soon be in disguise.

Of course I needn't have worried. Even with the additional handicaps of the shovel, coal chute, and toolbox he carried (I held the lantern), Hymie was virtually invisible to the residents of North Main Street. It was as if he moved in everyone's perpetual blind spot. Besides, given the evening's traffic in goblins, he was just one more clanking spook.

For the site of his rehearsal he'd chosen Catfish Bayou, a fetid sink just north of the Pinch, its banks bordered by ramshackle shanties and an old slave burial ground. To get there we crossed Auction Street, where the shops petered out and a row of dogtrot houses began. Though the only lights were the odd jack-o'-lanterns in windows, the moon was bright enough to upstage my oil lamp. It shone in the mud of the bayou, rippling sluggishly with what may have been the spines of snakes, and on the tin roofs and smooth headstones and the ring of fallen leaves where we halted. The place being deserted, I made a joke, which was only half a joke, about how its occupants might be returning soon. Since my chum didn't seem to know the meaning of fear, it was up to me to be jumpy enough for the both of us.

Indifferent to sinister surroundings, Hymie'd already shrugged off his load and set to work. He banged together some slats from his toolbox, making an upright trestle against which he propped the coal chute. At the mouth of the chute he placed a tumbled wooden grave marker and tamped it into the ground. (Seeing him so industrious, who would have believed he didn't necessarily know what he was doing?) When he'd completed his incline, he began to dig, heaving damp clumps of earth onto the coal chute and rambling between grunts about Houdini.

"One time he does one of his bridge leaps . . . unh . . . and there's a corpse stuck in the weeds which he unsettles . . . unh . . . at the bottom of the river . . . unh . . . so before the maestro can get free of his chains, the corpse floats to the surface . . . unh . . . and that's what the crowd sees first, this decomposed dead man . . . unh . . . then Houdini pops up right after."

I could see that the digging was taking its toll, so I offered to spell him a while, which surprised us both. If I'd forgotten I was no great shakes at physical labor, Hymie's laughter, as he leaned against a mossy headstone, reminded me soon enough. Moreover, here was this situation where a fat kid in a skeleton suit was helping his only friend dig his grave. Amazed at myself, I climbed out of the hole, turned in the shovel, and begged him once again to reconsider.

His answer was to slide back into the hole and carry on digging, reassuring me there was nothing to it. "I lie in the hole with my knees to my forehead, see, which makes a nice pocket of air. You can live like this ten, maybe fifteen minutes, long enough so the audience goes crazy with suspense. Then it's a simple matter to scramble up through the loose earth." By the time he'd finished explaining, the dirt was piled high in the coal chute, the excavation chest-deep, and he was ready to demonstrate.

He took wads of cotton from the pockets of his ragged cardigan and stuffed them in his nostrils, mouth, and ears. Throwing off the sweater, he unwound a long linen croker sack from his waist. He pulled the sack over his head, poking his arms through slits in the sides, the golem become a Halloween ghost. Then he curled up in the hole and mumbled something that the cotton in his mouth made unintelligible.

"What?" I knew better than to ask.

Possibly needing an orifice to breathe through as well as speak, he must have spat out the cotton, because this time the request came loud and clear: "Open the chute!"

"Guess again," I replied.

"Stuart, old pal," he entreated, making what was under the circumstances a tasteless crack, "this is a strictly kosher burial, no casket or nothing. All it wants is some Jerusalem mud to finish the job."

But I stood firm.

Undiscouraged, Hymie got to his feet and began to grope blindly in the toolbox at the side of the hole. From among the collars and shackles he eventually dredged a large three-pronged fishhook with line attached. This, after a couple of clumsy efforts, he snagged like a grappling hook on the soggy marker at the lip of the coal chute. Then he lay back down with the line in his hand, shouted, "Anthropropolygos!" (which I hadn't heard in a while), and pulled the cord. The marker toppled but the huge mound of dirt stayed put.

"For God's sake, Stuart," pleaded Hymie like his heart would break, "give it a shove! This is what I was born for!"

So I did it, if only to shut him up, to stop his accusing me of coming between him and the fulfillment of his destiny. All right, I thought, Hymie meet Destiny, Destiny, Hymie. Then I placed my hands against the hill of cold earth, which was taller than myself, and pushed, but it refused to budge. I pushed again and it began to inch glacially down the chute, spilling over the edge, dumping its weight in an enormous dull avalanche on top of Hymie.

In the moment before I panicked, I was angrier than I'd ever been—angry at myself for having let him sucker me into this, angrier at him for not being what he claimed. Never anybody magnificent, he was only the screwball Hymie Weiss, whom I could wait for till kingdom come without his ever crawling out of the ground.

Then I fell on my knees in the unpacked earth and began to claw my way toward him, burrowing from above the way Hymie was supposed to have tunneled from below. I dug until I was certain he wasn't going to meet me halfway, and was nearly done in before I remembered the shovel. Grabbing it, I managed finally to scoop out the hole to the depth where he lay. Then I tossed the shovel and went back to clearing away the dirt with my hands, unearthing him enough to lift his head by the filthy linen shroud. I pulled off the sack and unplugged the cotton, which the killing weight had yet to expel from his nose, but I knew all along it was too late.

He was stone cold, no hint of a pulse in his marmoreal neck, and his moonlight-flecked eyes, opaque as ball bearings, stared starkly from a hollow face. It was said that Houdini, using the techniques of oriental swamis, could breathe so shallowly it took a stethoscope to detect his heartbeat. But shaking Hymie, beating on his chest, I was unable to elicit even the faintest sigh; though a sound like a wind through venetian blinds came from his sphincter, and a foul gas enveloped us both. Plunked down next to him, I began to cry for help through my tears. When my voice broke, the fractured word subsiding in whimpers, I tried to close his gaping jaw; I lifted an arm that fell limply, like a marionette's.

After a while a couple of colored kids, come down I suppose

from the shanties, did in fact peer over the rim of the hole. They saw the stiff, pearl gray corpse in the arms of a roly-poly skeleton and, their curiosity satisfied, turned tail and fled. Or did they flee because they'd seen Hymie blink? He'd blinked once or twice as his eyes adjusted to the sight of me, then leapt to his feet and started to holler. I was hollering too, sitting splay-legged and pointing with one hand, holding onto my heart with the other. Then I remembered I'd yet to remove the rubber skull mask, and promptly did so.

"It's me, Stuie," I was able at length to inform him.

Hysterics ebbing, he caught his breath and said distantly, "Stuart," like he might have made my acquaintance in another world. When he attempted to grin, I thought I knew what was coming: he would tell me he'd been fine all along; he'd only been waiting for the suspense to build—after which I would pick up the shovel and send him back to wherever he'd been.

But instead of his standard assurance, he scuttled the grin and touched his own haggard features. He touched them the way a blind man might touch someone else's, hoping to recognize. "Stuart, I was dead," he confided in a voice thick with awe. "I was dead, Stuart," he repeated with growing urgency, hunkering down beside me in the hole. "Crushed under the weight of the clay. I wasn't alone, but I was lonely and I wanted to come back. So I escaped."

VIII. Metamorphosis

At first he said he couldn't explain it, then began to explain it. Death, he told me, was like being in an audience, looking toward a milk can or a packing case that contained your life. It was *your* life though you weren't in it anymore, and you could only see it taking place vaguely, as on the screen at the Idle Hour before the curtain was raised.

He told me everybody who was recently dead was there: "You name 'em. The Birnbaum kid, who was knocked over by a meat wagon? He was there. Mr. Klotwog, who died of that thing nobody will mention, and Mrs. Pinsky, who passed away in shul? They were all there. So I thought, maybe Houdini—we could put our heads together and figure a way to get out. But when I asked, nobody knew who I was talking about."

Instead he had himself been found, to hear him tell it, by a gaunt, bearded man in a dented bowler, holding a book. "'Pardon me,' he says, 'but I was your papa, Berl Weiss, that didn't live to meet you. And this was your mama, Chanah Sarah, rest her soul.' She's standing next to him, this pie-faced lady in a babushka. 'We been watching your monkeyshines,' he tells me, 'which it makes us to wonder is this our own sonny, eh Mama?' 'Gevalt,' says the lady in the babushka."

At that point I exclaimed, "Have a heart!" out of habit, though I didn't really want him to stop. He said he told them he was sorry if he'd disappointed them, but he was likewise disappointed, since they'd blown his theory of the magician's bastard child and all. Then he asked them if they knew the way out of there.

"'Give a listen, Mama,' says my papa. 'He wants out, this pisher, that's been trying so hard to get in. Well it ain't to my knowledge in the Five Books, the Zohar, or the Shulchan Aruk, the secret how to get out of here.' Then my mama speaks up, apropos I don't know what; she talks like this with a frog in her throat: 'Was you afraid? We was all the time afraid.' Papa gives a nod like she's hit on the heart of the matter. 'That's right, we was afraid of the Russians and the diseases and the whole gantseh megillah. Good riddance, says I. We was glad to leave the world.'"

This had set Hymie thinking: Was there something he'd been scared of? Certainly not danger or pain or even death, which he was here to tell me was no big deal. When it occurred to him to look back on his life from the other side, he saw how everything was faded already to shadows—everything, that is, but my sister in her smoldering anticipation, who was still lit up as bright as his own dead family.

"All right," Hymie admitted, as if he'd been bullied into confessing, "I was frankly afraid of her. But now I was even more scared that, if I didn't act quick, Miriam would turn to shadows along with the rest. And that's when it came to me, Stuart, how to jimmy the lock so to speak—which you'll understand is a professional secret I must take to my grave."

As he scrambled out of the hole and started for North Main Street, I noticed a definite spring in Hymie's limp. I pulled down my skull mask and hurried to catch up, following him back across Auction, wondering if there was anyplace I wouldn't have followed him to.

On the evening of my sister's wedding the entire neighborhood was gathered in the Anshei Sphard Synagogue. Women in the gallery wept openly or sniped in whispers; young men grumbled into their prayer books, as Miriam began circling the groom seven times. Veiled and trailing petal points of organdy and lace, she was a spectacle you could go snow-blind from looking too long at. Even Bernie Saperstein, despite the finery of his leather spats and silk lapels, looked humbled as she marched resolutely around him. In fact, he looked downright apprehensive, like a prisoner tied to a stake surrounded by savages.

Then she'd come to a full stop, my sister, and the two of them stood under the chupeh, facing the squat Rabbi Fein in his homburg reciting psalms. A hymn was sung and the blessing over the wine spoken, which was my cue to excuse myself. I rose from the front-row seat next to my father, who growled, "What's a matter, you got ants in your pants?" and made for the altar. I turned, sniffing the flower in my buttonhole. There, before God and my family—not to mention the Nussbaums (Uncle Shaky wheezing, Aunt Frieda shushing him from the gallery), the Forbitzes and

Seligmans, the shnorrers hoping to double as wedding jesters, all of them muttering in a commotion that swelled like a stirred hive of bees—I pronounced the French phrase and pulled the cord.

Muslin draperies fell about the bridal canopy. (The bolts of muslin had been easy to come by since Hymie had resumed his old job at the Emporium. As for the rest, the rigging of the chupeh and so forth, we'd managed it all quite handily after breaking into shul the night before.) The congregation held its breath as I counted down from ten, barking the numbers to drown out the noise of scuffling behind me. Then I declared "Behold, a miracle!" and parted the curtain.

Hyman the Magnificent, restored to the top hat and cloak of his original performance, was standing astonishingly erect in place of the groom. He was presenting his case to my sister, whose arms were folded, her toe tapping impatiently. The green fire in her eyes seemed to have melted the ice of her veil, thrown back to reveal her dark hair braided into a garland.

"You want kiddies, I'll give you kiddies," Hymie was promising. "We can use them in the act. They'll pop out of flowerpots and picture frames, and when they're older I'll teach them escapes. . . ."

"You're impossible!" accused Miriam, unfolding her arms in a gesture that released her bosom like doves about to take flight.

There was the sound of thumping and clanking that was Bernie, struggling in his chains, safe in a place known only to the magician and me. Meanwhile Rabbi Fein had evidently gone into shock, his mouth hanging open, the goblet fallen from his hands to smash on the floor. This didn't prevent him, however, from delivering the benediction—once Hymie, slipping a ring over Miriam's finger, had turned toward the little man.

"Blessed art thou, O Lord," said the rabbi, though his lips were never seen to move, "who plucked the bride and groom out of a hat. . . ."

THE ANNALS OF THE KABAKOFFS

I

1964

Every year at Cotton Carnival time, Itchy, black sheep of the Kabakoff clan, returned to Memphis with the traveling show called the City of Fun. When he wasn't running crooked concessions, making short change, performing his wild-man gaff in the freak tent, or propositioning local girls, he sometimes visited old haunts. He wandered the decaying length of North Main Street, where the only surviving business (and practically the only remaining building) was Kabakoff's General Merchandise. Satisfied that his grandmother Tillie was still a going concern, that she seemed even to have gained an employee or two, he might take the long bus ride out to his former neighborhood. For this Itchy always waited until dark, when a character as rough as himself, with his unkempt, sooty hair and matted beard, would be less conspicuous among the manicured lawns around the Kabakoff home.

He would prowl as he'd done since childhood, climbing trees to look in windows, determining that his absence made no difference at all. If anything, since his departure shortly after the death of his stepmother, Ida, the household appeared more settled. His father, Mose, who'd lost most of his hair and put on a few portly pounds (as became the founder of Kabakoff Publishing, Inc.), was more likely to be at home. He might be discussing some new enterprise with Itchy's half brother, David, a trim and precocious go-getter in an adjacent recliner, the two of them deporting themselves like diplomats. Then there was his half sister, Rose, whose generous dimensions had finally assumed a certain buxom symmetry. She might be entertaining a nervous beau in the upstairs rumpus room, enticing him into a slow dance to the lilting LPs of the Platters and the Lettermen. They might be holding hands on the sofa, watching the very TV in front of which Ida, during a power failure, had passed away.

But on this particular soft May evening, some six years after he'd left his father's roof, Itchy observed that Kabakoff's General Merchandise had closed early. His grandmother, decked out like an argosy in a billowing marmalade frock, a pillbox daringly tilted atop her blue wig, was leaving her apartment to enter a waiting taxicab. And when he'd taken the bus out east to his native subdivision of Something Wood, Itchy, approaching the house, encountered a crescent driveway backed up with cars. A glimpse through a window revealed a wedding in progress.

A canopy had been erected in the spacious living room, and under it stood a youthful rabbi with a neatly trimmed goatee. He was facing a pallid young man with the look of a sleepwalker, propped up next to Itchy's well-fed half sister in her glacier of white chiffon. They were flanked by a spruce brother David holding a jewel box, and Mose, tightly corseted in a tartan cummerbund, making numerous solemn chins as he gave away the bride. Then the rabbi was reciting the benediction, the groom stomping the goblet as if startled by a menacing insect, the bride throwing back her veil triumphantly. At the kiss (initiated by Rose), the groomsmen in matching tuxedos, the bridesmaids in uniform pastel gowns, and the seated onlookers, with Tillie in a place of honor among them, all shouted "Mazel tov!" as one.

Afterward some of the guests joined the receiving line, while most made for a lavish buffet set up in the dining room opposite. That was when Itchy, who'd been among other things a house-breaker and a sneak thief, climbed the trellis to an upstairs win-dow and slipped inside. He was in the bedroom that had once been the shut-in domain of Ida, mother of Rose and David, who'd died, as Itchy saw it, posthumously. What he was doing there he couldn't have said. Maybe he'd make a little mischief, a little revenge—who knew, as when in his life had he ever had a plan? He'd always been a creature of impulses he didn't quite under-stand, "creature" being the shoe with the likeliest fit. He was a grifter, an alibi agent, a shill, the intimate of human curiosities; he lurked in funhouse passages wherein he frightened lost girls, then offered to lead them through the mirror maze for a favor. Sometimes Itchy thought that, in the world he inhabited, he wasn't so much a person as some motherless figment out of one of his grandfather's books.

c. 1943–1964

"In the beginning was the Book." For a long time that was all Itchy could remember of old Yankel's crackpot homilies. Later on, especially during his travels with the carnival, he remembered other things: that the Book, for instance, had been given to the Jews by God at Sinai. Once in the world, the Book had spawned many others with various titles, though each additional volume was only a gloss (a midrash, his grandfather called it) on the orig-inal text. Written in an alphabet that looked to Itchy sometimes like flames, sometimes like the wings of black birds, in a language he never learned to read, the Book recounted the trials the Jews had endured on their long journey toward redemption.

"From the minute it was in their hands," Yankel said, his whiskered face a circuitry of creases and tics, "they got a choice, the Jews. They can live in the Book or in the world." But since events in the Book were roughly paralleled by what happened in history, the decision, as his grandfather was forced to admit, could be moot.

It was Yankel who'd named him Yitzkhok, calling him often by the affectionate Itchele, Itchy for short, though his father had dubbed him something entirely different. After the boy's mother had vanished and before he left for the War, Moses Kabakoff had given his son a joke of a name. But by the time he returned from overseas, it was Itchy, and even Mose couldn't remember when it had ever been anything else.

Yankel lived with his wife, Tillie, in an apartment over their general store on North Main Street, which was just above the river in a neighborhood known as the Pinch. Having bought the store with capital saved from decades of peddling, plus his wife's inheritance, he left it to Tillie—robust and capable, many years her husband's junior—to run the business. Meanwhile Yankel sat poring over worm-eaten books in his corner study, trying to recapture the days when he was the undisputed prodigy of Shatsk. Because Tillie had her hands full down in Kabakoff's General Merchandise, where it wouldn't do for the boy to be under foot, Yankel's sanctum served as Itchy's frequent playpen.

Later Itchy would remember other places from that time: the street itself, with its fast-talking shopkeepers hustling old clothes, old furniture, bruised fruit and claiming, despite the evidence of your eyes, that all was ripe and good as new. The Anshei Sphard Synagogue, where, from his grandmother's lap in the gallery, he'd grown seasick watching the skullcaps bob in a surf of blue and white shawls. There was the park in Market Square where they camped out with neighbors on nights too hot to sleep in the rooms above the store. Heat lightning flashed in a lavender sky beyond the roofs of North Main, and Itchy had asked if that was the War.

He would also recall the street he'd never seen, the one Yankel claimed to have found on his arrival in 1912, when "there was angels and devils that you had them in the Pinch in those days." But mostly what came back was his grandfather's study, a place minted in Itchy's memory in a coppery glow of dusk. Out the window the shopkeepers and their wives were always growsing, the newsboys shouting the names of faraway battles, the trolley spitting sparks like a dragon clearing its throat. Yankel would be currying his beard with dirty fingernails, yodeling over yellow pages, interrupting himself at every opportunity to tell tales. This while Itchy, temperamentally drawn to darkness, built himself a little shelter out of the scattered volumes and hid inside.

When Mose returned from the War with his silent bride, he showed himself ready to face his responsibilities. He took his son to live with him in a suburban enclave some miles east of the Pinch, for which Itchy never forgave him. After all, Moses Kabakoff, a hulking, driven man whose watchword was ambition tempered by principle, was a total stranger to the boy. So, of course, was Mose's wife, Ida, who spoke little English and was half a shadow. Rawboned and ashen, with anxiously darting gray eyes, she seemed as wary of her husband as was Itchy, who sometimes thought she invited his complicity. But after the shock of being torn away from the Pinch, which faded almost instantly to legend in his mind, Itchy kept resolutely to himself. This was already at age five a lifelong habit.

Once he'd snatched Itchy to himself, Mose behaved as if his duty toward his son were discharged; he was free to concentrate on his business pursuits. Years before he'd been apprenticed to Eli Shendelman, the printer, on North Main Street. Mr. Shendelman was now far past retirement age, and no sooner was he home than Mose had begun negotiating for his old boss's operation. Already in hock to the bank for the down payment on a ranch-style bungalow, he joined the new reform temple, which had a loan fund for returning GIs. He sealed the bargain and moved Shendelman's antiquated linotype into a mercantile plaza out east, where he set up shop. Working round the clock, he solicited jobs from all quarters, printing wedding announcements, political tracts, sectarian newsletters, business flyers, and Chamber of Commerce brochures. He worked feverishly, as if he thought the river was rising and you needed not sandbags but money to shore up the world against the flood.

For a while Itchy had insisted they take him back, though he was losing the sense of exactly where "back" was. Besides, who was listening? Ida was so remote, and Mose, on the rare occasions when he was home, remained preoccupied. The most Itchy could expect from his evasive father was a thoughtful frown, his knitted brow as severe as a visor. "Beats me how anybody could miss that dump," he would say as if to himself, running a hand reflectively through sparse copper hair. He might continue muttering aloud while he moved about the poky house, tuning a radio, correcting a picture frame, inspecting the fridge, anything to keep busy. At first Itchy supposed his father's perpetual motion was an effort to stay clear of him, though later he realized it wasn't personal; Mose wasn't so much trying to get shed of his son as he was the past.

Itchy would follow him stealthily, as stealth had become second nature, picking up the dropped crumbs of his father's boyhood, which he endeavored to trace back to the Pinch. That was how he learned how much Mose had hated it, the apartment with its acrid schmaltz odor cluttered with museum pieces: the samovar shaped like a pissing pygmy, the tallow-encrusted menorahs and biblical figurines, Yankel's library of mildewed books. Then there was Kabakoff's General Merchandise itself, full of butter churns, buggy whips, thunder mugs, Buster Brown outfits, worm cakes, bust developers, marriage manuals, incontinence bags—stuff that was an outmoded embarrassment even when Mose was a kid. This was to say nothing of the "relations," as he called them, whose freeloading and generally disgraceful behavior mocked Tillie's best efforts to make a decent home.

"What about my mama?" Itchy had ventured to interject once or twice, breaking his father's reverie.

"I told you," Mose would grumble, without looking up from whatever he was tinkering with, "she died."

"You said she disappeared."

"Died, disappeared, what's the difference?"

Whether giving in to reason or disinterest, Itchy would concede there was no difference, but Mose remained unappeased.

"What do you mean by eavesdropping on me when I'm talking to myself?" he'd snap. "You're a spook, ain't you, Itchy? You're not hardly here."

This was true, of course. Listening to his father's maundering, Itchy was transported back to his grandfather's study, where Yankel weighed the pros and cons of living in the Book. When Ida served her silent, tasteless fare, Itchy was again at Tillie's table, inhaling her savory stuffed chicken necks and enjoying her shoptalk. ("Ask a payment of Merle Cohen, you might as well give a corpse an enema.") But such memories were always ephemeral, no sooner surfacing than they dissolved. Meanwhile the neighborhood was rowdy with other boys Itchy's age, riding their bikes in the street in front of his house; they played football and staged wild whooping war games in the adjoining backyards. But Itchy kept a furtive distance, ducking from sight whenever they saw him, hearing them call out: "Lookit, it's the 'Bominal Kabakoff!" like he was something you spotted only once in a blue moon.

He was in school now, where he'd decided that by an act of will he could make himself invisible to his classmates. This seemed to work, or at least owing to his peculiarities—his custom of lingering under his desk after bomb drills, of spending recess in a tree—the other kids left him alone. In the meantime he'd learned to read, hungrily and without discrimination at first, content so long as his eyes pored over print. Because there were few books beyond the phone directory in the Kabakoff house, he brought them home at random from the school library; he kept them in constant rotation, usually careful to return them on time, but if he grew attached to a particular title, he stole it.

In this way Itchy duplicated, as best he could in his own matchbox bedroom, the atmosphere of his grandfather's study. Having already forgotten the tales of Yankel's travels, however, he came to confuse the old man's encounters with wandering souls and prophets, his brushes with temptresses, with fictional journeys through jungles to buried kingdoms. Elijah, Mottel Habad, the angel Raziel, and the golem-maker Rabbi Loew were replaced by Mowgli, the master thief Raffles, the Man Who Laughs, the Phantom of the Opera, Titus Groan. But even more than the reading, which tended to make him restless, Itchy simply liked having the books around. He liked stacking them in ramparts that he could roof over with a blanket, crawling inside at night to listen to cicadas and distant trains.

It was around this time that Itchy's lusterless stepmother became spellbound by the Philco television set, which Mose claimed they were the first family on the block to own. Spirited from a Polish refugee camp to a tract house in a treeless subdivision in Tennessee, Ida, like her stepson spirited from the Pinch, had yet to recover her bearings. Sometimes Itchy felt that he and Ida were in competition, each attempting to outdo the other's talent for shadowiness; sometimes, though he resisted the notion, he thought they were two of a kind. For a while she'd made gestures toward making a home, boiling cabbage, scrubbing woodwork, ministering to her impatient husband in his rare passive moments. (Itchy'd seen his father facedown on a bed while his wife lanced a boil or salved his hemorrhoids, acts suggesting an intimacy not confirmed by Mose's upright behavior.) But often Ida was subject to long bouts of lassitude, and once the TV had entered the house, she was captivated.

She took to gazing at its water blue glow as if through a window onto things meant for her eyes only. Toward every program—be it Milton Berle in hoop skirts or Molly Goldberg about to plotz or Liberace eclipsed by a grin, from Howdy Doody lost in space to Mr. Wizard holding fire in his hand—Ida evinced the same rapt fascination. "Oy a shkandal!" she might be heard to utter from time to time, having glimpsed another event worth breaking her silence for. Meanwhile she'd had a child, a daughter, Rose, and then a son, David, the following year. With each birth Ida appeared a bit more washed out, the turquoise veins beneath her transparent skin as pronounced as the turquoise numbers on her arm. Her babies, in Itchy's eyes, were offerings she presented to the television set, in front of which she placed their crib.

It was thanks to his half sister and brother that Itchy first came to realize he was ugly. Why else should they seem so threatened whenever he approached, the stout little Rose making a human shield of herself to protect her delicate baby brother? In a mirror Itchy could see that, in contrast to his paler-pussed family, his sloe-eyed features were dark. His face, with its prominent cheekbones, was the shape of a bicycle seat, his nose a beak, his unruly black hair like burnt kapok. Although you wouldn't have called him seriously misshapen, he'd always known he was different, and here in the vicinity of his ninth or tenth year he knew why: he was ugly and could never be loved.

Having felt little in the way of affection toward others, Itchy seldom looked to receive it from anyone else. But now that he was convinced he couldn't have it (love, that is) he missed it like he'd used to miss the Pinch, which he scarcely recognized during family visits anymore.

They'd gone back at irregular intervals to spend the high holidays with Yankel and Tillie. But Mose could never sit still in his parents' apartment, and he chafed at the ululations of the skeleton congregation at the Anshei Sphard shul. Since the meteoric rise of his business, he'd been asked to join the board of directors of the sumptuous Temple Israel, where, as he liked to put it, "The Book is the Book, the world the world, and never the twain of them should meet." There you had a resonant pipe organ and an energetic young rabbi in ministerial robes, instead of a handful of fleabitten old kuckers led by a cantor without the wind to blow his ram's horn.

North Main Street itself, never fully recovered from hard times, was in a sorrowful state of decrepitude. Not many members of Mose's generation had gone back there to live after the War, and few of Yankel's peers still survived. As a result, shops were boarded up, buildings fell into disrepair, weeds choked the alleys, and roots and vines wormed like serpents from under the paving stones. Kabakoff's General Merchandise, its inventory unaltered by Tillie (who replenished it from God only knew what prehistoric catalogs) in forty years, its ceiling fans in need of oil, was one of the last holdouts in the Pinch.

If only (as he phrased it) to keep from having to go down there anymore, Mose invited Yankel and Tillie to come live with them. On hand, when he asked, were Rose and David, who held their noses whenever they went to North Main, and on that day conspired in irreverent whispers over the prospect of their grandparents moving in. But Itchy, snatched untimely from the same apartment, saw the pattern in his father's largess. What might look to others like generosity looked to him like mere acquisitiveness, the Kabakoff impulse to redeem what might not necessarily want redeeming. In any case, Mose could well afford them, given the recent prosperity of his business.

Outfitted with innovative new machinery and a rapidly growing staff, the Kabakoff Press had lately required larger quarters, prompting Mose to relocate in a corporate development further east. Because the family had also outgrown their original residence, he'd built a new house closer to the press and more suited (as he said) to their needs. It was a barn-sized, mock-Tudor affair in an eclectic suburban compound of other mock-Tudors, colonials, and chateaux. Looking about his parents' cramped apartment with undisguised disdain, Mose assured them,

"We got room at our place, you could knock around a week without meeting a soul."

Tillie just shrugged and offered him another pirogi, while Yankel, sunk in an armchair and so shrunken with years that his feet no longer reached the floor, was obstinate.

"I wouldn't leave my books!" he proclaimed, lips twitching and eyelids fluttering in a furious semaphore.

"What are you, crazy? You can bring them with you."

"I shlepped them already over the ocean. Not another inch they don't budge."

Mose rolled his eyes toward a water-stained ceiling whence he saw no help forthcoming, then hung his head and sighed, "Give me strength."

In their spacious new house Mose saw to it that there were televisions in practically every room, including Itchy's. That way, a good provider, he made certain his wife would never be far from the programs that were her passion and sustenance. It was a needless expense, however, because Ida seldom left the bedroom she shared with no one. Slouched in the pink flannel housecoat she wore night and day (despite the extensive wardrobe that Mose had stocked her closet with), she looked as if lit from within by the glow of the TV. Though he tried not to, Itchy had sometimes pictured her naked: a neon skeleton with stringy, dishwater hair. Rose and David, who on the other hand had weaned themselves from television for hours at a time, were placed in the charge of a Negro maid named Hedda Bee. A squat, superstitious woman who (though illiterate) opened a scripture at every leisure moment, she avoided Itchy even more strenuously than did his sister and brother.

Normally the children saw their father only at the evening meal, which he bolted down and chased with bicarbonate in order to hurry back to work. Currently publishing, among other things, a shoppers' journal and two nationally distributed magazines—

one for hotrod enthusiasts, the other for naturopaths—the Kabakoff Press had achieved the status of a minor empire. Still, there were times when even Mose was moved to linger, and when he did he tended to dote on Rose and David as actively as he side-stepped Ida and Itchy. With little David, who was cranky and demanding, he was a bluff Goliath, ready to be toppled at his son's least petulant slap. Toward his butterball daughter his attentions could be more demonstrative, his favorite tease involving the tickling of her feet.

"Moses supposes his toeses are Rose's," he would chant. But where this had delighted the girl as an infant, it had since come to cause her no end of irritation. "Shame on you!" she'd snap, early proficient at the art of scolding; and perhaps remembering what store he set by his dignity, Mose would appear properly chastised.

Once in a while he took home movies of them, in which Itchy, though not necessarily in motion, was always a blur. He lavished gifts on them—dolls that talked and went potty, elaborate electric trains; plus the fads of the day, indispensable for the moment before they were discarded. Hula hoops and mouse ears crammed the drawers and closets; 3-D glasses, burp guns, and rocket radios littered the floors. He gave them pets that snarled and hissed at their half brother, personal phonographs to play the records of a local boy who'd become an international sensation. (On rumors that he cruised the area in a purple Cadillac, Rose and David kept vigil, as if—quipped Mose—for the Messiah.) Itchy couldn't complain that he hadn't also had his share of his father's free hand, but his gifts always seemed to be hints, like the sunshades and tennis skirts Mose gave his solitary wife. Instead of books he gave Itchy sporting goods, along with the exhortation that he should get out of doors more often.

"It's a rare opportunity you got to be a kid instead of a spook. Fields and trees you got. In the Pinch what did we know from a tree?"

He was referring to an undeveloped parcel of land beyond their compound, containing scrub woods, eroded gullies, and standing water infested with poisonous snakes. But unbeknownst to Mose, Itchy had been following his advice for some time, in lone excursions, usually after dark. Goaded by the example of the nightwalking mavericks in his books—which, having served their purpose, were no longer read—he stayed out to all hours, testing the limits of how little he was missed around the house. He explored the rough margins of his otherwise tidy neighborhood, creeping so unobtrusively that owls in chinkapins and foxes drinking from puddles of moonlight took him for granted. With a guttering candle he spelunked the tunnels of sewers, expecting at any moment to turn a corner into a subterranean laboratory or banquet hall.

He was forever anticipating transformations. From rooftops and tree limbs he spied on his neighbors through their windows, waiting for them to drop the masks of their ordinariness. Who knew when they might fold their newspapers and get up from their TV trays to perform some mad dance or blood sacrifice. Prepared by a diet of stories for surprising turns of events, it was the predictability of his neighbors' lives that seemed so consistently strange to Itchy. His own family, whom he also spied on, seemed equally strange: the boy refusing to mind the maid enjoining him to put away his toys; the girl painting her pudgy toes; the father unable to alight, pausing here to balance a bank book, there to muss a stubborn son's rust brown hair. Then there was the woman alone in her room, transfixed by Kate Smith, Boston Blackie, and Gorgeous George, her lips mouthing a phrase that Itchy after a while had by heart.

"Ma zol gornisht da leben tsa shtarbin."

On a bygone trip to North Main Street he'd asked his grandfather to translate. "Means we should none of us live to see ourselves die," he'd said. Itchy figured there wasn't much danger of that in his case, feeling as he did that he was somehow yet to be born.

By the time Itchy'd entered his teens, his Grandpa Yankel's tenacious health had finally begun to fail. This shouldn't have been surprising given his immemorial age, but the news was still a source of bewilderment to his grandson. Itchy had long nourished the idea that at some point Yankel had been overlooked by death for good and all. Hadn't the old man himself maintained that his associations during his military term with mountain Jews had taught him the trick of endless longevity? Besides, he'd always declared he couldn't expire before his studies had reached their conclusion, whatever that entailed.

Mose went dutifully to see his father several times on his own, then one bright Sunday in April collected his kids to take them on what amounted to a farewell visit. A couple of years had passed since Itchy's last trip to the Pinch, and he was amazed at how desolate it had become. Of the many businesses that once flourished in the neighborhood, only Blockman's Scrap Metal and Kabakoff's remained. Except for the old brick synagogue, converted to a nightclub with a shady reputation, everything else left standing was vacant and condemned. But Tillie still managed to eke out a living and then some, proudly assuring her son that she and Yankel needed nobody's assistance. In fact, thanks to its vintage merchandise at obsolete prices, Kabakoff's had become something of a tourist attraction, Tillie finding herself as much in the role of curator as proprietress.

In such desert surroundings the apartment, for all its claustrophobic clutter, was an oasis. Tillie bustled about as if her husband's dying were another of the curiosities she was famous for. She served tea and homemade strudel, brought up toilet masks and stereopticons from the store to amuse Rose and David, who were civil enough these days to feign a little interest. Mose stayed active, looking in on his father for brief spells, returning frequently to the parlor to scarf up more pastries and ask again for the doctor's last prognosis. Again he'd suggest they take the old man to the hospital, anticipating Tillie's, "He won't leave his books."

"How well I know," Mose would concede in exasperation, while Tillie gave no sign of apologizing for her man.

Sitting at the book-strewn office desk in his grandfather's study, Itchy tried to remember what it had been like to feel at home there, or anywhere else. Having chosen the study over the marriage bed as the scene of his final hours, Yankel lay supine on the very cot Itchy'd slept on as a child. Beneath the ragged quilt that covered him, the old man wore his baggy gray gatkes, his chin resting on a volume lying open over his shallow chest. Sunlight through the window limned his rigid features, his unfluttering eyelids, making him look like some sepulchral cast of himself; his labored breathing was a tune played on tissue-and-comb. But when he spoke, his rasping voice was still sharp, his nose riding the foam of his grizzled beard like a fin.

"How it is, Itchele boychik," he said, "is once you leave it, I'm talking the Book, you can't never go back again."

Itchy supposed he ought to be honored; Yankel was imparting deathbed secrets, like when the dying King Arthur gave up Excalibur. But Itchy had little use for old stories anymore, and his grandfather had become as good as a stranger. And as events went, death itself was not so impressive as he'd hoped it would be. So in response to the old man's confession, his grandson only grumbled under his breath,

"What if you never been there in the first place, I'm talking the Book?"

After Yankel passed away and was buried at his own request (and against Mose's protestations) in the swamp of an Anshei Sphard cemetery, Itchy was informed he'd inherited the old man's antiquarian library. "What do I want with that?" he complained in a bitter outburst that warmed his blood. Mose told him "Keep your shirt on," while Tillie assured him he would know where to find the books should he change his mind.

Still officially in school, Itchy at age seventeen was frequently truant. His teachers rarely bothered to admonish him, no doubt relieved the weird Kabakoff kid had the decency to make himself scarce. Or had they even noticed him missing? But there were consequences nonetheless, because for his poor grades and attitude he'd been held back a couple of levels. If his progress continued to stall, who knew but that his sister and brother, half a dozen years younger, might one day overtake him. Already they were showing signs of their father's zeal. Rose was active in the Junior Pep Club with an eye toward the Thespian Society; David, grown out of contrariness into ambition, aspired to the newspaper staff. For them, Itchy had always been a source of embarrassment, though they'd distanced themselves so thoroughly that most never suspected they belonged to the same Kabakoff clan.

Although he couldn't forgive them, neither did Itchy blame them very much. He was after all more of a sore thumb than ever, his cheeks erupting in pimples, his hair a tangled clump in a day of sleek pompadours. And though capable of inventing bold speeches to confound his enemies and break the hearts of girls, he seldom spoke to a soul.

In the meantime, demonstrating an early initiative, little David had begun accompanying his father to the press on Saturdays, where he was learning to cut and paste copy, and set type. Inspired by his younger son's resourcefulness, Mose broke precedent, approaching the elder with the proposition that he might like to do the same. "So you want to be a printer's devil or what?" he inquired. There followed a moment of mutual unease during which the question seemed to reverberate eerily. Then, before Itchy could appreciate the nature of the request, never mind give an answer, Mose had thrown up his hands and said, "Sorry I asked!" He walked away, apparently satisfied the subject was closed.

Itchy was busy in any case, cultivating his gift for sub-rosa skulking, which at night he put to practical use. Ranging farther afield in his spying activities, he prowled the gardens, swarmed the rooftops, and chinned himself on the balconies of the showy homes in his neighborhood. He crawled out on branches far enough to press his face to a leaded windowpane. Sometimes, having lowered himself onto a ledge, he discovered that the window was unlocked, then opened it and stepped inside. At first he never entered a room unless it was empty, but gaining confidence, he began slipping into bedrooms and tiptoeing past sleepers to test his nerve. As proof of his visitations, he left rubber reptiles under pillows; he knotted braids and turned paintings to the wall. He took mementos, initially objects that wouldn't be missed—a hair ribbon, a book; though he later began to lift more saleable goods. The watches, cameras, and so on he carried off to the pawnshop district on Beale Street, but other items—such as Wendy Fesmire's falsies, Loretta Steinke's garter belt, a pair of peach-scented briefs belonging to Eva Marie Duck—he hung on to, like souvenirs brought back intact from dreams.

Through their bedroom windows Itchy watched girls, many of whom were familiar to him from school, undressing. Often they disrobed before mirrors as if for lovers, lingering to admire their own coltish anatomies. They removed padded bras and gathered their budding breasts as if they might spill over, teasing the nipples till they stood up like stems, dancing a bit to make them jiggle. They squirmed their hips enticingly as they pulled on a chaste cotton nightgown. Entering their rooms while they slept, Itchy adapted his movements to the rhythm of their breathing; he snatched intimate garments, took them home, and from a single piece of rayon or silk reconstructed the entire girl in his mind. The next day he might see her in class and wait to feel shame. But instead he convinced himself that they exchanged subtle glances, hers signifying a thrilling awareness of having been debased.

Then came a windy night when Itchy clung to a branch outside Fuchsia Jones's window while she uncovered herself in front of her vanity. Suddenly the world went platinum; thunder cracked like the firmament's splintering rafters. In that instant the girl had turned toward the window, her eyes, which were saucered in horror, melting as they encountered Itchy's. That's what he could have sworn he saw: an invitation, the poodle skirt allowed to slide from her narrow hips. Then they were pitched into darkness, the power gone out all over the neighborhood, and Itchy drooped from his perch in dizzy elation.

The storm was becoming to the Kabakoff house, its interior mysterious with wisps of darting flashlights. Drenched to the bone, Itchy climbed the trellis and poured himself through his bedroom window. No sooner had he done so, however, than the rains abated and the lights came back on, as did the portable TV he'd left playing to fool anyone who missed him (Who missed him?) into thinking he was home. "Your Show of Shows" was in progress, Sid Caesar and Imogene Coca clinging precariously to a sputnik in flight. Each was blaming the other for their predicament, which had evolved after some confusion over placing a star at the top of a tree—it was a holiday show. Later Itchy wondered if this was the program his stepmother was watching when the power failed; because, when the lights returned and Mose routinely looked in on her, he discovered that Ida was deceased.

For some years it had been Rose and David's hilarious theory that their mother was a ghost. Conceding the possibility, Itchy had sneaked a peek in her bedroom. Truthfully, it would have made more sense to him had she just vanished, a natural enough means of departure for one so ethereal, but in death Ida appeared more present than ever. Rather than give up the ghost, it seemed to Itchy that the reverse had occurred: the ghost had given up a gaunt woman in a flannel housecoat, with a fearful rictus that might find an echo in every bow-shape and sickle moon.

Waiving his trademark dignity, Mose beat his barrel chest, tore the lapels of his paisley dressing gown. "Let's face it," he keened, "I was a miserable husband!" though once he'd rehearsed the lament, he didn't mention it again until friends had gathered to contradict him. Rose and David alternated between whimpering and fits of temper, as if Ida had expired to teach them a lesson they hadn't thought they needed to learn; while Itchy, as guilty of neglecting her as the rest, felt oddly abandoned. He was deprived of an unspoken fellowship, a creature whose irrelevance was as much an affront to the idea of a happy home as his own.

She was buried with the obsequies befitting the spouse of a prominent man of business, her imposing monument in the Temple Israel Memorial Gardens inscribed:

IDA LEYBUSH KABAKOFF

BELOVED WIFE AND MOTHER

1919–1957

FOR LOVE IS STRONG AS DEATH.

Her husband, lest his devotion be questioned, saw to it that the plot was subject to perpetual care.

He received the condolences of all and sundry, especially widows, some of whom discreetly suggested that "it was maybe for the best." But still Mose wasn't quite himself. For a while he kept close to home, restlessly proposing family activities to Rose and David, whose crammed social calendars foiled his good intentions. He renewed his campaign to coax Tillie to come live with them, but she insisted on staying near her business—"which it's a regular institution consecrated to my husband's memory." In his nervous, sullen rambling from room to room, Mose complained it was impossible to do anybody a favor. He resumed his old anti-nostalgic monologues, decrying his North Main Street origins, and it was his special dispensation to Itchy that he didn't discourage his eavesdropping.

Out of habit Itchy would prick up an occasional ear for some clue to his own pedigree. There were moments, in regretting aloud Ida's passing, when Mose did seem to confuse her name with someone else's—Lida, was it? But in the end such vague inklings couldn't hold his interest, now that Itchy already had one foot out the door.

Meanwhile the Kabakoff Press, become Kabakoff Publishing Incorporated, had acquired a momentum that wouldn't let its executive director play hooky for long. Recalled to the business, Mose embraced it with rededicated fervor, taking on a variety of new projects—a firearms digest, an Americanism review, a magazine for amateur sleuths. In the interim little David, proving himself something of a wunderkind, had graduated to technical mastery in the operation of the linotype. He'd also started learning to keep accounts. Rose, though increasingly plump, nevertheless had a solid sense of her worth, a virtue which, augmented by her father's bankroll, made her popular among her peers. The house was often full of her friends, their jocularity implying that Ida's passing had in a sense cleared the air. Now only Itchy's presence spoiled the otherwise convivial atmosphere.

But lately Itchy had found his own society. He was hanging around Beale Street, pawning his petty thefts at Kaplan's Loans, where no questions were asked, then spending the money in flyblown juke joints along the avenue. There, for the price of a bottle of hooch that he passed around, he could listen to old blues minstrels recalling their glory days. This was the time back before Beale ("where the haints," as they liked to say, "walk upright like natural men") had become a ghost street on the order of North Main. Obviously not colored, Itchy was tolerated as being also not quite white. He was poked fun at and put in the dozens where he suffered numerous insults to his hypothetical mama. But these were small dues in exchange for the privilege of hearing their tales about barrelhouses, packet boats, and medicine shows.

On a good day one of them might sing the song that "some white boy done stole it and made him a million dollar," a gripe that reminded Itchy of his grandfather bemoaning his exile from the Book. In their company, apart from cultivating more bad habits, Itchy began to find his voice. "I'm evil," he'd confided in a bluster conceived to suit the surroundings. "I'm a tom-peeper and a ace second-story man. I'm so horny I could shtup the crack of dawn." Although these boasts were submitted in all sincerity, the laughter that followed made him think he was also a bit of a clown.

Then it was May, toward the end of the Cotton Carnival season, and Itchy was strolling the midway in his black leather jacket and black dungarees. This was the outfit he'd chosen to consolidate his shadow condition. In school, where he still put in the odd appearance, the tactic had backfired, his getup calling undue attention to himself. But unlike on Beale Street, where he was generally regarded as a figure of fun, in his high school Itchy seemed to inspire fear. It was understandable because not only was he ugly, but the years of nocturnal acrobatics had left him sinewy and strong. Boys kept their distance; girls clutched their books to their bosoms, coloring as if they suspected him of spying on their secret thoughts. It was a conspicuousness that, if it flattered him, reinforced Itchy's feeling that it was time to move on.

What he liked about the midway was the sensation of being overwhelmed by a tidal wave of spectacle that swept you far from shore. There was something in the garish pandemonium that drew him out of the shadows and compelled him to throw away money on three-card monte; he was driven to eat the corn dogs that made him bilious after riding the Crack-the-Whip, which left him reeling. In a show tent Itchy applauded a down-at-heel magician called Madagaspar, who made indecent remarks while performing weary parlor tricks. Then a rockabilly band, featuring a midget accordionist in furry chaps, played "Little Red Caboose," and a pair of Negro comics, their lips daubed pink so that they looked like white men in blackface, came on to swap malaprops. After their skit, in which they were gravediggers assailed by an undead corpse, they doffed their fright wigs and auctioned off pearl earrings from Kuala Lumpur. They took bids on a woebegone blood-

hound with an august lineage and a tonic guaranteed to restore
whatever life took away.

In the burlesque tent blowsy women dropped spangled neg-
ligees and twirled their tassled breasts in opposing directions.
They made their bellies swell and recede like ocean tides, promising that this was nothing compared to what you'd see at the midnight show. There was a funhouse where Itchy negotiated tumbling barrels, shifting floorboards, and pitch-black passageways,
feeling perfectly in his element. He explored a hall of distorted
mirrors and thought that in some he looked almost handsome. At
the exit ladies crossed a grid that billowed their petticoats, affording glimpses of garters and nether frills. Itchy supposed someone
sat behind a panel and pulled a switch releasing the blast that lifted their dresses.

Some career, he smirked before the voice of his better judgment
whispered: *You could do worse.*

Of course an accomplished sneak thief such as he didn't have
to work. A professional now, what did he need that he couldn't get
by the simple act of breaking and entering? But on the other
hand, a carnival might make an ideal seat of operations, a place
where Itchy's peculiar talents would not go unappreciated.
Deciding, he felt the decision had somehow already been made.
He applied to a beet-faced fellow in a Stetson and suspenders,
introducing human oddities through a bullhorn from a bally
platform.

"You'll see Og the Albino Cyclops with his X-ray eye, a sight
that ain't for the infirm or the faint of heart. . . ."

A man, presumably Og, stood to one side of the barker, wearing a terrycloth bathrobe and a yachting cap pulled down to his
nose, a single peephole slit above the bill. On the barker's other
side, also in a robe, was a woman ("Flame the Illustrated Lady")
with a hard face and stringy red hair. Because neither showed any
inclination to display their alleged attributes, you were left to
imagine how they compared to their larger-than-life counterparts

on the painted facade. Then, as the barker vowed that still greater wonders abounded on the inside, the two sample show people turned and entered the tent. His shpiel completed, the barker stepped off the bally, tilted his hat to mop his brow, and proceeded with selling tickets.

"We got your ossified man, your Feejee mermaid . . . ," he was chanting mechanically, when Itchy stepped up and asked for a job. "Move along, son," scowled the carny, "there's paying customers here." But after a double take, during which he must have glimpsed something that made him relent, he handed Itchy a ticket and said to see him after the show.

The Feejee mermaid and an item billed as Harry the One-and-a-Half were disappointing, nothing but malformed fetuses pickled and exhibited in jars. The ossified man was only a leather-skinned stiff in an upright casket. But there were living anomalies as well, such as Teeta Tons-O-Fun, her buttocks the size of seabags spilling over a wardrobe trunk, and an unshelled peanut in short pants who called himself Victor the Ancient Child. There were Leo/Leah the Morphodite, Malcolm the Pig Boy, Mignon the Limbless Demi-Girl in her lacy infant's slip, plus of course the tattooed lady and Og, unmasked. His third eye, set lopsidedly in his forehead like a cheap paste gem, stared through the spectators from beneath its sleepy lid. Except for Teeta on her trunk and Mignon in her cradle, they all sat complacently on folding chairs in a half-circle of raised daises beneath a string of 40-watt bulbs. Holding up nickel photographs suitable for postcards, and quarto-sized fifteen-cent chronicles recounting their triumphs over impossible odds, they confirmed by their poker faces that they meant to give nothing away.

While the crowd jostled one another for the better view, Itchy hung back, not wanting to be identified with the rubbernecks. The barker was still working his audience, informing them that, for an extra two bits, he would reveal the most misbegotten creature the Almighty had ever mistakenly placed on this earth. When they'd paid their money and passed through a second tent flap, the man took Itchy aside.

"So, plug-ugly, what can you do for me?"

Suddenly unsure of how his special skills might translate themselves to a sideshow, Itchy was all the same determined to make an impression. He was emboldened, though he couldn't say why, by the proximity of freaks. The situation clearly calling for brass, he remembered a line he'd once heard from a Beale Street blowhard.

"I can fish, fight, fart, fuck, fly a kite, and drive a truck," he announced, then felt as if he'd invented himself on the spot.

The carny took his measure a moment, hawking up a bolus that filled his ruddy cheeks before he spat. Then he shoved the loopy kid toward the tent flap. Looking in, Itchy saw the bored audience watching a man like a mop in a dirty diaper, standing barefoot in sawdust while pensively gnawing a piece of raw meat.

"Think you could add some spice to this act?" asked the carny, and when Itchy didn't seem to understand, he explained, "The old rummy's teeth have played out."

If not quite as emphatic as he'd been seconds ago, Itchy nonetheless assured the carny that he was his man. He was told he could expect fifty a week, plus meals and accomodations when available, and whatever "fringe benefits" happened to come his way.

"Name's Julius Few," said the carny, extending a meaty hand, which he withdrew, frowning, before Itchy could grasp it. "Say," on second thought, "you're kinda young, ain't you? Your people know where you're at?"

Itchy entertained, then discarded, an impulse toward honesty. He had the unreasonable fear that, if he turned his back on the carnival in order to bid his family farewell, the carnival would be gone before he could turn back around. Whereas this was an unhappy prospect, it cheered him to believe that the reverse might apply to turning his back on the family.

"I'm a orphan," he said, which seemed to satisfy Mr. Few.

Although there was no question that it was his decision to run off with the traveling show, Itchy nevertheless had the sense that he'd been abducted; the carnival people had claimed him for one of their own. On the road the show was called the City of Fun, and in its way it was as much a throwback as Kabakoff's General Merchandise on North Main. Making its circuit of dusty towns in the Mississippi Delta, looping down through Alabama to winter in southern Georgia then trek back to Tennessee in the spring, the carnival attracted every type of misfit along the way. Not just freaks of nature, but vaudeville and medicine show veterans, as well as fugitives from justice, mental asylums, and marriage, fell into their nomadic ranks. Among them was an unspoken credo: although they might depend on the world at large for their subsistence, they were not technically speaking a part of that world, whose citizens they considered fair game. "Show me a mark without larceny in his heart," they challenged, and with daubed cards, gaffed wheels, and sleights of hand, they fleeced the yokels at every turn. They picked their pockets while reading good fortune in their open palms, sold them surefire remedies (one part molasses to two parts alcohol) for syphilis, walleye, pelagra, dengue fever, and lost youth. They hustled them pie-eyed into the burlee tent, where the marks witnessed acts so unnatural that they were afterward ashamed to face their wives.

As a consequence, the carnival was often at odds with a disapproving citizenry, who were all the same drawn to its lights and ballyhoo. Frequently, aroused suspicions and insufficient bribes would force the show to decamp at a moment's notice. But sometimes it was already too late, and, set upon by local toughs, the carnies had to hold their own.

At length Itchy came to the conviction that he was born to their company. He wasted no time in attempting to prove himself invaluable, willing and able to provide whatever might be needed. He could of course be stealthy where stealth was called for, light- and sticky-fingered when "peeking the poke," that is, inspecting the contents of a customer's billfold. He was nimble as a monkey at raising ridgepoles and fastening the struts at the top of the Wild Mouse ride. But what's more, never having claimed any particular personality for his own, he seemed suddenly capable of conceiving one to suit any purpose. A fast learner, he soon became fluent in the patter of the alibi agent and efficient at operating grab stands and complicated bunco games. Employing a theatrical bent hitherto unknown to himself, he shilled for the auction and demonstrated the effects of miracle cures in the more backward communities. He performed a turn as a ghost in one of Rufus and Bones's comic routines; planted in the audience, he swapped insults with Madagaspar the Great, the seedy magician who, as Feyvush Meyer, had been in better days a tumler at a Catskills resort. All this Itchy did in addition to his duties in Mr. Few's ten-in-one.

Which isn't to say he abandoned old habits. Early on the ladies had been aware of Itchy's leering; they saw him prowling backstage at the kootch show (where there was scarcely any call for discretion), spying on them from under the runway. Deciding that something ought to be done about such a nuisance, who they allowed was cute in a golliwog sort of way, they got together and drew lots. It fell to Miss Melba May, one of the senior exotic dancers, a woman of generous volume and pumpkin hair, to deal with the pest. She invited Itchy to her trailer and he went thinking she would ask him a favor or assign him a task, and still didn't get it when she greeted him in dishabille. The kick, he thought, had anyway gone out of just looking, since what did these women have to conceal?

Asked Miss Melba, "So whadja bring me?" which puzzled Itchy, who'd naturally come empty-handed. He was further confused when, making as if to search him for a surprise (mumbling at each button: "Miss Melba may, Miss Melba may not . . ."), she began to unfasten his fly.

"What are you doing?" he inquired when she had him in hand, his shock dissolving into fascination.

"Honey, you don't know by now," replied Miss Melba, backing him with her whiskey breath into a berth beneath a velvet matador, "it ain't no use for me to say." Then she cautioned him to just relax.

She pulled the cord at the waist of her kimono, releasing gallons of salmon pink flesh, while he protested that this wasn't right; it wasn't in the cards that Itchy Kabakoff should be loved by anyone. Straddling his hips with her heavy hams, she assured him this had nothing to do with love. But having hung on so long to the idea of himself as untouchable, Itchy wasn't about to let it go in a moment's heat.

"Look, I'm ugly!" he reminded Miss Melba in case she hadn't noticed, which earned him a gold-capped grin.

"Ain't it the truth," she sighed blissfully.

When the word got out that Itchy wasn't so much a boy as a demon, a regular sex fiend, other carnival ladies were quick to step in line. Among the first to have him round to her wardrobe was Flame LaTouche, who divided her time between the kootch show and the ten-in-one. She unwrapped a sarong to reveal her slack nakedness still clothed in illustrations, as if she were wearing the Sunday funnies, and offered him a crash course in art appreciation. (Itchy wondered if she'd begun, like his stepmother, with a spider bite of a tattoo that had spread into a glorious rash.) Next was Pagan Lee, makeup crusted like cake frosting to hide her mahogany skin, who lifted her sequined gown to advise him, "My burnin' bush want a word with you." Itchy noted that the women often had pet names for their private parts: beehive, organ-grinder, the Hot Box Hotel. He might be asked to place his jack in their pulpit or, as in the case of the statuesque Vivacia, "Would you-uns care to climb up on Mount Pleasant?" Sometimes they invited him to play various roles, for which he discovered a natural aptitude, such as janitor and schoolgirl or Quasimodo and Esmeralda—a favorite of the bookish Miss Lorraine Cloud. Once, throwing her chemise over his head, Boo Kay Jones, the Dixie Pixie, enjoined him to act like a woolly booger, and to his amazement Itchy seemed to know exactly how one ought to behave.

At first he missed the savory wickedness of watching through windows; he missed the bittersweet longing he'd always believed was his lot. Then Itchy found out that longing wasn't necessarily diminished by such serial encounters; entering their bodies didn't cure it any more than had entering their bedrooms. Accustomed to being the spectator, no sooner had Itchy experienced a woman than he had to repeat the experience to convince himself it was real. One woman only increased his appetite for the next. Besides, having allowed a talent like his to go unexercised for so many years, he felt an urgent need to make up for lost time.

With no reason to maintain an exclusive fidelity to the ladies of the City of Fun—they were anyway too aggressive when he preferred to instigate—Itchy preyed on girls from the towns they traveled through. He stepped out of shadows to lead them along the funhouse corridors. Outside, before they'd had a chance to recover from the first fright of seeing their guide under neon, he would ask for some kindness in return. He made lickerish suggestions over the gift of a piece of slum merchandise ("this here authentic Peruvian temptress love charm, that no man can look on without he gets the rise in his Levis"), to which they responded, incredibly, with gratitude. Some lingered after hours and followed him into thickets behind the carnival lot. Others left him instructions for furtively visiting their family's address, insisting he climb through a bedroom window like a burglar or an incubus.

These were rangy girls with glossy lipstick and loose chestnut hair, in thin cotton sundresses redolent of buttermilk and dimestore cologne. What they wanted was a good time with no strings attached in the company of an itinerant carny, with whom they might lose (as in the case of some) the nuisance of a protracted maidenhood. And while there was no shortage of willing young roustabouts to oblige them, broad-shouldered swaggerers with square jaws and ducktailed hair, again and again they turned to Itchy. It was as if he were some novel attraction, like a crystal-gazer or the Wall of Death, which they'd been told they ought to try at least once before settling down. Or was it his very unlikeli-ness, the moonstruck temerity of his believing he might be desir-able, that intrigued them? Strapping boys and men were in abun-dance, but as more than one girl expressed it, "Creatures like you ain't so easy to come by."

"I'll see can I fix that," Itchy had learned to reply.

They liked to pamper him, laughing at the incongruity of his greasy hair festooned in clover, delighting at the moment when he'd had enough and shook off his adornments with a "Feh!" They especially enjoyed sending him away with a keepsake through a window at dawn, confident they would never see him again. Sometimes, however, the maturer types could be more demanding, as take for instance the wayward preacher's wife in Hattiesburg. A cat-eyed, bouffanted woman in a hobble skirt, she lured him to a yew-shaded gazebo and implored him, "Defile me! Tell me you're a troll from hell!"

"I'm worse," Itchy assured her, beginning to enjoy the rough stuff. "I'm a Jew."

If ever he wearied of easy conquests, he might be moved to try his hand at tantalization. Like the Sunday morning he avoided the ritual boil-up, when the carnies deloused their clothes, and treated himself to a laundromat on the town square. Having caught the sardonic eye of a dishwater blonde in denim toreadors, Itchy orchestrated his wash to come out of the machine at approximate-ly the same time as hers. He stationed himself opposite her at the table where she'd begun to fold her laundry, folding his own for perhaps the first time in his life. For a while he followed her lead quid pro quo: if she folded a sweater, he folded a jacket, she a skirt, he a pair of dungarees. This until Itchy took over, determining the pattern as he accelerated the pace. Soon, breathing with mutual intensity, they were folding ever more personal garments. When he was wadding his threadbare longjohns, she was down to a lacy camisole, some silken briefs, then nothing at all. Her eyes were moist and heavy-lidded, her breasts rising and falling, Itchy's cue to stuff his clothes in the duffel, swing it over his shoulder, and turn with a wink to walk away.

But not all his encounters were fly-by-night, an important exception being Mignon the Limbless Demi-Girl. Limblessness aside, Mignon was possessed of a strong, small-bosomed torso, compact as a cello and with hardly any waist. Although the muscles of her jaw were strung taut from clenching utensils, her face was fine-boned and smooth, set with ardent gemlike eyes framed in a feathery bob. She spent much of her time recumbent in a rocking cradle in Madame Delphine's mitt camp trailer, alternately attended to by the fortune-teller and Leo/Leah the Morphodite. Often restless, though, she would sometimes topple her cradle without warning and scoot about the grounds in her muslin wrapper, like a broken doll borne away by wobbly ants.

Once, curious about his fabled prowess and with a famous itch of her own, Mignon had wriggled headfirst into Itchy's sleeping bag behind the cookhouse where he bunked. Thrust from dreams of leeches and snapping turtles into the conviction that he wasn't dreaming, Itchy howled and made to protect his vitals. But nuzzled rather than clipped, he eventually relaxed, settling back into sweeter dreams. Later, when his visitor emerged from the down cocoon, a process that left Itchy feeling like he'd given birth, there was nothing for it but to return the courtesy.

Dallying with Mignon, who pressed him to be energetic, Itchy tried to clear his mind of mean images, of inflating footballs and such. Despite himself he'd conceived for the girl a somewhat fraternal attitude, which precluded passion, as even Itchy recognized certain taboos. What he liked were the quiet times when they talked about life, she wanting the conventional things (a home, a family); whereas he felt the road was the ticket, not that it had made him content. Still, this was the nearest notion of a philosophy that Itchy had yet developed, just as intimacy with Mignon was his closest brush with friendship. It was a thing for which he found himself grateful, occasionally summoning the hardihood to tell her,

"You're maybe only half a girl, Mignon, but you're all woman in my book."

"I'm all human anyway," she might reply, grown pettish since their physical relations had cooled, "which it is more than I can say for you."

This seemed also to be the consensus among the other freaks, whose society Itchy nevertheless sought out. In light of his success with the ladies, he was coming to regard his own ill-favoredness as an advantage rather than a handicap. Then it followed that the fabulously deformed and disfigured should constitute a kind of aristocracy in Itchy's eyes. For their part, perhaps disapproving of his wanton ways, the freaks tended to tolerate Itchy more than accept him, which for the time being would have to do.

After Mignon, he felt a special attachment to Victor the Ancient Child, who at twelve was as desiccated and crotchety as an eighty-year-old man. (The story went that, seeing his missionary family devoured by cannibals who were saving him for dessert, Victor had aged several decades overnight.) Then there was Og the introspective albino, who looked as if molded from cookie dough, decorated with here a splayed nose, there a pair of meaty lips, and an off-kilter triad of eyes. That was how it was with the freaks: they had too much of one thing, not enough of the other, a difference that distinguishes mortals from creatures of nightmare. Mildly curious about their literary ancestors, Itchy revived for a period his longlost interest in books, which he borrowed from Og, a great reader of science fiction and Gothic romance. But only a passing fancy, his reading could never compete with his ongoing ache for the ladies.

Among the normals, the roughnecks and mugg joint operators, Itchy was generally kept at arm's length, the distance he'd grown accustomed to in school. But Rufus and Bones, the former vaudevillians, who had need of his gymnastic skills, endured the weird kid's occasional apprenticeship. So did Madagaspar, to whom Itchy was less a student of magic than of the toilet-mouthed old trooper's tired jokes.

Itchy guessed from the beginning that the names of the carnival folk were not the ones they'd been born with, that the stories in the freak biographies were apocryphal. Fond of mystery himself, he'd straightaway assumed his own alias, one with a touch of the sinister.

"Scratch, they call me Danny Scratch."

"He look kind of itchy," remarked Malcolm the Pig Boy, thoughtfully revolving the rusty ring in his snout, and the name stuck. Thereafter, when he began to eat bugs and pluck chickens with his filed teeth in the sideshow gaff, he was billed as Itchy the Wild Man.

But just as the ladies had failed to reduce his craving for more ladies, neither did his membership in such prodigal company dispel Itchy's loneliness. On the contrary, loneliness and desire had acquired a piquancy beyond anything he'd known before he left home. Now when he looked at his life, Itchy felt as though he were regarding a character in a book, about whom he was free to feel pity, fascination, alarm. Once, on one of his funhouse haunts, an old adage of Yankel's came back to him, how the world was nothing but a cloudy mirror of the Book. It was an idea that meant little enough to him during his travels. But sometimes around Cotton Carnival season, when the City of Fun returned to Memphis, Itchy wondered if his own shadowy tale might come clear in the telling.

He'd been poking about the upstairs bedrooms, including the one that used to be his, which was now a shrine to Kabakoff industry.

Any vestiges of himself had long since been erased in favor of framed awards and publications, the photographs of Mose and David shaking hands with visiting potentates. Then, having inspected his fill of drawers and closets, Itchy passed a tentative moment at the head of the staircase before making his descent under a crystal chandelier. He figured that his shaggy hair and whiskers, plus the changes wrought by six years, would serve for a foolproof disguise. If his black attire, admittedly not the most appropriate for a wedding, should trigger any recollections, the red kerchief at his throat ought to cancel them out. Besides, didn't the Jews have some time-honored tradition of inviting all manner of misfits to entertain at their wedding feasts? Thus assured, Itchy still hadn't a clue to what he might do next.

As if to announce his intrusion, the little orchestra in the marble foyer struck up a lively show tune, and Itchy pressed himself to the wall. "If I was a rich man, yadda biddle bum . . . ," warbled an oily singer in a velvet tuxedo, the hair at his temples folded like raven's wings.

The large rooms on either side of the entrance hall were clamorous with guests. They shuffled back and forth between the extravagant buffet in the dining room and the living room, where the canopy had been collapsed to make way for more tables. Some attended the musicians, swaying synchronously in their chairs. An old man with a rakish tilt to his yarmulke, inspired to youthful gyrations, tried to entice his wife into a dance, though she patently refused. But finally the music was no match for the hum of conversation, unhampered by mouths stuffed with smoked fish and blintzes, not to mention glazed ham. It was such a commotion that Itchy, moving gingerly among them, scarcely turned a head.

At the center table in the dining room, a broad bay window behind them, the immediate family sat facing the company. Flanked by Tillie and David, Mose interrupted his compulsive eating from time to time to field congratulations. Then he would look admiringly toward his full-figured daughter hoisting a rebellious bodice with one hand, spoonfeeding ambrosia salad to her wand-thin groom with the other. Beside the newlyweds the courtly rabbi was offering a lackluster couple, presumably the bridegroom's parents, the artificial sweetener. For the present Itchy was content to keep his distance, testing his anonymity instead on the guests in the opposite room. As he lurked about the long tables, there were occasional looks askance, puzzled expressions exchanged, lips silently inquiring, "Do you see what I see?" but that was all. So Itchy was tempted to push his luck a little further.

A frosty-haired gentleman with varicose jowls, forking some brisket into his open mouth, froze at the awareness of the kibitzer's pinched face next to his. At his ear Itchy was recalling one of his grandmother's mealtime maxims: "Rather than starve, it's better to eat a roast," he observed. Either the words or Itchy's pungent odor elicited a tic in the gentleman's left cheek; then a beat after which he coughed in appreciation, inserted the forkful, and began purposefully to chew.

So far so good, thought Itchy.

Just ahead was a suntanned matron under a petal pink beehive, chatting animatedly with a neighbor while smearing mustard on a slice of beef tongue. "We stayed at the Lido, but never again!" she was saying. "You know, they're letting in the shwartzes now." Then, prompted by an aroma, she turned her head to find a species of unwashed beatnik intently studying her plate.

"Myself, I never eat anything that comes out of a animal's mouth," he informed her, the professional swallower of live toads. " 'Course, there's others have problems enjoying a egg."

The woman dropped her knife and clutched the pearls at her freckled cleavage. With her free hand she tugged at her husband's sleeve, directing his attention from real estate to the empty space from which Itchy had already moved on.

He was at the strapless shoulder of one of Rose's bridesmaids, a slender girl with a swanlike neck and drooping lashes, whom he relieved of her glass of champagne. Holding it aloft, he began to propose a toast: "Here's to you and from you and to you again . . . ," then hesitated, his nose beginning to twitch. When he'd sneezed, he leaned forward to pluck a rubber worm from the girl's sleek hair. Crossing his eyes to examine its wriggling length, Itchy thrilled at the intake of breath all around; he saw the vein throb in the bridesmaid's forehead and asked himself if he was sorry. Then he shrugged, quaffed the champagne (into which he'd dropped the worm), and threw the goblet over his shoulder, satisfied that he'd passed the point of no return.

By the time he'd completed his tour of the tables, sampling random glasses and making a show of munching scraps and bones, Itchy had the attention of most of the guests in the room. The five-piece orchestra were still playing, the singer crooning mellifluously a song called "It Was a Very Good Year," as the intruder bounded back into the vestibule. Eyes closed in a transport of emotion through which he maintained his keyboard smile, the singer lilted that his seventeenth had been an especially good year for small-town girls. Hearing his cue, Itchy stepped forward to snatch the microphone from its stand. Behind him the singer's mouth worked mutely, the musicians ceasing (one instrument at a time) to play.

"When *I* was seventeen," said Itchy, crossing the threshold into the dining room, "the only date I ever had was with L'il Miss Fist, if you take my meaning." He winced as feedback shrilled over the speakers, blinked at the glaring lights from some friend of the family filming the event. In this movie, wondered Itchy, would he still figure as just a blur?

"Do I have to spell it out?" he continued. "Okay, so I *spent* (get it?) a lot of time jerkin' the gherkin, choking my chicken as it were. Which reminds me of the one about the lady in the butcher shop. She's inspecting this chicken, see, poking and prodding. She spreads its legs and sniffs, makes a face, says, 'Got any liver today?' 'Listen, lady,' the butcher's boiling, 'you couldn't pass that test and you're still alive!'"

The hush that had overtaken the entire gathering was so pro-
found that Itchy shut up as well. All eyes looked to the head table
for an explanation. Moses Kabakoff, founder of the feast, was
mopping his broad brow with the napkin tucked in his collar. He
dropped the cloth to reveal a face as perplexed as any other,
flushed from a sudden attack of indigestion. Was this some gate-
crashing commie meshuggah, which the country was full of, come
in off the street to make a mockery of his swank affair? Or was he
a surprise, a wedding jester secretly hired by a well-wisher to
entertain? If the latter, then his performance so far was pretty
tasteless, though you had to remember these were after all permis-
sive times. And in the end it might prove even more mortifying to
make a scene by cutting him short than to let his shtik run its
course.

Choosing the path of least resistance, Mose forced a laugh, at
which signal the rabbi followed suit. So did a good portion of the
guests, some of them even managing to guffaw.

Itchy showed his sharpened yellow teeth. "Thank you," he
said, laying it on in the manner of Madagaspar the Great, a.k.a.
Feyvush Meyer. "You're beautiful!"

From the lining of his leather jacket he tossed them party
favors—combs, billfolds, and valium tablets he'd lifted from the
pockets of the guests he'd been loitering among. "It's great to be
here at the nuptials of Rose and—," he fanned his lip in an unintelligible mutter, "—b-b-b-b. Gorgeous ceremony, wasn't it? What
with the swelling of the organ and the coming of the bride. But
seriously, I'd like to make a toast to the newlyweds." Again he
pried loose a glass of champagne from liver-spotted fingers.
"Here's to Love and Honor. They got rid of Obey, but at least we
still got Honor and once you've got Honor, keep on 'er."

There was more hilarity, albeit affected, which encouraged
Itchy to go for broke.

"So, darling," he said, resting a hand on the clavicle of a
tiaraed woman whose nostrils flared and contracted like gills,

"remember *your* wedding night, when your daddy told you he put a thousand-dollar bill in your glove? You're getting in the cab to leave on your honeymoon when you realize you forgot the gloves. You run back in the house and your mama asks, 'What is it, sweetie?' 'I forgot my gloves,' you tell her. 'Gloves-shmoves,' says Mama, 'you'll take it in your bare hand like I did with your father.'"

Itchy moved through spottier laughter to another table where a man in a seersucker suit sat gnashing his jaw, his lumpish wife covering the ears of a little boy whose eyes ticked like wipers to and fro.

"And this one," said Itchy, indicating the sullen husband. "On *his* wedding night the safety slips off, so what does he do? He goes fishing for it with a piece of straw, which he also loses. Likewise the toothpick he uses to find the straw. Nine months later out comes Junior here, wearing a raincoat, a straw hat, carrying a cane."

The woman had to unclap her son's ears in order to restrain her husband from springing at Itchy's throat. The phony laughter had dwindled to a measured chuckle or two, most of the guests sitting stone-faced or at best confused, while Itchy persisted, his brain teeming with indecencies he hadn't known he knew. Stretching the microphone chord to its limit, he leaned against the head table and confided in the sartorial rabbi for all to hear:

"I'm in the toilet at the Tupelo bus station, and the fellow next to me is pishing all over his leg and mine. 'You're from Memphis,' I tell him, and when he asks how I know, I say, 'Rabbi Pasternak up there, he circumcizes on the slant.'"

The rabbi made an aborted effort to smile, his mustachioed upper lip impersonating a caterpillar's death throe. Then he closed his eyes, perhaps in prayer. Reveling in the further temptation of fate, Itchy had advanced along the table as far as the newlyweds themselves.

"Ah, the blushing Rose and her stout-hearted b-b-b." Again he fanned his lip.

"His name's Nat," Rose peevishly submitted on behalf of the wilted groom.

"Nat." Itchy tasted the name. "Nat, my bucko, you must be looking forward to tonight, to the moment when you whip it out and ask your bride if she knows what it is. [in falsetto] 'It's a wee-wee,' she'll say, delighting you with her innocence. 'Well, dear,' you tell her [in earnest baritone], 'now we're married, you might as well know that it's called a shwantz.' [in falsetto again] 'Oh no,' says Rose, 'I've seen lots of shwantzes and this one is a wee-wee.'"

Aside from a cough, a cleared throat, there was not a sound.

Then Mose was on his feet. "That's enough!" he bellowed, flinging down his napkin and making a throat-cutting gesture in the direction of a white-jacketed steward. With brisk efficiency the steward gave a nod to a couple of subordinates before stooping to unplug the microphone. As the servants approached the table, Tillie had also risen, her veiled pillbox dangerously askew.

"Itchele," she cried, rubbing one forefinger against the other as if to make fire, "shame!"

Mose, David, and Rose swiveled their heads as one toward Tillie, then back to Itchy, whom the servants were discreetly taking hold of. Ordinarily so sober, Mose succumbed to a fit of blinking fidgets, casting about as if for something to hang on to. Catching sight of the abandoned microphone on the table, he groped after it like a tossed lifeline.

Meanwhile, even as he was being manhandled toward the door, Itchy wasn't finished. What he'd set loose tonight, no one should try and force him to contain. More than himself, he felt he was the voice of other ghosts at the wedding—of the silent Ida, say, and perhaps his own unknown mama, and old Yankel, who seemed now to be speaking to him from across the years. He was citing a passage from some pertinent text that Itchy repeated at the top of his lungs:

"It tells us in Talmud that Rabbi Ishmael's penis was like a wineskin of nine gallons' capacity. That's according to Rabbi Pinkas, whose penis, according to Rabbi Yakov, was like a wineskin of five gallons' capacity, though some report the measure as only three. And what of Rabbi Yakov himself?"

On that he was shoved outside, and the beveled glass door slammed in his face. "His penis was like a leaky Carpathian jug!" shouted Itchy, who seconds later had scaled the trellis, tumbled in the window, and was stealing down the staircase again.

Mose was attempting to speak through the dead microphone. Seeing his difficulty, the steward tried to plug it back in, which caused a momentary tug-of-war between the man and his employer. Finally the mike was working again, the chord stretched taut from the hall to Mose's hand, but while his face had ceased its involuntary twitching, the host had yet to find his tongue.

"I'm sure," he began, with a plaintiveness of tone enhanced by piercing feedback. He cleared his throat and started again. "I'm sure we all enjoyed the hijinks of my . . . of our stand-up comedian." He was trying hard to control the tremor in his voice. "But now I'd like you to join me in drinking a health to the bride and groom." As the guests held their shocked conversation to a respectful murmur, Mose began to sound less perfunctory, his bearing reassuming some of its lost composure.

"It's not every day," he continued, gaining heart, "that a father gives away his only daughter, his sweet Shoshonah, which the rabbi informs me is the lovely Hebrew word for Rose. So if you'll indulge an old man in a sentimental moment . . ."

"Who's old?" from a nearby table.

"Still bucking for that promotion, eh Harold," said Mose, prompting polite laughter all around. With order apparently restored, he felt himself risen in stature a full inch or two; he was back where he ought to be, in control. "But seriously, friends, if you'll permit me to wax sentimental, there's an old saying I just made up. . . ."

Upon which he let go a sonorous fart. Chronically disposed to gas, Mose had stuffed himself to excess at the banquet, which he was after all paying for. Tension had graduated to distress in his gut, aggravated to turmoil by the revelation of his uninvited guest's identity. Now that he'd allowed himself to slightly relax, the wind escaped him with the squeal of a slowly released balloon, then a flutter like a moist Bronx cheer.

Beyond a few gasps and unsuppressed titters among the children, there was stunned silence.

This was when Itchy, who'd circumnavigated the dining room, hugging the walls, seized the moment to spring to his father's side. Himself uncertain as to whether he intended to deliver the coup de grace or save the day—you never knew—he wrested the mike from Mose's stiff fingers. "That puts me in mind of the guy who poots in the hotel bathtub," he began, when the chord snapped free of its socket and Itchy fell backward into his father's vacated chair.

The chair toppled over, though not before Itchy'd glimpsed the host disappearing through a pair of swinging doors. In his absence the head table was in utter disarray. Plumped back in her chair, Tillie heaved a sigh so mighty as to waft her marmalade gown like a parachute. Brother David was standing, outrage vying with chagrin in his close-shaven features; then outrage triumphant, he signaled to the servants with the practiced aplomb of his father before him. The rabbi was trying to comfort Rose, who spat curses through her tears, while the groom and his parents stared forlornly into their crumb-strewn plates.

From either end of the table came the steward and his minions, accompanied by guests whose suits bespoke underworld attachments. Recovering from his pratfall, Itchy rose and vaulted over a floral centerpiece, then made at a sprint for the saloon doors that his father had lately passed through.

He upset a platter of picked carcasses, jostled uniformed chefs and maids (was that Hedda Bee on a stool ducking into an open scripture?), and dashed blindly out the back door. In the porte cochere Mose gunned the engine of a bottle green Lincoln Continental. When the car lurched forward, Itchy, hotfooting behind it, leapt on to the fender and embraced the mounted spare. Avoiding a driveway clogged with guest vehicles, Mose detoured across the lawn; he knocked over lanterns, careering downhill to the street, spinning tires and leaving a trail of screeching rubber in his haste to get away. Holding on with one arm, his tangled hair whipped by spring breezes, Itchy thumbed his nose at the men who followed from the house in pursuit.

Mose drove the city streets at death-defying speeds, switching lanes haphazardly, weaving in and out of traffic, taking corners on two wheels. But Itchy, although he had to hang on for dear life, was more exhilarated than afraid, the wild ride affording him an opportunity to gloat. What a shambles he'd made of his half sister's reception! And that the high and mighty Moses Kabakoff had humiliated himself, running away in disgrace—that was the frosting on the wedding cake. But even as he congratulated himself for squaring the record with a family that had as good as cast him out, Itchy wondered if revenge was his motive. Or had he merely been trying to get their attention?

"The bastards, they didn't even claim me after Tillie blew my cover!"

Try as he might, however, Itchy couldn't stay angry; he was enjoying his ride too much. He was delighted by his father's reckless slalom, the honks and shaken fists of the other drivers, their expressions when they saw the hairy figure fixed to the rear of the car. This was a homecoming to remember, so unlike the previous ones, when he'd looked through windows and felt only exquisite self-pity. Now, if he felt sorry for anyone, it was his fugitive father, whom he expected would get over it soon enough. After all, what had he done but break a little wind? Itchy snickered again to remember—damage like that, he supposed, knits itself pretty quick. Eventually Mose would slow down, pull over, take a walk to collect himself. Maybe Itchy would join him and they'd be reconciled over coffee at an all-night café. Or maybe Mose would never regain his dignity, his errant son compelled thereafter to lead him like a blind bear from place to place.

They were headed downtown, toward the river and the Cotton Carnival midway, when Mose veered abruptly south. He drove into a warehouse district in back of the train station, through dark streets beyond the reach of parades and festivities. Emerging on Riverside Drive, he hugged the bluff, then swerved up a ramp onto the Harahan Bridge. Itchy was admiring a claret moon above a broad expanse of black water, into which the skyline and the carnival lights poured molten gold. Then, halfway across the bridge, the car came to a sudden stop. The door opened and closed, and there were footsteps drowned in the shush of passing traffic, but by the time Itchy'd hopped off the fender to take a look, Mose had vanished over the rail.

II

c.1925–1938

As a boy on North Main Street, Moses Kabakoff was early fed up
with his family. His father, Yankel, was a special embarrassment
with his pudding-thick accent and yellow whiskers, his semiretired
withdrawal among his books. An old man already, he harped inces-
santly on the disasters of the Jewish past until he was blind to the
possibilities of the present day. Then there was Tillie, Mose's
broad-beamed mother, who despite her bustling practicality ran a
store whose outré merchandise was the laughingstock of the
neighborhood. If that wasn't enough, there were visiting relations—his uncles Enoch and Joseph, his disturbing Aunt
Laylah—who'd crowded Mose out of his own apartment. With no
visible means of support, they'd extended their stay for as long as
the boy could remember. Suspicious types all, they seemed to have
no surnames or to belong to any particular branch of the family,
though Tillie's chronic exasperation suggested that they must be
Kabakoffs.

It was no wonder that, after the age of ten or thereabouts,
Mose kept mainly to the streets. In this he was far from alone.

There was a whole new breed of kid in the Pinch who'd quite frankly had it with their parents' quaint Old Country ways. A number of them having also been shoved from their homes by shiftless relations, they were angry, and they expressed their general disgruntlement through acts of mischief and sabotage. They threw live catfish in the Russian baths and fastened corsets round the Torah scrolls, seeing which caused the sexton Mr. Supoznik to suffer convulsions. They trimmed the *mohel*'s famous fingernail as he slept and, in cheder, wrested his ferrule from the rabbi's hand, stomping it as they declared into a ploughshare. When Blockman the junk dealer had his May–December wedding, they sent his swayback mare, complete with bridal veil, hobbling down the synagogue aisle.

As they grew older, they had traded pranks for more fruitful enthusiasms. Some of the more idealistic embraced the coming age, as outlined in Workman's Circle pamphlets, and began hanging around with the freethinkers in Thompson's Café. But most of his cronies, Mose included, threw their energies into the real American enterprise of making a buck. They battled their gentile neighbors for the choicest corners to sell papers on, monopolizing the Pinch and commanding Main Street proper as far as Court Square. Those with bicycles ran delivery routes all over town, sometimes swapping their bikes for skiffs or inner tubes during flood season.

They scalped tickets and picked pockets during exhibition bouts at the Phoenix Athletic Club; booking bets on the side, they pooled their take to buy back more of the action. They owned a "piece," making crude speculations as to precisely which piece it was, of the homegrown welterweight Eddie "Kid" Katz. In a flotilla of dinghies they paddled across the river to the Mud Island still, where they haggled with bootleggers over a swill popularly known as "witch's piss." This they watered down even further to sell for twice its original price in the Beale Street fleshpots. They ran an illicit pipeline of policy numbers between

North Main Street and Beale, where his fellows often lost their lucre in crapshoots; they spent it on glad rags or caramel-skinned ladies in the rooms above the saloons. But not Mose.

Even then he was proud of his principled thrift, the horse sense that distinguished him from his screwball family. Let his mother stand behind a counter peddling unmentionables, his father bury himself in books, while their progressive son snatched from the teeth of the future all he had coming. Hadn't Mose heard it said more than once that limitless horizons were the birthright of his generation? Youthful exploits notwithstanding, at seventeen he thought it high time he found himself a career. After the Crash, where others persisted in what he'd come to regard as folly, Mose tightened his belt. Felonious sources of income having begun to dry up, he was lucky enough to snag a legitimate job, apprenticing himself to Felix Shendelman the printer.

Of course Mose's mother would have happily put him to work in Kabakoff's General Merchandise, but the place—with its freakish assortment of doll heads, Klondike caps, strangle food, and laughing cameras—had always depressed him. Besides, his dumb Uncle Joseph, so irrepressibly eager to please, was all the help that Tillie could stand.

Throughout the lean years Shendelman Specialty Printing managed to limp along. In fact, since desperation had driven many previously reluctant merchants to advertise, business wasn't half bad. Meanwhile Mose had made himself virtually indispensable. He'd learned slugcasting, lithography, letterpress, rotogravure; become fluent in a language whose specialized vocabulary included "quoin keys," "star wheels," "riglets," "mutts," "nutts," and "furniture." Seldom would you see him when his face and apron weren't soiled from the inks and chases, his fingers bandaged from grappling with machinery. Frequently keeping late hours, he grew accustomed to taking catnaps under the paper cutter, sometimes staying the night. In this way Mose was able to wean himself from the apartment, adopting the print shop as a second home, avoiding for days on end the muddle of the Kabakoff household.

He took to dodging the family, ducking out of sight whenever he saw one of them coming—Uncle Joseph, let us say, who, though well intentioned, could literally kill you with kindness. With a head the shape of a dented enamel doorknob, tiny eyes, and a thick hairless trunk like a sackful of cannonballs, he never seemed to know his own strength. All his life Mose had pleaded, "Uncle Joseph, do me a favor and don't do me no favors." But should the Pinch boys be outnumbered in a friendly brawl with the nearby Mackerel Gang, in would charge Mose's mute uncle, suspenders adroop. He'd lift the Irish kids in propeller spins and fling them all the way back to Goat Hill, thus spoiling everyone's fun. Send him for coal and he'd bring back a heap like Mount Sinai, for a chicken from Makowsky's market and he'd return with the coop. Let Tillie cry foul when some cracker tried to shortchange her in the shop, and Joseph would pick him up by the heels to shake out his pockets. The street still buzzed over his encounter with the boxing chimpanzee escaped from a carnival sideshow. It was an event after which even Kid Katz stepped aside for the dummy, and Jewel Pardue, on behalf of the local chapter of Ku Klux Klan, presented the Kabakoffs with a Hanukkah goose.

But where Joseph at least kept silent, Uncle Enoch on the contrary never seemed to know when to shut up. Him with his livid eyes and silver forelock, his mien of a dissipated matinee idol, sporting a seedy Prince Albert coat and puff cravat. Insufferably self-righteous, Enoch was forever boasting connections in high places, making references to some vague lofty status he'd held before an undeserved fall from grace. "All is vanity"—this was his favorite refrain, with himself a living reminder. He liked citing the more vengeful passages from scripture, the ones where God got even with man for his failings; though in his sanctimoniousness he often sounded to Mose like a man who meant to get even with God.

For all his carping, however, Uncle Enoch wasn't above helping himself to Yankel's store of bootleg schnapps. In his cups he was given to making amorous suggestions to any passing female, now and then stealing a pinch from the ladies who came into Kabakoff's. They would squeal—indignant, as in the case of the Widow Teitelbaum, though Mrs. Rosen tended toward covert glee—and Tillie would scold him: "Enoch, shame!" Then she would turn the reprobate out of doors. He usually went without protest, after which (much to Mose's relief) he might stay away for weeks at a time. But you could count on his turning back up when you least expected, looking chastened and the worse for wear, anyway until he'd recovered his bluster and started in crowing again.

Third in the trio of good-for-nothing relations was Aunt Laylah, whose charms Mose grudgingly admitted, though he was more scrupulous in avoiding her than either of his uncles. In a neighborhood where the least immodest accessory was remarked, Laylah dressed like a gypsy. "Like a poor man's Isadora Duncan," the ladies sneered. Where sensible shirtwaists over whalebone foundations were de rigueur, Aunt Laylah wore gauzy off-the-shoulder blouses, flounced skirts, and sandals with crisscrossed straps about her bare ankles. Where hair was pinned back or confined to snoods, she wore hers in loose midnight tresses, or gathered in crimson scarves to match her lips. She couldn't walk for sashaying her fluid hips while winking a dark amethyst eye at husbands whose wives would drive them indoors.

It was said that, before Mose's aunt, pretty girls in the Pinch had been ashamed of the distraction they caused. They were demure, hiding their lights behind a screen in the synagogue gallery, while the rabbi admonished the men to avert their eyes. But now, if anything they emulated Laylah, who never set foot in the synagogue, parading themselves past the show racks and liars' bench with scandalous hemlines, bold as you please.

She was certainly a different breed from the uncles, whose sister it was hard to believe she could be. Similarly, Mose was damned if he saw what brotherly traits Enoch and Joseph might have in common. As a kid he'd regularly appealed to his father to explain their precise relation to the visitors, the visitors' relation to one another. But Yankel's answers were so circumspect, so freighted with platitudes ("So maybe my zayde's rooster crowed in his grandmother's yard"), that Mose was always sorry he'd asked. In one respect, though, Aunt Laylah was like Uncle Enoch in that each shared the habit of disappearing for unpredictable intervals. "Good riddance," Mose would mutter each time she left, then count the days until she returned, more radiant than ever, a fact that made him feel jealous though he couldn't say why.

When he was little she'd been fond of teasing him, threatening to steal him from his bed and carry him away. "Where?" Mose would ask, wide-eyed and less skeptical in those days. Leaning close, she'd reply in a voice strangely musical despite its Old Country inflections: "To sitra achra, the other side, where the moon under the ground is bright like the sun, and the place where you come from you don't remember no more, only that it was black and white and flat like a page in a book." Then she would croon a lullaby without any words.

She was some piece of work all right. But as much as Mose in his childhood had admired her impish eye, her brimstone and gardenia scent, the rainbow sheen of her blue-black hair, that much did he resent her later on. In his mind she'd come to stand for everything that was queer and un-American about the Kabakoff clan. He even suspected that, during his wayward years, he'd been somehow under Aunt Laylah's influence, a perception that had helped him to break with his hooligan friends and seek out the more reputable situation at Shendelman's. As he did with regard to the rest of the family, Mose deplored his aunt's unconventional behavior, her indifference to gossip, her impetuousness; but most of all, now he was twenty-one, he deplored that she looked much the same as she had when he was twelve.

At night she sometimes invaded his dreams so that he woke up in degradation, his pajamas sticky and damp. This shouldn't happen to Moses Kabakoff. He was after all a regular guy, clean-living and foursquare, and not too bad-looking either. Pushing six feet, he was broad of shoulder and chest (and hip), with a scroll of wavy cinnamon hair—an appearance prompting comparisons, among women of his mother's generation, with the actor Boris Tomashefsky. You might have said he was quite a catch, and there were plenty of neighborhood girls to second the motion. Take that cute little slip of a Fannie Buderman, for instance, or the busty and much sought-after Berenice Malkin. Weren't they more than pleased to step out with him to such classy spots as the Masonic Building's roof garden, where they swayed to the dance magic of Elma Chigizola; or the moonlight serenades on board the Island Queen excursion boat? Penny-wise as he must be, Mose was no piker, nor were the girls unappreciative. Rather, they were keenly affectionate, lavish in their flattery.

"You're a mensch, Mister Kabakoff," they would tell him, tickling his chin with a feathered toque as they cozied up. "You'll go far."

But they all seemed frivolous when compared to his maiden aunt. Willing as they were, he didn't want them, and time and again he disappointed them by retreating into his single-minded industriousness. No amount of setting type or feeding spools of paper to insatiable rubber cylinders, however, could banish her entirely from his brain. More than the metallic-smelling inks or the pervasive stench of the river, her musk suffused the air he breathed. "It's unnatural," he told himself, though on the other hand, where did it say it was a sin to love your aunt? Only this, what he felt for Laylah, you couldn't exactly call love. In any case, Mose had no time for funny business; skills must be perfected, money socked away toward the day when he could quit this laughing academy they called the Pinch.

Meanwhile the atmosphere over North Main Street had grown somber. Members of Mose's old gang could be seen among the once exclusive ranks of luftmenschen, loitering on the corner in front of Jake Plott's barbershop. Their once brash manner, like that of the unshaven shopkeepers sitting carpet-slippered in front of their empty stores, was subdued.

Having settled into what promised to be a long apprenticeship, Mose waited out the hard times. Sometimes he wondered if, in a not too distant future, Mr. Shendelman might want to turn over his business to a younger man. Cultivating ambition, he suppressed his other desire, though it continued to annoy him like a wedged grain of sand aspiring to become a pearl. Still, for all his diligence, Mose wasn't unaware of the major tsimmes brewing in Europe, news of which had increased the general gloom. It seemed that over there his neighbors' friends and relations were being boycotted, legislated against, and driven into ruin. Then, according to rumors too numerous to ignore, they'd begun to disappear.

It was an event that turned out to be contagious. As if in sympathy with Jews abroad, the freeloading relations at home, those whose wornout welcomes had pushed an entire generation into the streets, were themselves beginning to vanish. Some of them had had offspring through ill-advised marriages or scandals, producing feckless, frequently misshapen children that were afterward persecuted as local figures of fun. Largely disclaimed by their parents, members of that unhappy brood tended to run away from home at an early age. But rather than follow the example of its missing issue, the first-generation moochers vanished not all at once but by degrees. This isn't to say they left a few at a time, but instead began to fade away until they were transparent in their very skins.

It happened like this: you'd see one of them on the sidewalk looking peaked—Sheldon Wolf's Aunt Mamie, say, who was under four feet in her shoes and pale as a yahrzeit candle on the best of days. Then you looked again and noticed how her face appeared to borrow the colors of whatever she passed by; it took on the burgundy of the bed jacket on a manikin in Zimmerman's window, the warpaint of the wooden Indian outside Levy's Candy Store. You saw a quarreling couple projected like a film on the forehead of Doc Seligman's swivel-eyed nephew, until you realized it was the Rosens bickering behind him across the street. It was the same with the others—Josh Bilsky's clubfooted Uncle Nasty, Sophie Mendelson's twin cousins Ruby and Max, gone plaid if they happened to be standing in front of a horse blanket, diagonally striped in front of a barber pole. None of them seemed to be comfortable with their newly acquired chameleon propensities, which the women tried to conceal with excessive cosmetics. The men donned extra clothing, long dusters, stocking caps, and gloves, muffling their faces like bandits despite the summer heat. But for all their efforts, they succeeded only in looking like fugitive coatracks, the women as if wearing empty masks, and in their mortification they began to flee the Pinch.

Due to the prevailing climate of fatalism, the citizens of North Main Street were beyond feeling awfully astonished. The old folks regarded the vanishing relations with a rueful melancholy, while their children and grandchildren, by no means uninterested in such an original method of departure, were far from sorry to see them go. Their longtime hostility toward "that bunch of spongers who do nothing but occupy space" had deepened throughout the dog years. Now it was with a certain albeit quizzical satisfaction that the young people witnessed their helpless fading.

"He don't hardly exist!" Thus Lenny Beard had exclaimed, indicating a practically vacant duffel coat belonging to his papa's putative stepbrother Al; only to be corrected by the more philosophical Nathan Siripkin. "He don't exist," said Nathan, taking the logic one step further, "never did. Fact is, he ain't even real."

It was a judgment that the majority of Mose's peers, himself among them, came to hold in common, and it made them feel somehow vindicated. Moreover, their stony dispassion, plus a willingness to forget the parasites once they were gone, seemed to accelerate the epidemic of dissolving.

Mose's own uncles and aunt were no exception. Uncle Enoch at first accepted his affliction with a stoicism that was itself transparent; he took the position, during its early stages, that semi-invisibility might have its advantages. This led him to show up more often in places where he had no business to be. But it hurt his pride that he was so little apprehended by the ladies, who naturally enough continued to shriek when he pinched their bottoms, then experienced no more than a wistful disappointment on turning around. Posed in front of mirrors, Enoch mourned his loss of definition, his spare but still prepossessing features faded to the merest outline, a circumstance that drove him to stop drinking. In the end he put aside all pretense of equanimity and invoked with unbridled bitterness the depths to which he'd fallen from his once celestial estate.

It was an unceasing lament that forced Tillie to stuff her ears, Yankel to scour his texts for good news, assuring the malcontent, "Together we will all of us be in the Book one day." Disconsolate, accusing everyone of having betrayed him, Uncle Enoch turned up his collar, pulled down his fedora as far as his pellucid nose, and left the Pinch for good.

Uncle Joseph hung on a bit longer. He was so busy with his self-appointed tasks—stoking the furnace until it belched like an erupting volcano, smothering a mildly interested customer in an avalanche of vicuna coats—that he scarcely noticed his own evaporation. Since his bumbling was habitual, it took him a while to realize that he was having trouble finding his fingers. In an effort to retard the process of petering out, he tripled his already prodigious intake of food, swallowing rafts of knishes, shoals of whitefish at a sitting. He butted doorposts, pummeled a head that was becoming as insubstantial as onion skin, as if violence to his person might restore his opacity. "Vos iz?" he would mouth in confusion, his tears more prominent than the pinprick eyes from which they swelled.

Tillie could only shake her head over her plundered larder, Yankel search in vain for some epigram. ("Like it says in Tractate Whatsit, disappearing ain't but a sixth part of death.") Even Mose, during his rare appearances in the apartment, felt sorry for Uncle Joseph, who'd been faithful after his fashion and had at least tried to earn his keep. But rather than offer sympathy—was it his problem?—Mose opted for the popular attitude, content to believe that Joseph had not been real in the first place. It was a sentiment that seemed to hasten his fading. When he was gone, vanished into thin air or fled before his total eclipse, Mose found it suddenly hard to remember what the dummy uncle had been like to have around.

With its diminished population the Pinch was never so quiet. Even the clatter of streetcars seemed reduced to a muted ticktock, and the newsboys, lest they be accused of bearing ill tidings, no longer cried the headlines aloud. The shopkeepers, with so few paying customers, didn't bother to hustle their wares anymore. This is more like it, thought Mose, though he knew better than to trust the tranquillity. For one thing, while he hadn't actually seen her, he knew that his Aunt Laylah was still around, her scent lingering in the sluggish air.

One afternoon, while delivering a bundle of flyers to Blockman's scrapyard at Auction and Front, Mose spotted her across the road on the river bluff. She was standing amid the blown milkweed and burdock, her floating hair and staring eyes clearly visible, though the rest of her seemed to have coalesced with the gunmetal floodplain beyond. The ghost of her former self, she was somehow more alluring than ever, and as he turned away, Mose discovered that what was spectral in his sight had already assumed a fierce substance in his mind's eye.

That night she entered his dreams again with a vengeance, as if disintegrating in one world gave her more currency in another. Mose woke up in a sweat under the paper cutter. To date he'd always enjoyed sleeping in the shop, and Mr. Shendelman, a widower, seemed amenable to having him nearby. There was a washroom in back, and on moonlit nights (like this one) the glow through the plate-glass windows blanketed the machinery in what looked like lavender moss. Lying beneath the table, whose mounted blade cast a shadow resembling a guillotine, Mose nevertheless felt perfectly cozy. Whatever mishegoss history might be cooking up across the waters, he was confident it couldn't touch him here.

Sometimes, however, the litany of horrors his father had chanted throughout his childhood would parade themselves uninvited through his head: the destruction of the Temple, the fall of Masada, the slaughter at the hands of the Crusaders, the Black Death massacres, the expulsion from Spain, Hetman Chmielnicki's pogroms. . . . If you repeated them enough, they might substitute for counting sheep, though this had never worked for Mose. He remembered that the lot of these nightmares were inscribed in the texts that, according to Yankel ("In the beginning was the Book"), made sense out of history—which certainly made no sense on its own. But Mose had no patience with books or history, just as he had no use for his maiden aunt, who spoiled his rest and infected him with a passion that mocked his conscientious enterprise.

Speak of the devil: when he opened his eyes, he could almost believe he saw her standing over his pallet, or at least her aromatic shade, three parts moonlight to one part heated blood. Then he realized that this was no phantom, her very translucence arguing the fact that she was real.

"How'd you get in here?" snapped Mose, banging his head on the underside of the worktable as he sat up. The doors were locked, the washroom window barred.

Aunt Laylah shrugged, allowing a fringed silk shawl to slip from her bare shoulders to the floor. "Call me Houdini," she said.

Naked but for an undershirt and boxer shorts, Mose wrapped his sheet tightly about him and crawled out from under the table. He took a stance with his back to the paper cutter, which seemed suddenly to menace from behind, and slid away from Laylah.

"You gotta go," he told her anxiously, glancing out the shop window as if wary despite the small hour of passersby. "Shendelman'll pitch a fit."

She laughed, tossing a mane of dark hair that was as scintillant as northern lights. "Didn't you notice, nephew," she twitted him, "I ain't hardly here."

"Then take what's left of you and scram!" Mose was amazed at his own belligerence.

"Nephew," she replied in the voice that swallowed the canary, "do your Tante Laylah a favor, why don't you."

She took a step closer, her comely form so vaporous that Mose thought he might be able to inhale her. "Leave me alone," he sulked, scooting farther away; then he borrowed some courage from what had lately become the watchword of his generation: "You can't fool me, you don't even exist."

At that she did indeed appear to fade another degree or two. She tried to compensate by broadening her smile, leading with her hips as she took another step forward.

"Moses supposes his toeses are roses," she whispered, reviving a rhyme she'd teased him with in his infancy.

Nonplussed, Mose lost his grip on the sheet but quickly drew it up again, girding it tighter around his loins. Having turned the corner at the edge of the table, he was backed against a bulletin board on the wall.

Still smiling, Laylah sighed and inclined her head. When she lifted her chin, Mose detected in her misting features—even her inky tendrils were dulled to spun-glass—a sadness he'd never seen in them before. He was studying her so hard that he looked clean through her, to the relic of a flatbed press and the gilt-edged SHENDELMAN'S SPECIALTY logo across the window. Then he squinted to get her back in focus, observing how the sadness was itself evanescent, and beyond it you could see she was afraid. All at once Mose understood that she was at his mercy; he could order her out of his life forever and she would have to go. But perceiving her fear had the effect of dispelling his own, and her frailty, complementing his power, made him desire his aunt all the more.

"Moishe," she was pleading, "I don't want to disappear."

She made a pathetic little gesture of surrender, shucking her skirt and petticoat in the process, peeling her embroidered blouse off over her head. Now she was phosphorous, a silver stain on the otherwise grainy blue atmosphere of the shop. More pronounced than even her brimming eyes, her coral nipples, her maidenhair, was the tiny, scarablike mole on her upper arm. "A love bite a bad angel give me," she'd once told her nephew when he was small.

The fact that scarcely enough woman remained for him to want only served to exacerbate Mose's longing. He held open the sheet, making wings to enfold them both, praying he would embrace more than air. There was warmth all right, and a sufficiency of lady-shaped suppleness that made him cry out, biting her hair to stifle the sound. Still it came, an attenuated groan such as the heart might make if you squeezed it like a rubber bulb. Then Mose felt that his resolve, his ambition—everything, in short, that he identified as himself—had escaped along with that groan; and the guy who was touching his nearly intangible aunt with electric fingers, pulling her down onto the iron bed of a greasy printing press, was nobody he knew. A ferocious nobody, just this side of pure instinct, who blurted such avowals as,

"I take it all back, don't nothing else exist but you!"

Aunt Laylah responded with a weird whistling exhalation of her own. Her smooth limbs surrounded him with their pungent ectoplasm, and while her breath cooled, her tongue scalded the tunnel of Mose's ear. Still convinced that he shouldn't go to blazes without a struggle, Mose continued to give as good as he got. He rolled them both from the unpliant rack of the printing press so that they tumbled off into Laylah's discarded clothes. In his transports, however, Mose could scarcely believe that, with all he now had of his aunt—"a spinster" she liked to call herself—he wanted more. He needed something more material than this diaphanous shadow; and his own heat, he decided, must be the agent to stir her flickering into a conflagration. But for all his urgency Laylah remained a gossamer wraith.

Groping behind him in a drowning man's motion, Mose found the storage shelf under the press, his hand making contact with the tubs of colored ink. He stretched to turn a key that popped the lid on one of the tubs. Reaching in, he scooped up a fistful of the mud-thick, resin-based ink and smeared it over his fluctuating aunt. Instantly she broke into arpeggios of throaty laughter.

Mose trembled sympathetically as he stroked her shoulders and breasts, giving her substance and form as he spread the ink. But the color he'd chosen must have been a deep blue, because although her body (as in some dark brass rubbing) became more opaque, it also merged more completely with the enveloping shadows. Undiscouraged, Mose remembered his boss's dictum: "Your three primary colors, that they can reconstitute all the other colors of the spectrum." Here he reached for a second sealed tub, sprung the lid, and dipped in. This time it must have been yellow, since details of his aunt—her left profile, a half-chevron of ribs below a breast, her sunken abdomen—were highlighted under his firm caress.

"You ain't invisible no more," he panted.

"Nu," said Laylah through her hilarity, "so rub it in!"

He carried on finger-painting his undulant canvas, feeling as if he'd wrung a secret from the very air. Then Mose saw that he was perhaps overdoing it, having heightened her color to an unnatural antimony. Not to worry, he told himself, stretching to scoop more ink from yet a third container, even as she tugged his shorts to his ankles and tore the undershirt off his back. With what he knew to be cardinal red he was endeavoring to subdue her starkness, daubing and kneading while she returned his gestures playfully. When he paused to catch his breath, the moonlight surprised him with a revelation of his handiwork: the tousle-headed harlequin creature he'd created. It made Mose wonder how she could still manage to inspire, despite his terror, his adoration.

Aunt Laylah interrupted her friskiness to offer him a savage grin. "Good job, nephew," she hissed. "Now I take you to yenne velt, the other world, which from here you can't get to except on a magical broomstick ride."

1939–1941

During his Aunt Laylah's unending pregnancy, Mose Kabakoff lay low, beyond the reach of idle tongues. News of the war in Europe, whether shouted at him from headlines or muttered from the mouths of local refugees (who'd begun to replace the vanished freeloaders), fed his disgrace until he felt somehow partly to blame. Meanwhile, with her color having rosily returned, his aunt disported herself on North Main Street at every opportunity. She was proud of her tumescent condition, self-possessed in bright maternity smocks, and if at all hurt by her nephew's avoidance, she never showed it. She gave the impression that, for her, being pregnant was an end in itself, and in fact, nine months having come and long gone, Laylah was now well into her second year.

Throughout her bold-faced gestation, Mose stayed holed up in Shendelman's, the former hostage to his own ambition become a prisoner of shame. He worked day and night, seldom slept, and lost weight, though nothing he did could make him feel he was making amends. Meanwhile, as if deliberately adding salt to his wounds, he kept an ear glued to H. V. Kaltenborn's baleful broadcasts on his boss's console radio.

Then the Japs bombed Pearl Harbor and all at once history presented itself as a way out of his fix: here was the chance to leave the Pinch and expiate his guilt at a single blow. It occurred to Mose he'd been a coward; the way he'd been hiding out from recent events, you'd have thought he bought his father's version of history—that it was nothing but a cavalcade of atrocities you escaped by living in the Book. Book-shmook, if anything could save you from life's incursions, it was money. But despite his long apprenticeship, Mose had yet to accumulate enough of a nest egg to start his own business. In the meantime he'd succumbed to an indiscretion that, beyond its obvious consequences, had made him an object of gossip and ridicule. Now, rather than try and elude the real world, which seemed to have found him in any case, Mose was eager to jump in with both feet. It was a solution to his problems he shared with most of the restless and largely unemployed young men in the neighborhood.

Entering his parents' schmaltz-fragrant apartment after dinner one evening, Mose announced, "In the morning I enlist." It had been months since he'd so much as taken a meal with the family, preferring to dine at Rosen's Deli or share some tinned salmon with Mr. Shendelman in his rooms over the print shop. Together they would pass a peaceful hour (peace having been in scarce supply at the Kabakoffs), listening to "The Court of Human Emotions" and Paul Whiteman's orchestra following the news.

"Mama, who's there?" called Yankel from his study.

Busy at the kitchen sink, Tillie looked over her shoulder toward the stranger in the doorway. "I think it's the prophet Elijah bringing us a bagful of shekels," she shouted to her husband. "Sit down, Elijah," she said, turning back to the sink as she uttered her stock greeting. "Have some noodles and sour cream, you look terrible."

"I ate already," challenged Mose.

Tillie was pouring a box of jade-green Epsom salts into an enamel basin filled with steaming water. This she placed at the feet of a flushed Aunt Laylah sitting slouched in a tatted smock at the kitchen table, her gravid belly like a dinosaur egg in her lap. Generally intolerant of the foolishness of boarders, Tillie had nonetheless doted on Laylah from the moment her condition was made known, and for her part the formerly maiden aunt accepted these attentions as her rightful due. She sighed blissfully, blowing strands of corkscrewing hair from her forehead while Tillie placed her swollen feet in the bath. Opening her eyes, she gazed at Mose with an undisguised fondness. It was the look he'd been dodging since their night together at Shendelman's, the one (so out of character) that left no question as to whose child she was heavy with.

"Cut it out!" snapped Mose, so that Tillie, again at the sink, turned abruptly around. "Who does she think she's kidding?" said Mose defensively.

Laylah bent her head to resume studying a dogeared edition of *Duties of the Heart* that lay open on top of her breathing belly. This was in keeping with the pantomime of piety she'd commenced since finding herself in the family way.

Then old Yankel, wire spectacles propped on his parchment brow, book in hand, padded in to investigate. "Feh," he said on discovering, instead of a prophet, his estranged only son.

"Look," Mose huffed, unbuttoning the button at his throat, "maybe you didn't hear me. Tomorrow morning I'm joining the army. I just stopped by to pick up some things and say so long."

Tillie waddled over to tuck a napkin in his collar. "Eat first," she commanded, shoving him into the chair facing Laylah, "then go to war."

"What war?" asked Yankel, plainly indignant at not having been informed.

"Oh funny," said Mose, "very funny. They're murdering the Jews and he wants to know what war."

"Nu, Moishe, since when don't they murder the Jews?"

This was too much. "Take your head out of the sand for once!" Mose shouted, throwing his napkin into the plate of noodles that Tillie had set in front of him. "This ain't just another one of your tall tales! Don't you know that civilization itself is at stake?" And for a few seconds he trembled in a fervor of righteous conviction: not for nothing had they named him Moses. Rather than merely running away to save himself further embarrassment, he was marching off to defend a persecuted people—that was it.

"Civilization?" mulled Yankel, as if he hadn't heard of it either. "Ain't civilization the bad dream you would wake up from when you wake up in the Book? It's like he says, the Rabbi Simon bar Yohai in *Midrash ha-Something.* You know what he says?"

Mose rolled his eyes. "No, what?"

Yankel raised a crooked forefinger and opened his mouth, then bent the finger to his temple, becoming pensive. "I'll go and see," he said, padding back down the hall toward his study.

Shaking his head, Mose complained to the water-stained ceiling, "This place is a bughouse." He stood up from the table only to have Tillie sit him back down again with a heavy hand.

"Don't talk like this ain't your home," she scolded, taking the dishrag from her shoulder to give him a swat. "Besides," Tillie cast a hesitant but meaningful glance toward Laylah, still serene in her reading, "you got responsibilities."

"What? Her?" Mose feigned incredulity. "She's not even human." He braced himself for the inevitable explosion, but instead of rebuking him Tillie just shrugged, as if what did "human" have to do with the price of eggs. Then she matter-of-factly stated the unspeakable,

"She carries your child."

"Child!" gasped Mose; he was getting excited. "You don't know what she's got in there. Give it a thump, it's maybe hollow. Maybe she turned into a hunchback in front—her kind can do that!"

Here Laylah looked up from her book with an expression of such withering defiance that Mose swallowed and felt himself shrink in his chair.

Yankel reappeared from the hallway with his glasses riding the tip of his nose. "Mama, you married a shmo," he confessed, "I have it in my hand all the time." Then he began to read haltingly. "'Man was created for the purpose of working at Torah.' So says Rabbi Simon, then adds Rabbi Barukh, 'In raising up the words to the Lord, blessed be He, you return them to their source.' This, according to Rabbi Elimelekh, is the essence of teshuvah, which it means repentance. . . ."

Mose got to his feet again, bellowing, "Let me out of here!" But before he could reach the door, Laylah herself unloosed a piercing cry, not unlike the ones he'd tried to muffle that night in the print shop. He turned to see how her body had gone rigid and splayed, as if her stomach were a stone she was pinned beneath. When she relaxed, the water poured from under her saturated smock like bilge from a pump. Watching, Mose was also doubled over, confused to find that he shared her pain, that the fear that twisted her ardent face likewise contorted his own. From where, he wondered, came this abrupt change of heart, that even more than he wanted to put an ocean between himself and the Pinch, Mose should suddenly want to save his aunt, which amounted (in the logic that now gripped him) to saving himself.

"Moishele," called Tillie, redoubling the knot of her hairnet in preparation for action, "be a good boy and run get Gittel Dewlap! So what are you waiting for?"

Still nailed to the spot by his gut-ache, Mose managed to suggest, "Don't you think Doc Seligman . . .?"

"This ain't Seligman's speciality. Now go!"

As Yankel began to rock in prayer, Tillie helped the stricken Laylah to stand. Risen from her chair, she cried out again, this time with a high haunted flutey sound that was half a laugh. Mose had to hold on to the doorjamb until it passed. Before leaving he looked to see that her sable hair, tumbled from the modest bun she'd tied it up in, was turning to snow.

He fetched the midwife from her dogtrot on Auction Street and together they made their way back to the apartment in the early autumn drizzle. A bewhiskered old eyesore in a kerchief and oilskin coat, wearing men's brogans, Gittel Dewlap was so named for the folds of flesh that hung in lizard wattles from her chin. She was what mothers had threatened naughty children with since before Mose was born, saying, "Do your business or Gittel Dewlap comes to give you a enema." Later on the kids themselves would invoke her in their taunts: "Louie and Gittel sittin' in a tree / k-i-s-s-i-n-g," though her sudden appearance reduced the boldest to silence. Even tonight Mose had balked before pounding at the vine-hidden door of her lamplit shack, but on his aunt's behalf he'd screwed up his nerve.

She rattled along with her wooden hamper at such a pace that Mose found it hard to keep up. As she walked she muttered to herself as if rehearsing the lines of a performance she was about to give. Then they'd climbed the stairs and entered the Kabakoff flat, where she plunked down her hamper; straightaway she began producing items whose virtues she cited peddler-wise, in a voice alarmingly like a little girl's.

"I got your birthwort for the easy labor, which I'm picking it myself by the crossroads that they hang the shwartzes at Fourth and Vance . . ."

Tillie greeted the hag in mid-bustle. Having unfolded some fabric screens around the hide-a-bed in the parlor, she was on her way to the kitchen where a kettle was whistling. Still she paused long enough to accept a soiled pamphlet from Gittel, along with the exhortation, "It's the piss-alter that you should read in it number thirty-seven, that's the one about the bad seed, out loud." To Mose's astonishment, as she proceeded toward the kitchen, his ordinarily imperious mama obeyed. He was further confounded when the old woman called to the study, "Yankel, put on your Shabbos suit," and his father emerged soon after in his gabardines. She handed him a ball of red twine, saying that he should tie one end to a leg of the birthing bed, the other to the Holy Ark in the synagogue; and though he rarely ventured out of doors these days, Yankel nevertheless did as he was told. He backed out of the apartment unraveling the twine, which if nothing else, thought Mose, would assure him of finding his way home.

As he stood there agog, the midwife gave Mose a scrolled scrap of paper that she told him to stick in the mezuzah. He unrolled it to see, instead of the Hebrew he'd expected, an inscription reading: SATUR AREPO TENET OPERA RUTAS. "What's this nonsense?" he wanted to know. Having removed her scarf to give her wattles free sway, Gittel Dewlap answered that it spelled the same backward and forward, as if that explained anything. When she'd scurried behind the screens, followed by Tillie with an armload of towels, Mose wadded the paper and threw it to the floor. Then, in a voice unmistakeably his aunt's, came a volley of incomprehensible syllables, some snatches of Yiddish gutter slang, and a series of cries that rattled the windowpanes. Mose promptly picked up the paper and stuffed it into the tarnished brass talisman on the doorpost.

The cries kept coming at regular intervals, but although they were no less terrible, each was slightly diminished in volume from the one before. Each sounded farther away. Biting his lip, Mose picked a path through the clutter of parlor furniture and approached the fabric screens. Behind them he could hear Tillie at her psalm-singing, interrupting herself to adjure the patient, "Laylah, sweetheart, if you don't want to plotz, bear down!" He heard Gittel promise, "I got here a nice piece felt, that when I would light it and hold under your nose, you will sneeze the little pishtippel out. I got also a spider web poultice to put after on your knish. . . ." Then Mose took a breath and poked his head around the corner of the screens.

His mama and the midwife were on either side of the bed, ministering to the prostrate woman, her smock rucked up to her breasts, her legs spread like a blanched letter *M* with its valley aflame. But how could this be his Aunt Laylah for whom Mose ached in such mutual travail? Because this one was old, older even than Gittel Dewlap, so old that there was less of her in this world than another—which perhaps explained why she was nearly transparent. Her hair was watery milk, her face a damp tissue, torn where her toothless mouth gaped open; her flesh was wrinkled cellophane except where it was stretched smooth over the dome of her belly. It was toward her belly that the midwife directed her attentions, rubbing it in circles like a crystal ball until its cloudy interior came clear. Then you could see the wizened creature within trying to nudge its way among the living, scrambling to escape its bloody burst bubble or drown in the attempt.

That's when Mose understood why she'd been in no hurry to have her baby, his aunt, since the thing could only arrive on North Main Street at the expense of its mother's banishment to someplace else. Beside himself with panic, he began to bawl,

"Don't let it loose, Aunt Laylah! Don't let go!"

"Moishe, shah!" scowled Tillie, flinging a wet compress at his head, as Gittel fixed on him her reptilian eye. "Do us a mitzvah," she said, suggesting that he go down to the graveyard and petition the dead to intervene. "Tell them, kinnehora, a speedy delivery."

At the kitchen table Mose hid his face in his hands, cursing superstition. What went on in this house, it was a crime against nature, and his own family were the guiltiest accessories. Trying hard not to listen, he still heard her wrenching cries, though they grew fainter even as they became more frequent, as if the sufferer were falling down a long hole. Meanwhile the rain outside had picked up, turning into a regular deluge, pelting the window till what remained of the birth pangs was drowned by the noise.

Mose raised his head. "Laylah?" he quizzed himself. "Why, I don't believe I ever made the acquaintance of any such person." Nor could he recall, Your Honor, a distant night in Shendelman's when she'd allegedly stripped his soul from his flesh like bones from a fish, and carried it off. Where they'd gone in their rapture ("Where the black pepper grows," she'd said), he couldn't say, never having been there; but although it perhaps wasn't heaven, it would do in the absence of same. It was the place he supposed she was going to now, and God help him, Mose wished that she could take him along.

Then there was a new noise in the apartment, muted but not entirely silenced by the storm—a strident hiccuping caterwaul. With a heart like a kettledrum, Mose was once again drawn to the parlor, where his mama and the midwife were trading folk wisdom behind the screens. "An only son," this was the cautionary Gittel, "is already half a heretic." And Tillie, sanguine, "A son can be sometimes a healthy affliction." Mose could almost believe they were talking about him until he turned the corner, peering over the old lady's stooped shoulders. This time he saw his mama seated on the bed, its sheets rumpled but otherwise showing not a trace of a recent ordeal. In her brawny arms Tillie rocked a wailing little homunculus.

"Mazel tov," she chirped, offering her son the infant, its cauled head and birdlike torso, simian arms and legs, covered in what appeared to be dark thistledown. "You got for yourself a fine baby boy."

Mose waited for neither the dawn nor the cessation of the rain before packing a bag to head for the nearest recruiting station.

"What'll we call him?" Tillie had appealed to his departing back.

"I should care," replied Mose without stopping, though as an afterthought he submitted, "How 'bout Jocko."

"That's a name for a monkey," barked Tillie, who got for an

answer an echo from the tiled vestibule at the base of the stairs.

"If the shoe fits-its-ts . . ."

But when Yankel came home from the synagogue, he proposed that they name the baby Yitzkhok, because to look at him made you laugh.

III

c. 1870

In his muddy market village of Shatsk on the River Dnestre in the
Russian Ukraine, the young Yankel Kabakoff was a scholar of
some renown. He was reading the weekly Torah portion by the age
of four and at six was already fluent in Rashi's commentaries. By
age eight he was so skillful at disputation that he could oppose
with equal zeal the famous arguments of Rabbi Hillel against
Rabbi Shammai or Shammai against Hillel. Sometimes he pro-
pounded arguments refuting them both. For his talents he was
deemed by many a second Ben Sira, the prodigy conceived when
Jeremiah's daughter bathed in a pool where the prophet had been
forced to spill his seed. At twelve, on the eve of his bar mitzvah,
Yankel was rumored to be composing a commentary to the
Tractate Berekhot, its pages stacked to the height of Goliath's eye.
It was reported (though there was as yet no evidence) that he
studied mysterious books, such as Rabbi Cordovero's *Looking
Glass,* and could conjure angels and demons, construct artificial
men. Needless to say, he had long since outstripped the dour

Rabbi Kirsky, who lorded it over the other boys in the ramshackle study house.

By comparison with his fellows at Rabbi Kirsky's "academy"—a combined cheder and yeshiva where a motley assortment of ages was crammed into a single stuffy room—Yankel was sturdy and hale. The truth was that he had no business among them, having advanced far beyond the curriculum, but the nearest formal seminary was miles away in Kharkov, and Yankel wasn't ready to leave home. Besides, he was fond of what he liked to call "our local community of scholars," where he was not above showing off.

Although the other boys had aged prematurely from the tedium of study, their bodies bent, eyes like dead embers, sidelocks spiraling like sprouts from their potato heads, Yankel thrived in the bookish atmosphere. He was straight-backed and clear-eyed, with a blush to his milk-fed cheeks, a thick shock of copper hair beneath his kipah. The others were full of involuntary spasms, flinching from the constant threat of the rabbi's cane; they struggled against letting their attention stray toward the window, trying not to look out past the crazy configuration of fish-reeking hovels and listing onion domes. Beyond them lay the river lined with birch groves and goldenrod, the hop fields sprinkled with scarlet poppies, which the boys tried hard not to imagine. But Yankel remained immersed in his studies, appearing literally to feast on the words of Torah. He read so intensely it was said that the pages faded under his perusal, so thoroughly did he absorb the essence of Holy Writ. Indeed, to those students who dared to suggest that the solution to their problems was not Torah but a flight from their wornout town, who proposed a wholesale return to Palestine, Yankel's answer was always the same:

"The text is our homeland."

For such remarks the Shatsker folk would point him out to visitors on market days, saying of him, "That one, he lives in the

Book. He'll make a tzadik, wait and see." His proud parents, Malkeh and Shlomo the Scribe, spoiled and indulged him, providing their son with what meager luxuries they could afford. A ruddy-faced, sweet-dispositioned woman, Malkeh was forever stuffing him with compotes and almond bread. As noted for her needlework as her kichel, which the baker arranged to buy from her, she quilted his yarmulkes in gay mosaics; she dyed the fringes of his prayer shawl with an ink the peddler insisted was secreted from sea monsters that surfaced only once every seventy years. In anticipation of his coming of age, his father Shlomo, with elaborate ceremony, had bestowed on Yankel his prized possession: the phylacteries that had belonged to his father's father's cousin twice removed, a not-so-distant relation of the Seer of Ostropol. He'd replaced the dead leaves of the verses inside them with new ones in his elegant hand.

It seldom occurred to either of them that their son had reached an age when other boys were apprenticed to blacksmiths or packed off to lumber mills and (God forbid) pigskin factories. What need had a genius like Yankel of learning a trade? He was after all considered such a catch, his praises sung so far and wide, that the matchmakers came from Kishinev and Odessa to make offers. They came as ambassadors from wealthy merchants whose daughters were veritable princesses, their dowries large enough to purchase kingdoms. But if his parents were in no hurry to see him married, Yankel himself was just as reluctant to enter an affiliation that might distract him from study. "After the wedding it's too late for regretting," he cited often, paraphrasing a proverb of Isaac the Blind. In time he would of course take a bride, if only to give him the ballast prescribed by Talmud for pursuing otherwise forbidden branches of learning.

This was in the years after the passing of the iron czar Nicholas, during the reign of Alexander, called the Little Father, who freed the serfs and initiated benign policies toward the Jews. He authored legislation allowing Jews to attend universities and practice professions outside the Pale of Settlement. In some instances they were even permitted to buy land and give testimony on their own behalf in courts of law. Best of all, he reduced their term of military service from the virtual death sentence of thirty years to five. Gone were the days of juvenile conscription, of the *khapers* who'd come to replace the goblins and fiends of grandmothers' tales. These were Jewish thugs paid by Jewish councils to snatch Jewish children from their families (usually at night but sometimes in broad daylight on their way to school) and turn them over to the army of the czar.

Not that all was schnapps and sponge cake in the world of the shtetl. There were still military quotas to be filled, boys torn from their lessons, their earlocks shorn, silk tallises exchanged for stiff uniforms. Many were said to have been baptized and were in any case never heard from again. Some Shatskers held that "a hidden hand" was operating behind the czar's back, making sure that abuse of the Jews was kept alive, and it was furthermore rumored that certain *landsmen* collaborated. ("Our rabbis and bigshots are in cahoots/ teaching our kids to be recruits," the song went.) The rich could still pay to have the poor sent in place of their own. As a consequence, if they weren't already damaged enough from poverty, families might further mutilate their sons; they might starve and dismember them, puncture their eardrums, expose them to the elements in the hope of their becoming consumptive and thus ineligible for the draft.

But Yankel, who spent his days resolving knotty legal questions and interpreting miraculous parables, was oblivious to it all. Ignoring anything that might interfere with his close scrutiny of sacred texts, he paid scant attention to the boys missing digits or coughing up blood. He likewise disregarded the ancient veterans of Fonya's army, kidnapped from their cradles and returned decades later like tongue-tied prophets. You'd see them sagging from the weight of rusty medals, hanging about the footbridge or the synagogue as if looking for their misplaced lives. Toward them, Yankel was as indifferent as he was to cherry blossoms or cornflowers or peasant girls in the flooded fields across the river, their skirts kilted to their thighs. To notice would anyway have been sinful, requiring as it must that he lift up his eyes from his books.

Of all those who paid homage to the prodigy, none was more lavish in his praise than Rabbi Kirsky himself. With fawning blandishments he held up Yankel to the other academy students as a young Akiva or Maimonides, a second Daniel. Over the years he'd welcomed the many occasions when the boy undertook to correct his teacher's discourse, a tribute to the success of the rabbi's instruction. He must have received, humbly, a multitude of such contradictions throughout the course of Yankel's illustrious career. Inevitably, however, there came an afternoon, just before the scholar's thirteenth birthday, when having swallowed a surfeit of assaults on his authority, the rabbi choked. A baggy-eyed compact little man, with an upturned beard like the toe of a harem slipper, Rabbi Kirsky discovered that he'd had all he could stand of the impertinent Kabakoff brat.

It happened in a balmy September near Rosh Hashonah, the season when reasonably healthy lads of military age were subject to immediate induction into the Imperial Army. (Yankel himself, when he thought of it, was confident he wouldn't be called up, concerned citizens having established a fund to buy his exemption.) In the study house, while his charges squirmed on hard benches and picked splinters from their behinds, Rabbi Kirsky had launched into a long-winded disquisition. This one was in reference to a page of Mishnah, wherein Rabbis Nathan and Eliezer debated whether the mythical golem should be allowed to participate in a quorum of worshippers.

"In the end they concur," declared the teacher, pretending to gaze out the window, though the class was aware he had eyes in the back of his head, "that the corpus of a counterfeit being is second only in impurity to that of a woman immediately following childbirth. Therefore he may not join the minyan." To punctuate the point, he turned sharply and cracked his reinforced rod over the shoulder of Braineh's Hershie, who was snoring at the foot of the table.

Then Yankel Kabakoff begged to differ. He rose from the book-laden table, his coat adorned in velvet patches, an embroidered yarmulke riding the crest of his wavy hair. A fine figure of a boy, if a little pudgy, he stood a head taller than his teacher, his voice raised above the creaking chairs, the bleating and crowing from the market outside.

"Rabbi Gershon, Light of the Diaspora," he began, "clearly states in response to Tractate Hagigah, generally recognized to have authority over the Semahot which you quote, that by virtue of the divine breath vested in him, never mind the holy stamp on his forehead—this is the *emet* for 'truth,' though some sources mention the four-headed letter *shin*—the golem should be a welcome addition to any ritual gathering."

That was when Rabbi Kirsky decided enough was enough. The many bitter pills he'd so often ingested, along with the groats he'd had for breakfast, seemed finally to have backed up on him. They filled his craw and distended the pouches of his cheeks, so that the students braced themselves for an explosion. But instead the rabbi only swallowed, emitted a quiet belch, and turned a sickly shade of chartreuse. He thanked Yankel for enlightening them with his usual perspicacity and dismissed the class.

Later that evening, after having sought advice from on high, Rabbi Kirsky paid a visit to the home of Reb Bimko the salt merchant. Like every other dwelling in that narrow street, known as Needle's Eye Alley, Reb Bimko's had a modest facade. Pale azure paint blistered on roughcast walls; rotting roof shingles exposed the laths beneath them, the mossy eaves providing a purchase for barking dogs. But this was just a front to keep from antagonizing the gentiles. Ducking under a lintel, you were led by a servant into sumptuously appointed apartments with rich carpets and tapestries, brass lamps and gilt-framed paintings overhanging the cushioned divans. On a sideboard spice boxes clustered like a miniature city around a silver samovar. Then you were greeted by Reb Bimko, the householder, who dressed conservatively during business hours but decked himself out like a pasha in the privacy of his domain. "Like God in Odessa," as the townspeople were given to say.

On Rabbi Kirsky's mind was the subject of Reb Bimko's wastrel son Henich, who was due to report to the induction center at the end of the month. It would cost his father a small fortune to procure his freedom. Also in the rabbi's thoughts was the undying grudge the salt merchant held against the Kabakoff family. This had come about when Reb Bimko sent Zalman the matchmaker to Yankel's father with the offer of his daughter Shifra's hand in marriage. As aware as anyone of Shifra's reputation, the scribe had been undiplomatic. "My son should want the cheap local stuff when he can have his pick of expensive imports?" he said. Zalman dutifully reported his answer to the merchant, though not before confiding it to half the inhabitants of Shatsk along the way. Humiliated, Reb Bimko had never forgiven the Kabakoffs, and it was his continuing resentment that the rabbi counted on tonight.

As he sat at the oiled mahogany table taking some peppermint kvass with the salt merchant, Rabbi Kirsky wasted no time in raising the issue of the draft: how it was highway robbery, this business of buying your children out of armed service.

"A king's ransom," conceded Reb Bimko, heaving a sigh that made his belly ebb and flow beneath his watered silk caftan, "but what can one do?"

The rabbi nodded in sympathy, then leaned a little closer, the tip of his beard like a beckoning finger. "Why give your hard-earned rubles to Haman," he said in accordance with the clerical tradition of answering questions with questions, "when you can do us all a mitzvah by keeping them here in Shatsk?"

At that moment Reb Bimko's wife, Feiga Tamara, a woman with a glued-on grin and a terraced wig like Madame Pompadour, entered with a tray of ginger pastries. Her husband waved her away impatiently, then bit into one of the morsels, frosting his charcoal whiskers with powdered sugar. He shoved the tray toward Rabbi Kirsky as if to say, Your deal.

The rabbi continued in a voice arch with implication. "Shmuel One-Eye the teamster, poor man, I'm told he's having a very slow season."

The merchant unfurrowed his brow as light dawned. Consolidating his various seamy operations, the notorious Shmuel had organized a syndicate of local gonifs and toughs. For a negotiable fee they would seize the sons of poor families and turn them over as replacement conscripts for their betters. This had not been lately such a lucrative sideline, however, because there remained so few young paupers that the army hadn't already claimed for its own.

A nod being as good as a wink to a man of Reb Bimko's shrewdness, he'd taken the rabbi's hint to its irresistible conclusion: he might save his son and settle with his enemies at a single blow. Now it was the merchant's turn to lean forward conspiratorially.

"Nu, so you think Herr Shmuel could use my business?"

"I think," replied Rabbi Kirsky, "that he and his would bless your name, that we should see it inscribed in the Book of Life for a prosperous year."

Having reached an understanding, the two men clinked glasses and sipped in satisfied silence, interrupted only when Reb Bimko muttered, "That Kabakoff k'nacher, that bigmouth, he's too good for my daughter? So let him be the Czar's son-in-law."

No sooner were arrangements made than the deed was set in motion, though some weeks would pass before it was done. First the Days of Awe had to be gotten through, when even criminal activities were suspended. Then, Shmuel and his boys being strictly professional, there was the matter of learning Yankel's routine in order to determine the optimum moment to nab him. Of course his movements to and from the synagogue, the bathhouse, and the bet hamidrash couldn't have been more predictable. But while he usually walked alone with his nose in a book, his feet in Ukrainian mud and his head as it were in Jerusalem, he seldom frequented other than public places. En route he made his way through a tortured concatenation of alleys, but to snatch him from these would have meant lugging him some distance to a waiting wagon. He crossed the market platz, an unholy babble of hawkers, haggling women, and caged fowl, where a kidnap might not even be noticed. Though why take the risk when he could be spirited away after dark, on a Sabbath eve when all of Shatsk was indoors?

Every Friday at dusk Yankel accompanied his father to the bathhouse. There, after a dip in the warm green water, they would sit on warped bleachers togaed in towels and thrash themselves with brooms. (During this exercise, much to the rabbi's chagrin if he were present, the other sitz-bathers might quiz the prodigy on obscure points of law.) They emerged from clouds of steam with erubescent faces, strolling toward the shul in identical black sateen. Following services Malkeh would meet them in her fancy sheitel, her pearls retrieved once again from the pawnbroker for the occasion. The house would be fragrant with challah and potted meat, its few sticks of furniture spotless, Shlomo's scrolls-in-progress stored in a corner for the holiday. Lighting the candles, Malkeh would wave her arms above the flames, gathering smoke to fuel her generous tears. She thanked the Lord for a son who'd brought them such naches, whose merit had secured her husband a seat by the eastern wall.

When they sat down to dinner, it was often in the company of some vagabond peddler whom Shlomo suspected might be the prophet Elijah in disguise. (Once it had actually been the broken-nosed Leon Deathwatch, a crony of Shmuel's sent to spy.) After the meal the knives would be covered, the zmiros sung, the eyes daubed with wine for a providential week. Then the guest departed and Shlomo and Malkeh would draw the patched canvas curtain hiding their feather bed. With Shlomo stripped to his talis koton and beaver hat, Malkeh in her flannel gown, they would commence their ritual coupling—a duty which, if performed on Shabbos, was certain to bring the Almighty closer to his chosen people. Rolling in noisy abandon, they were confident that their son remained insensible to their frolic; he was tucked away in his loft above the wood stove, poring over a volume of Abulafia or Halevi by hurricane lamp.

Or maybe he'd paused in his reading to contemplate some midrashic brain-teaser, as he did on this particular night. He looked toward the moon, a broken saucer beyond the dirty skylight, and pondered what it meant to have an extra soul on the Sabbath. Could you, for instance, depart from this life with one soul while leaving the other behind?

"If I should be someone else," he asked, after Rabbi Hillel, "then who should be me?"

It was during this meditation that the gag was stuffed in his mouth. Before he could utter any of the formulae for dispersing the enema lady or Lilith's minions, they'd muffled him and thrown a sack over his head; they trussed his torso and legs, then folded him, wriggling, over somebody's bony shoulder. Carried thus down the ladder, Yankel heard the impassioned groaning of his parents, who must have already begun to mourn him.

Outside Shmuel One-Eye sat grimly on the box of his wagon, his collar turned up, his cap pulled to the level of his eye patch, which fluttered like black bunting in the October wind. When his boys had dumped their burden in the wagon bed, he spat once and lashed his brace of horses, driving them at a gallop over the stone bridge in the direction of Kiev.

c. 1870–1875

Throughout the long ordeal of his abduction Yankel told himself he must be dreaming. He'd fallen asleep in his loft over a page of Sefer ha-Ma'asiyot, that was it. He'd been reading about the nocturnal mischief of certain species of Jewish hobgoblins: lantekh, shretelekh, the infernal sheydim for whom kidnap was the least of their crimes; and must have dozed off. Although it seemed he was blinkered and gagged, bouncing in the bed of a wagon in full career, in actuality he was only having a bad dream. Now if he could just fall asleep in his dream, Yankel reasoned, he would wake up again to a warm and familar world.

To lull himself he tried meditating on the characters of the Hebrew alphabet, an exercise much favored by the circle of Rabbi Mendl of Vitebsk. But the rattling wheels and the cracking droshky whip hindered even Yankel's celebrated concentration. He tried the breathing techniques of Rabbi ibn Latif, who advised inhaling through the nostrils of the soul, then crooned to himself one of his mother's cradle songs:

> *My Yankele will study Law*
> *The Law will my baby learn*
> *Great books will my Yankele write*
> *Much money will he earn . . .*

But nothing about the nightmare he was having was conducive to slumber.

By the time the wagon halted and he was lifted out, Yankel had abandoned any thoughts of sleep. Dragged bumping up a flight of stairs, he was spilled from the sack onto a parqueted floor and unbound. Stood up, he was left to sway on his feet, dizzy with exhaustion, aching from the bruises he'd sustained during the journey, and further abashed at having peed himself in fear.

If they were at all surprised by the manner of Yankel's arrival, the fiends who'd taken charge of him never showed it. They shoved him perfunctorily into the ranks of other boys huddled at one end of the longest room Yankel had ever seen. Portraits of bearded men in ermine-trimmed crowns decked the walls; crossed sabers and banners bearing two-headed birds hung from a mezzanine. His fellow captives, mostly peasant youths in belted overblouses, their demeanors running from docile to defiant, moved away from the stench of Yankel's nightshirt. There were Jewish boys also, puny specimens who (unlike Yankel) had not grown fat on Torah, fingering fringes and desperately clutching tefillin bags. These were confiscated without ceremony in exchange for the numbers assigned them by a devil in a braided tunic. And while they blinked and rubbed their eyes raw, he wouldn't go away, the devil who called himself "Sergeant major" with his face like a firebrick.

They were stripped naked and thrust into other rooms, hustled through a gauntlet of stethoscopes and cold metal prods, past committees who fired questions without waiting for answers, stamped documents without ever looking up. They were anointed in benzine, shorn of hair and sidelocks, which the barbers then cut capers with, using them for false mustaches and pigs' tails. They were trousered in breeches that fell to their ankles, greatcoats that swept the floor, boots so tall they couldn't bend their knees, and told they were soldiers now; they belonged to the czar. But skilled as he was in the logic of dreams, Yankel wasn't deceived. He understood that they'd been processed for devils themselves.

The sergeant major cursed them—"Offscourings! Yids!"— and droved them under armed guard out into the teeming streets. Kiev was the city that conscripts from Shatsk were routinely taken to, but Yankel knew enough to recognize the sprawling necropolis of Gehinnom when he saw it. How else account for such diabolical beauty? The avenues of russet-leaved locusts, the stone facades with intricately carved finials; the cavernous, gold-domed cathedral with its interior lit by red candles, a worshipper on her belly before a graven image. Graven images perched on cornices and the parapets of bridges; they loomed above the forested hills across the river. And what would you call the population but leering icons come alive to stare at them from the windows of horse trolleys and lacquered broughams? They stepped out of flame-belching forges to laugh at them, from behind steaming vats in bloody aprons, in peaked caps, bast shoes, babushkas, and chimney-pot hats; in cassocks, their beards parted like hammer claws around a crucifix.

The recruits marched until their heads swam and their feet swelled enough to fill their outsize boots. Some of the Jewish boys kept looking back as if in hopes that their mothers might be following close behind, an error for which they were punished with blows. The more anemic among them began to stagger and drop out, and Yankel wondered if this might'nt be the best policy. But when he saw how they were made to stand again and rejoin the ranks, in extremis though they appeared, he found the will to push on. By midafternoon they'd tottered into a barracks in some outlying district, no sooner arriving than they collapsed on hard berths. Instantly they were called back to attention. They were issued this and that—boot blacking, brass polish, a kit bag, a blanket, a rifle with bayonet. Those Jews with the strength to turn their heads glanced at one another and asked mutely, "What, no kipah, no prayerbook?"

They were herded into a mess hall where tin bowls of cooked water, afloat with distinctly nonkosher matter, were set before them on rough-hewn trestles. The older boys—largely Poles, Balts, Ukrainians—attacked their portions of swill with gusto, but Yankel's stomach rose up at the prospect. He was not alone among the Jewish boys, most of whom shoved their bowls away, though one said a brocha, took a taste, and promptly heaved. Another, clearly delirious, prayed aloud for manna to fall, while an unsteady third pitched face forward into his soup. No one bothered to lift his head in case he'd had the good fortune to drown.

After their light refreshment they were cursed at some more and made to march around the yard, this time in full battle gear. They were halted at dusk, propped up by their rifles like scarecrows, and interrogated as to their particular skills—a formality, though it might in fact result in their being assigned to an appropriate unit. As it turned out, some of the gentiles were already practicing wheelrights, journeyman carpenters, and cooks. There were even a few ex-convicts who proudly declared a talent for cracking safes. But most of the runty Jewish lads were too young to have learned a trade; they knew only about what had no application in Fonya's army—the Torah, the violin—and were thus designated cannon fodder.

Some came from provinces so remote that they'd never heard Russian spoken, and for their speechlessness they were cuffed and labeled cannon fodder. Some were merely too debilitated to answer. Despite his own bone-weariness, Yankel realized he ought to lie, say he was perhaps a cobbler's apprentice. But having never borne false witness in his mother language, it wasn't likely he'd succeed in an alien tongue. Besides, why should he conceal his identity when there was every possibility that his legend had preceded him even here? So when it came his turn, he explained in a mixture of Yiddish and fractured Russian,

"If it please your honor, I'm Yankel Kabakoff, gaon of Shatsk."

"Cannon fodder!" barked the chronically inflamed sergeant major, assigning him to an infantry detachment to be used for that purpose. He and his Christ-killing brethren were to be dispatched at dawn to an outpost at the ends of the earth, immediately following their baptism.

That night in his berth, amid a hybrid cacophony of whimpering and snores, Yankel tried to renew his faith in the unreality of his situation. He clung to the notion that, if he could sleep, he would wake to a cockcrow, Leibush Halbfunt the sexton calling all

Jews to come already to shul. A huddle of tin roofs, a river, a market, a tumbledown wooden synagogue—that was the world, and its windows gave on to other worlds more real than the village itself. There was the portable world contained in the books of heroes and martyrs and wandering patriarchs; the books of the Covenant outlining its six hundred thirteen mitzvot: the two hundred forty-eight positive commandments equivalent to the organs of the body, the three hundred sixty-five negative corresponding to the days of the year. You could count them until you began to drop off.

But Yankel had to admit that this present interminable hallucination was pretty convincing, compared to which the shtetl seemed more like the dream. A proverb occurred to him from a source he hadn't the energy to trace: "If the righteous so choose, they can make a world."

"Make a world," sighed Yankel. "I'm too tired to make water." Moreover, his fatigue and hunger were so absolute that they would not yield to sleep.

Morning came swiftly, announced by slaps and curses rather than daylight, but Yankel had no recollection of having dozed. Neither did he feel the least bit rested, his only solace that he was too spent to be afraid. Their "baptism" came when those who still refused to eat, Yankel among them, received benedictions from the sergeant major as he dumped bowls of hot gruel on their heads.

They were made to don the heavy greatcoats inside of which they freely perspired despite the early morning chill. Further encumbered with duffle, kit, and shouldered rifle, they were paraded again through the streets, but the few citizens abroad at that hour weren't laughing. The walking corpses in their ranks, spirits yet anchored to earth by the weight of their gear, no longer inspired levity.

By now Yankel had started to feel a certain estrangement from his own body. He noted with interest that his gut was constricting after a fashion that must have meant he'd begun to starve. In a matter of days he'd be dead and, in death, he would perhaps wake up to his own lost world. Of course, you might hold out the hope that, at the moment of extremest suffering, the angel Raziel would carry you off to paradise alive, like Enoch and what's-his-name. There you'd sit in a court of celestial rabbis, engaged in pilpul discussions with the Rambam and Meyer of Rottenburg. But Yankel anticipated no such intervention. As they slouched down the steps of an embankment in garish sunlight, it seemed to him there was anyway not a kopek's worth of difference between life and death.

At a landing stage along the river they were ordered aboard a rust-cankered steam packet and confined to the stokehold below decks. There they squatted on coal heaps in an oppressive closeness made more stifling by the heat from a throbbing cast-iron boiler. The firebox lit their faces, a misfit collection of gypsies, suspected anarchists and revolutionaries, and Jewish children with enormous eyes. Most of them looked as if they would bolt at the least opportunity, which was doubtless why they were treated more like prisoners than recruits. But the boys Yankel's age, lacking his bloom to begin with, appeared to have a head start on the prodigy with regard to dying. While Yankel might be shrinking to the condition of an ordinary yeshiva student, the other bochers were already several parts ghost. In this they heeded an unofficial imperial edict that went: the Jewish problem will be solved when one-third have emigrated, one-third converted, and one-third (here the government would provide needed assistance) died off. The last was apparently the present company's chosen alternative.

Bare-chested stokers fed the furnace and the packet was launched downstream to God knew where, upon which the boys began surrendering in earnest. Because there'd been conversation, furtive exchanges about a voyage from bad to worse, some of Yankel's fellows now had names. There was Shmulke of Uman, head like an onion bulb, who informed them between coughing up gobbets of his insides, "My mama put a note in the zayde's hand when he died." On reaching heaven his grandfather would pass the note on to the Lord, who would then intercede on Shmulke's behalf. There was cross-eyed Munya from Pskov who couldn't stop shitting himself, his trumpeting bowels rivaling the racket of the pistons and the churning paddle wheel. Such a stink he made that those to the left and right of him gave up the breakfasts they hadn't had.

There was Dovid Blum, a curly-topped cantor's son from Tchernobol, for whose moaning you didn't need a doctor to diagnose that he was suffering from a broken heart. When they'd been under way for no more than an hour, he stood and called out to an absent father, "Tateh, ich mach bar mitzvah far zich" ("I make a bar mitzvah by myself!") Then he stumbled toward the roaring furnace grate and dove in.

When the stokers tugged at his protruding feet, the ample boots came off in their hands. The gallery of recruits were transfixed by Dovid's stockinged toes, which curled too close to the flames for the men to get hold of. The burlier of the two, rolls of fat at the back of his glistening neck, tore a grappling iron from a beam and swung it into the fire. For all his brawn, however, the man had to pull mightily on the hook, as if an equal had engaged him in a tug-of-war from the other end. Finally the burnt Dovid Blum was retrieved from the furnace. The second stoker covered him with a tarpaulin, extinguishing the crackling torch of his hair; but not before Yankel and company had had a look at his face dripping tallow, bubble eyes drooling out of their sockets like yolks from broken shells.

His voice, though, remained miraculously intact. With a volume perhaps inherited from his father, Dovid's plangent soprano wail was louder than the chuffing engine and the farting Munya. Boys who were able to shake off their paralysis slowly stepped forward from the coal bins and stood over him. Having shed their coats and tunics in the swelter of the hold, they spread them on top of the grimy tarp—like you'd throw dirt on a grave, thought

Yankel, who did the same. Muffled but still amazingly shrill, Dovid's wailing persisted, prompting the boys to make a noise of their own. Although there were fewer than ten Jews present, and they not yet reached their majority, there were more than enough males to constitute a minyan. So they said Kaddish over the hill of greatcoats until the sounds emanating from under it were eventually exorcized.

Alerted to the disturbance, noncommissioned officers stormed below to break up the funeral with knouts. They directed the boys to carry the corpse aloft and drop it overboard, into sulphurous water that scarcely consented to splash. It was dusk and rations of a sort were being issued, the recruits told to line up outside a makeshift galley on the afterdeck. They were further warned that anyone refusing to eat would be forced to, and for those who didn't comprehend, there followed a demonstration—a funnel shoved down the throat of the colicky Chaim Fish, who was anyhow too far gone for such abuse to matter. Yankel received his tin of pork rind in broth, his cube of stale black bread, and recalled that dispensations might be made to save one's life. But since when did he want to save his life?

On the other hand, death out here on the river wasn't the event it was back in the world. In Shatsk you didn't so much die as you were invited to join the upper yeshiva. They scrubbed you and laid you out so tenderly, with a candle at your head; then they tucked you into a hole whose walls were boxed with the boards from your own prayer bench. The whole village turned out to escort you to the cemetery, that a like multitude of angels might greet your entry into paradise. But here death lacked dignity, not to say significance. To die was to do Fonya a favor that Yankel no longer felt so disposed to render.

"Besides," he recalled from *The Ethics of the Fathers* (or was it Onkelos?), "where there's no bread there's no Torah."

So he dipped the bread in his cup of bilge and gnawed greedily, somehow keeping it down, and afterward he felt a little less shaken. Before they were driven back into the stokehold, Yankel even noticed the sky. It was runneled in red like veins on the back of God's hand. The river reflected the color of the sky in that duplication of above and below specified in Kabbalah; they might be sailing down the Lord's own bloodstream, Yankel thought. But later the image of the reflecting river tended to outshine any allegorical references that found their way into his head.

The next day at sunset those who weren't too moribund were sent on deck again. This time Yankel observed how the steppe stretched away from them like nothing he'd ever encountered in holy books. Like a sea of violet grass. On the day after that they got cold porridge in the morning, and Yankel saw that they'd entered a sea of sunflowers, windmills listing like masts on the horizon. Another day, another sea, this one of acacias, that of blossoming hops. Although he'd never before paid much attention to external phenomena, Yankel supposed he must be in the presence of beauty. The psalms you might call beautiful, or the hymns of Solomon written in the language of birds, but that a landscape should similarly thrill the senses: this was news. In neither Hebrew nor Yiddish could Yankel find the words to describe it. Maybe Russian—for which he was acquiring a proficiency since having it shouted at him night and day—would prove more applicable.

At the town of Zaporozhye the boat docked and what was left of Yankel's company were marched down a gangplank into a gaudy bazaar. Brooded over by ancient Cossack watchtowers, the market sold everything from spices to carpets, weapons to wives. The mixed tongues of men vied with the tongues of beasts, some of which stood as high as the carved wooden balconies, an occasional monkey riding their humps. Reaching a station, the bewildered recruits were loaded into cattle cars that rocked and jolted out across a rolling plain. Through the slats those who cared to were able to spy vast orchards, vegetation that didn't know better than to flourish in a month when growing things were supposed to die.

They had a glimpse before the walls of Rostov of a sea that was neither feather grass nor grain, but pure shimmering emerald brine.

It occurred to Yankel that at least one of the days through which they'd traveled must have been Shabbos. How strange that its lack of observance should have been so unremarkable, without a bump or blemish in the atmosphere to advise you of its passing.

At Stavropol the train came to a full stop and the recruits were routed from their stupor; they were hustled through streets paved in pumpkin seeds, a slate-shingled town that hunkered beneath a bank of jagged dove gray clouds. On closer inspection the clouds turned out to be the snowy peaks of a deep mauve mountain range, and it was toward that distant fastness that their formal forced march inclined. Just beyond the town there were vertical pastures where gaunt men in astrakhan hats herded sheep on horseback. They carried daggers and pistols and sat ramrod-straight in their saddles, some showing fringes beneath their pleated shirts. Yankel had heard of these mountain Jews, who fought like demons, had several wives, and lived to astronomical ages. It heartened him somehow to know that, aside from their ritual fringes, they were in no way distinguishable from their neighbors.

On the long, punishing ascent to the cloud garrison more boys were lost. Death no longer needed a leg up from the conscripts themselves, because the deprivations of the journey were more than sufficient to do them in. There were also diseases, though seldom dramatic, a feeble cough or slight ague often signaling the final collapse. But Yankel, now that he'd decided that an untimely quietus was not for him, had set about trying to survive, adapting himself to the field rations of hardtack and boiled leather. In fact, although he slogged as listlessly as the others in order not to be noticed, Yankel felt he was beginning to thrive on treyf as once he'd thrived on scripture. Grown thin, he was becoming hard inside and out.

For a time Yankel composed letters in his head to Malkeh and Shlomo. Rather than console and reassure them, however, he angrily accused them of having countenanced his abduction; he catalogued in gruesome detail the indignities he was subjected to. But since, on the march, mail was neither incoming or outgoing, nor ever promised to be, Yankel supposed the best he could do with respect to his family was forget them. As a strategy this worked so well that he resolved to apply it to other areas of lingering irritation.

The Guzhny garrison was a stone-hedged aerie clinging to mist-shrouded crags high above the perpendicular city of Tiflis. Full of outcasts too sociopathic for more civilized assignments, the barracks were tense with hostilities. There were rivalries between primitive Georgians and sodden Cossacks, between Cossacks and wild Circassian horsemen, who frequently called one another out for duels. The ruffians bullied the fanatical spit-and-polish types, who in turn hounded the malcontents quoting Bakunin's *Revolutionary Catechism,* but all were united in their hatred of yids. When the remnant of Yankel's company arrived at the outpost after the crucible of their month-long trek, officers and enlisted men alike joined in continuing their persecution.

Having ruled out dying in harness, Yankel began to consider the other prescribed alternatives. Emigration was of course out of the question and conversion carried with it a stigma even among the gentiles; as witness Mottel Toches-Lekker, who'd kissed the rosary of the garrison priest, and was afterward thrashed for a coward as well as for being a member of a verminous race. So how should one proceed to live?

Briefly Yankel flirted with the notion of becoming a model soldier. But model soldiers were conspicuous, distinguished by rank and decoration, and lately Yankel was leaning more toward invisibility. It was a condition that he feared might not come naturally, though, to the once-famous prodigy of Shatsk. Then it struck him how, in a sense, he'd already begun to effect his own dissolution. By erasing his memory, Yankel covered his tracks; he lost his identity and thus became no one. And as no one, it stood to reason, he would scarcely be worthy of Fonya's regard.

Thanks to a traumatic journey the picture of his home had grown dim, and along with it much of the learning that flourished only in native mud. Further abetted through the rigors of the regimental routine—the maneuvers across chasms and raging torrents, bayonet drills on fields of ice, tedious footslogs interrupted by sudden skirmishes with furious slant-eyed bandits, the food that wasn't food, sleep that wasn't sleep—Yankel began to forget his Talmud by degrees. The first to go were the commentaries on the orders and tractates, then the orders and tractates themselves: the laws concerning the preparation of a red heifer's ashes to purify those who have contact with the dead; the laws governing adultery, murder, war, the duties incumbent on the first-born. Next he lost the threads of aggadah and midrashim, the tales of golems, dybbuks, and fallen angels, the tales of miracles. He forgot the one about what's-her-face, Queen Esther, who outwitted an enemy of Israel (or was it that she cut somebody's hair?) and Joseph, who fought a giant in a dream. In the end Yankel began to forget the Hebrew alphabet itself: the letter *mem* like a cat arching its back, the *shin* like a fleur-de-lis, elegant *gimmel* like a lady's boot, or was it her glove?

Eventually all the books he used to know became one book in Yankel's mind, a single Book that contained all the stories including his own. He was comfortable with this hypothesis, that the Book should bear the burden of remembering; it let him off the hook and made exile seem less like exile than the place where, for the time being, he happened to belong.

"Change your place and you change your luck," he announced to the other boys eroded by homesickness. When they asked where he'd gleaned that particular titbit of wisdom, Yankel shrugged and couldn't say.

It helped that there was nothing in this remote mountain stronghold to remind him of the past, though odd scraps of memory still surfaced now and then. He might be shivering at his sentry post, gazing from the ramparts toward a corona of moon above some dizzy pinnacle, when he remembered the Bird's Nest. This was the hallowed dwelling place of Messiah until such time as He should be called to earth to redeem His people. Or during patrols it might come to him that these fierce mountain Jews were one of the ten lost tribes. Didn't they live beyond a river that could have been the legendary Sambatyon, though in these parts it was known as Kura Gorge? And among the veiled peaks that shouldered one another like a battalion of headless colossi, blocking your path between the Black and Caspian seas, wasn't there one called Ararat? That was where, if Yankel weren't mistaken, a passenger boat had once run aground in a flood. But such associations were inconsequential, like shrapnel from bygone wars, pieces of which sometimes worked their way out of an old soldier's knee. The soldier would extract the shard with a blade, then throw it away as casually as a splinter, never thinking to keep it for a souvenir.

IV

Not long after the fiasco of his half sister's wedding, Itchy Kabakoff began to remember his grandfather's stories. They came back to him at odd moments following his father's leap from the Harahan Bridge, by which route the City of Fun had left town that very dawn. It was still dark out, a plum purple sky in the west, as the carnival convoy crossed over the river to Arkansas. But the bridge—Itchy'd seen it all from the cab of the truck he rode in—was lurid with spinning red lights, a circle of squad cars having surrounded a bottle green Continental.

As they traveled south through the Delta, zigzagging back and forth across the river, making stops at Stringtown, Dumas, Tallulah, Bewelcome, Itchy's thoughts regarding his father's leap grew increasingly tangled. On the one hand, he'd engineered the humiliation and literal downfall of the printing magnate Moses Kabakoff—a cause for, if anything, satisfaction: put it down to the settling of scores. On the other, he was more or less to blame for his own father's suicide. But was it Itchy's fault that a harm- less prank had gotten a little out of hand? Screw 'em if they couldn't take a joke. Guilt being something he'd never had in abundance, why waste it on a father who'd practically ignored him from birth? And if the son had hardly existed for the father, Itchy could assure the old (begging his pardon) fart that the feeling was mutual.

It didn't make sense that he should mourn the absence of persons who'd never really been there in the first place. Something else must have been eating him. After all, Itchy was no longer the shadowy character who'd joined the traveling show; his years on the road had turned him into a man of many parts. Or was it, instead, that he'd become many men? He was a shark, a seducer, an alibi agent, a human prodigy, now an orphan—though the irony wasn't lost on him that this last was what he'd long professed to be. No sooner had he found himself an orphan in fact, however, than he wondered if it was actually true. Never again would he have a chance to quiz his father on the subject of his first wife, whom Mose had always maintained was dead or vanished, depending on his mood. Eventually he'd refused to talk about her at all, which was fine with Itchy, who'd come to like the idea that he wasn't so much born as invented. So why should he wonder all of a sudden if she might still be alive?

That's how it went: despite his duties and diversions, the miles of pink dust and kudzu, Itchy couldn't break the chain of associations touched off by his father's plunge. In the end, via a tortured itinerary, his thoughts took him where they often led when he was troubled: back to his grandfather's study in its copper light. And there would be Yankel scratching under his crocheted skullcap as he offered up some half-baked proposition— the kind that was writ on water in Itchy's memory like the fortunes that appear and dissolve in a plastic eight ball. Or else the old man was telling the tales that had lately begun returning to his grandson, about his adventures during and after his years in the army of the czar.

Even as a child on North Main Street Itchy had suspected that his grandfather, mumbling over his books, was only pretending to study. At the least excuse Yankel would interrupt himself to impart some morsel of wisdom that Itchy was too young to appreciate. But he must have tucked them away someplace in his mind, like a legacy that awaited his coming of age, because twenty-odd years later here they were.

"When you die," he once found himself fingering on a dusty panel of the dormitory truck before he washed it, "the Lord, praised be He, won't ask why you wasn't Moses. He'll ask why you wasn't Itchele." Or touching up the Feejee Mermaid on the canvas of the ten-in-one, he'd been moved to paint a golden rubric: "Yankel says, 'Used to be me and the Lord, blessed be He, was that close, we would both of us pish in the same hole.'" "Yankel says," he scribbled on a business card out of a wallet freshly boosted from a lot louse, "'In Pentateuch our prophet Moishe Rabbeynu receives the Torah, that you read in it how Moishe Rabbeynu receives the Torah . . . and so on, world ain't got a end.'"

At first he felt compelled to relate Yankel's stories as they'd been related to him, haphazardly aloud. At a table in the cookhouse, say, where Madagaspar the flea-bitten magician was ragging Peabody the ventriloquist about his dummy Herbert ("I hear he had a bloodless circumcision, they used a pencil-sharpener"), Itchy might butt in.

"That puts me in mind [as what didn't these days] of a story my grandpa used to tell," launching into the one about Yankel and the Cossack who wanted to be as smart as a Jew. "So my grandpa advises him, 'Eat herring heads,' which he does, throwing away the rest of the fish, which Yankel fries up for himself. Weeks pass before the Cossack says, 'I don't think there's anything to this fishhead business,' to which my grandpa replies, 'See, you're already starting to get brains.'" By this time Itchy would have been all alone at the table.

He should have taken the hint from Rose's reception that he was no comedian, his theatrical repertoire limited to novelty turns. But the urgency that had come over him he couldn't contain, and again and again he tried to arrest the others with stories.

Take the time after Itchy, as good as his name, had picked up a case of the crabs in the town of Iuka. The relentless irritation in his pubic area reminded him how Yankel had once outwitted a Cossack who called him a lousy Jew. "So my grandpa, he challenges the guy to a contest to see who can stand at attention longest without scratching. . . ." But before he could get to the part about putting cooties in the Cossack's pants, his fellow performers—including Mignon the Limbless Demi-Girl, who was close to a captive audience—made their excuses and exited the short end of the tent.

"Don't take it personal," Og the Cyclops had paused to console him. "Mr. Few's got Tutty and Muldoon on the tube in his trailer."

As he watched them crossing the backlot through sapphire moonlight, Itchy wanted badly to tell them how much they recalled the creatures Yankel'd encountered after deserting the Imperial Army.

For years Itchy had gauged the seasons less by the weather than by where the carnival happened to be. They went north, they went south according to the climate: if it was Valdosta, Georgia, it must be winter; Memphis, it must be spring. Still, it was easy to lose track of what month you were in, never mind what day, so that birthdays often came and went without notice. When was Itchy's anyway, June 3rd or 4th?; it was a matter of indifference to him—until this year, his twenty-somethingth, when he remembered how Yankel had forgotten his own banner thirteenth. He'd also forgotten the holy days, which Itchy incidentally noted because old Madagaspar sometimes observed them. In Yankel's Guzhny garrison ("the Gehinnom of the clouds"), however, Shavuos, Simchas Torah, Yom Kippur Eve passed without so much as a ripple in the thin mountain air. Only duties—stitching tunics, reheeling boots, dragging overladen sledges with frostbitten fingers, counting lost boys after night patrols—distinguished one day from another. This for the entire five years of Yankel's service, at the end of which his discharge was deferred on account of a war.

No sooner would Itchy redeem one of Yankel's memories than he was driven to repeat it, often indiscreetly. Like the time outside Ten-Mile, Tennessee under a flatbed trailer with a hillbilly girl in a hiked-up Sunday dress. As he hovered over her, spare-haunched and priapic, his hair and beard tangled in elfknots, she said, "My name's Ray Lee Foot. What's yourn?" Then he told her a version of what Yankel, serving his own apprenticeship in depravity during a springtime expedition into Tiflis (which rhymed with syphilis), told a painted Kirghiz nafkeleh: "I'm the Passover satyr."

With another girl in Meridian, Mississippi, after it was over, Itchy recalled the acronymic of Maimonides, a philosopher Yankel was fond of misquoting. "Rambam, thank you ma'am," he said. And in the solitude he'd begun seeking more frequently, since the town girls also proved unresponsive to his yarns, Itchy remembered Yankel citing that "sex is the poor man's meditation." It was one of those chestnuts that had taken two decades to ripen.

More and more Itchy waived opportunities with the town girls. In the throes of his passion the floodgates of memory would open, filling him to capacity with episodes from his grandfather's past. The problem being that the memories would then displace Itchy's formerly unquenchable desire. Ironically, the more preoccupied he became, the more aggressively the girls sought him out. They followed him after he shut down the funhouse or wound up a short con on the grocery wheel; they waited until he emerged from the ten-in-one, throwing a robe over his dirty diaper and the fake fur plastered to his shoulders and chest. "Wild thing!" they catcalled, assuming cheerleader poses, so that Itchy resented the reversal of roles: that *they* should stalk *him*. What's more, he was frankly tired of wanting them, of taking without being asked for anything in return. A thief at heart, he rejected what was freely given. And if he were honest, wasn't he also a little tired of the road?

The show ladies taunted and cajoled him as well. "What's the matter, darlin'?" cooed Miss Lorraine Cloud, waving a feather boa under Itchy's nose until he sneezed. "Why ain't you come around tom-cattin' no more? You got jack-in-the-box disease?" "You pissin' pins and needles or what?" chimed Pagan Lee, a grin cracking her cosmetic mask. The Dixie Pixie professed in baby talk, "L'il Miss Twitchet misses her Mister Tallywhack," but Melba May, hoisting a sequined halter over rampant bosoms, told them to knock it off. "Can't you see the boy done had a attack of conscience?" There was teasing conjecture as to the location on his person of his conscience, while Itchy remained self-absorbed. He was thinking of how, during his peddling days, Yankel had sold among other things a remedy for what he called the Neapolitan bone-ache. On the verge of sharing this information with the ladies, he decided that they couldn't care less.

By now he'd understood that Yankel's nearly century-old exploits were no match for more immediate amusements, like sex and TV. But even erstwhile messmates such as the magician and Victor the Ancient Child seemed to remember they had errands to run, underwear to wash, whenever Itchy cranked up a story. Nor could he expect any encouragement from Mignon, with whom his intimacy had long since flagged.

"Save it for your memoirs," she told him, compensating for her limblessness with typically prehensile remarks. Propped up in her cradle like a throw cushion in an embroidered pillowslip, she'd unhinged her jaw to yawn.

"Not mine," corrected Itchy, slouched in the bead-curtained berth of Madame Delphine's trailer, "Yankel's."

But Mignon had struck a chord. Broadcasting tales like some Johnny Appleseed of memories, he'd been sowing them in barren soil, squandering them on deaf ears. Maybe he ought to be more frugal, Itchy reasoned; the truth was, since the stories didn't exactly belong to him, neither were they his to give away. The thing to do was to collect them, preserve them for . . . and here the logic foundered. If not his own show folk, just who was his proper audience supposed to be? In any case Itchy resolved to take his cue from Mignon.

"Have you got something I can write with?" he asked.

Mignon rolled her opal eyes but nevertheless obliged him, fishing a ballpoint from the handbag in her cradle with her teeth. "Sho I guesh oo musha loved him," she said as she passed him the pen.

Itchy took it and began there and then to jot notes on anything that came to hand, in the margins of the fortune-teller's dream books, on the backs of tarot cards. Without breaking stride he asked in an absent afterthought, "Loved who?"

"For God's sake," sighed Mignon, "loved Jesus, loved Elvis—who do you think, knucklehead? Your grandfather!"

Itchy looked up a moment, gazing into space (as represented by the star chart Madame Delphine had taped to the ceiling). Love was not a concept he was cozy with. Having never received it from another, he'd thus far withheld it from everyone else, but now he thought he could imagine what it was like. He recalled how Yankel, his own books long forgotten, saw the burning scrolls during the slaughter of the Jews at Ekaterinoslav. Smoke from black flames, barbed like Hebrew characters, clogged his nostrils, he'd said, and wreathed his brain in a lacerating crown. That's how much it hurt to remember, and that—assumed Itchy, making a note to the effect—was what love must be like.

For a while he was careless, leaving his notes in the wake of the carnival like a paper trail you could follow back to the past. It was enough just to know that his grandfather's tales had been transcribed. But increasingly acquisitive, Itchy grew reluctant to let them go; he stuffed his duffel with pages until he was forced to transfer his clothes to a cardboard suitcase. Then the suitcase also started to fill up with pages so that he threw out some of his clothes, Yankel's baggage having come to replace Itchy's own.

He wrote in pocket-sized spiral notebooks that ran out of paper at awkward moments, then wrote on whatever else was available: bingo cards, Madagaspar's starched collars, the cotton crotch of a cast-off G-string. He wrote on the back of a "true life" pamphlet recounting the exotic origins of the Wild Man of the Caucasus. Once, while painting a sluggish corn snake to resemble the deadly coral, Itchy inscribed the word *Lilith* along its cold hide. This was Adam's immodest first wife, one of whose daughters Yankel claimed to have met during his travels through the ruined towns. Needling the tips from his cage above a tub of water, Itchy reached through the chicken wire to snag a baseball hurled at a tin bull's-eye. On its casing he scribbled a detail from Yankel's description of the ritual mikveh in Shatsk.

There was the time during his blowoff bit when, with a razor concealed in his palm, he was about to slit the throat of a pullet and drink its blood. Suddenly reminded of an anecdote of Yankel's about cannibalism on the long march from the Anatolian front, Itchy interrupted his routine to make a note. Having set the chicken free, he made an additional note concerning the poultry that shtetl penitents whirled above their heads on Yom Kippur. That was when the manager Mr. Julius Few told him he'd finally done it: he'd graduated from nuisance to liability.

Writing about Yankel's wicked period, Itchy felt that his own impulse toward wickedness (his *yetser ha-ra*) was declining. Should this happen? After all, who was Itchy if not the shady black sheep of the Kabakoffs, just as Yankel himself during his military career had been shady—a scrounger and petty thief; though gingerly as regarded the latter, because it was written: "When a gentile steals, you hang the thief; when a Jew steals, you hang the Jew." Acquiring modest skills borrowed in equal parts from Esau and Jacob, he'd learned to make himself useful; he learned to sew, resurrecting the uniforms the quartermaster threw out for shmattes, then trading them for indulgences like trench knives, balalaikas, rawhide quirts. These he swapped on unauthorized visits to the Tiflis bazaars for apricots and salted fish roe, for sour cream, smoked meat, olive oil, vodka, and locust beans, which were bruited to have aphrodisiac properties. For his trouble (and toward assuaging symptoms presumably aroused by the locust beans) Yankel received small arms. He traded them to the alpaca-clad proprietors of the cliff-hanging brothels of Tiflis for women. They came in all varieties, speaking a babel of tongues, wearing smocks, beshmets, and nose rings, some with tattooed faces, some disguising childhood or advanced age with veils. Before smuggling them into the barracks, Yankel wasn't above sampling their charms, though careful lest he contract some disease against which the remedies he sold his fellow conscripts were admittedly useless.

All this he accomplished so adroitly and with such mercurial tact that he never forfeited his status of a nonentity. The soldiers seldom realized they'd dealt with the same provider twice. But just in case someone should take umbrage over finding himself beholden to a yid, Yankel laid aside a portion of his skin-trade gratuities for hush money and bribes.

Came the Russo-Turkish War and the Guzhny garrison, five hundred strong—with its mounted hussars in gold buttons and scarlet piping, its marksmen armed with the small-barreled Krenka carbines, the footsloggers in their varying degrees of seditiousness dragging the caissons and brass cannons—descended from the clouds. This was in the spring of 1877, and for all the hardships of the mountain outpost, you'd have thought the ensuing year was a banishment from heaven's high city; though by then Yankel had advanced beyond distinguishing between circles of the damned, negotiating one as well as another. Whereas the troops suffered short rations of green meat, stale sinkers, and candle tallow, Yankel traded camp followers to the officers for cognac and fresh game. He avoided rough bivouacs by waiving his IOUs in exchange for billets in the choir lofts of chapels and the stables of inns. His procurement activities, which put him in contact with the higher echelons, sometimes made him privy to orders concerning the movement of troops. This may or may not have contributed—Yankel had been vague on the subject—to the fact that, despite their extensive training, their impressive array, and relative proximity to the Armenian theater, it took the Guzhny battalion the better part of a year to find the war.

While dispatches were lost and maps turned out to be mysteriously in error, the rank and file succumbed to exhaustion and a multitude of infirmities. Of course the battalion encountered broad clues that the war had passed their way, but it always managed to have eluded them by a matter of days. They were further impeded by the rubbish left in its trail, blighted landscapes in which it seemed a trespass to be still alive. This was the case at Bayazid, where the bodies waiting for burial were piled willy-nilly like brushwood awaiting bonfires; and at Kars, recently toppled after a lengthy seige, its fortress walls sporting crucifixions, eyeless sockets surveying an immense kitchen midden of human scraps. About the brimming trenches what appeared to be corpses who hadn't yet gotten the message wandered erect singing hymns. (Here Itchy was reminded of what the old blues minstrels once told him: "On Beale Street your haint'll walk upright like a natural man," though by this point Yankel's memories had nearly eclipsed his own.) Whereas others tossed their gorge over such sights and smells, Yankel spied opportunities; at night in advance of detachments organized for the purpose, he'd gathered child recruits to compete with the carrion crows. Whereas the swarming birds were content to pick at spilled kishkes, Yankel's own feygelehs salvaged less perishable items, such as sabers, medals, and regimental swagger coats possibly infested with cholera. From packs and saddlebags they fetched him the diaries he sold to illiterates in need of written keepsakes, the ferrotype portraits of sweethearts he peddled to those who had none. They brought him officers' commissions, which he flogged to frightened infantry, suggesting that such papers might ensure them safe-conduct should they try to take French leave.

Eventually, in bitter January in the hills above Alaca Dagh, its ranks pruned by disease and desertion, the weathered remnant of the cloud garrison caught up with history. The forces were amassed in their terrible numbers, encamped from horizon to horizon, their tents surrounding the pavilions of the illustrious. A lucky few got to glimpse the czar's brother, the grand duke Mikhail Nikolaevich himself, and his high command with their visors aglint in the sun. What followed in a mandarin dawn, befogged from the steam of a thousand vats of shock brigade gruel, convinced Yankel, not much given to meditation in those days, that history wasn't his element. It didn't listen to reason, history. You couldn't nudge it and it was unreceptive to bribes. Try to bluff it and it calls yours, forcing you to slay or be slain. To his yingele grandson, who hadn't asked, Yankel had said that, should he want to know about the battle of Alaca Dagh, he could look in the traifeneh history books. His son Mose said the same about his own war to a son who couldn't have given a good goddamn.

On the heels of the armistice came other turns of events, conditions favorable to abomination persisting. As the soldiers had entered history, so had history infected the soldiers, whose ranks seethed with propagandists and mutineers. Suspected revolutionaries were deported to Siberia or executed on the spot. But the unrest in the army only reflected the unrest outside it, where strikes, demonstrations, and peasant insurrections proliferated across the land. Meanwhile Czar Alexander, the benevolent Little Father (though with such benevolence who needed oppression?), was murdered, and the new Alexander reinstituted a time-honored gloom. Because a Jew (a woman) had played a small part in the old czar's assassination, his son and successor revived the once-popular fashion of blaming a nation's troubles on the Jews. The newspapers made much hay of the idea, prompting anti-Jewish riots upon which the government turned a virtual blind eye.

Troops were sent here and there, ostensibly to quell the violence, though their role was never clear. Arrived at a scene of disorder, they were as likely to disarm the victims as the mob; and if they came early when the violence was still a rumor, they sometimes made it a fact, fomenting what they might have suppressed. Sometimes they set the example. They plundered and smashed, practicing first on furniture what they would later do to its owners, punishing them amid white blizzards of gutted mattresses, black blizzards of spiraling ash. They played ninepins with infants, violated daughters in front of their mothers, who were themselves harassed with the severed members of their men. They dragged old-timers by the beard to death's door, then refused them the coup de grace that would allow them to cross over the threshold. Afterward they hitched up and repaired to some nearby tavern, making jokes:

"Did you hear about the pogrom in Nemirov? It did ten thousand rubles worth of improvement."

Often among them was Private Yankel Kabakoff, veteran of the Russo-Turkish War, who (though undistinguished by a single stripe of rank) had made the army his home. Distinguishing himself was anyway not in Yankel's line of behavior, which in recent years had involved lowering a profile already flush with the earth. He'd also dropped certain suspect enterprises in favor of recommitting himself to invisibility. In this way he was an unobtrusive witness to the slaughter throughout the Pale of Settlement. He was there in the Podol district in Kiev, his hands not entirely clean, and in the province of Kherson, the towns of Brody and Lutsk, the Ukrainian villages along the Southern Bug and the Dnestre, where he sniffed the smoke from burning scrolls that jogged his brain.

• • •

In recovering Yankel's stories, Itchy felt he was more than Itchy, possessed of a raging afflatus that was sometimes unsettling. Occasionally, during their transcription, he might almost believe he was composing the stories himself, or it seemed that he was recalling not Yankel's past but his own. This was crazy thinking, of course, and it often made him wish that the memories would leave him alone. He wished there was some way to staunch their interminable flow, though any happenstance might start them hemorrhaging again.

Take for instance the night when all hell broke loose in the girl show, and the "Hey Rube!" went up, a cry that was never heard frivolously on the midway. This was in Hot Coffee, Mississippi, a mean-spirited little backwater where the fixers had long ago advised the carnival to "burn the lot"—that is, never return. But the Hot Coffees, who felt called upon to bear witness to outrage, were faithful devotees of the kootch dancers, whose tent packed them in every evening. They stayed late and paid extra for the blowoff, which included such props as snorting poles and soft-boiled eggs, and invited audience participation.

It happened during an innovative moment in Pagan Lee's contortionist act, the part where she used a fluorescent tube to shed light on the remoter regions of her anatomy. Meanwhile, stage left, in a generous if less educational routine, Miss Melba May was shouting, "Dinner is served!" At that point some of the observers—a branch of the Baptist Brotherhood was in attendance—began to despair of their immortal souls. One of them, said to have been a deacon and a kleagle in the local Klan, was commanded by the Lord to put a match to a bale of hay. Their collective heat fed further by the rising flames, others of the brethren did their righteous duty, carrying Pagan and Miss Melba (who complained she had two good feet) from the now-burning tent. Towheaded youths in bib overalls followed their example, fighting each other for the privilege of dragging more of the naked ladies out of danger.

At the call to assist their own, the carnies dropped whatever they were doing: candy butchers, ride boys, roughnecks, born freaks and made freaks alike, a tottering magician, a boxing chimpanzee, all came running. Never known to dodge a rhubarb, Itchy tore out of the ten-in-one; he leapt into the fray, aiding the roughies who sought to extricate the ladies from citizens bent on their salvation. He joined the bucket brigade at the kootch tent, where the blaze had already swelled to three alarms (which the county fire department chose to ignore), spreading to the nearby hanky-panks and grab stands. But in the midst of the pandemonium, the flames began to recall other flames: the torched ghetto at Bostok, which in turn had reminded Yankel of the tales of Rabbi Nachman, which his disciples were ordered to burn at his death. Breathing the smoke from the rebbe's incinerated stories, the disciples had inhaled an ecstasy so potent it scattered their wits.

Itchy wondered if his grandfather might have confused Nachman's followers with the population of Chelm, another village of idiots. Associations thus multiplying out of control, he abandoned the buckets and raced back to his kip behind the cookhouse to rescue his notebooks from the fire's path.

The carnival never recovered its former glory from the ashes of that night. Having lost so much property in the fire—its flat stores and concessions, the motordrome, the carousel—the City of Fun ("More like a ghost town," grumbled Mr. Julius Few) was reduced to a ragbag outfit no longer capable of supporting its large personnel. The die-hards stayed on: Rufus and Bones pitching patent medicines and Madagaspar making rude remarks, since what self-respecting show would take in such relics? Peabody the ventriloquist, whose dummy Herbert had perished in the flames, revived the old "Venus and the Professor" bit with Miss Melba May. But the senior exotic dancer, most of whose girls had drifted off with hustlers, wasn't the draw she once had been; so Peabody ended up an actuary in Picayune, Mississippi, and Miss Melba, though still in full control of her semivoluntary pectoral muscles,

took a job on a parrot ranch outside Mobile. Selling her trailer to
the show folks, Madame Delphine opened a school of cosmetol-
ogy—which she loosely interpreted as a marriage of astrological
readings and hair-styling—in Americus, Georgia. Og, Victor,
Leo/Leah, Mignon, and the other ten-in-oners naturally remained,
as where else could they go? Ditto Itchy, the Wild Man of the
Caucasus, though his heart wasn't really in it anymore.

The fact was that traveling shows like the City of Fun had
seen their day. These were interesting times for the country, featuring riots, celebrity murders, wholesale hysteria, events and
spectacles compared to which a carnival midway seemed tame.
Even Julius Few's human oddities now had serious competition
from the children of ordinary citizens, who took pills that
changed them into what they called "freaks." Their sons became
shaggy enough to rival even Itchy's own unwashed countenance;
the daughters wore garments as diaphanous as painted breezes,
leaving less to the imagination than a kootch dancer's fan. What's
more, there was a war on somewhere in southeast Asia, and the
natural hostility of small towns toward the carnival was heightened by suspicions that it harbored draft evaders. (This was often
true of the roughnecks, though in Itchy's case no draft status
applied; having never obtained a social security number, he technically didn't exist.) Even the formerly sanguine Mr. Few, teeth
clenched around an expired cigar, was heard to pronounce with
regard to their vagabond life,

"We're history."

With so many young men gone practically feral and wandering
the roads with sleeping bags, a girl no longer had to look to the
likes of an Itchy for reckless encounters. It was a situation for
which Itchy himself, who had other priorities, was not sorry. But
when a shapely young thing, hair cascading to the hem of her
brief dirndl skirt, presented herself in Andalusia, Alabama, Itchy
experienced a temporary reversal. The balanced life, he decided,
was one that never lost touch with the flesh. Besides, it was

Saturday night, Yankel's ghost was quiet, and he had a few hours to kill between lights-out and tear-down.

She'd become separated from a girlfriend in the mirror maze and was hopelessly disoriented, when Itchy gave her a hair-raising start, then showed her out. He was spending more time in the funhouse these days; he was working the hanky-panks, shilling the auction, steering generally clear of the freak tent since his last conversation with Mr. Few. The ten-in-one boss had complained that Itchy's wild-man gaff lately lacked a certain juno-say-kwa. "It needs spice, know what I mean? Glommin' geek stuff where you swallow live snakes and things till the pigeons puke. . . ." But Itchy had lost his appetite for reptiles and headless, twitching poultry. Moreover, he was becoming something of a finicky eater, having developed a recent aversion to mixing meat and dairy dishes; and so he turned in his loincloth and fake fur.

At the funhouse exit the blower lifted the girl's skirt, revealing the neat package of her lace-trimmed tush. Itchy switched off the speakers blaring ghoulish laughter and shut the place down, then stepped out under the harsh lights of the midway. She'd been joined by her friend, who, getting a load of Itchy, tugged at her arm to come on, but some shred of the old fascination must have held. At first she looked at him with something closer to pity than the fear-inspired lubricity he was used to—a look that took him off guard and made him want to retreat into mirrors and blind corridors. But in the end the girl shooed her friend away and gave Itchy a tentative smile.

Later, sans pants on a sofa in the parlor of her family's house on a street under an awning of live oaks, Itchy apologized for his performance. "Guess I'm out of practice," he sulked, suggesting that maybe if she allowed him on top . . . , when the lights came on. A pug-faced man with hooded eyes stood bow-legged at the foot of the stairs. He was naked but for his boxer shorts, their waistband strained by a beer-gut that bulged to the last notch of the gunbelt he was fastening on. Before he could draw the pistol,

Itchy rolled out from under the girl, who tumbled with him onto the carpet. Glad of an excuse to beat it, he scrambled across the floor with his pants in his teeth, diving through the screen of an open window into a chaos of crickets and frightened doves. Behind him he heard the girl's breezy bye-bye, her daddy's "Goddam werewoof!" which preceded the revolver's blast.

Making tracks, Itchy gained such a head of steam that he felt he could run all night, which as it turned out was what he did. Local cops were nosing about the lot when he arrived, inspecting mugg joints as a skeleton crew of roughies broke them down. Instinctively Itchy ducked behind the hoarding of the collapsed ten-in-one, where he was confronted by Mr. Julius Few peeling bills from a wad in his fist.

"Severance pay," he said without ceremony, handing the cash to Itchy.

At his employee's quizzical expression the boss explained exactly how he'd slipped up: he'd interfered with the daughter of the sheriff of Covington County. "They catch you on the lot," continued Mr. Few, "they'll lynch you and nail us for grifters. They'll put the kibosh on the City of Fun for the season if not the millennium."

"But how'd the sheriff know I was a carny?" Itchy knew better than to ask.

"They don't let hippies or niggers to cross over the county line, and you ain't so dumb as to believe he thought you was a person?"

He was amazed at how easy it was to leave. For the purpose of traveling light, Itchy emptied what remained of his wardrobe from the duffel, transferring from his suitcase the bulk of his accumulated archive. It occurred to him in a passing thought that, for all the years he'd called the carnival home, he was carrying away not one keepsake. Not a pitch book, a kewpie doll, none of the pairs of skivvies or locks of hair given him by his many conquests—he could do without the extra weight. What's more, having never been what you'd call sentimental, he took off without a single farewell. He told himself there wasn't time, though who was he fooling? To the show people he'd said good-bye already months ago. Since his grandfather's past had come to possess him, little that was exclusively Itchy had been available to anyone else in a while.

He lit out through mud flats and beanfields, confident they wouldn't catch him since he still maintained close relations with shadows. As he fled, certain details of his grandfather's flight from the Imperial Army came to mind, but Itchy resisted the impulse to stop and make notes. He'd crossed two counties, five silver bayous, hitched a ride on a fertilizer truck to Tuscaloosa, shaved his face and donned a cap in the Union Station men's room, and bought a ticket on a train headed north, before he allowed himself the luxury of jotting down one of Yankel's remembrances.

He arrived on North Main Street at the tail end of a summer that had begun in Memphis with a noted assassination. Sparks from the event kindled others elsewhere, and in the mayhem that followed cities burned. Where once he might have taken delight in the mischief, Itchy now preferred to lie low, seeking someplace where the ashes had settled. Figuring that no one would bother torching the Pinch, which had already fallen to rubble on its own, he turned up on an evening in late September. He paused under a streetlamp, savored a breeze that signaled the dog days were over, and penned the words "dead shtetls" on the back of his hand. This would remind him to continue at his next opportunity the chronicle of Yankel's travels through the smoldering towns of the Russian Pale. Then, seeing a light in a window above Kabakoff's General Merchandise, he trudged up the stairs to Tillie's door.

She answered his knock in a housecoat and hairnet, an excess of cold cream smeared over her nose and cheeks that made her look fit for the Dump Mable joint on the midway. Itchy blinked to erase the picture of his grandmother, in her golden years, seated over a tub of water daring the marks to toss a ball.

"It's me, Grandma, your Itchele," he said, doffing his cap to release runners of greasy hair. "I'm sorry what I did at Rose's wedding." The sentiment, pried painfully from his diaphragm, left a scalding in his chest.

Tillie took a pair of reading glasses from a pocket and held them to her nose, poking her face close to his. Having confirmed the family resemblance, she abruptly drew away. "Sorry don't bring back your papa," she snapped. Itchy hung his head as she added what he supposed was her final word on the subject: "A miracle it would take to bring him back now."

He lifted a brow as if to ask why that needed to be said, but it was more or less what he'd expected. He'd expected to be turned away. Outside his carnival element every door would be closed against him, and he would be forced to drift through all eternity with no place to rest his head. Such a sentence may have once had its romantic appeal, but not tonight. Tonight Itchy was tired. Satisfied that it was anyway useless to argue, he was about to retrace his steps to the street, but Tillie apparently hadn't finished.

"So come in, Mister Sorry," she said, an invitation that included a challenge, "and make for us a miracle."

Grateful if somewhat perplexed, Itchy followed her into the apartment, where he was surprised—though not overly—to find that she wasn't alone. In the parlor, slumped in an antimacassared wing chair, a long gentleman wearing a wintry formal attire was watching a rabbit-eared TV. A new addition since Itchy's day, the television, despite its terrible black-and-white reception, was a technological anomaly amid the surrounding antique bric-a-brac.

"Itchel, I got company," said Tillie, pausing long enough to point. "That's your Uncle Enoch who's visiting from out of town. Enoch, say hello to your wandering nephew, Isaac Kabakoff."

The gent turned his fine if dissipated features toward Itchy, the question mark of his iron gray forelock dangling above his somber eyes. He raised a simultaneous finger and chin in welcome or warning, it was hard to tell which, then turned back to his program: a decade-old amateur hour with a frenetic xylophonist on stage. Itchy supposed it not unreasonable that Tillie's television should show obsolete programs just as her shop dealt in vintage junk. Nodding "Pleased to meet you" to his stranger uncle's rapt profile, he started after his grandmother, who'd shuffled halfway down the hall.

"That one," she complained, ignoring the presence of another two guests as she charged into the kitchen, "trombenik! Turn off the TV, you'd think you were pulling his plug. I bet you're hungry, ain't you, Grandson?" She was stooping to pillage her icebox. "Let's see what I got. I got here some leftover compote and a nice stuffed chicken neck that you used to like. . . ."

Itchy visibly flinched.

"Him at the sink," Tillie continued, her head still in the fridge; though the hairless character washing dishes, his back as broad as a carnival donniker, suspenders dangling, needed nobody's indication. "That's Uncle Joseph. He don't talk much; come to think of it, he don't talk at all." She'd begun to set plates of food on the table, at which a woman sat fanning herself with an open book. "But he likes to help out. Oy, does he help out."

She shook her head and Itchy looked again, this time remarking the broken dishes and mangled cutlery in the drainer, the pool of water at his feet.

"And this one," Tillie went on, fussing with a ribbon around the seated woman's topknot, "this is the Tante Laylah that can speak for herself. Laylah," her voice skipping up the register until she cleared her throat, "meet Itch . . ."

"Itchy." Laylah complemented Tillie's squawk with a husky contralto, and accelerated her fanning.

The manufactured breeze was somewhat chilly. It stirred the curls that teased her pale cheeks, strands come loose from the thick black skein of her hair. Her upturned eyes, dark amethyst, appeared to be brimming with tears, while her full lips were part-ed in the barest hint of a smile. Spellbound, Itchy could not for the life of him have determined her age, that she was older than him being something he intuited rather than knew. The only thing he was certain of was that she was beautiful. She wore ear-rings, bracelets, a thin silk blouse swelled by breasts quietly aflut-ter from the rapid motion of her hand; she wore a red damask skirt with hemstitching, of the type preferred by fortune-tellers and lately young girls. Beneath the skirt there were most likely legs, slender and sturdy and smooth.

Itchy plunked himself down in front of food for which he suddenly had no appetite, already persuaded that for the first time in his outcast existence he was in love.

"Have a good nosh," prompted Tillie. "Here's some soda to wash it down. Forgive me I don't join you but it's time for 'The Millionaire.' That Enoch, he's got us all setting our clocks by the TV." Followed by a lurching, whey-faced, heavy-lidded Uncle Joseph, the old woman bustled out of the kitchen, though not before advising her grandson, "You need anything, just hol . . ."

"Holler." Again Laylah committed a private harmony, then hid her face behind her book. It was one of a pile that lay before her on the table, some with titles like *Her Hidden Flame* and *Black Dahlia*, the kind of back-numbered novelettes Tillie no doubt still stocked in Kabakoff's. Others, such as the one she held in her hand, had Hebrew letters on their leather bindings.

Itchy prodded a mound of horseradish with a celery stalk and tried to sound cavalier. "So what are you reading?"

"Rabbi Naftali's *Epistle of Holiness*," said Laylah, without lower-ing the book.

"Ah," replied Itchy, as if that were one of his favorites.

"It's a marriage and seduction manual," she added in a breathy whisper that caused Itchy to feel heat in the lobes of his ears.

"You ever read any, um, Gaston Leroux?" he asked, reaching back for conversation's sake to the brief literary moment of his childhood.

Laylah lowered her little volume to the height of a veil, revealing only the swimming gems of her eyes. Peering helplessly into them, Itchy caught a fleeting glimpse of his reflection before it went under. Suffocating seconds elapsed, after which he found himself sputtering for air. That's when Itchy became acquainted with love's first principle, the one he'd anticipated back in Madame Delphine's trailer: it hurt. It made you feel as if you'd been occupied by an entire other person. They poured themselves into you, displacing your organs and flooding your lungs till they burst, leaving your ribs to collapse like empty barrel hoops. It was finally too much, this love, especially when you'd already made such adjustments to accomodate the influx of Yankel's stories. Hadn't Itchy thrown out most of what he'd always identified as fundamentally Itchy to make room? Now desire was finishing the job that memory had started, and Itchy didn't seem to know himself anymore.

"Aunt Laylah," he submitted in agony, not to mention shame, because love also made you ashamed of never having loved before; and discarding *Who am I?* as untimely, he asked her point-blank, "Aunt Laylah, who are you?"

She placed her book facedown on the table and heaved a sigh that had its rumbling echo in Itchy's gut. "Didn't your bubbeh say it was time for 'The Millionaire'?" she wondered, rising to sweep out of the room. In her absence Itchy's body went limp as a rag.

In the parlor the family circle were gathered around the fake mahogany television set. It was sunk in a cushioned footstool, crowned by a buff-tinted photo of Yankel and Tillie (circa 1912), and a brass menorah out of which the antenna behind it looked to have sprouted. Uncle Enoch was in his wing chair, Tillie and the undershirted Joseph on the sofa, Laylah in a wooden rocker like a creaking pendulum. With the exception of Uncle Joseph, who appeared despite his open eyes to be dozing, all gazed intently at the snowy TV screen. On it a pie-faced, pompadoured man in a conservative tweed suit was receiving the word from a resonant voice offstage.

"Mike, in that envelope you'll find a cashier's check bearing the name of our next millionaire—"

Having slouched in to station himself behind the sofa, which he held on to for support, Itchy felt a clamorous need to be noticed. Here he was in the grip of such unsettling emotions and no one was paying him any heed. It was all he could do to keep from appealing to the lot of them, "Don't I belong here!," a sentiment he feared he might first have to prove. Recognizing the show they were watching as one of a score his late stepmother had been addicted to, Itchy decided he had nothing to lose by testing the water.

"How come," he asked, resolved to take nothing for granted, "you can watch a show that ain't been on since I was a kid?"

"Shah!" admonished Enoch, lifting his stiff neck from its celluloid collar but not deigning to turn around. "He opens already the envelope."

Tillie tugged at Itchy's sleeve to whisper, "We got funny whatchacallem . . ." She looked toward the inscrutable Joseph as if for an answer, and winked. "We got funny airwaves over North Main Street, or didn't you notice? You never know what you might pick up."

Another sharp "Shah!" from Enoch, who thereupon commenced to override his own authority. "This Michael Anthony," he speculated, meaning the man with the check, "he's maybe from the Mycaenas John Beresford Tipton an angel?"

"Angel-shmangel," scoffed Tillie, who tolerated no nonsense in her own home. "What are you, soft in the brain?" Then she remembered a pet figure of legend for whom she might be willing to suspend her own disbelief. "Could be he's the prophet Elijah that turns up from the blue with good news and money?"

"Could be." This was Laylah humoring, cutting her eyes in their mixture of prankishness and piety in the direction of the newly arrived. "Or could be is Elijah our vagabund visitor there."

Abruptly all heads turned toward Itchy, including the neckless boulder of Uncle Joseph's. Enoch harumphed and gave a horse-laugh. "Ha, why not Elijah? Why not Messiah himself? Hey, Messiah," here was the pot deriding the kettle, "you could use a bath."

Feeling in fact never so unsightly, a slovenliness compounded by the accumulated dust of all his years on the road, Itchy still found it in him to rally. "Kinnehora," he said, speaking syllables he couldn't recall ever having uttered before. But it seemed the sort of thing you said in such company, as did the old saw of his grandfather's that went: "May the Lord who preserved us from Pharoah and Haman save us also from the hand of Messiah." After which he ventured a self-congratulatory grin.

"Shah," said Enoch, again facing forward, apparently the signal for the others to do likewise.

"What'd I say?" Itchy wanted to know.

Tillie tugged and whispered over her shoulder, "Fresh towels I got in the hall closet. This crowd, if they sleep, sleep where they please. Uncle Joseph, he likes it down in the shop, Enoch don't budge from his chair, and to Laylah I gave your papa's old bed-room. But you can have Yankel's study."

Since, among the number of sensations that dogged him, exhaustion figured prominently, Itchy thanked her; he could use a little solitude to sort out his thoughts. Collecting the canvas duf-fel he'd parked by the door, he made his excuses, picked his way through the parlor, and entered the corner room.

He closed the door and opened the dirty window, half-expect-ing trolleys and hustling merchants. Instead he saw the single burning streetlamp, heard distant sirens and gunshots, though they may have been only backfiring automobiles. Itchy switched on the light, a dim overhead bulb in a cinquefoil fixture, its glow more like dusk than broad day. With the light, odors seemed also to have been released: moldering foolscap, dry-rotting plaster, insecticide. Nothing was changed. Fat volumes were still piled across the office desk, spilling onto the cracked leather chair and the floor. Books anchored the hook rug and buttressed the walls, providing pedestals for here a mousetrap, there a bottle of liver pills. So respectfully untouched had Tillie left his sanctum that her husband might have just nipped out for a glass of tea.

Exit Yankel, enter Itchy, who began to browse. He inspected the tomes his grandfather had rescued from burning villages, then shlepped around two continents for as many decades before dumping them in this depository. Here he'd tried to nestle inside them as he had in his childhood. But Itchy, too done in for reverence, questioned how effectively Yankel had been able to return— *teshuvah*, didn't they call it? What kind of return was it when he'd taken every occasion to interrupt his labors and tell his grandson a story? The same stories, by the way, that his own son had ignored a generation before. Hadn't Yankel said it himself: "Once you leave the Book, which there ain't no book but the Book, you can't never go back again." Still you had to hand it to the old kucker; he must've had some power of concentration, because the pages that Itchy was riffling had faded considerably under Yankel's long perusal. As if he'd absorbed their essence, the very words had paled to the point of illegibility.

Not that Itchy could have deciphered a single letter of any one of them. All the same, nobody could accuse him of coming home empty-handed. If Yankel had recovered the books themselves, his grandson had salvaged the stories that were the old man's oral whatsit, his midrashim on impenetrable texts. Having gathered and brought them back to their source, Itchy emptied them now from his bag in an avalanche of notebooks, a flurry of loose leaves—napkins, toilet tissue, and handkerchiefs blanketing the volumes already scattered about the room. And with this act he understood that his job was done. The passion for remembering had finally stopped haunting him, his fever subsided; or at least he was free for the moment to swap one fever for another, whose name was his (perhaps maiden?) Aunt Laylah.

Itchy reeled at the thought of her. In his weariness he ached insufferably, suffered exquisitely. This was how he'd always heard it happened: you were struck, you were smitten. One minute you owned your own fate, the next you belonged hook, line, and sinker to somebody else. It was kismet, or, as his grandpa might have said, *bashert*. Barely able to stand, Itchy turned out the light and peeled down to his shorts, shoving aside books to make room for himself on the camp bed. Folding onto his back, he groaned aloud, "All right, I give up," and felt that in surrendering to Laylah, he'd revived something of his old self. Couldn't he already sense a trickle of familiar energy, confined for a time to his head and heart, beginning to seep its way south? All it needed was perhaps a little shut-eye to complete the process and make him whole again.

But sleep wouldn't come. Restless, Itchy tossed from side to side so violently that he rolled off the cot, tumbling into the slush of notes on the floor. Lying there in the softer bed, he remained wracked with several kinds of desire, though it came to him how he might calm himself down. He began to crawl about in the coppery dark, snatching up random volumes and stacking them in a low palisade. When he'd erected three walls, Itchy pulled the mildewed quilt from the camp bed and threw it over the top. Then he slid under the canopy with his head poking out like a dog in a kennel and, wrapping a stray book in his jeans for a pillow, fell instantly asleep.

He dreamed he attended a family carnival. It was a two-bit mud show featuring such acts as Prof. Enoch's Delusions and Joseph the Albino Ape-Fighter. Tillie was in it too, pitching bust food, hair conk, and bibles from her seat in the Dump Mable joint, while Mose was on the bally working up the crowd for Fried Ida. This was the bit where, every night and twice on Saturdays, he strapped his wife into a replica electric chair. Madame Laylah combined mitt reading and kootch dancing, using a lightning rod for her snorting pole, so that the marks (Itchy among them) fell head over heels. But she was cool to Itchy's suggestion that they visit the synagogue tent, preferring instead a ride on the carousel, one revolution of which constituted a carny marriage. "Synagogue," he insisted, while Laylah coquettishly countered, "Merry-go-round."

"Syna-go-round!" Itchy asserted so forcefully that he woke himself up.

She'd stepped out of his dream to stand over him, her bare feet planted slightly apart, which left him looking into the deeper darkness beneath her skirt.

"Nu?" Laylah, was saying, caressing the books with a pointed toe. "This is a what, a wedding chupeh you maybe made?"

Embarrassed, Itchy sat up and frantically pulled the quilt around his shoulders, toppling the palisades. "It's just um . . . when I was little . . ."

She ignored his alarm to kneel beside him in the debris. Curious, Laylah took his fingers in hers, squinting in the half-light as she examined the inscription on the back of his hand. "What's this 'dead shtetls,' a hoodlum gang?"

Itchy reclaimed the hand, surprised at his own irritation. The veteran teaser, he didn't like being teased, though his impatience with his aunt's persistent queries wasn't a patch on his impatience with himself. He was angry with himself for being afraid. Why afraid, when she'd quite possibly come to offer the intimacy he was hungering for? Wasn't it anyway a little late for Itchy to fall prey to an emotion—large as a funhouse, it seemed—that he'd always prided himself on provoking in others? It should have been the other way around: he should have been the one to steal into her room, crouching over her slumbering form and seeding her dreams until they blossomed into wanton consciousness. That it was she who'd invaded his repose—beyond mortifying, it was downright creepy.

"I got also a tattoo," she was saying, unbuttoning her blouse to expose an alabaster shoulder, "what you might call it a birthmark."

At first Itchy refused to look. Hadn't he seen enough tattoos in his day, ladies with skin like comics left in the rain? But when Laylah cupped his chin to turn his head, inside of which his teeth were audibly chattering, he observed how the mark on her shoulder was as discreet as Ida's number; it was indigo and scarab-shaped, though when you blinked (a trick of the dark?) it might have been the cross between a flower and a flame.

That was all it took. Fear and mortification, never mind any other phenomena related to the natural world, assumed an immediate distant backseat to Laylah's arm. Urged by the pressure of her hand behind his neck, Itchy leaned forward for a closer inspection, so close that his lips grazed the birthmark. At the first contact with her marmoreal flesh, inhaling its fragrance of brimstone and gardenia, Itchy nearly swooned. He moaned like an ill wind.

"Mummedunumebm," he blithered into her shoulder, meaning, "I'm dead and in heaven."

For her part Laylah sighed contentedly. "Shaineh kind," she murmured, which even in his transports gave Itchy pause. Who before had ever accused him of being pretty? Not complaining, however, he continued tracing the sign on her arm with the tip of his tongue, encountering goosebumps. He slid his lips uphill and down, over her shoulder and down the top of her breast, moving with a compulsion he couldn't contain toward satisfying his sudden need to be suckled.

Her skin, albeit sour to the taste, was deliciously cool, while the tears she anointed the crown of his head with were scalding.

"Shlufen iz a gute shoireh, / Itchele vet lernen Toireh," she crooned to him tenderly, though tenderness wasn't exactly what he had in mind. "Sforem vet er shreiben, holy books will he write . . ."

"Eh?" Itchy paused in his progress, grown wise at last to her different agenda. Meanwhile Laylah had pulled him so tightly to her breast that it took all his might to break away, scooting backward from her on his hands. Still plagued by a question she'd yet to answer, he determined, despite the fear that had again seized his throat, not to let her off the hook this time.

"Aunt (ahem) Laylah," he managed, "who are you?"

Her perfect face was streaming tears that left phosphorescent tracks down her cheeks. In a single motion she rose to her feet and yanked the ribbon releasing the torrent of her blue-black hair. A few shards of light from the streetlamp beyond the window were trapped in her thick tresses, but she shook them out—darts and splinters showering the room—until the blackness was absolute.

"I am Laylah, daughter of Lilith, queen of the left-hand side of the Great Abyss. My papa was take your pick—Ashmodai, prince of darkness; Duma, prince of dreams; or Ketev Meriri, lord of the outhouse and wherever else he don't belong. Sometimes Mama, she likes to ride them at once all three. And so a succubus am I, that I come in the night to the men. I give them a suck, I give them a buss, a lek un a shmek, and they're waking up with dew in the pants."

She'd switched on the overhead light and was standing under its yolk yellow nimbus with folded arms. Beholding her thus, Itchy found it hard to hang on to himself. It seemed to him that he dangled from the clapper of a bell that was tolling within and without; he was swinging back and forth between terror and lust. *Bong,* okay he was scared, but even through his dread there was ardor. *Bong,* dread notwithstanding, how he wanted her! *Bong,* he wanted only to hold on and keep from dropping into giddy oblivion, glad all the same that her revelation had rung a bell.

"A shape-shifter, that's me," continued Laylah. "I might come as a cat or a spider or your own sweet betrothed, out of a mirror or a bottle of schnapps. But not no more since I got stuck here in the shape I'm in. This what you see," unfolding her arms to show empty palms, "is what I am from the time I jumped out of a burning book in Zhitomir. . . ."

The tolling had localized itself somewhere in Itchy's chest, restoring him the use of his extremities. Involuntarily he reached for his wadded jeans and began dredging their pockets for a pen.

". . . I jumped straight into the body of a pretty girl that her soul had fled premature on account what they would do to her the Cossacks. Where the soul departs, leaving in the bosom a hollow place, that's where I make my nest."

Because he was able, Itchy got to his feet, wrapping the quilt tighter about him. Presently he would fling himself into Laylah's embrace, which would no doubt have dire consequences, leave him blind perhaps and baying in the general direction of the moon— so be it. But first there was something else he had to do. "I'm listening," he assured her, scooting away. It didn't worry him that he might appear rude, so convinced was Itchy that Laylah was somehow behind his every impulse. This was literally the case, since, still talking, she'd followed him to Yankel's desk, hovering over him as he sat down in the leather chair and opened a book.

"But now I can't succubus," she lamented, bending to tuck a lock of his matted hair behind Itchy's ear. "I lost it how-you-say the knack. You hang around enough by mortals, you forget how to be bad, since who competes in this speciality with the mortals? One day you wake up with a conscience; you don't make nocturnal emission no more, you don't observe Black Shabbat. Oh, you still flirt a bissel, but you can't bear again no unholy babies. All you can do is be varts-froy, the midwife to somebody else's a baby, which I don't mean in particular one from the womb. Babies of the head and heart yet I deliver, even if it ain't circumcized, the heart. You tell me, is this suitable work for a lady ghoul?"

"I'm listening," repeated Itchy, though he wasn't, at least not to Laylah, which isn't to say he wasn't acutely aware of her presence. But where wonder may have had its source in her fetching contours, the fascinating rhythms of her deep-pitched voice, it had since spread to everything in sight. There was nothing that hadn't caught fire from Itchy's infatuation. Cherishing Laylah, you cherished for better or worse the very atmosphere she breathed. You loved the dust devils, the cockroaches, the disordered fragments of your grandfather's knockabout life littering the floor. You loved the warped volumes that would have remained inexplicable even if their printed pages weren't leached of ink; so faded, in fact, that if you wrote in them, the new words would be more distinct than the old.

"I don't like to kvetch," she was keening softly into his ear, "but just look at me." Itchy did not. "Tears I never had before I had you. I want to go home already to the Book!"

He'd begun to write, taking dictation from the voice that shared his head with Laylah's, which was the late Yankel Kabakoff's, if you gave credit where it was due. But on the other hand, wasn't it time he considered a voice grown this habitual as his own? While Itchy furiously scribbled, the demoness unraveled the knots in his filthy hair.

1968

As I fell from the bridge, a giant bird swooped down and snatched me by the seat of the pants. The earth passed far beneath me, and it was not till the bird flew over a mountain that I was able to tear myself from its beak and drop to the ground. I landed roughly and tumbled down the steep mountain slope. Reaching the bottom, I thanked God for preserving me, then noticed that the ground was strangely warm; the grass looked more like fur. All at once the earth started to move and I realized that, instead of a mountain, I'd jumped onto the horn of an enormous beast. I clung to the fur at the base of the horn while the animal plod-

ded all day, pausing at night to graze in an oasis before lying down to sleep. That's when I closed my eyes and leaped from the dizzy height of the animal's back, landing in soft sand which broke my fall. I fled for days without food or water and would have perished, had not the mirage of a glittering caravan turned out not to be a mirage. . . .

This, or something like it, was how Moses Kabakoff, stepping off a bus in his old suburban neighborhood in Memphis, imagined he would explain his travels to his grandchildren. He was sure that by now he had grandchildren. Of course, when you thought of it, the truth wasn't so terribly different, except that his exile had been self-imposed. For the past four years Mose had viewed himself as a penitent, a notion he'd developed during his free-fall from the Harahan Bridge.

No sooner had he leapt, on that ill-starred night of Rose's wedding, than Mose was made to reconsider his impetuous act. The awful velocity of his plunge had seemed instantly too extreme a retribution for such a petty faux pas. For this to make sense you would have had to tally against him all the crimes of his fifty-three years, beginning with a youthful indiscretion he scarcely remembered (though the fruit of its union still dogged him) and his black-market activities during the War, capping it off with his neglect of a phantom war bride (his marriage to whom was itself an effort to correct the errors of youth) and his bastard son, hard cases though they both were. Add to these a suicide—if public flatulence was disgraceful, how much more so suicide?—and you had quite a catalog of iniquities. As the black water rushed up to slap him into perdition, an estate to which Mose had never subscribed, he was heartily sorry for his sins; he promised a God he didn't believe in that he'd atone for them every one, if only he were allowed to survive.

It was an oath he regretted the moment he realized he hadn't drowned, though you might have made a case that he'd drowned indeed and been brought back from a watery grave. For hadn't he struck the river with an impact that left him insensible, so water-logged that his resuscitation, according to jocular deckhands, had required a bilge pump? He'd been spotted in his fall and fished from the drink by merchant sailors on a passing barge. As he lay among them, blue and sputtering in his soggy tuxedo, Mose had inspired an assortment of wisecracks. Hard-bitten veterans quipped they should throw him back; the younger men, some with their hair tied in queues, educated types but disenfranchised and taken to drifting, suggested (though it was night) that he'd flown too near the sun, (though they were inland) that he'd been spewed from a whale.

Mose was doubly grateful that neither captain nor crew were inclined to ask questions, but merely offered to put him ashore at the next town. At first he was tempted to let them; he could go home again as if nothing had happened and no one would be the wiser. Recovered from his dunking, however, lounging in a warm berth in a roustabout's borrowed overalls, Mose concluded over his coffee that he'd been spared an untimely death for a purpose. Was he or was he not a man of his word, bound in good faith to the pledge he'd made while plummeting from the bridge? Before returning he should seek in some way to make amends for a checkered past. Though, if he were honest, wasn't there something else?—a nameless longing that, in the absence of family and business concerns, was urging him to continue the voyage.

As an initial gesture of penance he offered them all his money. He would repay their kindness by handsomely defraying the cost of his passage, maybe endow their trade union, their orphans and widows fund; his largess knew no bounds. But it turned out that his wallet and checkbook had been lost in the river. In lieu of remuneration, short-winded and pot-bellied though he was, Mose offered to work off his fare. Uncompensated menial drudgery, that was the ticket; assign him any task and he'd tackle it with zeal and humility, working steadily until his labors had earned him the right to go home.

The captain, a fierce-faced man whose mustache made him look as if his nostrils were aflame, was nevertheless amused. At length, overcoming his official reservations, he gave out that he was willing, social security number or no, to put the foundling on the payroll. But Mose wouldn't hear of it, insisting that his services be rendered gratis or not at all. This he was in the end permitted, though not before he'd first had to forfeit his anonymity, since the crew, many of whom went by aliases themselves, had taken to calling him Sinbad.

They were carrying acres of sweet-scented hardwood downriver to New Orleans, where they would take on barrels of crude oil, hauling them back upstream to Dubuque and beyond. In the beginning, clumsy and out of shape, more accustomed to giving orders than taking them, Mose found it hard to make himself useful. But under the patient tutelage of fellow crewmen, especially the younger members who maintained that theirs was a job for poets and dreamers, he began to learn. He got the hang of keeping the cargo secure in all weather, battening it down with a variety of knots: cat's paws, diamonds, figure-eights—Mose was as pleased with knowing their names as with mastering their intricacy. He cracked eggs and stirred brackish soups in the galley, oiled screw pumps and tightened cogs in the sweltering boiler room. He scrubbed the head, poop, and promenade of the trim little tug that propelled the long concatenation of barges, at whose bow he sometimes stood watching the river at night. Sometimes Mose sat with others atop stacks of lumber, swatting mosquitoes and smoking the funny cigarettes whose glow he tended to confuse with lightning bugs. Similarly the shadows along the bluffs became the desperate characters (One-Rump George, Stacker Lee) that figured in the deckhands' tall tales.

Along with his fat wallet Mose also in time lost his paunch, his baggy jowls, and the frosty curls encircling his freckled pate boiled over his ears. He acquired a tan that caused his black bargemates to joke there might have been one of them in his woodpile; though Mose preferred to think of himself, in the fanciful moments that came to him now with more frequency, as a lascar. Off-duty he liked listening to the guitars and mouth harps below decks, the songs that were hymns to rootlessness. He read magazines with photo spreads of naked ladies whose well-wrought limbs made him weep, waking his desire for a wraithlike woman (more wraithlike than even his dead wife) who as yet had no face or name. He read dog-eared paperbacks passed on to him with evangelical earnestness by the younger crewmen. Mose, who'd boasted that he never finished a book, perused with interest the popular chronicles of Yaqui shamans dispensing sagacity, of Martians come to teach earthlings alternative ways. But his favorite was an account of his years on the river by an author who'd decoded sights—the mist curling among the cypresses, the hieroglyphs of half-submerged driftwood, the signal lamp flashes of yellow foxfire from a purple levee at night—previously mystifying to Mose.

From the young men he learned the watchword: "You're either on the barge or off it," implying that anyone not on board had missed the boat. He liked feeling a part of what he thought of as a floating island, at once in the wide world and outside of history. Astonished at how little he missed his family and Kabakoff Publishing, Inc., Mose now and again caught himself thinking, "It's lovely, God forbid, to live on a barge." He was thankful for having been rescued, glad if you must know to be alive, though he dismissed such sentiments as unbecoming a penitent.

Thus passed a couple of years. It took Mose that long to remember that he was supposed to be ashamed of himself, and, remembering, he got off the barge with regrets at New Orleans. Altogether too pleased with his altered appearance—he was toughened and appallingly hale for his years—he'd decided it was time for the real atonement to begin. He would seek out even more obscure circumstances, some meager situation that, when he found it, he'd recognize because it would feel a lot like home.

With its ramshackle pastel houses choked in clematis, their frames buckling under the burden of malarial air, New Orleans seemed an ideal place to wash up in. In a crumbling faubourg behind the French Quarter Mose came upon a community of destitute kids—"freaks" they labeled themselves with backhanded pride. Living mostly on the street, they slept five or six to a room in a paint-peeling camel-back appointed in wall-to-wall superstition. They survived by selling feather earrings, macramé bracelets, passing the hat after "revolutionary" theater performances in the Quarter. (This was a style of open-air theater involving public nudity and offenses hurled at the audience, which often resulted in beatings and arrests.) They fed one another out of a communal pot of red beans and rice, garnished with mushrooms said to have magical properties.

This was the authentic squalor, thought Mose, lower than which you could not sink. It occurred to him: *I jumped in the river but I never touched bottom.* Here, by way of a necessary prelude to restitution, he could touch bottom. For the novelty and presumed wisdom of his years—he must be wise to have so little regard at his age for dignity—Mose was welcomed into their derelict ranks. They applauded his willingness to don the outlandish shmattes from their collective wardrobe, his tolerance for their eldritch music, their utopian ideas. On a porch swing twined in scarlet trumpet flowers, breezes soughing through the broken jalousies, he sampled their books: *The Politics of Ecstasy, The Morning of the Magicians,* a poet who said: "Go love without the help of anything on earth."

That's easy for you to say, thought Mose, who all the same guessed he had nothing to lose by trying.

Though duly informed of the risks, he took potluck with them. Their food, he should know, afforded one glimpses of paradise, after which the world never looked the same. "It already don't look the same," replied Mose, remarking the kaleidoscopically painted walls and faces; but because he frankly didn't believe a word they said, he ate. He was anyway goaded by flattery to the effect that he must be "the most cosmic senior citizen on earth"; their assurances that, in his paisley kerchief and pirate shirt, with his third eye open, he was beautiful.

"Pretty I ain't with the two eyes I was given," he told them. "So how's a third supposed to improve my looks?"

But eventually, under the influence of a full belly and an expanded consciousness, Mose was persuaded. What wasn't beautiful? Certainly these kids in their rags of many colors, like Purim-shpielers from outer space, were a sight to behold. He watched them among rioting camellias, tossing the fortune-telling coins they claimed to have lifted from the eyes of dead gods. Whether plucking at palm fronds from the windows of the St. Charles trolley or being trodden under the heel of the law, they were a picture. They were so brilliant astride the raised sepulchres in a bayou cemetery that you might almost have believed death itself was beautiful.

Again Mose was left feeling shamefully complacent and beholden. He felt particularly beholden to the young girls for whom his age—when you compared it to, say, the life of a star—was immaterial. In their floppy hats, their toches-length gossamer shifts, their nipples like jelly beans, they calmed the wanting that still flared up in him sometimes. To show his appreciation he peddled their bracelets and earrings on the street. He endowed these items with a certain romance, especially appealing to tourists, by employing the furtive approach he'd used to good effect in his black-market days overseas.

"Right here," in sotto voce, "I got your gen-u-ine American deviant paraphernalia. Hey, I'm talking to you."

Then the community determined on printing an underground newspaper by means of a mangled rotary press salvaged from a riverside dump. "To penetrate the bullshit," they asserted without a trace of irony, "it's time we had an organ of our own." Working tirelessly to restore it, Mose fashioned from the old bones of gears, levers, and rusty flywheels a cottage industry. The paper, when it appeared, was a hodgepodge of articles with a shared philosophical bias; it viewed society through a Marxist perspective as illustrated by the conflict between the Morlocks and Eloi in H.G. Wells's *Time Machine*. Throughout its pages you were exhorted to transcend the depredations of history, engineered by fascist insects with the faces of your mother and father, and learn to live for love. There were editorials favoring something called "passive-aggressive resistance," cartoons depicting unnatural relations between political figures and aliens; there were listings of local bacchanals and inspiring quotations attributed to Bilbo Baggins and Joan of Arc.

The Lotus-Eater, as the paper's masthead declared it, enjoyed an instant popularity, due in part to Mose's energetic hustling around the Quarter. A substantial profit was realized, allowing the community, who now thought of themselves as a business cooperative, to rent an old building on Chartres Street. After renovations they assembled under one roof a printing press, theater (this in the courtyard that doubled as a café), and craft shop. For a while they provided a headquarters for the city's subterranean activities, surfaced in a perpetual costume ball. But in time the tourists, come in droves to get a load of the beatniks, edged out the very ones they'd hoped to see. Still they spent freely, and the thriving Lotus-Eaters Co-op, urged by Mose to make prudent investments, abandoned their decaying faubourg for independent efficiency apartments uptown.

"Can I help it that I got the Midas touch?" wondered Mose, the thought recalling the lyrics from one of his daughter's teenage LPs. Which reminded him that he had a daughter, a son (or two). He remembered also that this wasn't what he'd intended: in fact it was backward, this prosperity, since he was supposed to be suffering for his sins. A flop at penance, he coined a phrase: "Atonement begins at home." After all, what better expiation could you ask for than that your family should serve as witnesses to your disgrace? So Mose designated the craving that had started up once again in his heart as homesickness. Where suffering was concerned, why look beyond your own backyard?

He might have barged through the front door demanding sanctuary—it was still his house. But a gaunt man now with billowing sideburns in a headband and woven accessories, and a fringed leather vest, Mose was afraid of giving them too great a shock. First he should get the lay of the land, he decided, wading into the shrubbery.

It was a mild October night and the low windows about the house were open. Looking into the den, its paneled walls thronged with Chamber of Commerce citations, Mose spied two young men in their respective recliners watching baseball on TV. One of them, wearing polished oxbloods and a necktie despite the casual evening hour, he recognized as his son, the assiduous David. Though scarcely more than a pup, there was little about him (save his beardless cheeks) that seemed youthful. His pink eyes flickered beneath a worried brow; his sandy hair, if you looked close, had begun to thin. The other was his daughter's listless husband Nat, asprawl in his armchair in an attitude of surrender.

When the phone rang on the tray beside David, he picked it up and spoke impatiently. "So Max, what are you telling me?" Max Spiegel had been press foreman of Kabakoff Publishing since 1959. "All right, give the plates a diazo-polyvinyl bath and I'll look at them in the morning. What do you expect when you don't de-scum after every litho? And as for the Maybelline order, use the phototypositor yourself. That nephew of yours, he gets five fonts to the reel, he thinks he's Gutenburg. . . ."

Where pride might have been, Mose had only a sinking feeling; he moved away from the window, shambling around to the other side of the house. In the kitchen amid burnished copper was Rose, who'd let herself go since her marriage. Her heavily painted face had grown additional chins and her ankles, below a tent-sized

muumuu, were like harem trousers made of flesh. She was standing over a butcher's block preparing a plate of cold cuts, presumably for the men, eating one of every few pieces of salami she
sliced. At the table, making meandering rainbows with a fistful of
crayons while slurping soda from a straw, sat a carrot-topped little
girl in a quilted blue robe.

"My granddaughter," breathed Mose.

"Mommy," she was asking between adenoidal pulls at her
straw, "when can I have a baby brother?"

"I don't know, honey," said Rose, her voice a touch guttural.
"Maybe when that sad-sack father of yours gets his sperm
count up."

"Mommy," she persisted, "was I born on my birthday?"

"That's right, sweetness. Some coincidence, huh?"

"Mommy, when's my birthday?"

"Oo mo," swallowing a slice of corned beef, "perfectly well."

"I forget."

"Let's see," Rose considered. "The last time I looked, it was
still June 4th. You were born a year and one week to the day after
the first anniversary of your Grandpa Mose's—may he rest in
peace—fart."

Mose staggered backward out of the flower bed, bludgeoned
by understanding. He stood shakily on the lawn and assured the
implacable facade of his house that he could take a hint. "I get the
message." It was clear to him now that his physical presence in
these parts was a stupid redundancy; having stepped out of his
former life into legend, he was stranded there and could not
return.

"You're beautiful, I love you," Mose whispered to the windows, sounding in his own ears a little like a nightclub act. Then
he evaporated into the dark.

He went—where else would he go?—back to North Main
Street. Met by blight and desolation, he told himself, "This I
deserve." But instead of a mood more suited to a wasted landscape,

not to say life, Mose felt his spirits lift the moment he'd set foot in the old neighborhood. Then he thrilled to see it still on its corner next to the gravel heap that once was Ridblatt's Bakery: Kabakoff's General Merchandise, a beacon, its lights on upstairs and down. Without taking time to reconnoiter, he stepped up to try the shop door, and finding it open walked right in.

"Mama," he announced, because there she was, "I'm home!"

The years hadn't yet robbed her of her stoutness, her floral housecoat draping her barrel shape like a shower stall. With the hairnet over rollers resembling a radio chassis, her slack face a taffy pull, Tillie was in the process of stocking her shelves. Behind her was a walking column of boxes containing God only knew what, though Mose would have wagered sombreros, hair switches, foot batteries, bicycle bells. As it passed beneath a ceiling fan the wobbling stack was truncated, one box left precariously riding a wooden blade. The procession halted in front of Mose, who'd planted himself athwart an aisle with open arms.

"Mama."

Tillie squinted over the rims of her glasses. "Do I know you?"

"I'm your own lost boy, your Moishele, though some call me Sinbad these days."

Unimpressed, she eyed him suspiciously. "Since when does my Moishe, peace on his soul, dress up like a wild Indian?"

"I changed."

"You changed into somebody that ain't my son."

Mose sighed, it was too true. "Look," he offered, lifting a pantsleg, "I got this scar when I was bit by Plesofky's dog and this—" Tillie made a face "—when I sat on the stove. I wet the bed till I was seven. When I was nine you told Miss Tulip at the fourth-grade pageant, 'My son plays the front end of the donkey or nothing doing.' I remember the time you hid Lazar the bootlegger in the cellar and what he did down there with the ladies' galoshes. When I was twelve, I kept a copy of *The Physical Life of Women* under a floorboard, which you can check it out. . . ."

"Enough!" barked Tillie, and swatted him over the head with her clipboard.

"But that was forty-five years ago!" Mose protested.

"I have to make sure you ain't a ghost," explained Tillie, then swatted him again. "And that's for not writing."

"You know from the War I'm no good at letter-writing," Mose sulked, rubbing his head.

"It ain't the half of what you're no good at."

To this Mose would have happily pleaded guilty, but Tillie never gave him the chance. She cried his name ("Moishe, mein kaddishel!") and threw herself on his neck, sobbing mightily. Taken off guard, Mose stumbled forward with the burden of his mother, both of them crashing into the stack of boxes that tumbled all around. He struggled to recover his balance in time to save himself and Tillie from sprawling onto the floor. Having established them more or less securely on their feet again, Mose was free to regard his Uncle Joseph standing in the rubble, looking several degrees beyond peaked. Where he wasn't covered by an undershirt and his pants with their dangling suspenders, you could see clear through him. His thick biceps and the bullet dome of his skull distorted the objects behind him—the remnants table, a bald manikin that might have been his bride—as if they were viewed through the wrong end of a telescope.

Observed Mose: "I think this is where I came in."

Tillie disengaged herself, dabbed beneath her glasses with her collar, and straightened her housecoat with a shrug. "Your shnor-rer relations," closing her eyes forbearingly, "they sneaked back when the coast is clear. Now that it ain't nobody but spooks live around here, they're cozy again. This one, he helps me out like a hole in the head."

Joseph had begun to gather up boxes, dropping some in the process and trodding in their contents.

"How can you tell whether he's coming or going?" asked Mose. He was thinking of that distant contagion of disappearing encouraged by himself and his kind. But the return of his dummy uncle, couldn't you call it a vindication? proof that Mose's one-time loss of faith and his subsequent wandering penance had not been for nothing?

"Uncle Joseph," he tendered, eager to let bygones be bygones, "you don't have to vanish on my account. I believe in you, farshteyst? Fact is, I believe in everything. What I don't believe in, they ain't yet invented." Then, swelled by his own reserves of untapped credulity, he declared, "There's no place like the Pinch!"

"Ach, Moishe," Tillie clucked her tongue, "you come back to me a nincompoop."

She hustled him upstairs where he was delighted to find Uncle Enoch—it was just like old times; though in return for his effusive greeting Mose got only an irritated "Shah!" This wasn't quite the uncle he remembered, the one who was always ready with a laundry list of complaints, always boasting past glories and his influence among the mighty, lamenting a lost pair of wings. Now the old humbug appeared to be merely marking time, slouched in front of a television in a state of dissolution at least as advanced as Uncle Joseph's. He was glued to the screen, where a bearded prophet (bearing no resemblance to Charlton Heston or any other celluloid incarnation Mose knew of) was smashing the tablets of the Law.

"Praised be the Lord who permits the forbidden, eh?" muttered Enoch to no one in particular.

Having paused to puzzle over his uncle's words, Mose was nudged from behind by Tillie, telling him not to mind the wet blanket and shoving him toward the promise of a noodle ring. "This one's got your bowtie kasheh. . . ." Mose admitted he was famished; he was hungry for the sort of food that, though it might not induce visions, nevertheless enkindled your insides for days. After a few steps down the hall, however, what he heard over the hubbub on TV made him dig in his heels once again. Somewhere a deep velvet voice was singing.

Mose shuddered, his heart turned to ice and slid from his chest down into his underwear, where it promptly melted. That's how it felt sinking in, a realization finally so simple that he wondered how he could ever have forgotten. What he'd been calling "homesickness," it seemed, had always had another name. Funny how he hadn't dared to pronounce it, had willfully misplaced it so long ago, only to discover that he'd been looking for it—albeit by a somewhat scenic route—all his life.

"Mama," he asked, "where is she?"

"First have your supper, on you skinny ain't so becoming."

"Mama."

Then a lull among the Israelite rabble made it apparent that the voice was issuing from behind the closed door of Yankel's study, toward which, having about-faced, Mose was irresistibly drawn. He opened the door on a room suffused with a dazzling opalescence, which forced him to squint her first into focus before he could feast his eyes. Somehow it didn't surprise him that, while transparent, she was still youthful, though she had been impossibly old when last seen. It figured that for her the years were elastic, that she'd come back just as he remembered her on that faraway night in Shendelman's, a woman made of moonstone and vapor. She was standing over a bushy-haired party in a flannel bathrobe who sat busily scribbling at Yankel's desk.

"Sforim vet er shreyben," she sang into the scribbler's ear. "Vet er m'yehrtz-e-shem bleyben / God willing he'll remain . . ." On the last lilting note she turned to Mose.

It was a lot to take in at a glance, and Mose preferred to view the scene exclusive of a certain unanticipated element. Granted, he recognized the intruder as his own bastard offspring, and when the time came he would give him his due. He'd tell him what?—I love you, all is forgiven, and so on, in the spirit of his new generosity. Come to think of it, who wasn't he willing to forgive these days? But on the other hand, brooded Mose, why should the she-devil be singing to him?

"Laylah!" he cried out, then had to grip the doorpost as if his soul had passed a stone.

He expected, now she'd dropped the lullaby, that Itchy would also leave off his writing, but he continued with if anything more intensity. Even through his lathered excitement Mose could see that there was a connection between the rate of Laylah's vanishing and the momzer's accelerated hand. Still he stood waiting for her response, which would no doubt be something suitably acerbic: *Reb Hiawatha, vi gaits* . . .? He was almost disappointed by the warmth of her greeting.

"Mose darling, you're just in time to say to me good-bye."

Mose shook his head vehemently. "I said good-bye to you already in another life. Today goes like this: Laylah hello, I'm back, you're beautiful. . . ."

Her spectral features had gathered in an expression sufficiently forbidding to check that line of appeal. Having shut him up for the moment, she relaxed into sorrow.

"You're too late."

Shaken to his sandals, Mose fought to confine the evidence of his discomposure to a twitching jaw. This wasn't what he wanted to hear. "What do you mean, too late?" he asked to buy time. He was trying to ignore the suspicion, which accompanied his increasing alarm, that he was the victim of a conspiracy perpetrated by a demon and a half. Pointing toward the desk, Mose scattered a drift of loose pages as he lurched forward and demanded to know, "What's he writing?"

"*He*," Laylah forthrightly informed him, placing fingers like isinglass on the scribbler's shoulder, "has a name."

It cost him a considerable effort to make it personal. "Itch-ch-chy," he managed as if forcing a sneeze, "what are you writing?"

"A book," mumbled Itchy without looking up.

Mose nodded like it wasn't perfectly obvious, noticing how the kid was using an old volume of Yankel's to do his composing in. "But that one's already been written," he offered lamely.

Itchy didn't bother to dignify the remark with an answer. Meanwhile Laylah, gypsy raiment and all, was fading fast.

"Will you wait!" Mose flung about in his mind, trying on a command, an entreaty, before settling for a desperate truth, "I don't want you to go." Without her (this was his sudden conviction) what was the point of anything?

But she was resolved. "You got a home, I got a home, all God's children, never mind the devil's, got a home, which they should go there if they can find. Yoysef is a nuisance without he has some hussar's a head to break, and you see for yourself how oysgeputtert goes Uncle Enoch. Laylah, she also ain't having around here so much fun."

"Okay okay," Mose conceded, ruling out argument, which meant he was left with only a last resort. "I don't like to have to take off the gloves," he threatened, "but what other choice do you give me?" And again he called the kid by name: "Itchy!"

Itchy lifted his head, a certain exalted cast illumining his ebony eye.

"Criminal!" accused Mose. "Do you know what you're doing? You're disappearing your own mama is what!"

Sniffing impatiently, Itchy answered, "So what do you think, I was born again yesterday?" and continued his task.

Mose turned to the shimmering blue adumbration that was Laylah. "I won't let you go," he proclaimed. There was yet another course of action left open, and drastic though it was, he felt equal to it. He knew the antidote to this situation, and in his knowledge was power. With all of his aching concentrated in a single portion of his anatomy, Mose fumblingly undid the fly of his calypso pants, which fell to his ankles. His risen member, bald and inflamed as its owner, parted the curtain of his shirttails in an audacious debut. Gripping it like the neck of a broomstick stallion, he spurred himself forward at a headlong shuffle.

"Mose," protested Laylah, her voice emanating from a hollow distance, "not in front of the boy!" But she was laughing. In fact, nothing remained of her but laughter, her ribcage an evanescing silver glockenspiel tickled by the wind. Then there was only wind fanning the leaves of open books, a sultry breeze that Mose made frantically to embrace, clutching nothing at all. Elsewhere, in an empty armchair in the parlor, a concave cushion plumped itself back up, the television returning to its Indian-head test pattern. A stack of boxes downstairs in the store was suspended a second in midair before tumbling into the aisle, and in the kitchen Tillie paused while sucking the marrow of a wishbone to sigh a fond "Good-bye and good luck."

Mose groped a little more, then gave it up. His manhood drooped in front of him like a failed divining rod, pointing feebly in the direction of the scribe at work. Still hobbled at the ankle, Mose scooted over to the spot recently occupied by his first and only love. As he stood at Itchy's shoulder, his impulse was to snatch up the book and tear it asunder, this in lieu of doing the same to its single-minded author. Why he hesitated, Mose couldn't say, though it may have been due to the glimmer of admiration he'd suddenly conceived for Itchy's penmanship. You had to hand it to the little gargoyle: the letters were as neat as calligraphy, dark and defined, moving steadily across the page like black flames along a fuse.

The section at hand—Mose bent closer to read it—had to do with his own father's desertion from the Russian army. It recounted Yankel's travels through ruined villages collecting sacred books. When he couldn't save the books, he collected refugees—golems, devils, fallen angels—who'd escaped the books before they were destroyed. Mortals and mythic creatures alike were at large in the land, mingling (according to Itchy) like freaks and normals in a carnival. "Like some of them that you should have seen where I lived in New Orleans," Mose heard himself inject, relieved that Itchy ignored his kibitzing. But the damage was done, and, wincing from a stab of guilt that—deep as it was—missed his vitals, Mose read on. This cockamamy story, which you had to admit had its charm, was beginning to give him ideas.

"Tell you what I'll do," he submitted at last to his son, who never turned a hair but no matter. Mose had seen it all in an instant, how he had first to reclaim old Shendelman's antediluvian linotype from the basement of Kabakoff Publishing. On it, once he'd made the necessary repairs, they could print Itchy's chronicle tabloid-fashion, serialized and suitable for vending in Tillie's store. The tourists and browsers who frequented the place for its oddball merchandise would return every week for a fresh install-ment. Soon the word would spread and who knew but, with a lit-tle luck, syndication and film rights might follow; though they shouldn't get ahead of themselves. The principal thing was to make a living. Meanwhile, by the time they'd done publishing Yankel's story, Itchy would be well into writing Mose's own, which the father thereby proposed to dictate to the son.

"So what do you say?"

Without interrupting the flow of his composition, Itchy told him he should get in line. Then he turned to his papa and sug-gested respectfully, "You ought to pull your pants up. This isn't dignified."

1881—1912

It was in the Jewish quarter of the town of Durashna, or Monastyrschina or Ekaterinoslav, that Yankel again remembered there was more to life than death. He was among a detachment of soldiers who'd stepped in from a street of spiraling smoke and feathers to join rioting peasants in looting an old timber syna-gogue. Having plundered the ark of its Torah, they removed the crowns and silver breastplates, piled the scrolls in front of the bima, and set them on fire. A rabbi in a bloody white talis was dragged forward, hoisted to a rafter, and hung by a noose around his ash gray beard. The flames curled his toes and caused him to wriggle like, as the soldiers remarked, "a hooked jewfish." That was when Yankel's long dormant memory stirred, waking up interestingly enough on a scene from his childhood: the cheder boys were pasting the beard of a snoozing Rabbi Kirsky to the table with sealing wax. When he returned to the present, Yankel found himself backed halfway up a ladder whose brittle rungs collapsed beneath his every step. Only at the top did he think to ask himself, "Is this wise?" before scrambling into a loft and waiting to be burned alive.

Discovering a cache of old books, he burrowed under them; he pulled their splayed covers on top of him as if, thus already buried, he might be spared the fate of cremation. But although the flames scorched the rafters and blistered the ornamental animals on the walls, the synagogue remained intact. Hours passed and Yankel took courage, deciding that, insignificant as he was, he might now complete his obscurity by staying absent without leave. No one would even miss him until roll call the next morning, by which time he could be far away. That night when the pogrom had subsided, hastened by an eerie feeling that he wasn't alone, Yankel resolved to make his break. Convinced that they had somehow protected him and he ought to return the favor, he gathered up as many books as he could stuff under one arm and dropped from the loft.

He dropped clear through the charred floorboards, which splintered around him, and fell into the cellar below the shul. Dazed and multiply contused, mad to climb out of that fetid place, Yankel was helped in his efforts by a pair of peasants whom the noise of his crash had alerted. They hauled him up by an arm and a hank of coarse hair, and were briefly appeased at the sight of his uniform, but his frightened eyes and the books he made to hug to his chest at length gave him away. "A yid! A yid!" they bellowed triumphantly, until they themselves were set upon from behind. Then, released and falling backward into his hole again,

Yankel saw him framed in a moonbeam through a broken window: the broad, bullet-headed figure in a belted capote, cracking together like muted cymbals the peasants' skulls.

On his abraded hands and knees in the dark, Yankel had begun to grope for his scattered books, when the dispatcher of his enemies leapt into the cellar beside him. He grabbed the deserter by his free arm with a pincerlike grip and began to haul him into the deeper darkness. Torn between gratitude and terror, Yankel had no choice but to follow in blind career. "Where are you taking me?" he begged to know, getting not so much as a grunt in reply. To himself he sought to explain his whereabouts: in his youth Yankel had heard rumors of catacombs, tortured tunnels dug centuries ago under towns all over the Pale, where the Jews could hide out from Bogdan Chmielnicki's raids. Surely this was one of those. But no amount of reasoning could dispel Yankel's impression that this outsize mieskeit creature was leading him down the throat of Gehinnom.

When they'd negotiated what seemed like a dozen versts of choking pitch-blackness, Yankel was shoved up some stairs through a flimsy trapdoor. The scene he beheld, as he emerged from behind an iron stove, confirmed his worst suspicions. But nightmarish as it was, the compartment they were in proved to be only an outpost of hell, a poorhouse being used for a makeshift infirmary. There, under cover of the universal anguish—putrid air ululating with the cries of victims, the chants of healers, families wailing curses and prayers—the deserter and his silent companion were able to stay the night unnoticed. But having been billeted during his time in the extremest of circumstances, Yankel nonetheless slept with one eye open; this he kept trained on his hairless protector, who he'd concluded was not a human being.

At dawn, after Yankel had swapped clothes with a dead man, they set off together from the poorhouse. Why not? The deserter was in need of a bodyguard, and the other, having saved him once, seemed doggedly committed to ensuring his welfare thereafter. It was a service that more than compensated for Yankel's inclination to travel light. In weeks to come he was made to understand, through miming gestures and semiliterate notations, that he was in the company of one Yoysef, a human simulacrum escaped from the pages of *Sefer ha-Shem*. In Chapter Five of that text he'd been molded out of clay by Rabbi Eli the Lame for a Shabbos goy; he was created to help the rebbetzin with her housework and deal death, when necessary, to the enemies of Israel. At the death-dealing he'd been a fair hand, but his zeal for household chores was not matched by his competence, and his blunders resulted in the burning of his native village of Volograd to the ground.

At first Yankel challenged him. "Where's your tattoo?" he asked, pleased to have lately recalled some of the finer points of ancient mysteries. He was thinking of the famous golem of Judah Loew, sorcerer rabbi of Prague, who placed a mark on his creature's forehead that, when erased, rendered the thing inanimate. But Yoysef indicated that he belonged to a new generation of golem, made unblemished so he could never be shut down.

Do I believe this? Yankel asked himself, only to discover that the answer was again a resounding *Why not?* These days what wasn't plausible? If a child of history could dwell for a time exclusively in books, then by the same token shouldn't a character born in a book be able to enter history? Stranger things had happened, though no example sprang immediately to mind. Still, Yankel recognized a common bond between himself and the lumbering defective: they were both of them exiles, both hoping—it was Yoysef's artless ambition, which Yankel had also contracted—to eventually find their way back into the books they'd once called home.

Soon the deserter had in any case come to depend on his lunk of a sidekick. Though his domestic skills may have been wanting, Yoysef was a regular beast of burden, a tireless shlepper of the library that Yankel had begun to acquire; he was vigorous at wringing the necks of the chickens Yankel stole. In their various encounters with bandits, constabulary, and anti-Semitic thugs, the golem never failed to acquit himself well, making up for what he lacked in stealth and discretion with demoralizing strength.

Because the Jews were everywhere undesirable, and a Jewish deserter if identified would be shot on sight, they gave the towns (both thriving and smoldering) a wide berth that winter. Yankel allowed his hair and beard to grow, altering his appearance as often as the prophet Elijah changed disguises. He saw to it that Yoysef's glabrous features were kept muffled in woolen rags, except on those occasions when his naked visage was needed to inspire fear. In this way they passed for a pair of the dispossessed, just another rattleboned luftmensch with an overgrown half-wit in tow. They lived rough, often sleeping in open ditches and snowy woods, taking shelter whenever possible in a corncrib or stable. Hardships notwithstanding, there was seldom any shortage of camp fires to be shared with other travelers—for legions of them were wandering the roads, swarming over the fields, driven from their homes by torch and imperial ukase.

So beggarly were the lot of them that it was hard to distinguish between those uprooted from their native provinces and the odd fugitive from some desecrated holy book. After a while there seemed no point in trying. Now and again, though, Yankel might pause to consider if perhaps the Almighty Himself, fled from say the Book of Genesis, was among the wayfarers masquerading as an ordinary Jew.

In the spring Yankel and Yoysef sometimes risked the villages, where they might count on a handout or pick up a few kopeks performing odd jobs. (Yankel was always reluctant to volunteer them for the latter, since Yoysef's frequently bungled good intentions often succeeded in getting them run out of town.) Some of the more rural settlements, purged of their Jewish populations, had become veritable ghost shtetls, though a handful of demighosts usually managed to hang on. These congeries of rotten thatch, rusted tin, and termite-riddled logs surrounded by a moat of mud were all of a piece. Like Yankel's library, which he thought of as the several volumes of a single Book, all the villages were the same village with a variety of names.

Though one such hamlet, once they'd reached it after ferrying across a mist-shrouded River Dnestre, declared its uniqueness. The barren market, abandoned mikvah, moss-grown study house, and synagogue were not more remarkable than those of another village. But Yankel, remember, had been snatched from his bed on the Sabbath, when a pious Jew is in possession of a *neshomah yeseyrah*, an auxiliary soul; and while one had departed with him (and been subsequently damaged), the other had remained faith-fully behind. How else explain the seismic palpitation that ham-mered his breast the moment he'd set foot in that desolate place? It was the happy reunion with a longlost spare soul that allowed him to recognize his childhood home of Shatsk.

He was also able to identify the raggedy stick standing solitar-ily in the mud floe of an empty street as the honorable Meyer Hell-Beadle, caretaker of creaking shutters and broken glass. It was to him Yankel applied for word of the Kabakoffs.

"Kabakoffs?" the old idler reflected, scratching the bristled crop of his Adam's apple, and already Yankel was sorry he'd asked. "There was a boy, am I right? A scholar. They say he was carried off by the *sheydim*, that left in his place a book about—guess what? A boy carried off by *sheydim!*" He cackled unhealthily and blew ribbons of snot from his nose. "His parents? Like everybody else they moved away. So where else should they move, them that don't go to America?"

In the Shatsk cemetery, despite wildflowered meadows spread-ing out all around them, the Jews huddled together in death as they had in life. There was a low stone wall, some stunted ailan-thus and juniper, trees the Hasidim claimed had sprouted from the grave of one dead tsadik or another. They were supposed to signify posthumous fruition, these trees, though their leaflessness suggested otherwise. Among the cankered headstones were wooden markers of recent vintage, some planted at giddy angles in obvious haste. One with a lopsidedly blazoned Magen David belonged to Rabbi Isidore Kirsky, may his name be inscribed, another to Mordecai Bimko and his footstool, Feiga Tamara. On yet another, in a blackwash faded almost to transparency, Yankel could just make out the names of Shlomo and Malkeh Kabakoff.

What frustrated the deserter was not so much the loss of his parents, whom he'd buried in his mind long ago, but rather his inability to say Kaddish over their grave. Among his growing store of reclaimed memories, it seemed that the prayer for the dead, without which nobody rests in peace, was still notably absent. He looked appealingly to dumb Yoysef, then several plots beyond him, toward a lank figure standing under a gnarled branch in a formal getup that had seen better days. Taking him for one of Meyer's tribe, a mendicant mourner, Yankel approached him accordingly. From some nether depth of his pocket he dredged up a coin and offered it in exchange for the prayer. What he got instead of devotional words for his money, which the fellow hung on to all the same, was an irate earful.

"For what do you take me, some lumpen shnorrer?" One narrow brow was arched like an angry eel. "Boy, do you got the wrong party! You know who you're talking? Enoch, that's who, that they took me to heaven without I even have to die! There I became the formidable Metatron, archangel that ain't got no peer, who has exclusive the right-hand ear of God. You can read for yourself about me in the *Sefer Raziel,* which I ain't in it anymore, not since the Philistines tore up to shreds the book in the bet hamidrash. Wings I had—who could count them? One for every color of the rainbow, every day of the cosmic year . . ."

Speaking thus, he peeled off his patched Prince Albert, revealing a false shirtfront that curled above his pigeon breast. He turned around to show, between his scrawny shoulder blades, all that remained of his former glory: a fidgeting appendage, featherless and malformed like a pair of arthritic hands. Yankel assured him that he and Yoysef had intended no disrespect, and the angel was somewhat appeased. Come down off his high horse, he inquired, "You got perhaps a little schnapps?" When Yankel said he was sorry, Enoch dolefully repined, "The long and the short of it is, I don't get back in the book, I'm one shtupped seraphim."

As an alternative solution, however, he allowed that "in di goldene medina, I'm talking America, they maybe got there doctors can fix me back up. You ain't going by any chance to America?"

This was all Yankel heard in his travels, America; it was on every straggler's lips. "The Golden Land," they called it in a phrase that was uttered more often than "Zion," which you had to admit had a certain ring. In America you could put your sore feet up; you sat in the shade sipping kosher moonshine, feasting on watermelon borsht and ritually slaughtered buffalo. You unloaded your books and studied them at leisure, until America itself evaporated around you and you were immersed once again in a luminous perpetuity.

So in answer to the angel's request Yankel told him, "Why not?"—though something always seemed to postpone their going. In the meantime the years intervened, Yankel acquired more books, and yet another member was added to his party. He made her acquaintance one summer night in a privy behind an inn in Volhynia, where he and his companions were entertaining for their supper.

This was their custom: Yoysef would execute feats of strength—lifting a bewildered donkey or a bench of tipplers on his back, putting a dent in the blade of a plough with his head. Enoch, who'd been a shoemaker before his apotheosis (stitching leather, he bound together the lower and higher worlds), now thought himself too good for even an artisan's tasks. However, when not too sodden or deeply involved in some lecherous pursuit, he might stoop to performing a few parlor tricks. With what tired magic remained to him in his fallen state, he made cards rise out of marked decks; he removed eggs from the ears of an audience for whose gullibility he made no attempt to disguise his disdain. As an extra attraction, and for a few kopeks more, he might be induced to show off his increasingly atrophied wings.

For his part Yankel had worked up a pitch to get the attention of strangers. He'd fabricated stories, which conscientiously avoided any taint of the supernatural, of how Yoysef had come by his enormous strength and how Enoch had developed his sleight of hand. At some point he'd had the idea of writing down these spurious biographies and flogging them along with the knickknacks he'd begun to sell. Then came the night, during their performance for a bunch of muzhik farmers in a puncheon-floored taproom, when Yankel went out back to relieve himself. Facilities being scarce on the road, he was looking forward to relaxing in the outhouse, foul though it was, with a smoke and a luxurious defecation. But just as he'd dropped his trousers and settled himself over the hole, a hand shot up between his parted knees.

Yankel let out a howl and froze while the hand grasped his shrinking member, then cast it aside, searching for something more profitable. That's how Yoysef found him when he'd torn the door from its hinges: his legs flung wide, jaw agape in petrified fascination as he watched an arm snaking out of the closestool to pick his pocket. The golem grabbed the arm at the wrist as it retreated from Yankel's pants with a couple of coins, and hauled a kicking, beshitten she-devil out of the hole.

Once they'd cleaned her up—Yoysef holding her thrashing limbs, Enoch pinching his nostrils while Yankel scrubbed her with pumice and benzine; once they'd gotten rid of her filthy pinafore and procured more fetching apparel from passing gypsies, she turned out to be pretty. Very pretty. And the stir caused by her beauty struck a responsive chord in her own shapely breast. In no time she'd assumed the habit of admiring herself in mirrors, which she'd previously been accustomed to peering out of from the other side. Her name was Laylah, daughter of Lilith by Ashmodai, etc., and her adjustment thereafter to (roughly speaking) human society was swift. She was the first to admit she'd grown weary of dwelling in root cellars and toilets. Such places had been good enough in those disembodied, shape-shifting days before she'd abandoned her respective book, namely the *Zohar*; but since she'd found herself trapped inside the body of a solitary maidele with no recourse to inhabiting others, with apparently no way back into her book, she'd become lonely and in need of a little fellowship.

Yankel and friends were pleased to welcome her into theirs. For one thing, she was a treat to look at, and beyond her accomplishments as a petty thief, she could also sing. In a long career of lurking about the beds of male children, she'd picked up quite a repertoire of standard Yiddish lullabies. Her a capella renditions had curious effects on her listeners, pacifying them and making them free with donations. Frequently, while she sang, her audience might drop off in a doze during which they were prone to spilling their seed. Of course her strong suit was still corruption, but in a climate where life was so cheap, where Jewish fathers sold their daughters and the daughters sold themselves for an unsalted crust, Laylah's skill at luring men into sin seemed pitifully redundant. Instead she preferred to content herself with tantalizing her victims to the point of delirium, leaving them to attend as best they could to their ravening lust.

Among her immediate circle there was relative harmony. Yankel, who liked to think of himself as keeping his hand in with the ladies, drew the line at female demons, and for Laylah had conceived a strictly fraternal affection. What Yoysef felt for her, beyond protective—his organ, although trunk-sized, was always recumbent—was anyone's guess. Only Enoch, subject to all manner of unseemly appetites, made advances, though Laylah rebuffed them unconditionally, announcing she would have no truck with angels. It was anyway more fun to tease him to distraction.

Meanwhile they stayed fixed on the idea of America as an ultimate destination. This included Laylah, who'd needed little per-
suasion, imagining there a population ripe for depravity. But what
was the hurry? "It ain't going nowhere, America," Yankel had
pointed out, untroubled that, for all their journeying, neither
were they. His own lack of urgency sometimes puzzled him,
though when they weren't dodging barbarous outbreaks or their
collective resolution to get back to books, he had to admit that
the road had its virtues. It afforded a freedom compared to which
the much-vaunted liberties of the New World remained an
unproven abstraction. So who was to say they were wasting time?
On the road you felt you were as good as on a river, whose banks
appeared in constant motion while you and time stood still.

Usually they traveled on their own, cherishing their indepen-
dence, but it was natural with so many itinerants abroad that on
occasion they should hook up with others. From time to time
they were camp followers, joining the ranks of high-spirited fus-
geyers, young people who'd pledged to walk all the way to
America and were glad of a little diversion en route. There were
smugglers with whom Yankel and company, recognizing no bor-
ders, sometimes allied themselves, helping run goods and illegal
immigrants into Poland for a price. There were countless peddlers
with whom they traded entertainment for merchandise—profane
Yiddish novels, nostrums for curing melancholy and parasites,
amulets against vampires and czars—which Yankel marked up and
resold.

This was the period that saw the beginnings of Yiddish theater, wandering troupes of glorified Purim-shpielers playing the
market squares and wine cellars all over the Pale. Their presenta-
tions consisted largely of breast-beating melodrama leavened with
broad burlesque, which they interrupted at random intervals with
sentimental songs. Among the companies of ragtag professionals,
escapees from books were known to turn up now and then, called

upon to lend authenticity to traditional roles. Thus, when
Yankel's bunch crossed paths with a party of strollers from Vilna,
Yoysef the golem was conscripted to play an idiot in an open-air
production of *Kuni Lemmel.* Enoch, whose wings had by now
dropped completely off (his ego compensatorily inflated), proved
a natural in such title roles as *The Banker Tyrant* and *The Bigamist.*
Whenever a script provided opportunities for self-aggrandizing
histrionics and incorrigible behavior, he shone. Yankel himself was
invited to take a part as a homesick soldier in *The Recruits,* but
despite his flair for disguises, he opted instead to hawk sundries
before and after the play.

Asked to interpret a variety of characters, from temptresses
and traduced maidens to girls possessed by snarling dybbuks,
Laylah found herself much in demand. She was featured in a number of stock pieces, such as *Daughter from Hell,* Goldfaden's
Capricious Peninah, and the crowd-pleasing *Braindele Cossack,* in which
she was riveting as a lady bluebeard. Whatever her part, she managed to provoke sensations in her audience—of mainly menders,
grinders, and bluff wagoneers—that even her ballads and cradle
songs couldn't quell. (Indeed, it was her singing that left them
without a dry eye, or pair of pants, in the house.) She might have
been a star had not her disturbing stage presence aroused such
controversy. But the rabbis objected, exhorting their communities
to shun these indecent displays, which in turn gave the local
authorities a license to intercede on moral grounds. They used
any available pretext to throw Laylah in jail, the better to ogle her
and worse at close quarters. Then the players would be forced to
pay ransoms to prevent Laylah's captors from doing her some
serious harm, or vice versa.

In the end the manager of the Vilna Troupe had to let Yankel
and his creatures go. Didn't he have enough problems with the
anarchists in his ranks, the loudmouths who threatened to usher
in Messiah with a bang? Rumors to that effect had already

prompted the government to outlaw Yiddish theater in certain cities and towns. So who needed the additional headache of a troublemaking succubus, thanks all the same?

About their walking papers Yankel wasn't complaining; on the contrary, he preferred it that way: just him and his traveling sideshow. They would continue to front for his retail ventures—the hustling of unpatented medicines and linen burial shrouds, quite a popular item in those days—and it would be like before. His companions, however, were full of regret. Having been permitted to enter again into legends, every evening and Shabbos matinees, they had all of them, Yoysef included, become stagestruck. Away from the theater they pined, their discontent translating into an even more ardent nostalgia for the stories they'd fled. After a while, grudgingly reminded of his own long delinquency, Yankel also succumbed to the general malaise. Keen though he remained for commerce, he wondered if he hadn't socked away enough of a nest egg already. Maybe it was time to settle down to his studies, and to take, if only as an accessory to scholarship and a means of perpetuating his line, a nice haimesheh bride. Because it was true that, while his little band of immortals had scarcely aged a day since they'd met, Yankel himself wasn't getting any younger.

But there was always the next town, with its promise of market crowds anxious to be fleeced, though the towns where they were welcome had become fewer every year. More and more they'd burned their bridges in places where Yoysef, demonstrating his prodigious strength, had accidentally broken a dray horse's spine; where Enoch had insulted some petty official or been caught with a kulak's wife, and Laylah had incited a free-for-all with her fluid bones. There were places that no longer tolerated Yankel's flim-flam. In the Ukraine alone they'd already been run out of Brailov, Poltava, Olensk, and Korostyn. It was the same in Belorussia and Galicia, in the Polish provinces of Lublin, Bialystok, and Lodz. It was getting hard to remember where they were personae non grata and where unknown, whether this was the platz or that the goat-bleating courtyard where they'd committed some fabled unpleasantness. Finally they seemed to have exhausted much of the continent, traveling clear into the next century—from which, agreed one and all, there could be no turning back. The moment had come for them to push on to America.

In the free city of Danzig they greased the necessary palms for their papers, leaving the more uncooperative bureaucrats to Laylah's wiles. Booking their passage in the steerage section of a barnacled SS *Wilhelmshaven,* Yankel cautioned his creatures not to arouse undue curiosity; they'd yet to gauge the laws of the high seas (never mind the New World) with respect to denizens of Jewish lore. Then, judging from the prudence observed by others among the passengers—who attempted, even as they upchucked jointly over the rail, to conceal vestigial wings and horns— Yankel suspected there might be more of their kind on board. Still they kept their own counsel, uninspired in any case to make further mischief in those rolling compartments awash with human spew. Even Enoch, emptying his dinner pail to the sharks, was too bilious to get into trouble. After three weeks of a rough but otherwise uneventful crossing, they arrived, entering America by a backdoor, so to speak, at the port of New Orleans.

It was hard to tell, in that tropical city, whether they were suffering from a lingering seasickness or a stupor caused by breathing the dense jasmine air. Here was the Golden Land, a fact they'd scarcely begun to appreciate before Yankel, with what presence of mind he had left to him, was herding them out of town. Nobody protested. Made docile by so much cloying, intemperate beauty, they willingly stumbled on in search of something familiar. Besides, it was a habit of too many years to shed overnight, their wandering. Accosted at a crossroads by a transplanted Litvak jobber, a bent spindle of a character whose optimism seemed out of place, Yankel had himself outfitted for a tripod and keister man. That way they'd have a store of articles to placate the natives with. In addition to the usual line of household notions and quack remedies, Yankel carried novelty items such as dream books, John the Conqueror root, mojo hands. These latter, he was told, were much coveted among "colored" folk, though what color he'd neglected to ask.

They traveled the rutted backroads whose junctions sported wooden crosses advertising redemption, which they agreed resembled Old Country highway shrines. The slack-faced rustics, who eyed them so inquisitively, dipped their snuff and combed their horses' manes with their rifle stocks Cossack-style. The silos were like watchtowers, the liver brown Delta land stretched away as rich and treeless as Georgian steppes. The sharecroppers' shacks, shingled with tarpaper, sided in Hadicol signs, tumbled on rotten piles into shtetl mud—or so they insisted. But who believed?

Nevertheless, their courage increased with the crumbs of language they gathered from the loose lips of farmers' wives: *the daughter up tooken with Count No-Count, the man his dojigger done mashed;* or from a garrulous planter's mouth to Yankel's ear: "Dry it is as the funnament of old Miss Fanny." Quick studies all (excepting Yoysef), they were soon speaking a species of pidgin Yinglish and had begun to make themselves understood. Gingerly at first, they tested the water, starting to offer entertainments in the wagon yards of Itta Bena, Napachechaw, and Coffeeville. In Tallulah and Bewelcome, taking heart, they performed in the courthouse squares, under hanging oaks whose moss-decked branches resembled rebbes' beards, or so they said. The yokels they swindled generally treated them well. In fact, having seldom encountered an authentic Hebrew, they tended to defer to Yankel as a person of the Book. They sought his views on their prospects for salvation, on certain biblical passages that he pretended to know, then made a note to look up later on.

By the time they reached North Main Street in the city of Memphis, they were feeling their oats. (Afterward Yankel would find texts to prove how it was written that the street had been their destination all along.) This was a sunny September morning in 1912, the year a brickmason was on trial in Kiev for blood libel and the HMS *Titanic* went down. Located in a poor district called the Pinch, North Main had been until lately a lawless street of bordellos and saloons, a place of epidemics, frequent fires, and floods. Relics of its earlier days were still in evidence: here a drunken Indian, there a cadaverous refugee from an Irish potato famine. In front of the feed store sat an old Confederate soldier, fossilizing in his moth-eaten butternut, a buff-skinned ex-slave perched on a bottle crate nearby. But now that the strangeness had begun to have a not-so-unfamiliar ring, Yankel's party was presented with a host of familiar strangers; because the population of the Pinch was mostly given over to a mercantile element of recently immigrated Jews.

Like Yankel they'd come across this farflung outpost carrying the bundles containing their life and livelihood, and in some instances their holy books. And since North Main Street had looked to them a lot like the ends of the earth, rather than go farther and fare worse, they put down their bundles. They put them down in the skunk cabbage and bitterweed along the river bluff, where some claimed their bundles immediately began to sprout roots. But Yankel had another reason for tarrying, having spotted a zaftig redhead in a sable shirtwaist bustling out of a corner candy store.

"Who is she that she looketh forth like the dawn?" his memory passed down to his mouth from centuries ago.

Her name, which she blushingly assured him was none of his business, was Tillie, and young though she might be, she'd been (for his information) recently widowed. Her late husband, Mr. Olswanger, a consumptive custom tailor (may his remembrance be for a blessing), had left her perfectly comfortable, thanks very much. Secure in the knowledge that she was quite a catch, that she had a head on her shoulders not to mention her other assets, she was in no hurry to remarry. But just supposing she were, what interest could she have in this Yankel Bag-of-Bones, this mangy goat of a greenhorn who was old enough to be her father (may his etc.), if not older? Him with his cockeyed stories, which despite herself she couldn't get enough of; with his peculiar companions, his impertinent suggestion that she put away her weeds, combine her fortune with his, and open a store.

Wasn't the neighborhood lousy with such types? Self-styled scholars, they used their devotion to study as an excuse for idling away their days, while their foot-weary wives were left to mind the shop. Then there was the issue of their so-called "relations," a pestilent brood. Hardly human, with small regard for common decency or private enterprise, they overstayed their welcome, eating you out of house and home. They poked their noses in places they didn't belong. Interfering in the lives of ordinary citizens, who might have offered a more spirited resistance, they confused the races and created scandals. Already you had a situation where these sons and daughters of eternity were routinely taking up with the sons and daughters of time. In the ensuing mishmash, who could tell anymore where one left off and the other began . . . ?

Postscript

When the great Hasid, Baal Shem Tov, Master of the Good Name, had a problem, it was his custom to go to a certain part of the forest. There he would light a fire and say a certain prayer, and find wisdom. A generation later, a son of one of his disciples was in the same position. He went to that same place in the forest and lit the fire, but he could not remember the prayer. But he asked for wisdom and it was sufficient. He found what he needed. A generation after that, his son had a problem like the others. He also went to the forest, but he could not even light the fire. "Lord of the Universe," he prayed, "I could not remember the prayer and I cannot get the fire started. But I am in the forest. That will have to be sufficient." And it was. Now I, Shlomo the Scribe, sit in my study with my head in my hands. "Lord of the Universe," I pray, "look at me now. I've forgotten the prayer. The fire is out. I can't find my way back to the place in the forest. I can only remember that there was a fire, a prayer, a place in the forest. So Lord, this'll have to do."

Permissions

STEVE STERN was born and grew up in Memphis, Tennessee. His first collection of stories, *Isaac and the Undertaker's Daughter*, received the Pushcart Writer's Choice Award and the title story of that collection won an O. Henry Prize. His second short story collection, *Lazar Malkin Enters Heaven*, won the Edward Lewis Wallant Award. He is also the author of two previous novels, *The Moon and Ruben Shein* and *Harry Kaplan's Adventures Underground*, and two children's books, *Mickey and the Golem* and *Hershel and the Beast*. He now lives in Saratoga Springs, New York, where he is Associate Professor of Creative Writing at Skidmore College.